P9-BYF-977

"LET ME MAKE LOVE TO YOU," HE SAID SUDDENLY.

"*Please* let me make love to you. I've asked you every way I know how. My God, Elizabeth. I feel like I've been thrown back into the Victorian age. I feel like your father's in the next room, shotgun on the wall. This is weird . . . this shouldn't have to be so hard. . . ."

He cut off a groan deep in his throat and said, "Ah, the hell with it," and yanked her against his chest, trapping her hands flat against him and covering her mouth with his in a hard, frustrated kiss. Liz opened her mouth to say something, to protest or to agree, she never did know which, and he thrust his tongue into it, filling it, beating back her words, beating back her thoughts. . . .

Time After Time

ANTOINETTE STOCKENBERG

A DELL BOOK

Published by
Dell Publishing
a division of
Bantam Doubleday Dell Publishing Group, Inc.
1540 Broadway
New York, New York 10036

The trademark Dell® is registered in the U.S. Patent and Trademark Office.

ISBN: 0-440-21676-1

Printed in the United States of America

Published simultaneously in Canada

August 1995

10 9 8 7 6 5 4 3 2 1
OPM

For Diane

ACKNOWLEDGMENTS

My gratitude to the following for their helpful input: Dr. Howard Browne (as always) and Dr. Samir Moubayed; Mike Muessel of Oldport Marine; Seaman David Parry; Newport Officer Teresa Hayes; Vicki Lawrence; and especially my sister Diane, whose kids had *better* remember all those birthday extravaganzas.

Jane, thanks for the copper beech and the view.

Chapter 1

*L*iz Coppersmith and her friend Victoria raised their wineglasses to the brooding mansion on the other side of the chain-link fence.

"Not a bad neighborhood," said Victoria, the taller, more whimsically dressed of the two. She dropped into a plastic lawn chair, shook out her red permed curls, and straightened the folds of her star-print sundress. "You'll do lots of business over there," she predicted, "or my name's not Victoria."

Liz had heard her say "or my name's not Victoria" a thousand times since they'd met five years ago in a grief-management group. And every time, Liz had to resist saying, "Your name *isn't* Victoria, dammit." Victoria's name was Judy Maroney, and if it weren't for her stubborn, persistent, rather amazing amnesia, Liz would be calling her Judy, not Tori, at that very moment.

"If I do get any work out of them, Tori, it'll be thanks to you. You found me a house in a perfect location."

"I did, didn't I?" said Victoria, pleased with herself. "Call it intuition, but I was sure you'd like it, despite that dull little ad in the paper. I mean—a four-room house? I have more *bath*rooms than that, and I live alone."

They both turned back to look at the sweet but plain two-story cottage that now belonged to Liz. It was exactly the kind of house that children invariably draw; all that was missing was a plume of Crayola smoke from the red-brick chimney.

"It's no castle," Liz conceded with a cheerful sigh. She jerked her thumb toward the intimidating mansion to the east. "But what the heck—it's close enough," she quipped.

She went back to gazing through the chain-link fence. The grounds of the estate were magnificent, even for Newport. Ancient trees, presided over by a magnificent copper beech, threw shimmering pools of shade over an expanse of well-kept grass. In the sunny openings between the trees were huge, wonderful shrubs—viburnums and hydrangeas and lush, towering rhododendrons. There were no flowers to speak of; only a green, understated elegance. It was like having her own private deer park—except without the deer—right in the heart of Newport.

Too bad the chain-link fence and barbed wire separated her from it.

Liz reached up and plucked a strand of the rusty wire as if it were a harp string. "This has been here a *long* time," she said.

"If I were you," said Victoria, "I'd think about getting a tetanus shot." She frowned in disapproval. "Barbed wire. Who do they think they are, anyway?"

"You mean, who do they think *we* are," Liz corrected. "Obviously they don't trust my side of the neighborhood." She glanced again at her tiny cottage, the smallest house on a street of small houses. "And let's face it, why should they? We don't exactly radiate wealth and prosperity."

"Never mind," said Victoria with an airy wave of her coral-tipped hand. "That will come. It's your karma. I had a vision."

Liz laughed and said, "You and your crystal ball just might be right. After all, yesterday—the very day I moved in!—there I was, talking through this fence to their house-keeper. I suppose they sent her over here to make sure I wasn't in some prison-release program, but I liked her, even if she *was* a spy. Her name is Netta something, and she was as chatty as could be. Apparently her boss is some workaholic bachelor—"

"Uh-oh. No business there," said Victoria, sipping her wine.

"That's what I thought, too, at first." Liz raked her rich brown hair away from her face and cocked her head appraisingly at the Queen Anne–style mansion.

"But then I found out that his parents stay at the estate— East Gate, it's called—every summer. It's been in the family since it was built, a hundred years ago. Besides the parents, there are a couple of semi-permanent guests staying there now as well. They must do *some* entertaining." Liz smiled and said, "Naturally I found a way to let it drop that I was an events planner."

"Did the housekeeper even know what that was?" asked Victoria.

"I made sure of it. I told her I design weddings, dinners, birthdays, dances, receptions, fund-raisers, charity events— the works."

"In other words—"

"I lied." Liz's deep brown eyes flashed with good humor. "Hey—if I told her I arranged kids' birthday parties at Chuck E. Cheese, you think she'd have been impressed?"

"You did what you had to do, Liz Coppersmith," agreed Victoria. "You planted the seed."

"Yeah. That was the easy part. The hard part will be to provide references who're old enough to read and write."

Victoria said, "If you need references, don't worry. I'll come up with references."

And she would, too, because—unlike Liz—Victoria had money to buy anything she wanted.

It wasn't always that way. Less than six years earlier, Victoria—Judy Maroney then—had crossed the Rhode Island border with her husband, two children, and not much more than high hopes that her husband's new job at the Newport Tourist and Convention Center would give her family more stability than he had at his old job in the defense industry. The family was eastbound on Route 95, just a few miles behind their moving van, when they were sideswiped by a drunk driver and ended up broadside to two lanes of east-bound traffic.

Judy's husband, Paul, and their four-year-old son were killed instantly. Their daughter, Jessica, who would've been two in a week, had lived another forty-eight hours. Judy Maroney, behind the wheel, was saved—just barely—by the driver's-side airbag.

And she could not forgive herself, both for being at the wheel and for surviving. That, at least, became Liz's theory. How else to explain the post-trauma amnesia that had no medical basis?

Judy's mother-in-law, to whom Liz had once spoken, had a different theory. She believed that Judy, rejecting the unspeakable horror of her loss, had invented a new identity to get around having to face that abyss. Hence the single—and now legal—name "Victoria."

Whatever the reason, Judy Maroney had for all practical purposes died in that crash. And the woman who replaced her—Victoria—had never once, to Liz or to anyone else, alluded to the accident. Tori was pleasant, she was friendly— by far the most cheerful member in the grief group—and she was totally amnesiac.

The accident had resulted in a huge settlement for her. Money hadn't given Judy back her memory—it certainly hadn't given her back her family—but it *had* given the woman named Victoria lots of people willing to call themselves friends. Or references. Or whatever she wanted.

"Hey, you," said Victoria behind her. "Have you heard a word I said?"

Victoria had an almost spooky knack for knowing when Liz was focusing on her amnesia. Liz was forced to back up mentally, searching her brain for the last of her friend's light-hearted babble. "Of course I heard. You think I should give my house a name."

"I really do. Houses sound more important when they have names. How about 'West Gate'? Or 'Harborview'? Or—I'm quoting you, now—'Bigenuf'?"

"I was talking about the mortgage, not the house," Liz said, laughing.

She set her wineglass on a nearby stepstone and turned her attention back to the imposing mansion to the east. Since yesterday, it had held her in its thrall.

Privilege. Tradition. Wealth. Elegance. Lineage. It was all there, on the other side of the barbed wire. Everything about it was the opposite of her own life. Liz had been born and raised in Newport's Fifth Ward, a working-class neighborhood of ethnic families that—until the yuppies began moving in recently—had changed little over the past century. Privilege in the Fifth Ward meant getting a parking place in front of your own house; tradition meant meeting with the same people every Friday night for a game of Pinochle.

"Do you think I'm being too ambitious?" she suddenly asked Victoria. "Do you think I should work my way up through the Point and the Hill before I go after East Gate and the rest of the Bellevue Avenue crowd?"

"Heck, no," Victoria said cheerfully. "This is Newport! The town has a long tradition of society-crashing. Where would the Vanderbilts be if they'd taken some slow-but-sure route?"

Liz turned to her friend with a wry look. "I'm not trying to break *into* society, Tori. I just want to be able to make a little money off it once in a while."

Victoria came up to Liz and put her arm around her. "And you will. You'll make tons of money. And you and your little girl will live happily ever after in a big house of your own. If that's what you want."

Together they gazed at the shingled and stuccoed Queen Anne–style mansion, sun-washed and golden in the evening light. After a moment Victoria said, "Where *is* Susy, by the way? With your folks?"

Liz nodded. "She's been feeling ignored, what with the flurry of moving and all. My parents have her overnight."

"Lucky for you they live in town."

"Isn't it, though?"

Liz was very aware that her friend's own parents were dead. Even if they'd still been alive, Victoria wouldn't know them. The amnesia was so bizarre, so sad, so complete. When Liz met Victoria in the grief group, she herself was on the ropes emotionally. For a while she believed that as she pulled out of her numb state, Victoria would, too. Then she realized that being left by a husband—even learning there'd be no more children—didn't come close to losing one's whole family in a car crash.

"You're doing it again," said Victoria. "Drifting."

"Sorry. Did I tell you that someone in the mansion has two kids?" asked Liz. "I saw them playing outside. There's a little blond girl who's my Susy's age; I think her name is Caroline. And there's a two-year-old boy that the house-keeper has to chase after every minute."

"You're thinking they'll be playmates for Susy?"

Liz's laugh was the dry laugh of a working-class townie with no illusions. "Not unless I attack this fence with cable-cutters." She turned and began walking back to her new little home, a cozy twenty feet away from where they stood.

She added, "I just meant, with kids around you're always celebrating something or other—baptisms, bar mitzvahs, birthdays, graduations, weddings. The kids could end up be-ing my ticket to Bellevue Avenue. Besides," Liz said with a musing smile, "it'd be fun to do something for those two. They looked *so* sweet."

Netta Simmons was on her hands and knees picking up pieces of a broken soup bowl when a plate of steamed vegetables went flying over her head, smashed up against the eighteenth-century inlaid sideboard, and came dribbling down the polished wood not far from where she knelt.

That's it, the housekeeper decided, tossing the soup bowl pieces into a plastic pan. *I quit. After thirty-eight years, to have to put up with* this?

Leaning on one knee for support, Netta got to her feet with a painful "oof" and turned to face her tormentor.

"Caroline Stonebridge—" Netta began, her lips trembling in her jowly cheeks.

"Caroline, sweetheart, that wasn't called for," said Cornelius Eastman from the head of the table. "You could have hurt Netta. Now, come—be a good girl and say you're sorry."

The five-year-old blonde with the Shirley Temple curls turned her steel-blue gaze on Netta and said, "I'm *sorry.*" Under her breath she muttered, "That I *missed.*"

Instinctively the housekeeper turned to Cornelius Eastman's son: handsome dark-haired Jack, him that she had practically raised from scratch, him that would've cut off his hand before he'd ever raise it to her in anger—with or without a plate in it.

Jack Eastman stood up and threw his napkin on the table in disgust. "This is impossible, Dad!" he said angrily. "Send the brat to bed without supper—God knows she has no use for it."

"Now, Jack—" his father began unhappily. "I know it's not easy for you. You couldn't have had this—situation—in mind when you took over East Gate. But what can we do? Caroline is a fact in my life, whether—"

"I don't *like* broccoli," said little blond Caroline. "And Netta knows it."

Netta saw Jack clench his jaw, a good sign. She folded her arms across her chest and waited with a kind of grim hope: maybe the son would overrule the father and lock the little monster in the carriage house for a year or two.

But no. In a controlled voice Jack said to Caroline, "When and *if* we can bribe a new nanny to take care of you, you can go back to eating all the junk you want. Until then, you will eat whatever Netta prepares for the rest of us. If you *ever* throw one morsel of food again, you will eat in the kitchen, in a high chair, like your little brother. Now. Either finish your supper or go to your room."

Caroline stuck out her lower lip and said, "You wouldn't talk to me like that if my mommy was here. When is she coming back? I want her here." The child began a wailing refrain of "I want my *mom*-mee . . . *mom*-mee . . . *mom*-mee . . . ," kicking her chair leg for emphasis.

Netta shook her head; the girl's lament was a routine event by now. Caroline's mommy was a thirty-year-old woman named Stacey Stonebridge who'd rocked the Eastman household when she showed up seven weeks earlier with a boy in her arms and a girl at her side. The girl, she'd announced blithely, belonged to the elder Eastman.

No one much doubted the truth of Stacey's story; that was the sad thing. It hardly paid to bother with blood tests and DNA analysis. Stacey was pretty, leggy, and young, but most of all, blond—which is how Cornelius Eastman liked them a few years ago. Now that he was in his seventies, he seemed to have gone back to raven-haired beauties. But a few years ago? Oh, yes. Blondes couldn't miss.

Mrs. Eastman had taken one look at Stacey, packed up her bags, and removed herself to Capri for the remainder of the summer. This time, Netta knew, the hurt went deep. It was possible that tall, blond Stacey was the last straw. Time would tell.

Caroline's wailing continued. Cornelius Eastman rubbed his silver temples with manicured fingers and said fretfully, "Now, Caroline, we've been through all that. Please don't pound. Your mother is at the clinic. You want her to get well, don't you?"

Stacey? Not a chance. She's much too fond of her pills and her bottle. She's not ready to get well. Netta knew it, Jack knew it, and so did the elder Eastman.

Caroline pushed her plate away with a morose look. She was getting ready for the next phase of her tantrum: self-pity.

Cornelius turned to his son and said, "Where's the damned breeder, anyway? Didn't you say he'd be here at six?"

Jack glanced at his watch. "That's what he said. Well, have fun. I can't wait any longer. I'm off to the shipyard—"

Caroline began to sniffle. "I just didn't want broccoli, because it's my *birth*day. I shouldn't have to eat broccoli if I'm being five years *old*." Tears began rolling freely. "And I *don't* even have a *cake*." She turned to the senior Eastman with big, glazed blue eyes. "Dada? Do I?"

Oooh, she's good, thought Netta. That Dada-thing that she'd come up with: it always made Mr. Eastman melt visibly.

He was doing it now. "Of *course* we have a cake for you, darling," the old man said, his face creasing into a hundred lines of happiness. "Would we forget you on your birthday?"

"She knows we have a cake," Netta snapped. "She's already dug a trench through the frosting."

"Forget it, Netta," said Jack tiredly. "It's not worth it."

They were interrupted by the ring of the doorbell. Caroline stopped sniffling at once. Cornelius Eastman grinned broadly. Jack shook his head with wary resignation. And in the adjacent new kitchen, installed expressly so that Netta wouldn't have to fuss with the dumbwaiter and the old basement cook-area anymore, Caroline's little brother Bradley let out a welcoming shriek.

The puppy was here.

Cornelius Eastman himself went to get the door, with Caroline right behind him. Jack got up to leave.

"Jack Eastman, where do you think you're going?" said Netta.

The next sound they heard was a high and relentless *arf-arf-arf-arf!*

"Oh, lord," murmured Netta, "your father really has gone and done it."

A white ball of fluff came cannonballing through the dining room, hardly stopping long enough to pause and sniff Netta's skirt, then Jack's trousers, before racing to the nearest table leg, lifting its leg, and peeing.

Caroline, who was in hot pursuit, stopped short with a scandalized look. "He's a *boy* puppy! I thought I was getting a *girl* puppy!" She dropped to all fours and began crawling under the table after the dog.

Arf arf arf! Arf arf arf!

"I'm sorry, honey, that's all they had," said her amused and silver-haired father, lifting the damask tablecloth.

Arf arf arf!

Netta thought that Cornelius Eastman didn't look sorry as much as glad to be done with the week-long hunt for a female Maltese. And *no*body seemed sorry about the wet stain on the Oriental rug.

"But I had a *girl's* name all picked out," Caroline lamented as she lurched in vain after the bouncing white mop.

At that point Netta had to dash into the kitchen to fetch Bradley, who'd cleared his own tray of food with one sweep of his arm and was screaming incoherently. It was his way of saying, "I've finished dinner, thank you so much, and now I think perhaps I'd like to join the others."

Arf arf arf! Arf arf arf arf!

The elder Eastman was chuckling at Caroline's distress over the puppy's gender. "What name did you have in mind, sweetheart?"

"Snowball," said Caroline in a pout.

Bradley, on the loose now, went charging after the puppy and succeeded in coming away with two clumps of long white hair, which clung like angora mittens to his still-sticky hands.

Arf. Arf arf. Arf arf arf arf arf arf arf!

Jack, a bachelor who had never in his *life* been surrounded by this kind of chaos, said in a loud voice, "Will somebody *please* get that animal under control?"

Netta wasn't sure which animal he meant. She grabbed the one closest to her—Bradley—and began cleaning his hands with a wet washcloth as the brown-haired boy squirmed and screamed to be let down.

Arf. Arf arf. Arf arf arf.

"You can still name him Snowball, honey," said Cornelius Eastman over the ongoing din. "Snowball is for either."

"Well, I guess . . . but . . . well, all right." Caroline sighed, then gave them all a sweeping look of wide-eyed innocence. "Can we have my party now, then?" she asked. "And my presents?"

Arf.

There was a pause. Even Snowball paused. Finally Cornelius Eastman said, with a sheepish expression, "You said if you got a puppy that you didn't *want* a party, honey."

Caroline managed to lasso Snowball with her arms and squish him onto her lap. "No, I didn't," she murmured, studying the dog's moppy face intently. "I said a puppy *and* a party."

"You said a puppy *or* a party, dammit!" snapped Jack.

" *'And,'* " said Caroline, still studying the dog's face.

The two men—seventy and forty—exchanged looks. Netta watched them, mesmerized by the family resemblance. Eastman genes ran true to type: the hawkish nose, the fierce blue eyes, the thick brown hair. Oh, gravity had taken its toll on the father and softened the once-square line of his jaw. But he was still a good-looking man. Paul Newman could take lessons.

Jack began to reason with the girl in a calm, carefully controlled voice. "You don't really know anyone here, Caroline. Who would we invite? Maybe when your mother gets out of the clinic and you all go back to Aspen—maybe then would be a good time for a birthday party."

Caroline looked up at the older of the two men. "Dada?" she whispered as a tear rolled down her cheek. "Can I?"

"Of *course* you can have a party," Cornelius said gruffly. "You're only five once. By all means. Arrange one for Caroline, Jack."

"You must be kidding. You know I'm flat out at the shipyard—"

"Yes, I suppose you're right," Cornelius Eastman said, annoyed. He looked at his housekeeper. "Netta? Would—? No, no, you have more than enough to do already," he said quickly, withering beneath her baleful look.

He turned back to his son. "Well, Jack, I guess you're the only one with the resources. Have Cynthia at the shipyard look into it and make the arrangements."

"Dad, that's absurd," Jack said sharply. "She has her hands full, especially this week. We're revamping our billing system—"

Netta leaned closer to Jack's ear and said, "If I could have a word with you, sir. I think I can help you out." She picked up her basket of broken crockery and led the thoroughly irritated son into the relative quiet of the kitchen.

It distressed Netta to see the household in such chaos. It

used to be such a quiet, well-ordered place. Too quiet, perhaps; but at least Jack could bring his work home every night as he struggled to keep the family shipyard afloat. Now, he hardly ever bothered coming home before they were all asleep.

Could anyone blame him? His own mother had fled from East Gate, even though she and Cornelius had lived there every summer of their long marriage. Could anyone blame *her*? To have her husband's illegitimate daughter under her own roof, over her own objections. *Well*. It was all scandalous, it really was.

Not that Netta hadn't longed for the sound of children under the old slate roof. But they were supposed to be Jack's children, happy children, *nice* children, and Mrs. Eastman was supposed to cherish them, the way a proper grandmother should. But she wasn't the proper grandmother! And in any case, she was in Capri. It was all such a mess.

Netta closed the door on the barks and shouts and turned to her adored Jack. He did look bad: tired, and worn, and used up with worry over the failing shipyard and his mother's hurt. As for Cornelius Eastman, well, he was obviously slipping into dotage, insisting that Caroline and Bradley stay at East Gate.

But that wasn't today's problem.

"What is it, Netta?" Jack said irritatedly. "Have you found the perfect nanny for our little Caroline?"

Netta snorted. "*That* machine hasn't been invented yet. No, but I do know someone who can take this birthday party off your hands. You know the little cottage to the west? It's been sold to a nice young lady named Liz Coppersmith. She designs—I think that's how she described it—events for people."

"This is a birthday party, darlin'," Jack said, helping himself to a mug of coffee. "Not a wedding. I'm not inclined to waste money on frivolity just now."

"You never are, Jack," said his housekeeper with a dry
look. "Not if you can pour it into the shipyard instead. But
you heard your father. He wants a party for his dau . . . for
Caroline."

"Yeah, well, he also wants the yard to stay solvent," Jack
said with a black look.

"He's on the fence about that, and you know it," Netta
said flatly. "*You* want to keep it. But your father—he's tired
of the struggle, and he'd maybe like to sell. So don't go using
that as an excuse, my boy."

Netta had no need to mince words with Jack. It was one
of the perks of having basically raised him. His own mother,
though she loved her son, would not have felt so free to
scold.

Jack took a sip of the just-brewed coffee, burned his
tongue, swore, slammed down the mug, and said, "*Fine.
We'll have the damned party!*"

"It's only a little thing," Netta said, wrapping her ample
arm around Jack's waist and giving him two quick squeezes.
"It won't make the difference between bankruptcy or not."

Jack laughed softly and swung his own arm around his
portly housekeeper's shoulder. He turned to her with a
brooding, troubled look in his deep blue eyes and said, "You
understand, Nettie, that the birthday party will in effect be a
coming-out party. We can't keep this charade about my
'cousin' Caroline going much longer. Especially now that
everyone's up from Palm Beach for the season."

Netta gave him a sympathetic smile. "Well, if the gov-
ernor of Rhode Island can come clean about his past," Netta
said softly, "I guess your father can, too. I only wish your
mother wasn't taking it so hard."

Jack's look turned bitter. "Yeah. After all, she knew she
was marrying an Eastman. She was bound to have to share
him with another woman sooner or later."

"Don't be fresh!" Netta said sharply. "That's your father you're talking about."

"My father; my grandfather; his father before that," said Jack in an even tone. "As we know, the tradition goes way back."

Which is why you've never married, my dear, thought Netta. *You're looking for the perfect wife, mother, and mistress all rolled up into one. You want to be the first in your family. Ah, you dreamer, you.*

She shook her head and sighed.

Jack mistook her sigh and said with his old roguish smile, "I'm too old to stick in a corner, Nettie. So now what?"

She spun him around and faced him toward the door. "I'm going to send you back to the table and stuff you with birthday cake, that's what. Maybe sugar will help."

The swing-door opened just then, and Jack's father poked his head through it. "Netta, Netta," he said in a harried voice, "I need you out here. The kids are—the dog is—*help* me, Netta," he begged.

Netta shooed both men out ahead of her and thought wearily, *They're hopeless. Where are the women? Who's going to organize this foundering kingdom?*

Chapter 2

"Why can't I stay in the house, Mommy? I just *got* here."

"I know; I know," said Liz, running a brush quickly over her daughter's sleek brown hair. "But it's too wet outside to play, and Mommy's going to make a big, big mess breaking through the ceiling to get into the attic. So you go on to the restaurant with Aunty Tori, and by the time you get back from lunch, I'll have the plaster all cleaned up outside your room, and you can come and go wherever you want."

"Because I've hardly been in my own house so far, you know," Susy said, clearly feeling shunted around.

"We've only owned it for three days, honey," Liz reminded her. "Got your money?"

Susy opened her plastic purse and pulled out a neatly folded five-dollar bill, then put it back inside. "Yes."

"Good." Liz turned to Victoria and said, "Thanks a bunch, Tori. I didn't expect to have to have the attic ready for the roofers so soon. But if they're really willing to re-shingle the dormers this week—"

"—they need to inspect the rafters before then. No problem. We don't want rain dripping on our Susabella, do we?" Victoria said, pinching Susy's nose lightly.

Off they went. Liz made one last pass around the second floor, searching for some sign of an old covered-up entry to the attic. Nope, nothing: the entire ceiling was plastered smooth.

For the life of her, Liz could not understand why there was no access hatch. Granted, the attic was no more than a crawl space, but it could provide at least a little extra storage—something the cottage had in short supply.

The most logical place to cut the hole was over the landing in the hall between the two bedrooms. Liz wrapped a red bandanna around her hair, slipped a pair of goggles over her eyes, and did some preliminary drilling here and there to figure out where the gap between the joists was. Then she picked up the jigsaw and attacked the ceiling.

The sawing left a thick cloud of dust and a shocking mess of plaster, lath, and horsehair on the plastic-covered floor of the upstairs hall. But as the opening began to take shape, Liz could practically hear the attic sucking in deep breaths of fresh air.

She set up a stepladder under the new opening and popped her head into the space above. The smell of damp wood dashed her spirits; damp wood meant rotten wood. Fearing the worst, she aimed a flashlight into the recesses of the long-forgotten attic.

Not too bad, she decided after a quick scan of the timbers. No rot, no bats, no bees. There was a little dampness along a rafter where she knew she had a leak, but that was all. *Good little house,* she found herself thinking affectionately. She was about to climb back down the ladder when the beam of her flashlight fell on something rectangular straddling two joists at the far end.

It was a small, canvas-covered, metal-strapped trunk, the kind people used to haul around on steamers when they plied the Atlantic. Sealed away, who knew for how long? Here, in the tiny attic of her tiny house. A buried treasure.

With an eager, thumping heart, Liz hoisted herself up through the opening and began crawling on her knees from joist to joist toward the trunk. It was slow going. Halfway there, an exposed nail ripped her jeans and tore her thigh. Liz let out a cry and pulled away, whacking her head on the roof's low ridgepole. *Damn!* Now she hurt in *two* places. Worse, she was beginning to feel claustrophic in the unlit space. She took a deep breath to calm herself and resumed her crawl.

When she reached the trunk, she was frustrated once more: it wouldn't open. Liz had the sense that the trunk wasn't really locked but was simply used to being closed. She banged on the metal catch with the palm of her hand once, twice, until it hurt too much to continue.

This is idiotic, she realized eventually. *I'll haul it down-stairs—somehow—and open it there.* She muscled the sur-prisingly heavy little trunk from one joist to the next and was rewarded with the sound of the lock snapping open on its own.

Despite her curiosity, Liz hesitated before opening the lid. The one thing she did *not* want was to have something fly up into her face when she did. A flashlight would help; but the flashlight was lying next to the sawed-out opening, throwing its beam only vaguely in her direction, and she hadn't the heart to go crawling back for it.

Ho-kay. In we go, she decided. She flung the lid open with a sudden motion.

Nothing flew out. Liz could see, by the slits of sunlight from a vent at the opposite end of the attic, that the trunk contained papers and letters. Captain Kidd's treasure, it was not.

Obviously the contents weren't valuable enough for the owner to remember where he'd stored them before he'd had the attic sealed in. Disappointed, Liz was about to close the lid when she saw, tucked in the darkest corner of the trunk, another, smaller box.

She reached in and took it out. It was a lacquered box,

seven inches wide and three inches high, about the size of a Victorian tea caddy. Even in the near-darkness she could see that it was lacquered a brilliant Chinese red and decorated with an elaborate floral design. Still hunched over, she fumbled awkwardly with the thing, trying to open it. But it was clearly designed for a key, and she had no key.

She shook it. It sounded empty. It felt empty. The chances were it *was* empty. But Liz had a fierce, sudden, irrational desire to believe it held treasure. She began an awkward, painful crawl back to her sawed-out opening, leaning on her forearm instead of her hand, which was holding the box.

She was on her last joist when the doorbell—a hand-cranked, ear-splitting contraption from long ago—jangled loudly, jolting her upright into the ridgepole again.

"Ow!" she cried, reeling from the pain. She leaned down through the opening into the hall and yelled loudly, "C'mon up, *dammit!* It's open!"

Expecting Victoria and Susy, Liz was surprised when a male voice called politely, "Anybody home?"

If he was a serial killer, he wasn't a very bright one. "Up *here,* I said," she repeated, rubbing the goose-egg on her head. "Who is it?"

"Your neighbor to the east. Jack Eastman," he answered as he ascended the bare, varnished stairs.

The voice was rich and deep and had that touch of Ivy League affectation that Liz so disliked. Clearly he wasn't there as part of any Welcome Wagon. She wondered why he'd driven all the way around to her side of the barbed wire. It never occurred to her to climb down the ladder to greet him. Instead, she waited for him just the way she was. Upside-down. Like a bat.

She was still hanging there when Eastman reached the landing beneath her.

"I'm looking for Liz Coppersmith," he said, clearly refusing to believe he'd found her. "Of Parties Plus?"

"Yessir! May I help you?" asked Liz, snapping to attention at the magic word *parties. Nuts.* This was a business call, then.

"Let me just get down from here," she said hurriedly. "I'm sorry about the mess. I was poking around, and . . ."

Still gripping her red-lacquered box, she scrambled onto the top rung of the stepladder—the one all the signs said not to step on—and promptly sent it flying out from under her as she fell backward, more or less into her new neighbor's arms.

He staggered under the weight of her fall but recovered gracefully, which was more than Liz could say for herself. She felt like Lucy Ricardo after a bout with Ricky. It didn't help that her head was wrapped in a ratty bandanna, her jeans were torn, and her face was covered with plaster dust.

He held her by her shoulders longer than he needed to. "*You're* Parties Plus?" A half-smile—too condescending by half—relieved the sternly handsome lines of his face. "Really?"

A shiver—indignation? resentment?—rippled through Liz.

"Yes. Really," she said coolly, reacting as she always did to condescension. She knew she should be used to it; Newport had more snobs per cobblestone than any other town in New England. On the plus side, they formed a solid base of customers for businesses like hers.

Smile, she told herself over the annoying hammering of her heart. *You need the business.*

"I tried the number in the Yellow Pages," Eastman said, "and I got a not-in-service message." His tone suggested consumer fraud.

"Oh, that," said Liz. "I was in the process of moving my Middletown office to Touro Street here in town, but a sprinkler went nuts in the new place, so I won't be able to move in for a month. In the meantime I'm operating out of my house. The business phone goes in tomorrow. All of my clients know my home phone, of course,'' she added, implying that she had lots and lots of them.

It was obvious to her that he wasn't impressed. Why should he be, when they were standing in a pile of construction rubble?

Liz suggested that they continue their discussion downstairs. On the way down she tried to convince herself that she was in fact wearing a smart linen suit and that he was buck naked—anything to level the playing field.

The living room, with its charming brick fireplace, was only twelve feet square. Earlier in the day Liz had been regarding the room as cozy; suddenly it merely seemed small. And that was Jack Eastman's fault. Right-side up, he looked truly formidable: six-two, broad shoulders, arms that convinced her he worked out regularly. His thick brown hair was sun-bleached and surprisingly untidy for the impeccably casual clothes he wore. He was deeply tanned.

Another rich and idle yachtsman, without a doubt.

She thought of her father, still saving up for an aluminum skiff and an outboard motor, and had to repress one of her frequent surges of resentment for the moneyed class. *Why him and not Dad?* was her thoroughly blue-collar thought.

''Have a seat,'' she said, reminding herself one more time that there was money to be made from that moneyed class.

Eastman opted for the damask wing chair that went so well with her country-cottage chintz, but—she couldn't believe it—he didn't fit. The wings crowded his shoulders.

''Maybe you'd be more comfortable on the sofa,'' she suggested.

''It doesn't matter,'' he said impatiently, glancing at his watch. ''I understand from Netta that you do birthday parties. We have a five-year-old, ah, guest who's staying with us. Can you arrange a party on the premises for a week from tomorrow?''

Ta-dah! Exactly according to plan. Liz grinned broadly—

and tasted plaster dust. She'd forgotten all about looking like Lucy Ricardo; it was obvious that she was going to have to go all out to overcome this disaster of a first impression. "I'd be *delighted* to do it," she said enthusiastically.

"I know it's short notice—are you sure you'll be able to fit us in?" he said, irony flashing in his sea-blue eyes.

Clearly he thought she had no other business at all. It stung.

"Well, that depends," Liz said, slipping mentally into that smart linen suit. "Some themes are more elaborate than others. But we should still be able to do something nice in that amount of time. I was thinking that the little girl—it *is* for that adorable little blonde, isn't it?—I was thinking that, like most kids, she's probably into dinosaurs."

It was the first thing that popped into Liz's head, but she quickly warmed to the idea. "Oh, I don't mean some big purple Barney hulking around and passing out party hats, but something more fun. Your grounds are *so* extensive—maybe we could do something with big cutout dinosaurs placed all over . . . a kind of Jurassic Park. We could create an entire prehistoric—"

"Hold it." Eastman stood up. Frowning, he said, "Nothing prehistoric. Nothing historic. I had in mind some balloons and streamers, that sort of thing. And a cake—even though Caroline's already had one. Some little nonsense presents. And I guess food of some sort. They eat at these things, don't they? Plan on—Netta tells me—about half a dozen kids and an average number of their parents. If you need anything else, talk to Netta." He glanced at his watch again. "Now. What's this going to run me?"

"Oh." Utterly deflated, Liz could think of nothing else to say, so she said it again: "Oh."

This wasn't exactly the commission she had in mind. Jack Eastman was not only a surly host, he was a cheap one. She sighed and thought that he must be from old money. Newport had plenty of that.

Still, it was a start. She did some quick calculations and came up with a rock-bottom estimate.

He frowned and cut it in half.

"Oh, I don't think so," Liz said, breathless at his insulting counteroffer.

Eastman shrugged. "I'm sorry to have taken up your time," he said, and he headed for the door.

It was all happening so fast. Her entrée to Bellevue Avenue—boom! Gone! Just like that.

"Wait!" she cried.

He turned around. Liz swallowed hard and said, "Okay. Since you're a neighbor. But I don't mind admitting—"

"Oh, don't do it as a favor to me, Miss Coppersmith," he said quickly. "Do it because you want the business."

She did. Damn him. She did. "I'll do it," she said with a tight, offended smile.

"Fine. I'll leave you to it, then. G'day."

He let himself out. Liz marched up to the door, threw the bolt, and muttered, "G'day yourself, you cheapskate."

The whole interview was too embarrassing to dwell on; Liz pushed it from her mind and went back to retrieve the red-lacquered box from the floor of her bedroom, where it had landed after flying out of her hand when she fell from the ladder. She carried it over to the west-facing windows for a closer look. How odd that her visitor hadn't been the slightest bit curious about it. Or perhaps he was, but was too well-mannered to show it.

It was a beautiful box, lacquered to a slippery, brilliant finish and covered with an all-over pattern of intricately painted flowers and twining vines, all in deeper, richer colors than the Chinese red background. Its hinges were hidden, and its lock—the size of a fingertip—was recessed into the wood. An exquisitely made thing, and probably valuable.

She would not be able to open it without damaging it unless she had a key.

Or some little tool? She held the box to her breast and stared absently out her bedroom window, trying to think of what might do.

As usual, she got caught up in the view. From her hilltop perch she could see glimpses of Newport Harbor and of Narragansett Bay beyond it. At the moment, a big freighter was picking its way through a flock of tiny, feathery sails as it headed down the bay for other ports of call. The ship was high in the water. Whatever its cargo—cars, electronics, clothing—it had been emptied at the Port of Providence; now the ship was going back, probably to Asia, for more.

Liz tried not to think of the lost jobs the freighter represented and daydreamed instead about the magic of maritime trade. She knew—every Newporter knew—that much of Newport's old wealth had come from its deep involvement in trading with eighteenth-century China. From teas to trees to silks to willoware, everything pretty once seemed to have come from the Far East. Shipowners put the best pieces aside for themselves, and sold the rest, and got richer and richer. No one begrudged them back then—not if it meant they could have pretty blue dishes on their tables and silk dress goods for twenty-five cents a yard.

And red-lacquered boxes like the one Liz held in her hands. That it came from China, she had no doubt. Probably it had been offloaded from some square-rigger right here in Newport harbor in the days when Newport was still a major port of the United States. She was cradling a small token of the commerce that had enabled more than one man to build himself an imposing mansion on Newport's Gold Coast.

She thought of Jack Eastman and wondered where *his* money had came from. He had a certain Captain Bligh glint in his eye that made her think he could easily take a ship around the Horn. On the other hand, he looked like he'd be just as comfortable in the give-and-take of a trading session dockside. Heck, hadn't he just proved it?

Well, he might have his empire—but she had her red box. And she had no intention of destroying it, only to discover it was empty.

But it *wasn't* empty. It couldn't be. What Liz needed, she decided, was a locksmith; he'd be able to pick the lock in two seconds flat. She dusted herself off, changed, and was on her way out the door when she saw Victoria pulling onto the graveled parking area in front of the rose arbor—the rose arbor that had sealed Liz's decision to buy the house.

Victoria had Susy in the front seat of her BMW. As always, Liz's heart sang a bright song at the sight of her five-year-old daughter. As always, the thought hurtled through her mind that, if Keith had had his way . . .

But he hadn't, and for that, Liz was more grateful than anyone else on earth.

"Hi, honey," she said to the child. "*You* must've had a good time."

Her daughter waved through the open window and unbuckled her seat belt in a very grown-up way, then got out and skipped over into her mother's waiting arms for a hug.

"Aunty Tori let me get a milkshake for dessert!"

"And you were able to drink it all?" asked Liz, glancing at Victoria with amazement.

"Well, no," Susy confessed. "Aunty Tori had to help me a little."

Victoria reassured Liz by holding her thumb and forefinger two inches apart. Two inches of milkshake wasn't so awful; Susy'd have her appetite back by suppertime. "Well, just so you know you can't have a special dessert like that *every* day," Liz said gravely.

"Oh, *Mommy*," said Susy, as if she were well aware that she didn't have a prayer.

For Liz, one of the the hardest things about sharing Susy

with her parents and Victoria on a regular basis was trying
to keep Susy's diet honest. It was so tempting to let them
ply her with treats, so tempting for Liz herself to bribe Susy
whenever she had to farm her out on a sunny weekend or a
big holiday—which was inevitably when Liz had to work.

Life would've been so much easier if Keith had chosen to
stick around.

Susy was peeking into the shopping bag that sat on the
ground next to her mother. "What's this, Mommy? A present
for someone?"

Liz smiled at her daughter's subtle fishing expedition and
rumpled her dark-brown hair. "It's a box I found in the
attic," she said, lifting it out for her daughter and Victoria
to see. "It's locked, so I'm going to take it to someone who
can open it for me. Do you want to come?"

While Susy considered her options, Victoria asked, "For
heaven's sake—how did you get into the attic?"

"Jigsaw," said Liz, rolling her eyes at the memory. "I
made an ungodly mess; I haven't even swept it up yet. I
found a trunk of old letters sealed away, and this was in with
them."

"No kidding?"

Susy was tugging at her mother's hand. "Mommy? I think
maybe I don't want to go. I think . . . maybe I should have
some quiet time," she said with a tentative look in her big
brown eyes.

Stomachache, dammit. Liz threw Victoria a scolding
glance, then said to her daughter, "Okay, sweetie. I'll take
the box to the locksmith some other time."

"Liz, just go—I'll stay with Susy," said Victoria amiably.
She held out her hand to the little girl and said, "You can
have quiet time while I tell you another adventure of the
Princess and the Magic Petunia."

Susy was all for that, which left Liz with mixed feelings.
Her daughter's early years were precious ones, and on Liz's

deathbed she was going to want every lost moment of them. She felt guilty for wanting to open the box—but she wanted desperately to open the box.

"Okay, then, sunshine. I'll be right back."

Jimmy's Lock and Key was located in a peeling colonial house, one of the many historic buildings, most of them updated, that lined both sides of downtown Thames Street. The concept of gentrification, however, had not yet occurred to Jimmy; his ancient, tattered shop was a jumble of new brass hardware, carousels of key blanks, and boxes of mysterious metal innards. Liz laid the red-lacquered box on the painted plywood counter and said, "Can you get it open without damaging it?"

Jimmy, a bulldozer of a man who could probably pry open a locked safe with one arm tied behind his back, picked up the box in his thick, stubby hands and said, "Shouldn't be too hard. Where'd you get it—flea market, or antique shop?"

"Neither. It was in the sealed-in attic of the house I've just bought, along with a bunch of old letters. Isn't that weird? If this box was bigger, I'd be afraid of finding someone's bones in it," Liz said with a self-conscious laugh.

"Or ashes," said Jimmy, shaking it back and forth the way Liz had.

Ashes! She hadn't thought of ashes. "Can you pick the lock?" she asked with more dread than before.

Jimmy shrugged and reached under the counter. "Won't need to, maybe." He brought out an El Producto cigar box and flipped open the cardboard top. "Let's see what we got in here," he said, pushing an assortment of tiny keys around in the box. "Sometimes we get lucky."

His eye lit on a little brass key that must've looked promising. He picked it up and tried inserting it. No luck. He tried another. Ditto. Liz's hopes began to sag. Then he pulled out a third key, a tiny key turned dark with age, and tried that one.

"Well, well," he said, obviously pleased as the key turned smoothly in the lock. "Nothin's frozen."

What Jimmy did next showed he had an instinct either for chivalry or for caution, Liz never did figure out which: He turned the box around to face her so that she could open it herself.

Liz bit her lower lip and laid both her hands gently on the lid. She'd half convinced herself that there was an important letter wedged inside, or a map—a treasure map left behind by Captain Kidd. But she did not want ashes.

Slowly, expectantly, she raised the lid. Almost at once her ears seemed to ring, as though somewhere in the far, far distance, someone were playing an instrument. A chime, perhaps: a single-noted chime whose echo began to fill the room with its extraordinary tone.

She was confused; she thought perhaps the box was some sort of music box or that—bizarrely—it was rigged to sound an alarm when opened. But the tone stayed with her, filling her head with its melodious note.

"Well? What've we got?" asked Jimmy.

"I . . . what?" Liz asked, hardly registering the question.

The inside of the box was lined with rich black satin, and on the satin sat a heart-shaped pin. The heart itself was open and gold, shaped into a twining leafy pattern. The inside point of the heart ended in a tiny red stone sitting on five gold petals. It was very pretty, but worth less, probably, than the box it was pinned to.

"Are you all right, miss?"

The single, chiming note became more intense as Liz reached into the box and gently released the heart from its satin anchor. "A pin," she murmured. Her own heart had taken off at a flyaway rate; her hands began unaccountably to tremble. The silvery ringing in her ears—was she about to faint? "It's a pin," she repeated in a whisper, unbelievably distressed.

"Oh, yeah," said Jimmy with a sideways tilt of his balding head. "Very nice. Got any idea how long it was sealed away?" he asked.

"I . . . don't. The house was built in the thirties," Liz said, shaking her head, trying to rid herself of the ringing sound. She took a deep breath or two and looked around the shop in confusion, then said, "Do you have an appliance somewhere that makes some kind of high-pitched sound?"

"The fridge out back drives me nuts," Jimmy volunteered.

"No, no . . . this is more . . . beautiful, than that."

"Beautiful?"

"And scary."

"Scary?" He frowned and said, "An *appliance*?"

"Maybe your neighbors have chimes hanging outside?" she asked him without much hope.

"Chimes! Don't get me started on chimes," Jimmy said, snorting. "Damned clanging pipes. As if we don't have enough noise blastin' outta car speakers all summer long. The traffic eventually dies down—you can catch an hour or two of quiet at night. But chimes! All day, all night . . . chimes just keep chiming. Chimes in the city," he said pontifically, "are not a good idea."

"Yes, like that," Liz whispered, ignoring his speech. "You have some nearby?"

"No," he answered grimly. "Not anymore."

She needed some air. She slid the pin back into its satin cushion and closed the red box. The silvery, penetrating sound ceased at once.

That left Liz more disturbed than before. She wanted to lift up the lid, just to test the box, but she was so grateful for the quiet, the peace, that she let it stay closed.

"I guess my ears *were* ringing," she said in a clumsy lie. "How much do I owe you for the key, then?"

Jimmy flapped a beefy hand at her and said, "Ah, nothin'. It's just an old key."

"Thank you," Liz said, still in a subdued voice. "That's awfully nice." Afraid that she wasn't seeming properly grateful, she took a business card from her purse and handed it to the locksmith. "If I can ever return the favor..."

Jimmy read the card. "Parties, eh? Well, I got grandkids, and no mistake. Do you have one of them Barney getups available?"

Liz smiled wanly and left with her red box and her new old key.

Chapter 3

*O*ne mystery was solved, anyway: There was no treasure map, only a pretty little pin.

But now a new, more daunting mystery faced Liz: What had produced the strange and melodious chime-note? She glanced at the red box sitting innocently on the front seat alongside her as she crawled through downtown traffic on her way back to her cottage. As it happened, she was trapped behind a Jeep blasting rap music; it was all she could do not to march over to the driver and rap him on his damned head. Jimmy was right. It was all so rude.

She tried not to think about the traffic or the box and instead turned her thoughts to the Eastman birthday party. She could save money by making the cake herself: say, a giant Mickey Mouse head, with eight-inch cake-pan ears. It would be the pièce de résistance of the affair. No one would ever remember that the decorations were skimpy; everyone would go home raving about the huge Mickey Mouse cake. Good. The cake idea was good.

She glanced again at the red box beside her. *Had* she imagined the sound? By now, she was as curious as Pandora. She took a deep breath, then lifted the lid an inch. Nothing. Thank God, nothing. Relieved that *that* was over, Liz swung up to Bellevue Avenue, hoping against hope that traffic would be slightly less crushing there than on narrow Spring Street, the only other northbound street to her cottage.

Wrong. On a steamy Friday in June, Newport traffic came in only two versions: horrendous and murderous. Obviously she should have walked, but old habits died hard. The Fifth Ward, where she'd been brought up, was just a few blocks too far from downtown to be easily walkable. Then, after she married, she and her husband had rented a little ranch house in Middletown, farther up the island, because it was close to both their jobs at Raytheon. But now she had a house smack-dab in the middle of everything. Walking was the only way to go.

Eventually Jack Eastman's exquisite manor house loomed ahead. With its steeply pitched roofs, multiple chimneys, intricate shingles, and half-timbered stucco, the house was one of the finest and biggest Queen Annes in a town that overflowed with them. Liz could still remember pedaling down Bellevue Avenue on her way to the beach when she was a child, liking the Queen Annes more than any of the French chateaus, Italian villas, or granite castles that lined the famous avenue. Something about the brooding Gothic lines of the shingled English style appealed to her.

And scared her, of course, which she loved.

Liz turned off Bellevue Avenue toward her house and then, entirely on impulse, she pulled up in front of the Eastman mansion. She had a question for Jack Eastman. She could have asked it by phone; but she had changed into a stylish skirt and a new knit top, and she wanted to prove that she didn't *always* look like something the cat dragged in.

Scanning her image in the rearview mirror of her minivan, Liz poked her thick blunt-cut hair back into place, then decided that maybe she needed a bit more lipstick.

And a little mascara.

And a touch of eye shadow.

Whatever it takes to make him see that I'm—I'm— What? Professional? Hardly. A professional would have called first before dropping by. She strode up to the front door, trying not to listen to the little voice running around madly inside her head screaming, "You idiot! You just want to show him you can look pretty! You idiot!"

But it was too late for second thoughts. Ignoring the doorbell above the discreet brass nameplate engraved with the name "East Gate," she lifted the heavy dolphin doorknocker and brought it down in three sharp thumps.

Netta answered the door immediately, as if she'd been hovering on the other side. Startled, Liz said, "Oh, hello, Netta. Is Mr. Eastman in? I wanted to ask him about the cake and, if it was convenient, to look arou—"

She was interrupted by the very gentleman in question, whose outraged voice thundered from behind a set of closed paneled doors off the massive, portrait-lined entrance hall, itself as big as the whole first floor of Liz's toy cottage.

"What the *hell* do you think you're up to, inviting those slimeballs on the property!" she heard him shout.

The hair on Liz's arms stood on end as she murmured, "This may not be the right time—"

"Dear, it surely isn't," the housekeeper said uneasily.

Liz heard another man's voice, obviously attempting to calm Eastman down, and then Eastman again, interrupting him.

"You want to hang out with those sewer rats, go ahead— but do it in their sewer, not the shipyard! If I see them there again, I'll run them off myself!"

Again the other voice, soothing and yet urgent.

Then Eastman's voice, hoarse with rage: "Are you *crazy*? You mess with them, you'll end up in jail! You think they're along for the ride? They want the *land,* you bloody old fool! Not the business!"

Then the other voice, also angry now.

And then Eastman again, cutting him off. "They'll do whatever they have to do to get it! You bloody, bloody old fool!"

Then the door opening. Then the door slamming.

And there he was, face to face with Liz for the second time that day, except, of course, that now she looked pretty.

"Mr.—Mr. Eastman," she said piteously. "This may seem like a trivial question . . . but I wanted to know . . . chocolate cake?" she asked in a faltering voice. "Or white?"

Still flushed with fury, he stared blankly at her for a moment. "The question's not only trivial," he growled at last. "It's goddamned stupid!"

He brushed past her on his way out, leaving Liz—for the second time that day—agape.

"He doesn't mean that, dear," said Netta apologetically, wringing her hands. "Truly. I've never seen him this angry. He would *never* talk to someone like that."

"I see," said Liz, shaking with indignation. "Then I guess we both imagined it!"

"I mean, he's always a perfect gentleman," Netta said.

"With gentle ladies, you mean," said Liz grimly. He'd looked at *her* . . . answered *her* . . . stormed past *her*, as if she were some low-life panhandler.

"I mean with *everyone*," his housekeeper insisted. "But Mr. Eastman's been under tremendous strain. You simply can't imagine . . . ," she said, her voice trailing off. She was shaking her head and looked exactly the way a housekeeper in a Gothic mansion should look: distressed, old, and loyal to the bone.

But Liz was unmoved. As far as she was concerned, Netta's master was ruder than either chimes *or* rap music. "Well!" she said crisply, tapping her foot on the marble floor. "Now that I'm here: would you like to show me where the event is going to be held?"

Netta furrowed her brow with uncertainty and studied the closed doors. "Yes," she said, suddenly making up her mind. "Why not?"

She knocked once on one of the paneled doors and then

opened it. Liz followed her into what was obviously East Gate's Great Room, a soaring affair of dark and gleaming elegance. From the parquet floor and exposed timbers to the deeply silled windows topped by panels of stained glass, everything about the room suggested excessive wealth and power. Nothing about it was timid or subtle. Nothing about it was even remotely feminine. It was a statement of pure male dominance.

The seating was grouped into several arrangements of sofas and chairs, most of them covered in dark, rich tapestries, each grouping with its own exquisite Persian rug. One armchair stood out from the rest. It was the only one in the room, made of tufted leather, with big rolled arms. Obviously it was an old favorite, worn soft by generations. In that chair, which was positioned in front of a massive fireplace heaped with ashes, sprawled an older, thinner, and altogether calmer version of Jack Eastman.

He'd been deep in thought when they walked in. He, too, seemed angry, although there was no hint of a scowl on the etched features of his still-handsome face. Liz decided, on the spot, that *this* man would never permit himself to scowl: it would take too much energy.

When he realized that Netta had someone with her, he stood up from the leather armchair and said pleasantly, "I beg your pardon."

He looked expectantly at Liz. He had the same blue gaze as Jack Eastman—and yet not the same at all. There was something about the way he looked at her. There was no doubt about it: he was taking her in, from her head to her toes. Liz was glad, after all, that she was well dressed.

"This is Mrs. Coppersmith, Mr. Eastman. Mrs. Coppersmith is planning the—oh, what is it? The *event*," she said.

"Ah. Good. Has Jack supplied you with a guest list?"

Liz shook her head.

He turned to Netta. "Round up the usual suspects for her,

then, would you, Netta? Make sure you include children. We must have some somewhere.''

He took up his wineglass and raised it to them in an amiable toast. ''Well. I'll leave you to it, then,'' he said, and he left.

Netta sighed and relaxed visibly; it was obvious that she had no heart for confrontations such as the one the two women had just overheard. She tweaked the belt on the simple brown dress she wore, pushed her plastic-rimmed glasses back on her nose, and adjusted the set of her broad shoulders into normal-business mode.

''All right, then. The party will be in this room. The ballroom is far too big,'' she added, ''and besides, it's pretty much unfurnished. I don't know if you've planned a menu yet, dear, but Mr. Eastman—Jack, that is—doesn't want red wine served, or anything with barbecue sauce or ketchup, because of the rugs. We'll roll up the one in the corner and have a couple of children's tables there. The adults will eat buffet-style.''

''That's fine. Do you have trays, nesting tables, that kind of thing?'' asked Liz. When Netta frowned, Liz said, ''No problem—I'll bring them.''

''We don't entertain much anymore,'' Netta explained. And then she added with a petulant sigh, ''I hope the boy's springing for more than rolled baloney slices and olives on toothpicks.''

The boy, as Netta termed him, was hardly springing for *that*. ''Don't worry about a thing,'' said Liz reassuringly. ''I guarantee that it'll be a birthday everyone remembers. I'll call when I get a little farther along with the plans.''

She took one last look around the handsome room with its priceless rugs and rare antiques. The Eastmans could easily entertain royalty here, but apparently they chose not to. Liz's parents, on the other hand, didn't have room to swing a cat, and yet they were always entertaining someone or other in their chips-and-beer fashion.

Ah, well, Liz thought. *F. Scott Fitzgerald was right: The rich* are *different from the rest of us.*

Three quick right turns brought Liz spiraling back to her tiny cottage on its dead-end street. It looked smaller now than ever, but Liz didn't mind: Unlike East Gate, it made her feel welcome.

Inside the house she yoo-hooed for her daughter.

"In the kitchen, Mommy!" yelled Susy cheerfully.

Ah, good; all better, Liz decided as she strode the half-dozen steps down the opened-out hall to the kitchen.

Susy looked up from her coloring books with her usual happy grin. Victoria, who was sitting at the table opposite the child with her back to the heavenly view of East Gate, was completely immersed in a letter she was reading. Almost as an afterthought Liz noticed that the table was covered with letters—some in packets, some out of their envelopes, the rest scattered on the floor like snowdrops across a lawn in March.

"We cleaned up your whole mess," said Susy proudly. "You hardly can tell anything, except for the hole in the ceiling."

"Victoria!" said Liz. She understood at last where all the letters were from. "You brought down the *trunk*?"

Victoria tried to tear herself away from the letter: her head moved in the direction of Liz's voice, but her eyes stayed glued to the heavy linen stationery. At last, having finished, she looked up. "What?"

"Are those from the attic?" asked Liz in an annoyed voice.

"Of course they are," said Victoria, surprised at her tone.

"Susy, go out and play with Toby. I just saw him stalking some birds again. Make him stop."

Susy rolled her big brown eyes melodramatically and said, "You weren't even looking. You just want to talk to Mommy by your*self*." But she slid down from her chair anyway and ran out to the backyard to amuse herself.

Victoria held out the letter for Liz. "Look at this," she said in a hushed, almost awestruck voice. The skin of her face, under its scattering of freckles, was pale, almost translucent. "*Look* at this."

Liz took the sheet from Victoria and scanned it. "All right," she said. "I'm looking. So what?" But she wasn't looking at all; she was too upset that Victoria had beat her to the letters. Surprised by the petulance in her own voice, Liz observed, "It's dated July 1881."

"Exactly. Over a hundred years ago. Now look at the signature."

Liz turned the letter over. "What incredibly flamboyant handwriting," she said, still feeling misused. "It's as bad as yours."

"*Exactly!*" said Victoria, her beautiful green eyes dancing with triumph. "Read it!"

"Hmph. It looks like Victoria something."

"*Victoria St. Onge,*" said Victoria, flipping her long red hair over her shoulders. She scooped up a handful of letters and held them up to Liz as if they were gold nuggets. "These are almost all from her. It's beyond coincidence," she said in a low, breathy voice.

"What? That you're both named Victoria?"

"More than that, Liz!" her friend insisted. "Listen to me. I know you think I tend toward flakiness, but just listen. *She lived in this house.* Victoria St. Onge lived in the house that *I* tracked down for you. Didn't I track it down? We both agreed I did," she insisted almost feverishly.

She began a wild shuffle through the letters, looking for

one particular one. "Not only that, but—okay, you tell me—
how have I decorated my house? In what scheme?"

"You mean, in high Victorian style?" asked Liz, baffled.

Victoria slammed a fist on the table like an auctioneer.
"Right again! *This* Victoria," she said, tapping the letters
with her forefinger, "was *my age* during the high Victorian
period."

"I'll bet lots of people your age named Victoria have done
up their houses in Victorian style. So what?"

"My God," whispered Victoria. "I can't believe you
don't get it. What *motif*," she said slowly, as if Liz were in
the final round of the College Bowl, "what *motif* have I
featured in every room of my house—in my bedding—even
in my bathrobe?"

"What? Your thing about angels?"

"How's your French?" whispered Victoria, more to herself than to Liz. "*Ange* or 'Onge'? Close enough, don't you
think?"

It was, at last, beginning to dawn on Liz that her friend
was serious. "Victoria," she said gently, "Everyone's into
angels nowadays. *I* have an angel."

"I gave it to you!"

"What*ever*!" Liz snapped. Victoria was fragile; her entire
identity was a piecemeal, makeshift affair. Liz knew it and
respected the fact—and still lost her cool. "Are you *nuts*?
You think, what? That you're a reincarnation of this Victoria
St. Onge?"

"Who else can I be?" Victoria asked ingenuously. "I don't
know who I am. I have amnesia. In the hospital I pluck a name
out of the blue—Victoria. I buy a Victorian house, do it up as
a period piece, fill it up with all kinds of angels, then I find *you*
a house, then *you* find the trunk, then *I* happen to haul down
some letters . . . my God." She smiled a truly angelic smile, as
if she'd fallen off a cliff and landed unhurt on a cloud.

"Who else," she repeated as a tear rolled out, "*can* I be?"

Liz, worried now, laid the letter she was holding on the table, then bent over behind her friend and wrapped her arms around her shoulders. "You can be anything you want to be, kiddo. Haven't you always told me that?"

Victoria turned and pressed her cheek to Liz's, then sat her friend down in the chair alongside. "There are little things as well—like the fact that she rinsed her hair red with some kind of tea and henna mix—and the fact that she liked Johann Strauss. Didn't I just buy the complete collection of his waltzes on compact disc? You were with me at the Music Box, accusing me of being an impulse buyer."

She lifted a packet of still-bound letters and pressed it to her breast. "Don't you see, Liz?" she asked in a plaintive voice. "Isn't it as obvious to you as it is to me? Judy Maroney *died* in that car accident, along with her husband and two children. And Victoria St. Onge stepped into her body and started it up again. It explains the amnesia. It explains so many things."

"But why?" Liz asked, despite herself. "Why would this Victoria St. Onge do that?"

Victoria lifted her shoulders in a smiling, forlorn shrug. "I don't know. I'm hoping I find the answer in these letters."

"Which reminds me," said Liz. "The box."

She ran out to the car to retrieve it, then laid it on the table between them. "The locksmith had a key that fit. Look what was inside," she said, lifting the lid, not without trepidation.

But she heard no chiming sound, only blissfully deafening silence.

"Ah, how pretty!" said Victoria, taking up the pin. "I love it. Do you suppose it was hers?" she asked in her guileless way.

"It could have been, I guess. I'll tell you what," Liz said impulsively. "*You* have it."

Victoria colored and said, "I wasn't hinting for it. I just meant—"

"No, take it. To be honest, I'm not sure I like it as much as you do. It made *me* feel . . . odd. I feel almost guilty, in fact, dumping it on you."

"That's crazy! It's charming! Well . . . thanks, Liz. Really."

Liz thought Victoria would put it on then and there, but instead she slipped it into her handbag. *She feels as if she's stolen it from me, poor thing.* To reassure her, Liz said, "This box is worth a pretty penny, I think. More than the garnet pin, by far."

Victoria lavished endless praise on the box, holding it and turning it this way and that. Finally, she said, "But why do you suppose it's shaped like a sarcophagus? Something to do with end-of-the-century morbidity?"

"That's not the shape at all!" Liz said, too sharply.

"Sure it is. Look: the left side is wider than the right."

"That doesn't make it coffin-shaped! It makes it asymmetrical, that's all." Liz wanted to change the subject. "Are these all the letters? I thought there were more."

"There are; this is all I could carry from the attic in my arms." Victoria fished out one letter from a pile on the table and handed it to Liz. "Here's the most recent one I've found so far. It's dated 1935."

"Four years after the house was built," Liz said automatically.

"Yes. Your land used to be part of the East Gate estate— actually, it was a little service road to East Gate. But it was sold off to a Portuguese builder who tried to keep busy during the Depression building houses on spec. Probably that's when the East Gate people put up the barbed wire. Anyway, Victoria St. Onge bought the house new from the builder. She was around eighty by then, so she—I?—must have been a feisty old broad," Victoria said irrepressibly. "She paid sixteen hundred dollars for this house—and she complained bitterly about it.''

''Gee. That doesn't sound like you at all; everyone knows you go through money like water,'' said Liz, falling in with her friend's fantasy.

''Don't be smart. Anyway, read the last sentence of the letter. It's very distressing. Very . . . I don't know.''

Liz flipped the letter over and read the wobbly handwriting: *Stupid and wrong,* it said, *and now it's too late.*

''Huh. Well, this doesn't say much. She could be talking about anything, from picking the wrong wallpaper to the current president. What does the rest of the letter say?'' Liz went back to the letter's greeting. ''Who's Mercy?''

''Her sister.''

''Hmm.'' The short letter was a rambling, disjointed mess, bits and pieces about different people, all of it rather pointless and certainly mundane.

''Almost all the letters are to Mercy,'' Victoria explained. ''The sisters were almost weirdly close. I get the impression that Mercy was some kind of healer.''

''Wonderful,'' said Liz dryly. ''This gets better and better.''

Victoria got up from her rush-seated chair and stared out the window. But she wasn't seeing Susy, lying in the grass with the cat on her stomach; and she wasn't seeing the cool green oasis surrounding East Gate. Liz was sure of it.

''Know what else?'' Victoria murmured. ''Victoria St. Onge was—if you laugh, I promise I'll leave—a spiritualist.''

Liz confined herself to a skeptical pursing of the lips. ''Gawd.''

Victoria turned around. Her normally serene, almost spacey expression had been replaced by a burning, focused intensity that Liz had never seen before.

''That's what she was, Liz Coppersmith,'' she said. ''And

like it or not, that's what we've got. At least it explains some of my psychic skills.''

"Oh, come on. You're intuitive, I'll grant you. But *psychic*?''

"Liz—do you remember what you told me over cappuccino that last night of our grief-management class, when we declared ourselves graduated? That no matter what strange road my amnesia took me down, you'd walk down it with me?''

Liz remembered the moment very well. She'd been thinking of her husband then: of how after the baby was born, he had abandoned them both and taken off for California, just when she needed him most. She was going down for what felt like the third time when her mother talked her into joining the grief group. Within weeks, Victoria had quietly stepped into the breach left by Keith.

The gratitude that Liz felt for her that night over cappuccino was profound. Victoria had become an everyday part of her life. She'd supported Liz's decision to start up Parties Plus; lent her money, advice, and time; baby-sat Susy almost as much as Liz's parents had. She'd become the sister Liz never had.

"Yes. I remember,'' Liz said to Victoria, more humbly than before.

"Well, this is the road I'm going down,'' said Victoria quietly. "And I'm a little scared.''

"Okay,'' said Liz with a reassuring smile and a nervous shrug. "I'll get my walking shoes.''

Chapter 4

"Watchit watchit! You're bending his ear!"

"For pity's sake," Victoria said, frazzled, "he's got another one. There'd still be plenty of cake for everybody. Why are you being like this, Liz?"

"Because everything has *got* to be perfect." Liz slid one hand toward the middle of the huge cardboard tray that held the flour-and-sugar version of Mr. Mouse himself, and with her other hand she slid back the side panel of her minivan. "Easy, easy! Keep it level! Oh, this damned fog—it's going to wreck the frosting."

"I know this is your Bellevue Avenue debut, but come *on*. You're out of control, Liz."

"Okay, in he goes. Eee-zee-e . . . good. Don't tell *me* about control," Liz snapped, once the cake was secure on the floor of the van. She took the clipboard from the front seat and ran one last check over her list of party preparations. "*I* haven't been obsessing over some moldy letters for the last week."

"You said you wanted to do the party prep yourself on this one!" Victoria said, taken aback. "You said if I baby-sat Susy while I worked on the letters, it would work out well for both of us!"

Liz hardly heard her. "Trays . . . flowers . . . puppets . . . favors . . . programs . . . *shit*. Where'd I put the candles?" She looked up wildly.

"They're in your carryall. If you'd let me take the letters to my house in the first place, I'd probably be through them all by now."

"No! The letters stay here."

"Why?"

"I don't *know* why. Right now I don't *care* why. We've got one hour before guests start arriving. I *knew* I should've taken the cake over earlier. Why I thought I had to make a grand entrance with it . . ."

In an obvious attempt to end the bickering, Victoria suddenly laughed and said, "The cake *deserves* a grand entrance, that's why. Look at it: it's spectacular!"

Indeed it was. Mickey's head—with its huge glossy ears, bug-eyed grin, and bright yellow bow tie—was a thing of beauty, if not exactly a joy forever. It had far exceeded Liz's expectations. Susy liked it so much that Liz had to promise to make her one for her own birthday in September.

"You're right," Liz said, taking a deep breath. "Everything's going to be fine."

They got in the van and began a reverse spiral of three quick left turns to get to East Gate. The top part of the hill was very steep; Liz began fretting that the cake would slide. "I don't know why I didn't just hand the thing over the barbed wire to Netta," she said petulantly. "This driving around every time is ridiculous. What I need is a gate in the fence between my house and East Gate."

"What you need is Prozac," said Victoria, staring at her friend. "Why are you being this way?"

Liz eased into her last left turn as if she were ferrying a load of TNT. "You weren't there when he called me stupid," she muttered.

"He didn't call you stupid. He said your question was stupid. And it was, especially considering the circumstances. For gosh sakes, the cake is of *Mickey* Mouse. Chocolate *and* white. *Obviously*. No, there's more to this than that." In her serenely blunt way Victoria said, "Liz Coppersmith—do you have the hots for this guy?"

"Hots! I don't expect to have hots until menopause. Are you crazy? Who has time to have hots?"

"Okay, okay. Just curious. Personally, I was *quite* smitten when he dropped in on us in the Great Room yesterday. He's one heck of a hunk."

"Yeah. Until he opens his mouth. Why can't he be more gracious about this party? 'No thumbtacks in the woodwork, please.' God. I'd hate to be a kid on Christmas Eve over there. He probably makes them lay their stockings flat on the floor."

"You're overreacting. He's the heir apparent. Naturally he wants to pass on the family homestead in good shape."

"To *whom,* may I ask? The man's a bachelor, and with that personality, he's likely to remain one."

"Don't kid yourself, madame. I've checked around. He's dated every new—not to mention recycled—debutante in town, and every one of them thinks she has the inside track. He must be doing *some*thing right."

"Really?" The news was not only surprising to Liz, it was disappointing; she wanted to believe, somehow, that the curmudgeon despised all women equally.

She pulled the minivan onto the graveled drive of the shingled mansion. Victoria, impressed all over again, said, "Quite a nice little cottage."

Liz laughed sardonically. "*I* have a nice little cottage. He has a nice little *Cottage.*"

"At least it's not chopped up into condos like half the other mansions in town."

Netta, dressed in festive attire—brown with mauve trim—was scurrying out to them with a childishly eager look on her face. "The cake at last?" she asked, thoroughly caught up in the party spirit. She peeked into the van, oohed and ahed, and said, "Let me run get the trolley for it."

While they waited for Netta to come back, Victoria said, "What about this Caroline business? Doesn't this long-lost-cousin bit sound fishy to you? Would someone like the Eastman clan really lose a cousin? They seem like the type that keep track of their stuff."

"Hmm. Well, that's the official version, anyway," said Liz, but she was thinking, *I shouldn't have worn teal; I clash with the mouse.* "The puppets!" she cried. "I forgot the puppets!"

"In the bag with the candles, dope," said Victoria, swinging the carryall over Liz's shoulder. "I'll take in the cake with Netta. You clear a path ahead of us."

"Yes. All right." Liz spun on her heel and plunged through the massive double-doored entrance as if she were charging into an unexplored rain forest.

She was all too aware that she was being absurd, but she considered the birthday party a watershed event in her career. She'd committed virtually every cent of the agreed-on cost to an eager new caterer in town, while she herself worked basically for free. From the hours of her labor to the flour in the cake, Jack Eastman wasn't paying for any of it. Liz had accepted that fact and was treating it as an advertising expense. But it made her want, that much more, to blow the man's socks off.

She passed Cornelius Eastman in the entry hall and they exchanged greetings. He was clearly in a relaxed and expansive mood today. He said genially, "You look *very* nice today, Ms. Coppersmith. And so does everything you've done. I'm quite impressed. As for Caroline, she's absolutely thrilled."

"I'm so glad to hear it," Liz said.

It was just what she needed to hear. Feeling suddenly calmer and more confident, she went into the Great Room, which looked, well, great. Liz had confined the decorating scheme to Mickey's colors--red, white, black, and yellow--

and had made big cutouts of Mickey, Minnie, and all their friends, which she'd located around the room with sticky tape. She'd stripped her yard and Victoria's of every red, white, and yellow peony they had and placed huge bunches of them in big black vases that Netta had produced from somewhere.

The effect was childlike and elegant at the same time, guaranteed to please even the most discriminating client.

Liz's client was in the room right now, as a matter of fact—probably scanning for thumbtack holes. He was standing next to the massive fireplace with its elaborately carved overmantel, one arm leaning on the mantel edge. He wore the classic Newport uniform: khakis, white shirt, lemon-yellow print tie, and blue blazer. If there were anyone alive who looked more like the lord of a manor than Jack Eastman, Liz hadn't met him yet.

They said hello, and Liz, hard pressed to keep the triumph out of her voice, asked him directly how he liked what she'd done.

He smiled—wryly, it seemed to her—and said, "I have to admit, you've managed very well."

Only because I took out an equity loan, you skinflint, thought Liz. But she merely smiled back and said, "It was just the right theme for your budget."

He laughed out loud at the quip, and Liz turned pink with pleasure. *Damn,* he had a nice laugh. It thrilled her to wring one out of him; she'd never made a rich man laugh before.

"What's all that business over there, with the folding chairs?" he asked, pointing to her little hand-painted puppet theater.

Liz reached into her carryall and pulled out a mop-haired puppet. "I have a little Punch and Judy routine—without the punching, of course. Sometimes small children can get overexcited at these things. I've found that a puppet show calms them down and makes them easier to pack up for shipping home at the end of the party."

"*Excellent* idea," he said, with the first real enthusiasm she'd seen since she met him.

"I'll try to get them out of your hair as quickly as possible," she said dryly.

He got defensive. "*I* like kids," he said as Liz walked over to the theater and tucked her puppets out of sight. "If they're well managed."

Liz tried to bite back a retort. No use. She turned to him and cocked her head. "They're not Fortune 500 companies, you know. They can't be made structured and efficient. That's not what being a kid is all about." She was thinking of Susy, a dream of a child who nonetheless had a will of her own.

"That's ridiculous," Eastman said testily. "When *I* was a boy, children were seen but not heard." He sauntered over to her, hands in his pockets, a cool and appraising look in his eyes. "And I was a boy, believe it or not, in the second half of this century."

"Well, I'm afraid time has passed you by, Mr. Eastman," she said. "Nowadays children are encouraged to express themselves. What's the point of keeping everything bottled up inside? God knows kids are under enough pressure. You have to be willing to allow them to let off some steam once in a while."

"Fine. Just so long as they don't let it off here. But that, of course, is why I've hired you."

He glanced outside at the thick wet fog pressing against the triple-hung windows of the Great Room. "It's a shame this couldn't have been an outdoor affair," he said in a gloomy voice. "Kids belong outdoors."

Liz laughed softly. He was arrogant, intolerant, and very, very obviously a bachelor. "You *do* understand," she said, "that the kids aren't actually goats, don't you?"

His full lips settled themselves in a neatly compressed line. "I wouldn't push it, Ms. Coppersmith," he said at last.

But she did push it. "I'm sorry," she said, though clearly she was not. "But after this last week, I couldn't be sure. After all, you have no goats or children of your own," she added blandly. *Ah, well,* she thought. *There goes my career on Bellevue Avenue.*

His reaction was surprisingly mild. "Just because I don't have kids doesn't mean I *won't* have any," he said simply. And then came the unexpected blow to her stomach. "I'm no different from you or anybody else."

Liz sucked in her breath the way she always did when she was blindsided that way. She never knew where it would happen—talking to someone in the supermarket, the library, the playground. Always the presumption was the same: that sooner or later she would have more children.

But I can't have any more, you intrusive busybody! That's what she always wanted to shout. But the words would never come, and she'd always had to settle for saying exactly what she told him now.

"I have a daughter I absolutely adore."

Which was none of his business either.

"Ah. I didn't realize you were ma—"

"Divorced," she said tersely.

Liz was spared the rest of his speech when Cornelius Eastman rolled a trolley bearing her masterpiece into the room, followed close behind by Netta and Victoria.

"Jack, you have got to see this cake," his father said with a big grin. "Where's Caroline?"

"I think she's outside with Snowball," said Netta. "Someone should look at that dog," the housekeeper said to no one in particular. "Caroline says he's not feeling well."

"She probably gave him her ice-cream bar," Cornelius said with a friendly wink at Liz. "She's the sweetest little kid."

Jack snorted, then stalked out of the room while Liz decided that he was the worst father-material she'd ever seen.

The guests began trickling in at three. Despite a bleary sun that had finally dragged itself out to do halfhearted battle with an equally listless fog, the weather was chill and damp, and the youngsters were kept indoors. Besides a couple of very bored teenagers, there were half a dozen children between the ages of four and six, which was a pretty good turnout considering that none of them had ever met Caroline or her little brother Bradley before.

It struck Liz that the adult guests were unusually curious about Caroline and not overly involved with their own offspring. She had plenty of opportunity to study everyone's reactions, since she was constantly in the thick of things, acting as game host and drill sergeant to the energetic, romping, screaming kids.

It was Caroline who romped and screamed the most. Liz was amazed by the child's relentless energy. *Hyperkinetic,* she decided, and wondered whether there was any way she could tactfully suggest that someone have Caroline see a pediatrician. But who was in charge? Caroline Stonebridge's mother, Netta had hinted, was being treated somewhere for substance abuse. So where was the father?

"Is Caroline always so . . . exuberant?" Liz asked Netta after pulling Caroline off a smaller, shyer child who was whimpering for help. The children had just finished making their own little party hats, but Caroline had taken a fancy to the smaller girl's pretty pink version and had unceremoniously yanked it off her head.

Netta sighed and said, "I suppose we have to make allowances. Caroline told me she's never had a birthday party before."

"Ah!" That explained why Caroline didn't understand

that the Mickey and Minnie party favors were supposed to be for her guests and not part of her permanent collection.

"Her mother's problems go way back," Netta murmured in a gossipy aside. "They say it was a strain on everyone."

"I can imagine. But where's her fa—? Oh! No, no, no, sweetie, that's not a toy!" Liz said, chasing after Bradley, who, since he was younger than all the rest, could've used a full-time prison guard of his own.

"Now, *there's* a boy who needs a good strong father," Netta told Liz. "Too bad no one knows who or where he is. Here. Let me take the little bruiser off your hands for a while," she said, snatching the fireplace poker out of the boy's grip. She began shepherding him out of the room.

"No, Netta, you're busy with the caterer—"

Too late. In any case, a sharp scream sent Liz running to Caroline's latest victim, a chubby little tyke who was being pinched out of his turn at the beanbag toss.

It was exhausting. Liz had a slew of activities planned, from the beanbag toss to a pin-the-nose-on-Mickey game, because she dreaded having the children bored and roaming the room. That was her job: to keep the kids away from the antiques.

Some of the parents did put in a hand once in a while, but generally speaking Liz was on her own. As she chased around the room steering the kids away from one Ming vase or another, her thoughts, perhaps inevitably, harked back to her ancestors. Four generations of her people had served four generations of these people; the most recent was her father, who before his retirement had served as full-time gardener to a wealthy socialite on her thoroughly landscaped ocean-side estate.

That background of domestic service was a big part of why Liz had wanted to have her own business. The sudden loss of her husband's support and the desire to be with her daughter were other reasons, certainly; but mostly, Liz wanted to break with tradition and be her own boss. It wasn't until the food was being served that she had a chance to take a good, hard look at herself.

Self-employed businesswoman, my foot, she decided. *I'm a nanny, and an unpaid one at that.*

As soon as the children showed signs of being finished with their food, but before they actually began throwing it, Liz went into the kitchen to light the candles on the Mickey Mouse cake. She was wheeling it out on a serving cart when Caroline suddenly appeared ahead of her, arms akimbo, like Jesse James in front of a train.

"I don't *want* them to have my cake," she said, her round cheeks flushed with anger. "I don't *like* them. Especially Heather. She made fun of my shoes. Because they don't have Velcro."

"Oh, she didn't mean that, Caroline," said Liz, nervously eyeing the flaming candles. *Not now, for pity's sake. Have this tantrum some other time.*

"Tell Heather to go home," said Caroline, stamping her foot.

Liz glanced down the empty hall. No help there. "Caroline, go back and join the others, please, or you'll have candle wax all over the frosting."

"What about my shoes?" she demanded. "They only have *buckles.*"

"I'll see what I can do," said Liz in desperation. "Now hurry. *Go.*"

"All right, but I don't want Heather to have the ears," Caroline said with one last glance at her cake. "She can only have Mickey's chin."

She stalked off, and Liz, convinced by now that her career path had taken a detour into hell, rolled Mickey Mouse, his candles blazing, into everyone's midst.

The cake was a big success. Caroline, who was an incredibly pretty child, was all blue eyes and dimples as she blew

out the candles. Everyone cheered. Miss Caroline Stonebridge—whoever she was—was now officially five years
old.

Netta, having somehow hypnotized little Bradley into taking a nap, was on hand to help serve the cake, which eased
things considerably. After that, adults and children alike
gathered around the birthday princess to watch as she opened
her gifts.

Caroline displayed a side that Liz had not yet seen: an
almost grown-up graciousness, coupled with pretty compliments and artful glances at the adults who'd paid for the
extravagant presents. Later in her life it would be diamonds
that prompted those looks of pleasure; but for now it was
toys.

One gift particularly pleased the little girl: a spectacular
Madame Alexander doll, done up in long blond locks and
lacy nineteenth-century dress. Liz had seen the exact doll in
one of her most upscale catalogs; it was worth hundreds of
dollars.

Netta picked up the tag from the wrapping and read it
aloud for her. "Oh, *thank* you," the child said, turning to
Jack Eastman with eyes that danced with pleasure. "I really,
really love it!"

Jack Eastman! Liz turned to him with an astonished look.
For this, she'd worked for free? So that this spoiled brat
could have a doll that Susy could only dream about?

Jack Eastman was standing in back of the guests, across
from Liz, his arms folded across his chest. "You're welcome," he said grimly. But he was watching his father as
he said it, with a look that Liz couldn't begin to understand.
Some kind of power play was going on—that seemed clear
enough. But why and over what—those questions she
couldn't answer.

There was one last gift—an envelope from Cornelius Eastman, the family patriarch. He was sitting in the leather arm-

chair alongside the beautiful mother of one of the bored teenagers. He interrupted his chat with her to watch Caroline open his card and hand Netta the check inside without so much as a glance at it.

Netta's eyes opened wide. She flushed and said, "I'm sure Caroline is very grateful, sir."

Cornelius made some offhand, dismissive remark and went back to his tête-à-tête, and Liz and Netta began cleaning up the wrappings.

Feeling herself like an indentured servant, Liz was reconsidering whether to bother with the puppet show. But the children were getting into Caroline's presents, upsetting her, and Liz was forced to distract them while Netta spirited the gifts upstairs.

As she sat the children—a little too forcibly—down in their chairs, Liz wondered anew that East Gate housed neither wife nor mother. The mansion seemed oddly empty with no one but poor old Netta shuffling around in it. Liz shook her head. A bachelor and an apparently estranged husband: these guys were hell on women. Well, it wasn't her lookout. All she wanted to do was finish this godforsaken assignment and go home.

Her standard routine was to sit alongside the kids and wait with them a minute or two for the show to begin, then announce that she was going backstage to see what was holding it up. Today she did just that. Her heart, meanwhile, started to beat more excitedly, as it always did before a performance.

What the heck, she thought, fully in the spirit of the show as she slipped the puppets over her hands. *It's not the kids' fault I can't drive a decent bargain.*

She peeked through the hidden peephole and saw their faces all aglow with expectation. She was completely enchanted by this part—by the little squeezy things the children did with their hands, and the way they grinned and nudged one another with their shoulders as they waited and watched.

They were so full of joy, so willing to be made happy. Their eyes were huge; they didn't want to miss a thing. It made no difference how rich or how poor, how blond or how brown they were; kids at a puppet show were all the same, and Liz loved them desperately, every one—even Caroline.

Showtime.

Up popped the girl-puppet, a wide-eyed charmer named Misha. "Oh dear oh dear oh dear!" Misha said in Liz's high-pitched voice. "If I can't find him, I don't know what I'll do!"

Out strolled the boy puppet, a mophead named Kris with a skateboard on his shoulder. "Can't find what, Misha?" he asked in a slightly less high-pitched voice.

"My pet turtle," explained the girl-puppet. "He's gone! I think he ran away!"

"If he could run, he wouldn't be a turtle," the boy-puppet said breezily. "What's his name?"

"Tommy," said the Misha-puppet. "Tommy Turtle."

Through her peephole Liz was surprised to see Jack Eastman stroll over and join several of the parents who were standing off to one side, where they had a view of the show and the children at the same time. She watched nervously to see how Eastman would react to her innocuous little script. He looked, she had to admit, bemused but rather bored.

Okay, she thought. *It's not* Phantom of the Opera. *But you're not exactly a Broadway producer, pal.*

Kris the boy-puppet was busy peeking under the drapes and calling Tommy the turtle, when up popped another boy-puppet, a big hulky kid wearing a baseball cap. "Yuh?" he said in Liz's deeper voice. "What do you want?"

"I want Tommy."

"I'm Tommy."

"*You're* not a turtle!" said Kris, much to the delight of the laughing kids.

And meanwhile Liz was watching the oldest and pickiest

member of her audience,—and he was actually smiling. Smiling! His face, earlier so tight with repressed anger, had an expression a lot like the ones the kids were wearing. Liz couldn't take her eyes away from him; he was so much more attractive in this unguarded moment. She liked everything about him just then, from the way his dark hair tumbled over his forehead to the way he folded his arms across his chest, relaxed and at ease for once.

Then she saw him notice the children themselves, all of them gleeful and enchanted by the puppets' antics. It was as if he'd glanced out a window and discovered half a dozen rainbows on his property. His expression mellowed still more, into one of tender, surprised delight.

And Liz decided, right then and there, that either she was in menopause or she was in trouble.

She had to force herself to stay on top of her plot—to bring up the dopey-dog puppet on cue and to haul out the turtle-basket for her puppets to drag around. She'd done the skit a hundred times, but never with her heart in her throat the whole while.

As intensely preoccupied as she was, Liz still was able to notice two-year-old Bradley, apparently escaped from his nap, toddle into the room with Snowball in his arms. Because of the seating arrangements, no one else in the whole damned Great Room was able to see him plop down, puppy on his lap, against the back side of one of the sofas.

Liz groaned inwardly and thought about yanking the curtains shut in an impromptu intermission and removing at least the dog. But the toddler and puppy seemed content enough for the moment. She decided to let them be.

Warily, she hurried through her lines.

"Ow, ow, ow," cried Misha-puppet. "This rocky beach is hurting my feet!"

Kris-puppet reached down and brought up something for his audience to see. "I found him! Oops. Nope. It's a stone."

"Here he is!" said Misha-puppet. "Oh," she said, disappointed. "Another rock. Do you think he swam into the ocean?"

At this point Kris, who knew all about land versus aquatic turtles, was supposed to have given a little speech explaining the difference, and Misha was supposed to have decided that her turtle was smart enough to stay on land and close to home where it was safe, and all the puppets were supposed to have begun heading home because it was getting dark and where of course they would've found Tommy Turtle.

However.

Liz glanced over to where Bradley was sitting and noticed that Snowball had moved a couple of feet away, where he was now in a squatting position over the antique Heriz carpet.

"Oh, no!" screamed Misha, out of character. "*Bad* dog, Snowball!"

At the sound of the name Snowball, Bradley turned around, took in the situation in a glance, and scrambled to his fat bare feet. "Snowbaw poopie! Bad Snowbaw! Poopie poopie!"

Little Bradley made a waddling dash, right through the poopie, for the runaway puppy. Liz shook the puppets from her hands and shot her head up into the theater, surprising everyone except maybe Snowball, who clearly was used to being screamed at and chased from hither to yon. She watched, frozen with horror, as Bradley tramped dog poop from one priceless rug to the next in his pursuit of the puppy.

Jack Eastman, who had no idea what was going on, naturally seized on Snowball and hauled him out of the room. By the time he got back, it was very obvious, to him and to everyone else with nostrils, that the party was over.

"Good God!" he said with an expression of disgust. "What the *hell*—?"

Liz had already tackled Bradley to the floor and handed him over to Netta for hosing down, but that didn't make her feel any less guilty about the social disaster that had taken place on her watch.

"I'm so *sorry*," she said, mortified. "I saw Bradley bring in the dog . . . but I had no idea the dog was sick . . . oh, lord," she said, trying not to retch, as the guests began fleeing the house.

Jack Eastman was amazed. "You're telling me you *saw* what was going on?"

"Well," she said lamely, "sort of."

"For goodness' sake, it's nothing that can't be fixed," said Netta, rallying to Liz's defense.

But Cornelius Eastman wasn't so sure. "It's so runny . . . I don't know . . . the Kirman looks bad."

"I'll clean it," Liz volunteered. "A little Woolite—"

"Woolite!" Jack said, unsure, apparently, whether to laugh or scream. "*Woolite?* And for this you expect full payment?"

It was so gratuitous. Did she really need this fresh humiliation? She lifted her chin. "I've learned to expect nothing from you, Mr. Eastman. Neither courtesy nor respect. Why should you confuse me with a payment of money due? If you'll excuse me, I'll get a bucket of water."

She turned and found herself face to face with Netta, who was clearly at the end of her patience with everyone.

"You'll do no such thing, child. You're working for peanuts as it is." She turned to the men and said, "*I'm* the one who didn't put Bradley in his crib; you can blame me. And what's the fuss, anyway? Those rugs have been in the family for a hundred and fifty years. You think no one's ever messed on them before? This isn't a museum. It's a home—or at least it would be, if everyone would start acting like a *family,*" she said, sweeping them up in a look of withering contempt.

That was when it hit Liz. *Caroline Stonebridge is the old man's love-child,* she realized belatedly, remembering how he'd beamed every time Caroline came into view. And that meant she was Jack's half-sister. *And Jack doesn't like it one damned bit.*

And she couldn't care less.

"Go home, dear," said Netta. She jerked her head in the direction of the two men behind her and murmured, "Save yourself while you can."

Suddenly Liz was completely exhausted. The climax, after a week of feverish anticipation, was so completely crushing that she thought she'd never coordinate an event again. And yet the very next day she had to do a Mexican birthday for a mob of seventh-graders at a Taco Bell. *Was* life everlasting, then?

She tried to put on a good face. "Good-bye," she said briskly to the men. "Thank you, Netta. I'll come back for my things tomorrow."

She brushed past them all and was promptly accosted in the hall by a reproachful Caroline. "You gave everybody cake from the *ear,*" the child said, apparently oblivious to what was going on. "*I* wanted the ear."

Liz stared at the child in amazement, then led her to the cake, which sat on the tea cart, still in the hall. "You want an ear?" she said. "Fine."

She took up a knife and lopped off the intact ear with a stroke that would've made Van Gogh cringe, then slapped the eight-inch circle on a plate. "Here. Have an ear."

Then she turned and marched toward the heavy paired doors at the end of the softly lit hall. She was approaching the massive grandfather clock that graced the near entry when her head began to fill with the sound—the angelic, heavenly sound—of the chime-note that she'd heard at the locksmith's.

It's the grandfather clock, tolling the hour, she thought, catching her breath.

And then, whether it was the thick fog, or the lateness of

the hour, or the state of her exhaustion—she saw a shadowy, vapory, and yet oddly clear figure of a dark-haired man, well-built, wearing buttoned trousers and a loose flowing shirt with ominously dark spatters on it. The apparition was leaning, with arms folded, against the grandfather clock.

Watching her.

Stifling a cry, Liz stopped dead in her tracks. Before she could make up her mind what to do, the hallucination passed, although the sound—the single transcendental chime-note— did not. Liz took a deep breath and hurried past the clock. The chime-sound followed her as she fled through the fog to her van, parked off to one side of the mansion's graveled drive. Her hands were shaking uncontrollably as she struggled to fit the key in the ignition.

I have to get away from here, she thought distractedly. *Away from him . . . it . . . them. Oh, God. I have to get away.*

Chapter 5

◆

$\mathcal{V}$ictoria was in stitches.

"This gives whole new meaning to the term *party pooper*," she said, grinning, as she and Liz dunked doughnuts in Liz's kitchen the next morning.

So far Liz had told Victoria only about the party—nothing more. "I don't see what's so funny," she snapped. "My long-awaited debut turned out to be my unexpected swan song."

"You should've let me stay on and help," said Victoria.

"How could I? I wasn't getting enough to pay either one of us. Not to mention, the son of a gun is stiffing me."

"Oh, he'll pay what he owes, surely," said Victoria, still smiling. "Although *you* should know, of everyone, that you're supposed to collect the balance before the event."

Liz eyed the ransacked box of Dunkin' Donuts. "You didn't want this last chocolate one, did you?" she asked, lifting it out. "I'm feeling very insecure right now."

Their kaffeeklatsch was strictly hit and run. Liz had some photocopying to do and dozens of jokes and riddles to assemble for the Taco Bell birthday gig. After that she had to pick up Susy from kindergarten because she'd promised her that Mommy, not Gramma, would go with her to the dentist for her cleaning. And after *that*, she had to retrieve her party gear from East Gate.

But for now, Liz was bursting, after a night of tossing and turning, to finish her tale of fear and woe.

"You brought the pin?" she asked unnecessarily. It was in plain view, on Victoria's frilly white blouse. "Can I have it? I want to try something."

Victoria gave her friend a puzzled look but said nothing as she unfastened the pin and laid it in the palm of Liz's hand. Liz frowned, studying the bauble intently, listening all the while for strange heavenly sounds. She felt and heard nothing. It wasn't surprising; she had as much psychic ability as a potato.

She took the red-lacquered box that was sitting next to the Dunkin' Donuts box and slipped the garnet pin back into its black velvet lining. It was, she supposed, a vague attempt at being scientific. But the results were disappointing; she could not induce the maddening sound, no matter how many times she opened and closed the lid.

Liz shook her head and swore under her breath. "It must be like some kind of genie," she muttered. "Once it's out, you can't get it back in." She removed the pin and handed it back to Victoria.

With a look almost of relief, Victoria pinned the gold heart through the fabric that lay over her own heart. "*That* had nothing to do with Caroline's birthday party," she said shrewdly. "What's going on, Liz? You're as tense as a cat in a kennel."

Liz sucked in a lungful of air, then blew it out through puffed-up cheeks. "It's too dumb to tell, really," she said.

She meant it. With sunlight pouring through the big un-curtained windows, and a warm west wind fluttering through the lofty, spreading branches of the leafed-out trees, and the sweet-smelling promise of summer wafting through the screen door—on a morning as gloriously normal as this, it was embarrassing to remember how she'd trembled with ter-ror in her bed just a few eerie, foggy hours earlier.

But remember it she did. "I . . . um . . . think I may have seen a ghost," she confessed, gently closing the lid of the red-lacquered box.

"Excuse me? As in Casper?"

"He wasn't nearly so cute." Liz shuddered and closed her eyes; she could see it all so well. "His clothes were spattered—with blood, I think."

Liz was able to describe in detail the fleeting apparition that she'd seen by the grandfather clock in the entry hall of East Gate, but she had infinitely more trouble explaining the chiming sound that she'd first heard in the locksmith's shop.

"It's like a ringing in the ears," she said, struggling with the concept, "but it's a more beautiful sound—enchanting, even. I think the sirens' song in Greek myth must've sounded something like it."

"But the locksmith couldn't hear it? And no one at East Gate?"

Liz shrugged. "I guess not."

"What happened *after* the chime-sound?"

"Who knows? I shot through the doors like a bat out of hell."

"This is *wonderful*," said Victoria, clapping her hands together. "You hear about these ghosts in Newport mansions all the time, but you never know what to believe. If *you* saw a ghost, though, then all the other stories must be true as well," she concluded cheerfully. Apparently she meant it as some kind of compliment.

Liz shook her head, bemused by her friend's logic. "Could I have a multiple-personality disorder, you think?"

Victoria laughed and said, "Can you afford more than one?"

Suddenly it hit Liz: What if someone decided she was unstable? Would they take Susy away? The thought was more horrific than anything Liz had experienced so far.

"This is all pure fantasy on my part," she said emphatically. "I was tired. I was *upset*."

"Not in the locksmith's shop, you weren't," said Victoria with a crafty look.

"Stop it! You know what these old houses are like. East Gate is no exception. Their personalities are so intense. . . . I think we project all that atmosphere into some kind of human form . . . we create the ghosts ourselves," Liz said in desperation.

Victoria merely smiled. "I see. So after what you considered a bloodletting of a social event, you came up with a bloodied ghost. Interesting. But you still haven't explained the chime-sound."

"Oh, just—stop it," said Liz tersely. She began stacking the cups and saucers. "I'm sorry I said anything."

She decided to shift the subject from *her* neurosis back to Victoria's. As she loaded the dishwasher she said, completely without irony, "Have you learned anything more from the letters besides the fact that you and Miss St. Onge share a fear of snakes and a love of chocolate?"

She resisted the impulse to add, "And by the way, who the hell doesn't?"

Happy to be asked, Victoria promptly answered, "As a matter of fact, I played the piano last time, too. I'm probably Frédéric Chopin's oldest fan. And I had a green thumb; I'm willing to bet that I planted some of those peonies you gave away."

From one surreal conversation to another. Liz gave silent thanks that no one from the Department of Children, Youth and Families was overhearing this. The one thing she had to do was keep Susy out of it. This would pass. All of it would pass.

But if it didn't?

Liz found herself running water to fill the sink, despite the fact that the dishes were now sitting in the dishwasher.

"Victoria—I know that asking you if you believe in ghosts is like asking Queen Elizabeth if she believes in monarchy. But tell me this," she said, turning off the water and facing her friend. "You claim to be a reincarnated spiritualist. Have you actually ever . . . seen a ghost?" she asked in a voice humbled by fear. "Either time around?"

Victoria's porcelain-pale face turned a little bit paler. "Not *this* time around," she admitted. "But *before*, when I was on the way up in Newport society . . . I might have conducted a séance or two."

"I didn't know Victoria St. Onge was a social climber," said Liz, surprised. Clearly she was going to have to read the letters, starting today. "During these séances, then: Did any kind of—spirits—ever appear?"

Instead of answering Liz, Victoria bit her lip and stared out at the huge copper beech that flung a deep, wide shadow over the grounds of East Gate. "People thought they did," she murmured at last.

"People?" asked Liz, alert to something in Victoria's manner. "What about Victoria St. Onge?"

Victoria looked back with eyes brimming with tears. "Oh, Liz—I think we might be a fake!"

She jumped up from the little pine table and dashed into the living room with Liz following in confusion. It was in this room that Victoria had organized all the attic papers as chronologically as possible before she ever began to read them. It had taken all week, but eventually she'd ended up with thirty-seven shoeboxes spanning the years 1880 to 1911, and then 1931 to 1935. The first six shoeboxes were arranged neatly on the bluestone hearth of Liz's brick fireplace; the rest were taking up a big chunk of her upstairs bedroom.

Victoria fell to her knees, pulled out the shoebox marked 1881, and plucked a letter tagged with a Post-it label. In her softly shirred blouse and gauzy white skirt, she looked like some New Age secretary to Saint Peter.

"I hope I'm wrong," she said fiercely. "Tell me what you think. This was written when I was—she was—twenty-nine, not so young anymore, but still managing to make her presence felt in circles that mattered. Victoria St. Onge had just arrived in Newport for her first summer here."

Victoria unfolded the letter and in a faltering voice at first, then more confidently, read the words which presumably she herself had written over a century earlier.

" 'My dear Mercy,' " Victoria read aloud.

It is the middle of the night, and I have only just returned from a champagne feast hosted by Ambassador Schilling in honor of his "dear friend," the Duchess de Tino. Before I retire, I must write and tell you everything—everything!— while it is fresh in my mind.

Let me say at once that Newport is both the prettiest town, and the most vulgar, that I have ever seen. It is, quite simply, the perfect place for us. A mad gaiety abounds here which is much in need of a spiritual corrective. I think, dear sister, that between us we can restore the balance.

You must come just as soon as you can. I have no doubt that my hostess, who suffers the painful afflictions of rheumatism, can much benefit from your healing touch. And she has recently lost her third husband, of whom they say she was fond.

Victoria looked up at Liz and said, "When I first read this part, I took what she said at face value. Everyone knows that Newport entertained on a decadent scale back then. I thought she believed she could do some good. And Mercy, too—I *do* believe in faith healing," Victoria added with a defiant lift of her chin.

"As we know," said Liz in her dry way. "What made you have second thoughts about Victoria St. Onge?"

"Well, she seems a little too enthusiastic about the material world for a spiritualist. She raves about all of it, from the canopied dancing pavilion on the grounds to the two-hundred-foot-long red carpet they rolled out to it from the house. And she *loved* the dinner menu—four different kinds of fowl, six of seafood . . . blah, blah. Okay, now listen to this part about the woman she was actually staying with, the recently widowed Mrs. Gundrun."

I have it in mind to reunite, if ever so briefly, Mrs. Gundrun with her dear Eckhard. I understand that when he was alive, the lady was completely under her husband's influence and spent her considerable fortune according to his instructions. We shall see.

Victoria made a funny little grimace, then said, "How does that sound to you? Snotty or genuine?"

"I would have to say snotty."

Victoria sighed. "To me, too."

"Did she ever get them together?"

"Well—see what *you* think." Victoria took out several sheets of stationery from the 1881 shoebox and handed them to Liz.

The letter was written in a hurry; the handwriting was annoyingly illegible. Liz curled up in the wing chair that was too small for Jack Eastman's shoulders and began to read.

My dear Mercy,

I was disappointed, as you can well imagine, to learn you have decided to prolong your stay in Baden-Baden. I cannot blame you, of course. The hot springs there have great allure for the wealthy infirm, and where they provide no benefit, surely you, dear sister, can step into the breach. With whom do you stay? Write me with more care than you have taken so far. You are much too brief!

As for me, I like my little Newport very well indeed. After a month here, I have settled into a pleasant routine. If the weather is fair, some of the bolder of us head for the shore. I don my silk stockings, my corset, my pantaloons and my black wool dress, then I slip into my bathing shoes, put on my largest veiled hat, take up my black parasol—and voilà! I am ready for bathing at Easton's Beach, a pretty crescent of white sand that is oriented, praise heaven, to the prevailing breeze.

It hardly seems fair: No sooner do we ladies get wet up to our knees, when the flag is run up signaling us to evacuate the beach so that, beginning promptly at twelve o'clock noon, the men may have their turn to bathe—and they bathe, I may add, completely unencumbered!

But the afternoon beach is perhaps the only thing that society ladies do not control in Newport. The wealthiest women are very powerful here—indeed, they can hardly be anything else, since their husbands are away all week in Boston and New York tending to the families' vast fortunes. If it is true that Saratoga was created for the amusement of sporting men, then it is equally true that Newport exists for the amusement of ladies of high fashion.

Make no mistake, sister dearest—the competition to reign socially over all others is a vicious sport here, being fought to the death. At the moment the queen is undeniably Mrs. Astor of Beechwood, but that may easily change. A grander ball, a bigger mansion, a more titled guest list—any one of these factors could result in an overthrow of the monarchy.

Liz looked up from the letter. "This is historically very interesting, but—what about the séance?"

"How can you not be fascinated by it all?" asked Victoria, disappointed in Liz's lack of interest. "That's my *life* she's writing about. One of them, anyway," she added without a smidgeon of humor in her voice.

"I have to take Susy to the dentist."

"Oh, go to the fourth page, then."

Liz did so.

When it is foggy and we are forced to stay inside, my skills are much in demand. It is very puzzling to me how a Newport grande dame can dissolve in tears as her departed husband begs her to seek guidance from someone like me, now that he himself is gone—and the next day, how that same lady can demand that I guess the content of each of her guests' purses, and explode in shrieks of gaiety when I am right.

I must close for now; we are off to a picnic in a few short moments. Tonight there is to be a rather grand affair at Château-sur-Mer, an imposing castle on Bellevue Avenue. (Everyone in Newport seems to crave his own European-style palace; I predict that more will come.) I wish you well, dear sister.

"Wow!" said Liz. "I see what you mean. Is she or isn't she?"

Victoria began nervously rearranging the cheerful clutter of framed photos on the painted mantelpiece in Liz's living room. "Exactly," she said, obviously distressed. "On the one hand, she seems able to summon a widow's dearly departed—knowing beforehand what he's going to say."

"But on the other hand," mused Liz, "she's able to guess what's in women's purses. Not that that's so hard," she added.

Victoria moved the framed photo of Liz's daughter to the back, her mother to the front. "So you think she *is* a fake?"

"Heck, I don't know," said Liz, feeling a little preempted by Victoria and her spiritualist. "Read some more and find out."

"How can I do that?" asked Victoria, turning to her with a stricken look. "You know I'm going to Martha's Vineyard for the next week. And you're not letting the letters out of your house!''

Once again, the guilt. Victoria was younger than Liz, prettier than Liz—unless you happened to prefer nice-looking brunettes to knockout redheads—and much, much richer than Liz. And yet time after time, Liz found herself deferring to Victoria out of pity. How could she not? Victoria had no *memory;* and if she had, her tragedy would be twice as profound.

"Okay," Liz said. "Take the first two shoeboxes with you. That should keep you going. But whatever you do, please, please don't lose them."

"I'd never do that," said Victoria, eagerly scooping up the boxes. "It'd be as bad as losing a family album."

She gave Liz a quick good-bye hug and went off to pack.

Liz was left feeling funky and restless and at the same time somewhat paralyzed. What was she supposed to do now? Sit around and wait for her ears to ring?

It wasn't her style. Elizabeth Coppersmith had a long history of meeting crises head-on. When Keith took off right after Susy was born, Liz had reached deep down and come up with a new career in party planning. By giving up sleep and with the help of Tori and her parents, Liz had managed—without a cent of child support—to hold on to both her pride and her credit rating.

She decided to tackle this latest combination of setbacks head-on as well.

Between the apparition and the ruined rugs, Liz much preferred to deal with the rugs. She'd simply offer to have them all cleaned, no matter what the cost, thereby demonstrating that she was both successful and gracious. After a quick call to Netta, she put on a happy face and a new skirt and drove the minivan over to East Gate to collect her gear.

In the bright morning light the Queen Anne mansion looked far more charming than spooky, convincing Liz that the ghost had been a combination of fog and her imagination. After Netta admitted her into the marble-floored entry hall, Liz tested her confidence by pausing and admiring the grand-father clock, a Chippendale mahogany longcase of museum quality. There was nothing spectral about it; it was just your ordinary fifty-thousand-dollar clock.

"I'm sorry I haven't had time to pack up your things," said the elderly housekeeper, dressed today in workaday brown and black, "but Bradley is home from day care today. A summer cold, I expect; the poor dear is limp as a rag."

Liz apologized profusely for having walked out before fin-ishing the cleanup. "I don't know what came over me," she said ruefully. "I really lost it, especially with Caroline."

Netta threw open the doors to the Great Room, which smelled pleasantly of carpet cleaner, and said, "You didn't do anything I wouldn't have done. Mr. Eastman and I had a good chuckle over it later when I told him what you did with the cake."

Scandalized, Liz said, "You *saw* me? You *told* him? *Which* Mr. Eastman?"

"Well, that would be Jack, of course. I would never have told his father. Mr. Eastman—Cornelius Eastman, that is— is a bit on the blind side when it comes to the child. But Jack—"

Netta locked her arthritic hands over her stomach in a prim way and said, "Jack is not what you call your modern male. In many ways—I suppose it's the schools he was sent to— he harbors old-fashioned notions. About children, certainly. And—this I hate to admit—about women. Yes. He's a bit, what do you say, chauvinistic," she said with obvious af-fection.

Despite her own hostility to Jack, Liz liked his house-keeper very much. There was something about the woman's ample size and lisle stockings, something about the kind and faded blue eyes behind the plastic eyeglasses, that made Liz want to confide completely in her.

"This was my first event for influential clients," she said, almost wistfully. "And I think I blew it big-time."

"Now that's just silly. Several of the guests commented on how clever the decorations were. It's not your fault that Snowball got diarrhea. Which is exactly what I told Mr. Eastman—Jack, that is. He did overreact at the end. For goodness' sake, look at the rugs—there's no harm done.

"It's the strain," Netta added, shaking her head. "The shipyard's in bad trouble financially. It's not easy watching a hundred-year-old family business fade away," she said with a sigh. "People aren't buying pleasure boats . . . the fishermen are hurting . . . regulations are strangling everyone . . . taxes are up. Jack tells all this to me, you know, because no one else seems to care."

The housekeeper paused to listen for something, but whether it was for Bradley's crying or for approaching footsteps, Liz couldn't tell.

"Then, too, they've had such terrible luck lately," Netta went on, lowering her voice. "Did you see in today's paper about the toxic spill they found there yesterday evening?"

Liz didn't get the morning *Journal,* but she nodded sagely, as if she knew all about it.

"I don't understand what's so toxic about turpentine," Netta admitted. "In my day it was just something you cleaned paintbrushes with. The police think it might have been vandals. Be that as it may, it's the shipyard that's responsible. My poor, poor Jack."

She sighed again, a deep, heartfelt release of love and emotion for her poor, poor Jack.

Liz didn't exactly want to hear about Jack's troubles—just as she was *quite* sure Jack wouldn't be interested in hearing about her own—but she made a sympathetic sound anyway.

"Maybe things will turn around once Mrs. Stonebridge returns," Liz said, implying that she was more intimate in the family's affairs than she really was. "Families have a way of pulling together." She added innocently, "Stacey Stonebridge is, what, a cousin of Jack's?"

Netta's eyebrows did a quick little lift. She leaned more closely to Liz, as if they were sharing a box at the opera, and said, "Not a cousin. And nothing to do with *Jack*. If you get my drift."

Liz got it. She nodded and said, "These things happen," which meant absolutely nothing but seemed like the right thing to say.

"Well, I'd like to stay and help, dear," said Netta, "but I have to interview a nanny in ten minutes, and—"

"No, no, please—I'll be fine. Thank you so much, Netta. Truly." Liz had to resist an urge to hug the overworked housekeeper.

Netta gave Liz's forearm a little squeeze. "His bark is worse than his bite, dear."

She left Liz on her own. The first thing Liz did was stalk from rug to rug like a beagle, hovering over the areas of offense and sniffing for vile smells. She was stooped over the Aubusson, the oldest and most beautiful of the carpets, when Jack Eastman walked in on her.

"Good morning, Elizabeth," he said from behind her.

Liz whirled around so sharply that her blunt-cut hair slapped up against her cheeks. The sound of her given name on his lips sounded shockingly intimate to her; the tone of his voice, even more so.

"Ah! Hello, Mr.—"

"Jack."

"Mr. Jack," she said, unable to resist twitting him. At the same time she was saying to herself, *Why did you do that? Be nice. Maybe he'll pay the rest of the bill.*

He was dressed in working khakis and a dark polo shirt

that showed off his strong build and rugged good looks one heck of a lot better than some prissy old blazer and lemon-yellow tie. *He's going sailing,* Liz decided. Poor, poor Jack.

"I had to come back for my briefcase," he explained unnecessarily.

"Ah," Liz said. Not going yachting, then. How too, too bad.

He seemed to want to chat. "I've been so distracted by this mess at the shipyard that I walked out without it. Every damned bureaucrat in Rhode Island is down there, crawling over the spill." Obviously he, too, was assuming that Liz had heard about the crisis.

She began to wonder if the spill was serious. "How much solvent actually poured out?" she asked, becoming alarmed.

"Someone knocked over a fifty-gallon drum. It wasn't properly sealed—which I can't understand—and now there'll be hell to pay."

"Not exactly Chernobyl, then," Liz said with an ironic smile. She picked up the nearest Mickey Mouse cutout she could lay her hands on, just to have something to do, and began fussing with the two-sided tape on it.

She thought he'd be on his way in search of his briefcase, but he surprised her by coming the rest of the way into the Great Room and perching his buns on the rolled arm of the leather chair. He seemed to be in no hurry, apparently pleased to think that here was yet more labor coming to him for free.

Liz didn't like it: didn't like having him watch her, didn't like having him stiff her, didn't like having him out-stressing her. Dammit! She resolved not to engage in his game of one-upmanship by either meeting his glance or matching his stare. She simply ignored him. For all she knew, he could be counting the squares in the parquet floor.

"I'm sorry for the way I've behaved," he said out of the blue. "I've been taking a hell of a lot out on you. I hope you don't take it amiss."

Amiss. Who talked like that anymore besides lords of manors? "I'm sure you have weightier problems than most," she said, without meaning a word of it.

"Look, I've decided to pay you the money that's due," he said more stiffly. "I've told my secretary. The check's in the mail."

That made her turn around and smile. It sounded so low-rent, coming from him. "Of course it is," she said sweetly, mostly to irritate him. Clearly she was still smarting from his treatment of her.

His cheeks flushed deeply. Something about his embarrassment made him look almost like a kid to her, a kid in prep school who's been caught picking on someone littler than himself. Which is exactly what he'd been doing up until now.

He stood up and sauntered closer. "I said I was sorry," he drawled. "Surely you can forgive a first offense."

"Not if it was your second," she said instantly. It was Liz's turn to color; she remembered the moment all too well. "You ran me down in the entry hall a week ago after having words with your . . . with someone."

For a moment he looked blank. Then his expression settled into an ironic smile. "I remember now: chocolate cake or white. You're right. I'm a cad," he said in a softly mocking, oddly seductive voice.

Just for that, Liz decided to take all her peonies back. She wrapped her left arm around one black vase, then marched across the room and wrapped her right arm around another. "Where I come from," she said primly, "people only apologize when they mean it."

"Elizabeth, I was only teasing you," he said, amused by her reaction. "Hasn't Netta given you her little speech yet about my bark being worse than my bite?"

"I assumed she meant Snowball," Liz said, sweeping past him with the vases in her arms.

Where she was taking them, she had no idea. She detoured into the kitchen, completely flustered by his behavior. For a man in a hurry, his banter sure did seem idle.

Liz yanked the flowers out of each of the vases and tossed them onto the stainless-steel counter of the sink, then began a pointless search through all the marble-topped cabinets for something cheap and plastic to transport them in. And meanwhile, Jack Eastman still seemed to have some time on his hands before he had to punch back in.

"Maybe I can help you," he said from way too close behind her. "What're you looking for?"

"A plastic Kool-Aid pitcher," she snapped, without daring to turn around.

But he turned her around. "What exactly is your problem, Mrs. Coppersmith?" he asked without letting go of her shoulders.

Hot, hot, hot! Overwhelmed by the sizzle in his touch, Liz said, "My problem is, you don't drink Kool-Aid, and I'm afraid to borrow the crystal martini pitcher."

He let out a short baffled laugh, and then apparently it hit him: She resented his wealth. "Did you know you have an attitude?" he asked, squinting amiably into her brown eyes.

Oh, God, I do know it, and if I don't get it under control, I will never, ever, be able to make one red cent off these damned rich snobs.

"Do I?"

He grimaced. "I said I was sorry, I said I would pay you, I said I was harmless," he repeated in careful English, as if she'd just stepped off a boat from Norway. "Don't you think it's time to stop beating me up over our rocky start?"

"Our rocky start on the road to where?" she blurted. Really, it seemed—obviously she must be wrong, but it *seemed*—as if he was coming on to her.

Or not. He let go of her, then walked over to the sink, picked up a deep red peony the size of a cauliflower, and presented it to her. "I'd like you to do another event for me," he said with a very level, very serious look. "Would you be willing?"

"Is this a trick question?" Liz asked, confused by the signals he seemed to be sending.

He laughed. "You're not a very trusting person, are you?"

Liz remembered Keith, remembered how she came home from a trip to her obstetrician a week after Susy was born—and found a note from him on the kitchen table. A year later, she was still so traumatized that she had to sell the table.

"I've learned that the only person I can really trust is myself," she said tersely. "What event did you have in mind?"

"A company picnic for the second Saturday in July. We used to have an annual cookout at the shipyard, but then things got tight in the recession and we had to drop it. Ironically, things are so much worse this year—morale is so low—that I think we have to find the money for one," he said, his brow furrowing. "We have to."

Hey, just hock the clock, thought Liz. Aloud she said, "I couldn't possibly bid my time as cheaply as I did for the birthday." She handed him back the peony.

She saw—she thought she saw—a flicker of annoyance in his eyes as he took the thick-stemmed flower and laid it gently on top of the others. "I don't expect you to work for nothing," he said easily enough. "But I *would* like you to bring some magic to the event, the same as you did here. It'll be an outdoor affair, but if it rains, we'll move it into one of the boat-storage sheds."

He slipped his hands into his back pockets and rocked slightly on the heels of his deck shoes. "Well? How about it?"

If ever a job offer sounded like a double-dare, this was it. Everything about the man seemed to be taunting her, from the pose he struck to the words he chose. Liz had worked with ornery clients before, but never with one so rich, handsome, or unforgiving. If she blew this assignment, it was good-bye to the Gold Coast.

"I have just two questions," she said grimly. "Will there be dogs? Will there be rugs?"

"Dogs, no rugs. And kids, lots of them," he added with a dry little smile. "My secretary Cynthia will tell you what you need to know. Just call her, or stop by the yard."

Liz allowed herself a small smile in return. "Okay. I'll work up an estimate. But I think you should know: Magic doesn't come cheap."

He picked the peony back up from the pile and slipped it through her fingers and then, with no warning at all, began to lower his mouth to hers. Then he stopped, pulled back, and smiled.

"We all need a little magic in our lives," he whispered before he sailed out of the kitchen.

Liz was left in a state of shock. Her cheeks were burning and she forgot, quite literally, to exhale. So she'd been right after all—he *had* been coming on to her.

Sexual harassment, she decided with a kind of cynical triumph. Exactly what she'd have expected from a man like him. She touched the big red peony to her lips.

The question was, how much was sexual, and how much was harassment?

Chapter 6

The reporter from the Newport paper simply wanted Liz to confirm a few facts.

He was writing a feature story on Jimmy Screener, a life-long Newporter who ran a locksmith shop on Thames Street. Jimmy was chock-a-bloc with interesting anecdotes, the reporter explained, and one of the most recent ones concerned Liz.

Was it true, he asked, that in her attic she'd discovered a cache of old letters and an antique box with a pin in it?

"Well, yes, it's true," Liz answered reluctantly.

And was it true that they'd all been sealed away? Could Liz tell him a little more about that?

Liz had no desire to tell him anything at all, but she didn't want to seem as if she were hiding something, so she said, "The entrance to the attic had been plastered over to blend in with the rest of the ceiling. It was done, I would guess, over half a century ago."

"Was the pin very valuable?" asked the reporter.

"No, it's just a garnet pin."

"And the letters? What were they all about?"

"I've hardly had a chance to look at them," Liz said, which wasn't true. She was bleary-eyed from having read through the night. "Most of them were written by a woman named Victoria to her sister Mercy around the turn of the century."

For some stupid reason Liz added, "Victoria was a kind of spiritualist."

"Hey, there might be a story there," said the reporter, eager about the possibilities. "Would you mind if I looked them over?"

Nuts! "Well, maybe eventually," Liz said vaguely. "I'd like to go through them myself before I decide. But I have your name; I'll be in touch," she said, easing out of the reporter's grip.

She hung up, not without promising that she'd give his paper first crack. For the first time, it occurred to Liz that she might not even be the lawful owner of the stuff from the attic. What if someone from Victoria St. Onge's estate came to claim them? The thought was profoundly unsettling. For whatever reason, Liz felt deeply connected to the material she'd found.

Overnight Liz had learned enough about Victoria St. Onge to convince herself that the lady was a genuinely gifted con-woman. She was the kind of person to whom people were forever saying, "Why, you've read my thoughts exactly!" But she was also as cynical as they came. Her remark to Mercy that the summer colonists in Newport were like sheep in a pen—"easily spooked, and easily fleeced"—was fairly typical. Presumably Victoria always kept her shears sharpened and handy.

She was also either a thief or a kleptomaniac: "I took the scarf," she wrote in one letter, "because it was rather pretty, and because Lucy was altogether too vain in it."

Worse, she was not above a bit of prostitution. How else to explain the extravagant diamond brooch presented to her by a lovesick suitor? "George told me," Victoria had written gleefully to her sister, "that in the privacy of my sitting room I am less a *St. Onge* than I am an *El Diablo*."

All in all, a picture of Victoria St. Onge was emerging that wasn't very pretty. It was impossible for Liz not to think about her own Victoria, tucked cozily away on Martha's Vineyard with the first two shoeboxes. Was she, too, becoming disillusioned? And if so, would this be the end of the reincarnation nonsense?

Liz drifted into the kitchen, with its irresistible view of the East Gate estate, and let herself get lost in the peaceful majesty of the scene before her. After two weeks in her new house, she could safely say she'd never seen the same view twice. Every day it grew richer, fuller, greener; every day the light was new and different. Liz understood, at last, why some artists paint the same scene dozens of times, trying to get at its essence.

She herself couldn't decide whether she preferred morning light to afternoon, bright days to foggy ones. She liked the garishness of the noonday sun, but she loved the subtleties of a rainy day. Dawn always seemed more wonderful than sunset—until the sun went down. Liz was overwhelmed by the beauty of the summer season, aware that she had the rich red blaze of fall, the pristine snows of winter, the sleepy greening of spring still to look forward to.

And—unlike Jack Eastman—she wouldn't have to pay property taxes on any of it.

Liz thought of Jack, thought of the near kiss. To call it a kiss would be a bit of a stretch. She closed her eyes and relived it—again—and chewed her lip over it—again—and thought, again, that he meant it as a handshake, nothing more. Dammit.

"Anyway, who cares?" she murmured to herself. Did men like Jack Eastman ever really ask women like Elizabeth Coppersmith on dates?

She let herself drop back into the fantasy. Assuming he weren't her client, would she say yes? Jack was good-looking, powerful, rich. He could, when he wanted to, be charming. He had a seductive laugh. He knew all the right people. He was a very eligible bachelor.

Or—would she say no? Jack was vain; bossy; ungenerous. It took a major effort for him to be charming. His laugh was arrogant. He knew all the wrong people. He was eligible, all right, but he was a *bachelor*—the most selfish kind of male.

Interesting. Liz couldn't imagine *what* she'd say—if he ever asked her.

After picking up Susy from school, Liz fed her some lunch and dragged her off to the Newport Library. Liz wanted to find out when Victoria St. Onge died. For that matter, she wanted to know *if* she died.

The last letter Liz had of Victoria St. Onge was written in early 1935, a rambling note done in a shaky hand. The woman would've been about eighty-five years old by then and was obviously failing, both physically and mentally.

Nonetheless, Victoria St. Onge came across in the letters as someone so intense and manipulative that Liz was ready to believe—well, just about anything. Finding a date of death would be oddly reassuring to Liz in the mood she was in right now.

The mood was: *jumpy*. Liz's breakthrough to the attic had cost her a lot in peace of mind and hours of sleep. Chimes . . . ghosts . . . claims of reincarnation. Liz was convinced that the only way to get her life back to normal was to read through the letters, get to know Victoria St. Onge as an ordinary—if cunning—human being, and dismiss her from her thoughts forever.

She was far less confident about what to do with her amnesiac friend on the Vineyard.

After plopping Susy down under the watchful eye of the children's librarian, Liz squirreled herself a few feet away in the Newport Room and began leafing carefully through bound and yellowed copies of the *Newport Daily News,* beginning with the ones from early 1936. The crumbling newspapers, with their simpler, gentler themes, were naturally fascinating to Liz, a Newport native, but she made herself focus on her mission: to find out when Victoria St. Onge died.

By the time she came to the year 1939, Liz not only knew when, she knew how.

"So how's the Vineyard working out?" Liz asked Victoria in a resolutely cheerful voice when they talked on the phone that night.

"Better than my wildest dreams," Victoria said happily. "You remember the internist who treated me after the accident? I told you about him—dark eyes, beard, funky sense of humor? He's here, on vacation too, and boy oh boy, he's *alone*. He's a windsurfing nut. So guess what? I've decided that *I* want to learn."

"You, windsurf? I don't think so." Victoria was the most unathletic woman Liz had ever known.

"I know—I fall constantly. Ben thinks it's hysterical. This morning I fell right out of my top. Unfortunately, the water's so damned cold that we had to go out and buy me a wetsuit." Victoria sighed and added, "I hope that's not the end of the attraction."

"If that's all he cares about . . . ," Liz said, in a motherly way.

"Well, it's not as if he can love me for my *mind*."

"Victoria—you lost your memory, not your mind. And anyway, he knows it. Stop being so defensive."

"You're right. God, he's such a doll. Funny, patient, kind. Too bad his ex-wife couldn't handle his years of med school. But not too bad for *me*."

"Go for it, kiddo," said Liz, suffering an odd and unexpected pang.

"Are you reading the letters? *I* haven't had the time I

thought I would," Victoria confessed without guilt. "One thing's clear, though: Victoria St. Onge was a conniving little . . . whatever. She did make some enemies. I'm surprised she lasted so long."

"Yeah . . . ," Liz said in a vague way.

"What?" said Victoria at once. "What did you find out? Who did what to her?"

"Good lord, Tori—you've read my mind!" said Liz. Immediately she thought of the other Victoria—the other mind-reader. It was too eerie. With a wince in her voice, Liz said, "I was at the library, so I thought I'd do a little investigating. It turns out that Victoria St. Onge was—well—murdered. In 1939."

"*Murdered!* How?"

"Um . . . a blow to the head."

"Now *that* pisses me off. That was supposed to be a safe time to live. I expected to die in my sleep! Really, it's too much. The streets aren't safe. I may never come back, you know? Maybe I'll just buy a house on the Vineyard. Ben and I were looking at these *adorable* teeny-tiny cottages at Oak Bluffs. . . . "

Victoria's bouncing back and forth between lives had Liz reeling, but at least she wasn't taking the news tragically. Obviously Dr. Ben was a hell of an effective distraction. Relieved, Liz said, "Look, I'd better let you go. Susy's been waiting patiently for her bedtime story."

She was able to get off the phone without having to explain that before the final blow to the head, Victoria St. Onge had suffered a brutal beating at the hands of a thirty-year-old con-man who'd been living with her—thank God, in some other house than Liz's—at the time of her murder. The murderer's name was Johnny Ripen, and he was sent to jail, at the end of 1939, for life.

It was all so predictable. A senile woman with no family and a fair amount of money—along comes a charming ne'er-do-well, and the rest is history. How brutally ironic, Liz thought as she walked her daughter upstairs to her room: the con-woman got conned, and she paid with her life.

After she put Susy to bed, Liz washed up with every intention of turning in at seven-thirty herself; she was desperately behind in her sleep. She washed Susy's milk glass and her own tea things and began heading up the stairs, then made the mistake of glancing at the pine seaman's trunk that served as her coffee table, where the letters were stacked like full-color slides of another age.

Just one, she told herself. *And then I've got to get some sleep.*

After turning off the ringer to her phone, she settled into the down-filled cushions of her chintz sofa and picked up a letter at random. It was dated in July 1890; she read through it quickly, looking for—she didn't know what. For answers. For clues. For something to explain the red box and the chimes and the ghost and Victoria's bizarre behavior.

My dear sister,

I am out of sorts today with what I fear is the grippe. In any case, I am too weak and trembly to take part in the endless round of boredom that has become known as the Bellevue Avenue coaching parade.

You left Newport too soon, my sweet. Yesterday there was a great to-do when Mrs. Olivia-Pemberton had her coachman cut directly in front of Mrs. Vanderbilt's maroon barouche-and-six. (I was approaching from the opposite direction in Peter Trumble's phaeton and saw it all. It truly did happen.)

Mrs. V. will never, of course, forgive the impertinence. My advice to Mrs. Olivia-Pemberton is to cease construction on her Versailles folly, pack up her bags, and return at once to New York. She is quite through in Newport. Perhaps Bar Harbor will take her.

"Tough town," Liz said, smiling, as she laid the letter back on its pile. It was interesting to learn that Mercy had managed to visit Newport after all. Liz would have to read back from the letter to find out what scams *she'd* been up to. It was like a historical soap opera.

She picked up another letter—absolutely, positively her last of the night. It was dated in late June of the following year.

Dear Mercy,

I have made inquiries about the mystery man who so enchanted you at the Black and White Ball. Only one man there dared dress all in black, without even a shred of white. He is, alas, a younger brother with only modest prospects.

Even less encouraging, he is known to be a wild thing, taking up society's best women and then breaking their hearts. He is an artist by vocation, if not by trade. I understand that his parents, despite their disappointment, dote on him to the extent that they have allowed him to build a small studio on the grounds of their estate.

In any case, I hardly see how he will ever have enough money or ambition to suit you. His older brother, who manages the family empire in New York and on this island, would be much more worthy a catch for you—but he is engaged to be married. It will surely be one of the most extravagant nuptials ever to be celebrated here; I am desperate to receive an invitation.

Write me as soon as you arrive at Biarritz. I assume you stay at the Palace until you are taken up somewhere.

By now, Liz had made up her mind that little Mercy was a gold-digging masseuse; she saw nothing in the letter to dissuade her. And yet this particular letter, of all the ones she'd read, held Liz fast. She read it through again, disappointed that Victoria hadn't named the brothers in question.

What good was a mystery man if he stayed a mystery?

He was an artist; too bad. Newport society didn't take kindly to Bohemians—look what a hard slog it had been so far for Victoria and Mercy. On the other hand, the two sisters were still in the game, so who knows? Mrs. Astor's rule that you had to be rich for three full generations before the money cooled down was obviously being bent every day. Maybe you *could* be an artist and get away with it. Especially if you had an older brother to lend you an air of respectability.

Liz had no trouble imagining the wild young brother in black. Melodramatic, temperamental, egotistical—oh yes, she could see him now, swashbuckling his way through a quadrille. Had it been a masked ball? So much the better.

She curled her legs underneath her, propped her chin on her hand, and gave herself an invitation to the Black and White Ball. Why not? Fantasies were free. Like most Newporters, Liz had toured the biggest and best of Newport's mansions (run as museums now, and open to the hoi polloi); she had a pretty good idea what a castle-size ballroom looked and felt like.

Liz let the fantasy wrap itself around her like warm sleep. It was such an easy, pleasant thing to do, and her bed upstairs was so empty.

All she had to do was corset her waist to an impossible size, strap on a bust improver, slip a white gown by Worth over her head, encircle her neck with a dog choker of creamy pearls highlighted with an onyx medallion (her bit of black), pile her thick brown hair on top of her head—and she was ready for him.

He strode across the ballroom floor with the quick, easy strides of the dark hero in every woman's dreams. Heads turned; fans fluttered; there was a rustle of taffeta and silk as blue-eyed debutantes jockeyed to be noticed. No matter. It was brown-eyed Liz—Elizabeth—and no one else that he wanted. He took the full dance card that dangled from her wrist and tossed it aside, then swept her up in an immensely graceful waltz that she knew all the steps to.

He was strong, well-built, utterly in command. His touch was electric, thrilling; it left her giddy from the shock of it. His scent was all male—and maybe a little turpentine, which puzzled her, but she let it pass. He spoke not a word, but she let that pass, too: words seemed unnecessary between them. She wanted to see his face, but his elaborate mask hid all but his jaw with its faint shadow of a beard.

And when the dance was done, he ignored the cutting glances and hostile stares of every other woman at the ball and led Elizabeth through huge French doors onto an exquisite balcony. There, under a brilliant canopy of stars and with the sound of the ocean crashing against the granite ledges of nearby Cliff Walk, he pressed her up against the marble balustrade and kissed her deeply, repeatedly, hungrily, begging her to let him make love to her, pounding her into submission with words of love and deep, wet kisses.

And she said yes.

And then they took their masks off . . .

And Liz bolted upright out of her daydream on her down-filled, chintz-covered sofa.

"Damn!" she said aloud. "That's who it was! My God! Damn!"

He wasn't a murderer at at all; he was an *artist.* That wasn't blood on his shirt; it was *paint.* It was bloody paint! *The ghost lounging against Jack Eastman's clock was Victoria St. Onge's mystery man.*

Still goosebumpy with desire for the rake in black, and

completely confused about how and why she was so convinced that he was her ghost, Liz plunged into the 1891 shoebox and began to read. She went through one letter after another, searching for an identification; her eyes ached and burned until she whimpered from the pain of sleeplessness. She found herself nodding off, like a tired sailor slumping over the helm of a boat during the dog watch, and still she read. Finally, bitterly disappointed, she fell into a sleep that was deep and senseless.

Except for the sound: the seductive, haunting chime-sound that penetrated her oblivion—and every once in a while, turned into an arrogant laugh.

"*Mom*-mee . . . I'm going to be late for *school,*" wailed Susy, tugging at her mother's sleeve.

Liz awoke with a start and stumbled out of her exhaustion, murmuring automatic reassurances to her daughter as she quickly got Susy dressed, fed, and into the car. On the way to school Liz rolled right through a stop sign, forgot to signal almost every turn, and only by the grace of God remembered that a red light meant you probably didn't have the right of way.

"Mommy, why are you driving like this? You remind me of Aunty Tori," Susy complained.

"I'm sorry, sweetie," Liz said, distracted. "I'm thinking about something else."

"About the picnic for the people who work at the boatyard?" Susy asked. For some reason the child was fascinated by the upcoming event. "Do you think they'll get to go for boat rides?" she asked wistfully. "That would be so much fun."

"I'm afraid the picnic isn't going to be so much fun at all," Liz said. How much fun could you have in an asphalt-covered boatyard?

"Amy said there would be boat rides," Susy persisted. "She's so lucky she gets to go."

Amy's father, a neighbor of Liz's parents, worked as a welder at the shipyard. *So.* The employees were getting their hopes up. Liz took it personally. How was she going to make this event work?

"Don't worry about some dumb old boat ride, Susabella. *You* get to go to Disneyland in a couple of weeks."

It continually surprised Liz how enthusiastic Susy was about boats and boating. She seemed to have salt water in her veins; where did she get it from? On the rare occasions when they'd been invited out on the water, Susy had proved absolutely fearless. Liz would've signed her daughter up for sailing lessons, but Susy was a little *too* fearless. If anything ever happened to her . . . Well, nothing was going to happen to her. Period.

Liz dropped her daughter off just ahead of the bell. She considered visiting the shipyard but decided against it for the simple reason that she looked and felt like hell. Instead she went directly home, hoping to catch an hour's nap.

It was not to be. The answering machine blipped four times when she checked it, a lot of calls for less than an hour's absence. Then she remembered that she'd turned off the phone ringer before she'd begun reading the letters; the calls could have come any time since then.

Liz rewound the tape and listened, pencil in hand, for what she hoped would be inquiries from folks who lived on Bellevue Avenue.

Again her hopes were dashed. The first three messages were from the local historical society, the local psychics' society, and a graduate student named Grant Dade. All of them were interested—as a result of an article in the paper— in her cache of letters.

The fourth call was from Jack Eastman.

She returned that call first. Liz assumed it would be about the picnic; but it turned out that Jack, too, was interested in the letters.

"So your cottage has a big dark secret," he said in a lazy, intimate drawl.

"My house is too *small* to hold anything big," she said, flushing with pleasure at the low, almost sexy sound of his voice. "And as for it being a secret—well, I doubt that a town crier could've spread the word any faster than the *Daily News*."

She filled him in on the other messages. He seemed genuinely interested, which left her genuinely pleased; it wasn't often that she'd seen him anything else than self-absorbed.

"You *did* know," he said, "that your house is built on land my family used to own?"

Ah, yes, she thought. *Back to me, me, me.* "Of course," she answered, remembering what Victoria had read in the other Victoria's letters. "My land was part of an access road to East Gate."

"Not always. Originally there was a small artist's studio there. The studio got torn down a couple of generations ago, and the land started being used for access after that. Eventually it was sold off to make the boundary line more square."

He might as well have dropped the artist's studio on Liz's head. "Oh, really . . . how interesting." She tried to keep her voice from shaking as she asked, "Do you happen to know who stayed there?"

"I said it was an artist's studio," he said, a smile in his voice. "I don't imagine it was a plumber who used it."

Oh my god. Oh my god. Liz's heart took off on a wild thump, racking her chest, leaving her voice stripped of emotion as she said, "I see. Not a plumber."

Not a coincidence, either. Victoria was right. All that stuff about karma . . .

"Hey, come on," said Jack in a cajoling voice. "I was only teasing. Boy, you sure can dish it out more than you can take it." He let out a short, musing laugh. "What a thin-skinned little newt you are."

An artist's studio. "Is that why you called, then?" she asked weakly, oblivious to everything he'd said after that. "To find out about the letters?"

Obviously he was mistaking her faintness for chilliness. "No, that was supposed to be the friendly chitchat part that preceded the business part," he admitted dryly. "I called to find out how the picnic plans are coming. My secretary tells me she hasn't heard from you yet. Naturally I'd like to be sure—"

"That I can handle it? A commission as small as this?" She laughed with fine bravado, considering that she was in a state of shock.

"I'm glad to hear it," he said, coolly now. "In that case I'd like to see your preliminary workup. Is the day after tomorrow at eleven too soon?"

Liz felt as if she were being summoned into the principal's office for skipping school. "Eleven is fine," she said, rallying herself. "I'm absolutely sure you're going to love my proposal."

Chapter 7

"**I** have nothing! No proposal, no ideas—nothing!" Liz said to Victoria late the next afternoon. "I haven't even *thought* about the picnic. All I've done is read the damned letters, trying to find out who the damned apparition was—is—was."

Victoria, who'd cut her vacation short and was feeling as glum as Liz was feeling frantic, shrugged and said, "What's the big deal? Just make sure there's lots of good food. Nobody's going to pay attention to color schemes or party themes at a boatyard."

"But Jack said he wanted *magic*," Liz wailed.

Victoria poured another spoon of honey into her tea and stirred it languidly. "So? See if you can get your artist pal to make an appearance."

Liz, leafing madly through her Rolodex, looked up and said, "How can you be so flippant? *You're* the one who got me into this. *You're* the one who convinced me you were *her*. *Now* look at you—you're not her . . . you're not you . . . you're just a mooning, moping . . . teenager! God! One little fight with your new boyfriend—"

"It wasn't a fight," Victoria murmured. She dropped her head over her bone-china teacup and inhaled the bergamot scent as if it were a restorative. "It was a parting of the ways."

"Well, either tell me what it was about, or cheer up," Liz

said, plunging back into her Rolodex. No *way* was she going to find a decent caterer on such short notice.

"He wants me to be Judy Maroney," Victoria said in a dull, weary voice. "I told him Judy Maroney was dead, and that there's nothing I can do about it."

Liz stopped in her tracks. "Ah," she said softly. "I'm sorry, Tori. I didn't realize—"

Victoria shook off the tears that were glazing her deep-green eyes and said, "He's convinced I have psychogenic amnesia, that I can go back to being Judy Maroney anytime I want. He can't believe I've really tried."

"Well, forget Dr. Ben, then," said Liz softly. "What does *he* know?"

"I didn't dare tell him about Victoria St. Onge," Victoria added with a crooked smile. "You can imagine what he'd think about *that*."

"Do you still feel, you know, connected to her?" Liz ventured to ask. "Knowing what a—"

"Stinker she was? Yeah," said Victoria, sighing. She flipped a long, frizzy red lock of hair over her shoulder. "The best spin I can put on this is that she has some unfinished business to take care of."

"Don't we all," Liz agreed tiredly. "I'll be doing this stupid picnic on my *death*bed."

That brought a smile from Victoria, and immediately they both felt better. Victoria said, "What can I do to help?"

"Nothing right now," Liz said. "It's mostly phone and computer work. I may throw in a couple of sketches—did I tell you I went through the shipyard this morning? Acres of asphalt, and a dozen bank-possessed boats sitting high and dry in their cradles with For Sale signs on them. Bor-ring."

"I hope you didn't say that to Jack."

"No, he's out of town until late tonight. My point is, the boatyard's just so—I don't know—hard-edged. Masculine. Picnics should be about grass and shade and families."

Victoria snapped her fingers. "Have it at East Gate!"

"Oh, right," Liz said with a snort. "He was reluctant to let his *relatives* on the property for Caroline's birthday. I can see him opening it up to welders and mechanics."

She sighed and glanced up at the three-foot-long calendar clock that hung on the kitchen wall, ticking as relentlessly as a time bomb.

"Three o'clock!" Liz said, panicking all over again. "What was the point of dumping poor Susy on my parents?" She picked up the latest packet of unread letters and scowled at them in sheer frustration. "I'm ignoring my family, ignoring my work, ignoring everything except these godforsaken *letters*!" she cried, flinging the batch in a sliding heap across the kitchen table.

Exactly at that moment they heard the old-fashioned *br-r-ringg* of her hand-cranked doorbell. Much later that night, Liz wondered about the significance of the visit; but for now, it merely represented an interruption she was in no mood to have.

Which explains why she was downright surly when she flung the door open to greet a ponytailed young man with droopy eyes and wire-rimmed glasses who introduced himself as Grant Dade, fifth-year graduate student at nearby Brown University and author-in-progress of what he hoped would be a published doctoral dissertation titled "The Rise of Spiritualism in Two Ages of Excess."

"Got a minute?" he asked with a John Lennon smile.

"*Mis*-ter Dade," said Liz, exasperated, "I thought I told you on the phone this morning that I won't be making the letters available until sometime in the future."

"If I could just . . . if you could just hear me out. One minute. *Please,*" he said, with the fierce resolve that only doctoral students almost through with their dissertations can muster.

She sighed and gestured him in. "I've told the historical

society and the—well, one other group—the exact same thing," she explained, folding her arms eloquently to back up her refusal. "So you needn't feel singled out or anything."

She refused to sit down, hoping he'd get the message, but then Victoria wandered out and invited him to have a seat, so there they all were: ghostbuster, reincarnated con-woman, and crazed researcher. A nicely balanced group with a certain amount in common.

Mr. Dade rolled back the cuffs of his denim shirt and gave his pitch. It was his theory—or would be, if he could just be first to get it published—that toward the end of every age of lavish spending, a backlash sets in of increased spiritualism. You could trace the pattern all through history, he said, but he himself was concentrating on comparing the Gilded Age of the 1890s to the decade of the high-flying 1980s.

Victoria, dressed in her favorite New Age star-splashed sundress, said, "Really! So you don't think it's just typical end-of-the-century soul-searching? With an approaching millennium thrown in to boot?"

"Not at all—God, no!" said the student, his eyes glittering with maniacal conviction. "I mean, think about it! In Gilded Age Newport—maybe the most concentrated example of excess since Rome—people thought nothing of budgeting three or four hundred thousand dollars for the summer's entertainment. For nothing! For fun!"

He leaned forward in the wing chair; instinctively, Liz sat back in the sofa, easing away from him. He was too intense, too intent on converting her to his theory.

He narrowed his eyes. "It was *obscene*," he said, hissing the word through clenched teeth. "Think what that money was worth a century ago. Consider the mansions: The Breakers; Rosecliff; The Elms; Marble House. They cost millions of dollars—millions of *1890s* dollars—and were used a lousy six to eight weeks a year. And the people who built them made *two stinking dollars a day*!'' he said, sneering in disgust.

Liz was becoming more and more uncomfortable; he was making her feel like Nero's wife.

She could see that he was struggling to calm himself so that he could go on. To some extent, he managed to succeed. His voice became dry and professorial as he suddenly sat up straight and said, ''However, at the same time, spiritualism was making itself felt as a genuine force here. Mystics, esoterists, occultists—many of them the offspring of wealthy atheists—came forward to combat the Vanderbilts and Astors and Belmonts.''

His lecture ended abruptly. ''That's why I need to see the letters,'' he said, eyeing the shoeboxes furtively. ''Those *are* the letters, aren't they?''

He forced himself to look away from them, to concentrate on Liz instead. ''Please . . . I'm so near the end of my dissertation. . . . I could read through them here, if you like,'' he begged in a suddenly pathetic voice. ''I'll pay you rent— I'd be no bother.''

Mad as a hatter, Liz decided. Maybe all graduate students were. The pressure must be phenomenal. Not that she'd know: her only exposure to academe was a few evening courses at a community college before Susy was born.

Looking warily at the stressed-out, teary-eyed graduate student now confronting her, Liz decided to cut the interview off once and for all. ''I understand your enthusiasm, Mr. Dade, but if I gave you access, it wouldn't be fair to the others. I've already stated my plans,'' she said firmly. ''I'm sorry I can't help you.''

She began walking to the door, assuming that he'd take the hint. When he stood there, apparently in disbelief, she repeated, ''I'm *sorry*.''

Something in her tone got through to him. He flushed

deeply—whether in anger or embarrassment, she couldn't say—and muttered, "I hope you reconsider."

He got up and walked past her, but when he reached the door, he suddenly turned to her with a chilling look and whispered, "I really do."

She took a step back, then watched through the front screen door as he climbed into a beat-up red Volvo and made a four-point U-turn on the narrow, lane-size street and tore out of there.

"He's pissed," said Victoria evenly. "Did you get his license?"

"I never thought of it," Liz said with a sinking sensation. "All I know about him are two syllables: Grant and Dade."

"He goes to Brown," Victoria added. "He must be all right."

Liz gave her friend a sideways look. She hated it whenever money talked instead of common sense. But there was no point in getting into *that* discussion again. For one thing, Liz was well aware that she had a blue-collar chip on her shoulder the size of Rhode Island. For another, she just didn't have the time.

By eleven o'clock that night, Liz felt reasonably confident that Jack Eastman wouldn't kick her out of his boatyard office the following morning. The proposal wasn't to die for; but at least the food would be good, thanks to a last-minute cancelation that had freed up a favorite caterer of hers. If only she knew what to do with the kids! Boat rides were the obvious choice; but even she, a landlubber, understood the liability complications that boat rides would create for the shipyard.

She stretched at the little Shaker desk that she'd set up for temporary office duty in the kitchen, and yawned, tired beyond measure after the last few nights. There would be no letter-reading tonight. She was sick of Victoria St. Onge's outrageous handwriting, sick of the hassle that the letters had brought into her life. In any case, she hadn't found a single new allusion to the rakish younger-brother artist. If he was so dashing, where the hell had he dashed off to? Liz slumped in the near-dark of her desk-lit kitchen, too tired to move, too weary to care.

Normally she loved a night like this: thick, thick fog, with only the shrill, distant scream of the warning siren on the Newport Bridge and the low, flat moan of the foghorns in the harbor drifting through the window screens. But tonight she wasn't altogether comfortable with the soupy silence; it was more eerie-scary than eerie-neat. She wished she had Susy with her, or Victoria staying over.

Dammit, she thought. *I've let that graduate twerp get to me.* She resented it thoroughly. What right had he to force himself into her life? And for what? So that he could add a few more footnotes to a piece of writing that no one would ever read? She had a good mind to call Brown the next day and complain to his department head.

She stood up, yawned again, and surveyed the rubble from a day of last-ditch planning: papers on the desk and floor— dirty dishes on the desk and floor—and cookbooks and brochures everywhere. Liz was a tidy person by nature (she had to be, to live in a house that small), but tidy was the last thing on her mind right now.

Sleep, blessed sleep was her only thought as she turned her back on the mess and dragged herself up the stairs. She brushed her teeth, changed into a man's extralarge T-shirt, and went to bed. In less than two minutes, with visions of picnic tables dancing through her head, Liz fell fast asleep.

The sharp crack of one dish against another was like the crack of lightning before a squall. Liz jerked up on one elbow, eyes wide open, mind still off in dreamland. Her first, irrational thought was that her mother was fixing a snack for Susy. Her second, less irrational thought was that it was awfully late for snacks.

Someone is in the house. It didn't seem possible. Intruders were things that happened to other houses in other towns. Not here! *Please,* she prayed, *not here.*

Then a second, sickening sound, of someone bumping into furniture. And her without an upstairs phone. A business phone in the basement, a home phone in the kitchen, and zip-nada upstairs. *How dumb, dumb, dumb can you get?*

She had no Mace. Mace was for those other houses in other towns. And she certainly had no gun, not with a child in the house. If she were a witch, she could maybe cast a spell, but her psychic skills seemed to have come and gone.

The fakeout. It was all she had. If you could repel an attacker with screams and shouts, you ought to be able to do the same with a burglar on another floor. Without taking the time to second-guess herself, Liz bolted from the bed with a loud commotion, deliberately knocking things over and screaming, *"Jim, Jim—Call the police! Get the gun! Do something!"* and then began stomping down the stairs the way she imagined a two-hundred-pound Jim would do.

It worked. Halfway down the stairs, she heard the back door slam.

She paused, her heart knocking wildly in her chest. Then, still working on instinct, she ran to the back-door yard switch and threw it on, infusing the thick wet fog outside with bleary white light. She was in time to see a man—he certainly was no ghost—drop down on the other side of the barbed-wire fence and flee, stumbling, into the murky shadows on the grounds of East Gate.

She ran to the phone and punched in the number of East Gate to rouse the house there. Jack Eastman picked up on the first ring. His voice sounded annoyed, which was understandable; it was one in the morning.

"Jack! Quick!" she said without introducing herself. "Look out your windows for a burglar. I just chased one out of my house!"

"Jesus! Call the police. I'll be right over."

He slammed the receiver down before Liz could argue with him. She was baffled by his response; why rush to the barn after the horse had escaped? He should be guarding his own homestead. She ran to the front windows to wait for his car, and then, like a fool, ran barefoot out into the street to look for red Volvos. The street was quiet, the houses were dark; she lived on the kind of block where people had to get up early and go to work, party town or no party town.

No Volvos. By now, Liz was shivering violently, and not just because the fog was cold and clammy: it was her first-ever bout with crime, except for the time her watch got stolen from under her beach blanket. The charmed life she'd been leading was officially over. She scurried back into her still-dark house—another disillusioned, frightened statistic.

When she saw the shadowy figure looming in her kitchen again, she let out a scream that could be heard all the way to her parents' house.

"Elizabeth, for God's sake—it's me!" cried Jack, fumbling in the dark. "Where the hell is a light switch around here?"

"Oh—*Jack*," she said, dizzy with relief. She pulled the chain of an old glazed lamp that stood on the foyer table.

Apparently he'd just got home; he was still dressed in gray trousers and a long-sleeved white shirt. The shirt was spattered with blood.

She threw up her hands involuntarily. "Oh my god, you've killed him!" she cried, by now beyond the reach of simple logic.

"Are you all right?" he said, reaching her in three long

strides. He grabbed hold of her arms with his bloody hands. "Did he hurt you?"

He was wearing a tie, even. She'd never been rescued by a knight in shining business clothes.

"No . . . I was upstairs . . . he was an oaf . . . he tripped . . ." Her voice trailed off in confusion as she stared at the dark stains on his crisp white shirt.

She took hold of one of his hands and turned it palm up. "Is this paint?" she asked in a daze. She drew her fingers across the red sheen that covered the palm. "Is this some kind of joke?" It *was* blood, of course; but she thought she smelled turpentine, which confused her still more. Nothing made sense. How had he gotten into the kitchen?

"I scratched myself climbing over the barbed wire," he explained tersely. "C'mon. Sit down. You're shaking like a paint mixer yourself." He wrapped one arm around her and walked her to the wing chair, then sat her gently down in it. "Don't lean back until I wipe that blood off your arm," he said.

"Oh, thank you," she answered with bizarre politeness, impressed by his thoughtfulness.

He was on his way into the kitchen, but he turned and gave her an appraising look. "I guess the scare is sinking in. You look pretty pale for a dark-eyed girl."

"No, no," she said. "*You're* the one who scared me. When I saw you standing by the clock."

The clock, the paint, the blood . . . wait—he's the wrong one.

"Sorry about that," he answered from the kitchen. "I banged on the back door, but no one answered. I didn't know what—anything could've happened to you."

"I thought you were coming by car," she called back over the running water. "I went out to wait for you."

He came back into the living room with a wet dish towel

in his hands. "Dressed like that?" he asked with a bland half-smile.

Liz looked down at the extralarge T-shirt that she was wearing—that was *all* she was wearing—and felt her own blood do a U-turn from her feet back up to her face. She slammed both hands down between her thighs, pinning the T-shirt to the cushion, and slapped both thighs together in a gesture that was more pointless than prim. "I forgot," she explained numbly. "I was excited."

Again the half-smile. "Aren't we both," he agreed, extricating one of her hands from the viselike grip of her thighs. He sat down on the chair's tufted hassock, rolled the sleeve of Liz's T-shirt back, and began wiping her upper arm clean of blood drops.

Liz stared, fascinated, at his ringless hand. It was callused and deeply tanned, in vivid contrast to the starched whiteness of the French cuff of his shirt. His nails were blunt and clean but were neither manicured nor buffed; obviously he did honest-to-god labor when he wasn't wearing pinstripes. He may have been rich, but he sure wasn't idle. It was all very confusing.

"Other arm," he said, the way a father might to his child.

Liz held out her left arm dutifully. Her heartbeat, which had finally slowed back to normal, began to pick up the pace. He was so near. His hair, thick and dark and with a few odd strands of gray, had that rumpled look she associated with him. *Probably from trying to pull it out with worry over the shipyard,* she decided.

He was shockingly handsome. Liz wondered how he'd managed to stay unattached all these years. He had to be really selfish or really picky, she decided; there were no other possibilities. She stared intently at his profile, with its shadow of a beard so vaguely familiar to her, and wondered what he'd look like, say, wearing a mask.

Jack glanced up and caught her gaping at him. She said

awkwardly, "You really are scratched up. Aren't you worried about tetanus?"

He shrugged and held his hands palms-up her for inspection: there were several scratches and punctures, but the bleeding had stopped. "You own a boatyard, you get regular booster shots," he said. "Puncture wounds and boatyards go hand in hand."

She shuddered again, upset by the thought of him gripping the barbed wire. He said, "You'll want to put something on; the police should be here any second."

"The police? I didn't call the police," she said blankly.

"What?"

"I saw the guy running; he wasn't carrying anything. And you were on your way—it never occurred to me."

"Oh, for God's sake," he said in disgust. "Where's the phone?"

Chastened, she pointed to her little Shaker desk and waited while he made the very brief call. After that he made a second call.

"Dad?" she heard him say. "Anything?" He listened and then said, "All right. Put the alarm on. I'll be back in a while. . . . No, we haven't spoken to them yet; she didn't call them. . . . How do *I* know why not? Maybe she believes in guardian angels. . . . Yeah. Bye."

He hung up and surveyed the mess around the desk. His cheeks were flushed; obviously he'd had time to work himself into a snit.

"Look at this place," Jack said angrily. "The guy tossed it. How the hell are you so sure nothing's missing?"

"*He* didn't toss it," said Liz, embarrassed. "*I* did. That's how I work. And it's a good thing, too. If he hadn't stepped into my dishes, who knows how far he'd have gotten?"

She folded her arms across her chest, but that had the effect of hiking her T-shirt higher, a luxury she couldn't afford, so she settled for yanking the sides of the T-shirt down low, which flattened the fabric over her breasts—also not a good idea.

"How'd he get in?" Jack asked, with a burning look that left her unsure who it was that was getting in where.

"I—don't know. I must've forgotten to lock up. I was very tired."

"Ah. I see. Right through the old door. Well, that saves wear and tear on your window screens, I suppose." He muttered something she couldn't hear, then ran his hand distractedly through his unruly hair. "What'd the guy look like? Can you tell me that, at least?"

The implication that she was an absolute dodo rankled. "I certainly can," she said crisply. "I only saw him from behind, of course, but he was a tall male in pants and a shirt."

"Excellent," Jack said with a thin smile. "That means we can quickly eliminate all the short men in dresses we come across."

"Why are you being this way?" Liz said angrily. "*I* didn't commit the crime!" She brushed past him and began picking up books and dishes at random, then turned around sharply with an armful of debris and found herself nose to chest with him.

In a voice that was a husky, electric mix of fury and frustration, he muttered, "Get upstairs—and get dressed—*now*."

He was right, of course. What was she *doing*, prancing around the kitchen half naked?

"All right!" she said. She dumped the cookbooks on the counter, the dishes in the sink, and then swung around to face him, her bottled-up confusion of emotions easily matching his own.

"But let me tell you *this*," she hissed. "That stupid barbed wire isn't worth *squat*! *You* got over it! *He* got over it! All you're getting for your effort is a possible case of lockjaw. And—and let me tell you *this*," she added, more furious now than before. "It makes me feel like I'm in a concentration camp—that's what *all* of us on this side feel like: a despised struggling working class, huddled in the shadow of your greatness. I'm embarrassed—do you hear me?—I'm *embarrassed* to have my friends come over and see that barbed wire. What kind of message does it send about my neighbors and me? We're all good people. We pay our bills. We have jobs, we have children, we love our parents, and we cut our lawns. Who do you think you *are*?"

"You're upset," he said in answer. "You're taking it out on the barbed wire."

"Who the *hell*," she repeated softly, "do you think you are?"

Without waiting for him to tell her—and she was sure he had a grand opinion he was just itching to express—Liz turned and went upstairs to dress.

She was pulling a sweat shirt over her T-shirt and jeans to ward off the waves of shivers that kept washing over her when she heard the deep rumble of a car engine much more powerful than any of the compact cars her neighbors owned. She glanced out over her window boxes. Yep. Newport's finest, as prompt as could be, despite it being their busy hour for arrests—bar-closing time.

She righted the lamp she'd knocked over earlier and thought how grateful she was that Susy was with her grandparents. Then she went back downstairs, dreading to see Jack Eastman's face. He'd shredded his hands in an effort to save her, and she'd responded like an ill-mannered, mean-spirited bitch. Her parents, who'd brought her up better than that, would've been scandalized by her ungrateful outburst.

Jack and two policemen were all standing in the living room, filling up most of the available space. It was odd, sensing so much testosterone coming from there. Ordinarily the room was filled with a soft feminine presence—Susy; Victoria; Liz's mother, who baby-sat so often. It was a room of ivory, rose, and grass-green colors; cold blue and gray and white didn't belong there at all.

The three men turned as one to look at her—The Victim— and Liz began immediately to blush. She had no intention of being the object of anyone's sympathy, even though part of her was so grateful for their protection that she wanted to dispense hugs all around. The younger of the officers, flash-light in hand, nodded to her and then headed for the back door.

"I know who did it," she announced with a lift of her chin.

"Yes, ma'am?" drawled the older officer, waiting patiently for more.

Liz glanced at Jack, who was watching her with a look fiery enough to scorch her eyebrows. He didn't like it at all, this B-movie revelation of hers. Well, too bad. She would've gladly told him her suspicions, if he hadn't been so busy treating her like a child.

"A young man named Grant Dade was here this after-noon, pestering me for access to some historical papers I found in the attic of this house, which I've just bought," she said calmly. "When I declined, he became angry and stalked off. A friend of mine was here at the time; we both had a bad feeling about him."

"Are any of these historical papers missing?" asked the officer.

"Well, no," Liz said, glancing at the shoeboxes stacked neatly on the hearth. The only shoebox missing was one Victoria had borrowed earlier. "I intercepted him before he got the chance."

"Mr. Eastman tells us you got a look at the perpetrator," the officer said carefully. "Were you able to make a positive identification?"

"Well, no," she said again. She gave them her descrip-tion, such as it was, of the burglar, and then gave them a much better description of Grant Dade and of his whereabouts.

"For God's sake," said Jack, unable to contain himself any longer. "You mean to say you couldn't notice a footlong ponytail on a man whose back was to you?"

Liz said coolly, "When I first saw him, he was dropping to your side of the fence in a stumble. He was bent over; the ponytail wouldn't have shown."

"You have no proof at all!" said Jack. "You're blaming an innocent man!"

"How do you know?" she asked.

He flushed and looked away.

The older officer cleared his throat. "Well, now, let's take this one thing at a time. I'll write up the report, and you can sign it, Mrs. Coppersmith, and then we'll see about having Mr. Dade in for questioning and to check his hands. Is there someplace I can—?"

Liz motioned the officer toward her kitchen desk, still sitting serenely in the middle of her mess. Maybe her mother was right after all: Always do the dishes and straighten up before bedtime.

Jack said, "If you don't need me anymore, officer—"

"No, that's fine, Mr. Eastman. Thank you. And better see about those puncture wounds," he advised in a friendly way.

Liz turned to Jack and said, "Would you like a lift around? Or do you plan to go back the way you came?"

He glowered and said, "I'll walk, thanks." He added, "About our meeting tomorrow—"

Canceled, of course, she thought glumly. *Give my regards to Bellevue.*

"Under the circumstances, I think we ought to put it off a day. Same time Saturday all right with you? I'll be at the shipyard all day."

She nodded, feeling like a jerk. He'd behaved rationally through the whole thing, whereas *she'd* been—well, a jerk.

"Look, I want you to know . . . I'm grateful," she murmured, bowing her head. "And sorry."

"Sure," he said curtly, and he left.

"At least let me pay for the shirt!" she called out as he hit the street.

He turned around. In the darkness, she couldn't see the expression on his face. But she was pretty sure she heard a snort before he turned and began walking away.

It annoyed her; everything about him annoyed her. She ran down the steps after him, ready and willing to take him on again. But it was too late; in the blink of an eye, he'd been swallowed up by the fog.

Liz turned on her heel and began marching back up her steps when she suddenly heard the chime-sound. But coming from where? From the pear tree? The holly bush? The inside of her head? She froze in place. She knew the sound so well. It was haunting her nighttime dreams and her daytime reveries. She knew it like the sound of her own thoughts.

She shuddered, unwilling to suffer any further torment on this endless night, and went inside.

Eventually the officers left, and Liz, jumpy as a cat now, began—at last—to attack the mess in her kitchen. It took five whole minutes. She could hear her mother's voice: *Was that so hard?* She was about to turn off the lights and head upstairs when she remembered the packet of letters that she'd hurled across the table earlier when Victoria was over.

The packet wasn't there anymore.

"I *knew* it!" she cried triumphantly.

Shit.

Chapter 8

*L*iz returned home the next morning from amending the Crime Report at the police station and found Victoria sitting on the front steps, shoebox on her lap.

Victoria, wearing a big straw hat and a lavender sundress, waved one of the letters at Liz as she pulled the minivan onto the graveled parking space. "Where have you been?" the redhead cried. "I have news!"

"*I* have news," Liz said grimly.

She got out of the van, pausing at the foot of the steps to take in her little cottage. It *looked* the same—just as sweet as could be, with its lemon-yellow paint, deep-green shutters, and white picket fence. The pink climbers on the rose arbor were in the last stages of bloom; she could smell the scent from where she stood. Even Victoria was the same, with her fey outfit set off by the ever-present heart-shaped pin. Everything was the same.

And nothing was the same.

Liz sat on the steps next to Victoria and brought her up to date on the events of the night before.

Openmouthed, Victoria said, "This is unreal! My God— do you think it *was* Grant Dade?"

"That's the message I left on Jack's machine this morning," Liz said, pulling off an espadrille from her foot and knocking out a stone. "Who else would want a packet of hundred-year-old letters?"

"Jack really climbed over the barbed wire for you?" Victoria asked in a dreamy voice. "How utterly romantic."

Liz said, "You wouldn't have thought so if you'd seen him—or me," she added wryly. "We looked like a scene out of *Friday the Thirteenth*."

The trouble was, it *did* seem romantic. Every time Liz thought of it, her stomach fluttered in a way it hadn't since—well, since she'd made her last dumb mistake. Uh-unh. She didn't *want* this to be romantic. Heroic, maybe. Neighborly, for sure. But not romantic.

"He was just being nice," she said lamely.

Victoria gave Liz a knowing grin. "Ri-ii-ght," she said. "Well, we'll find out pretty quick if Grant Dade did it. If his hands look anything like you've described Jack's, it'll be obvious."

"Unless he was a ghost," said Liz, standing up and tipping Victoria's hat off her head. "C'mon in—I'll make tea."

She slipped her key in the lock and pushed the door open. The cottage was so small that, standing in the front doorway, Liz could gaze directly through the back kitchen windows and see the view of East Gate and its superb grounds. It made her fall in love with her house all over again every time she opened the door.

This morning, however, the view was different. Liz could see a workman standing on a ladder on the other side of the chain-link fence, just about eyeball to eyeball with Victoria and her.

He was taking down the barbed wire.

"Whoa," said Victoria in a husky voice. "This is heavy-duty *devotion*."

In her recap of events to Victoria, Liz had skipped her little diatribe about the concentration camp. She realized, as she watched the workman roll up one of the strands of barbed wire, that she'd shamed Jack into this. Couldn't she have just waited? He might have done it on his own. Eventually.

"Now he'll be able to get here with a lot less fuss," said Victoria slyly. "For those midnight trysts of yours."

"Now criminals will be able to get over *there* with a lot less fuss," Liz said with uneasy candor.

Victoria looked at her, surprised. "The robber barons live thataway," she said, jerking a thumb toward East Gate.

"But the petty thieves are all on this side," Liz said morosely.

"Hey—what's with you, missy? This is a *good* thing."

"I know, I know . . . but . . ." She almost hated to see the barbed wire go. It had Jack's blood—sacrificial blood—on it.

Had she been misjudging him?

She sighed and pressed the monitor button on the answering machine. There was one message, in a deep, baritone voice: "Elizabeth; Jack. It's false logic to say that Grant Dade coveted the letters, the letters were stolen, *ergo* Grant Dade is the thief. If you need help with that one, give me a call."

"Ho!" said Victoria, delighted. "He's right, you know."

"I sounded too smug when I left my message," Liz admitted, rewinding the tape. "It's a mistake to sound smug around him. He takes it so personally. . . . Oh, well; it doesn't matter. I'll make tea while you read me your exciting discovery."

"*This* isn't as big a deal as *that*," said Victoria, waving her hand theatrically at the workman by the fence. "But it does deepen the mystery about our artist-ghost."

"Wonderful," said Liz dryly. "God forbid the mystery should be solved."

"Oh, but it will be!" cried Victoria. "And when it is, the mystery of *me* will be solved. It's all connected. I know it is."

"What if Victoria St. Onge *never* names him?" Liz dared to ask as she filled her big copper teakettle—a gift, like every

other copper object in the house, from relatives in Portugal.
"What then?"

"In that case I'll die," Victoria said simply. "But she'll name him. Okay. Ready?"

My dear Mercy,

I write you from my stateroom aboard the SEA GOD-DESS, to which we adjourned after viewing a tennis match at the Casino in what can only be described as bone-melting heat. I became quite angry at the players for continuing to play in such perishing conditions. If only someone had col-lapsed of stroke! The rest of us could have boarded our yachts for lunch that much sooner and enjoyed the cool sea air that is now tumbling through the large open porthole above my writing table.

I have a delicious bit of gossip to pass on to you. Do you remember the masked marauder who so stole your heart at the Black and White Ball several years ago? I had occasion, with a group of two other gentlemen and three rather reck-less ladies, to tour the young man's studio yesterday. I'm sure I wrote that he was an artist. Well, he is, and quite a good one at that, but his talents seem to me to be terribly misdirected.

He paints nudes, *my dear Mercy! Or rather, one particular nude, in quite breathtaking detail. The subject is quite beau-tiful, with pale, porcelain skin and deep auburn hair, rich and flowing in every portrait. Unless he has idealized her, I may say without exaggeration that her form is as lovely and slender as ever I have seen.*

In every painting—there are seven or eight in his studio, of varying sizes—she is wearing, as her only adornment, a band of deep green around her neck. The velvet neckband, I think, is what enables her to retain a certain dignity in her bearing. Certainly there is nothing lascivious in her expres-sion, but only a rather wistful and loving look.

Here I must confess to an embarrassing encounter with the artist himself. The nude portraits had been stacked in one corner of the studio, facing the wall. I was curious about them—you know how I can be—and was in the process of browsing through them when your young artist, whose attention had been diverted, caught sight of me. He became quite angry—as I say, it was most embarrassing—and immediately afterward ushered us all out.

We were puzzled by his manner, but the mystery was explained to me just now over lunch, and that is why I write to you, while events are still fresh in my mind. Mrs. Le Fevre explained to me that the auburn-haired woman is—or was— an upstairs maid of the artist's parents.

After learning of their son's passionate involvement, the parents of course dismissed the maid. But I have it on Mrs. Le Fevre's authority that the artist is quite madly, seriously in love with the girl and refuses to give her up. Can you imagine? This town is quite the hotbed of scandal. In any case, I shall keep you posted of developments.

Victoria, who'd read without pausing, now looked up and said to Liz, "The rest of the letter describes the polo match she went to after her lunch aboard the yacht, and the ball she attended that night. Do you want to hear it?"

"Does she mention the artist again?" asked Liz, barely emerging from the trance she'd fallen into while Victoria read.

"Nope."

Liz shook her head. "Never mind, then." She filled two cups from the copper teakettle before realizing that she'd forgotten to boil the water. "I know who the artist is," she murmured as she emptied the cups, filled the kettle, and started over.

"Liz!"

"No, that's not true," Liz amended quickly. She was remembering her not-necessarily-logical conclusion about Grant Dade. "I know where the *studio* was. No, that's not true, either," she said scrupulously. "I *think* I know where the studio was."

"For God's sake, stop sounding like a lawyer! *Where?*"

"Here. The studio—*some* studio, anyway—was built on this property, and then it got torn down and the property became a service access to East Gate. Jack told me."

"Why didn't you tell me this before?" demanded Victoria.

"I don't know; it got lost in the shuffle, I guess. It's been a busy couple of days."

"So the younger-brother artist-ghost is an *Eastman*?" Victoria's voice dropped an octave as she said the name. She laid the letter down on the table and nervously began to smooth its edges, as if she'd been somehow disrespectful of it.

"It makes sense," said Liz with a limp smile. "I saw the apparition in Eastman's house. A studio once existed on this property. Ghosts don't haunt places arbitrarily, do they?"

Victoria frowned. "But how does Victoria St. Onge fit in? And for that matter, why would she buy a house on this side of the tracks—or fence—or whatever?"

"It *doesn't* make sense," Liz agreed, instantly reversing herself. "Victoria St. Onge was a social climber. She had some money; she could've bought something better than a tiny house on a street occupied by millworkers and fishermen."

"But if she really could channel—aha!—then maybe the Eastman artist ended up being her spirit guide; maybe *that's* why he's hanging around. He's waiting for me to resume my mediumship duties!" cried Victoria, sliding back into her alter ego.

Suddenly tired of the endless, bizarre speculation, Liz snapped, "How can you possibly say that? They were both alive at the same time, he threw her out of his studio, and his ghost—if it was his ghost—appeared to *me*, not to you. Get a grip."

Undaunted, Victoria said, "Good points. Okay; we'll just have to keep reading. But let's read chronologically from this letter on—this random sampling is too confusing. I'll get the 1895 shoebox."

"Oh, no. Oh, hell," said Liz, looking up with a blank, ashen look. "Those are the letters that were stolen."

"Ah," whispered Victoria.

The single, heartwrenching syllable was the exact same response Liz had given her doctor when he told her she wouldn't be able to have any more children. *Ah. A postpartum infection. Ah.*

Ah. It was the sound of hope dying.

"Then we may never find out who he is," Victoria said in a dazed, dull voice. "I may never know why Victoria St. Onge has come back in me. This isn't supposed to be how karma works. . . . I can't—this isn't fair," she said, tears beginning to trickle down her pale, freckled cheeks. "Burglars aren't fair."

"Victoria," Liz said gently. "I've done some reading. Reincarnation—you know it's supposed to begin at birth, don't you? Not at thirty?"

Victoria made an effort to bring herself under control, wiping away her tears with the heels of her hands; wiping her nose on the back of her wrist. "Not necessarily," she said with a tremulous lift of her chin. "There's another possibility. You've never heard of the walk-in process?"

"Walk-in?" said Liz, amused by the term. "You mean, as in a hair-styling salon?"

Victoria said softly, "Okay. Never mind."

"No, no, Tori, I want to hear! Really I do. I'm sorry. This stuff is just so new to me. I haven't been probing this—this arena of knowledge the way you have. Now tell me: What's a walk-in?"

Mollified, Victoria tried to explain it as well as she could. "Sometimes a problem on earth is so pressing that a soul-mind doesn't have time to be born and develop. The soul-mind takes the drastic step of assuming an adult's body—with that adult's permission, of course—so that it can go about its task more quickly."

The teakettle began hissing away; Liz took it off the burner again and filled two cups. "I see," she said cautiously. "So Victoria St. Onge took over from Judy Maroney with a definite, urgent purpose. Yes. I see."

She brought the mugs over to the table and said, almost casually, "Then where does Judy Maroney go for the duration?"

Victoria shook her head. "I don't know."

"And another thing—wouldn't it seem reasonable for Victoria St. Onge to know the history of the adult form she was assuming? For example, if the person had any allergies or was diabetic or whatever?"

"You're making fun," said Victoria with a look of despair.

"Oh, Tori, I'm not; I'm not. Believe me," said Liz, reaching over and squeezing her friend's wrist. "But I can't help wondering how these things work. Reincarnation was confusing enough, but this walk-in process—it's like using express mail instead of parcel post, but there's nothing in the envelope when it gets there. You see what I'm saying? What *is* the task at hand?"

"I don't know," Victoria said, the tears beginning to flow all over again. "It's in the letters. We have to keep reading. And we have to find the ones that are missing."

• • •

Saturday was all-out gorgeous, one of those superb June days that bring the crowds flocking to Newport. Bright, dry, sunny, and warm, with a smoky southwest breeze to keep things comfortable—Newport did June better than anyone else on the East Coast. Providence might be warmer in April, and Bar Harbor might be cooler in August; but June? June belonged to Newport.

"Can we go for a boat ride when we get to the shipyard, Mommy?"

Liz bent down to retie her daughter's shoe and said, "I don't think so, honey. Mommy has to talk with Mr. Eastman about business. It shouldn't take long, but you're going to have to be very, very good and very, very quiet."

She unzipped her daughter's Little Mermaid backpack. "Do you have all your Madeline books? And your colors, just in case there's a table you can use?"

Susy nodded solemnly and said, "Maybe if I'm good, you can take me for a boat ride after."

Again this obsession! Liz smiled noncommittally and said, "Let's go—we don't want to keep Mr. Eastman waiting."

The news that Liz's parents were driving to Massachusetts for a funeral had come as a blow. It was Liz's fault, of course; she took her parents so much for granted that she hadn't even heard her mother's remark that they'd be away Saturday until early afternoon. Too late to find a sitter; they were all at the malls.

Even Victoria wasn't around. After helping Liz coordinate a high-energy bridal shower on Friday for a group of Boston professionals who were renting a house in town for the summer, Victoria had driven off early to Point Judith and caught a ferry for Block Island. (Dr. Ben was possibly a part of the scenario, but Victoria didn't say, and Liz didn't pry.)

It's so much harder when there's only one, thought Liz,

giving in to a little self-pity. But she wasn't comfortable feeling sorry for herself, not when there were so many single parents shelling out hard-earned wages for day care and struggling against greater odds than hers.

She scanned her image in the shield-mirror on the hall landing, dissatisfied with the outfit she'd chosen—a button-front canvas skirt and a salmon-pink blouse—despite the fact that it was no better or worse than the other seven or eight she'd tried on that morning.

Heaving one last sigh, she loaded her clipboard, her proposal, and her daughter into the minivan, hoping Jack wouldn't notice that she had a papoose in tow. Professional, it wasn't. And Bachelor Jack, who apparently had zero tolerance for anything short that had the same number of hands and feet as little bratty Caroline, would probably consider Liz more unprofessional than most.

Too bad. This is how I do business. He can like it or lump it, she thought as Susy babbled happily in the seat beside her.

But Liz hoped, more than she ever thought possible, that somehow Jack would be willing to like it.

She had every intention of parking in front of the long, low building that housed the shipyard office, but after they drove through the ten-foot-high chain-link fence, they saw that the yardhands were in the process of launching a big fishing boat. Susy, instantly forgetting all her promises, begged to watch.

Since they were a little early, Liz parked the minivan out of everyone's way and, holding Susy's hand, sidled up to a small group of onlookers for a closer view.

Out of the water, the boat looked like a beached whale hanging in slings. Liz pointed out the neatly painted name on the bow: *Miss Betty.* She recognized the boat; it was a local lobster boat, and it had been around for as long as she could remember. Over the years it had been bumped from one dock to another as Newport's boatyards and waterfront businesses were torn down one by one and replaced by dense, often ugly condominium projects.

The old docks—once chock-a-block with working boats and rich with the smell of fish and salty shouts of men offloading their ice-packed cargo—now sat filled with plastic yachts, unused for the most part except on occasional weekends when their owners were able to break away from Wall Street or their medical practices.

And meanwhile, *Miss Betty* and her kin continued to play their ever-more-frustrating version of musical chairs. Liz was neither sailor nor fisherman's wife; she considered herself an impartial witness to the waterfront's development. But she knew, just as everyone in the boatyard knew, that unless the trend were reversed, the aging *Miss Betty*'s days in Newport were numbered.

Liz leaned closer to her daughter's ear and, over the noise of the Travelift, said, "We're just in time. Isn't this exciting?"

"Look, Mommy!" said Susy, pointing to the operator of the Travelift high above them. "It's Mr. Eastman!"

Indeed it was. Apparently he'd been inside the boat, checking things over. Now, high above their heads, he took command of the Travelift controls and began easing the giant-wheeled carrier forward, driving it onto two steel-edged channels hardly wider than the wheels themselves. Below the *Miss Betty* was the water, lapping softly at the bulkhead in the wake of passing boats.

Jack was focused completely on the task at hand; Liz was certain that he hadn't noticed them. She preferred it that way. Like the time she had studied him from her secret peephole inside the puppet theater, she was able to just . . . absorb him, somehow, drink in the sight of him, without worrying whether her lipstick was right or her repartee up to his standards.

He was in his element. With his windswept hair and his square-cut chin, in working khakis and a navy polo shirt, he was infinitely more attractive to her than he'd looked in business clothes on the night of the burglary. Oh, she'd heard vaguely about men and their love of Tonka toys, but *this* man on *this* Tonka toy—well, they looked right together, that's all.

She felt something lurch and then tighten inside her. Defense mechanisms, probably; without them you could easily be made a fool of by a man like him. Seduced, abandoned, and there you'd be: a fool.

Once was enough.

The Travelift came to a halt, and Jack yelled down to a man who was standing on the other side and ahead of the launching area: "Mike! You all set?"

Mike was apparently the owner, a man of about sixty with grizzled hair, a deeply weathered face, and arms even bigger than Jack's folded across his chest. He nodded silently, as if words cost money.

Jack gave him an upward lift of his chin in response and then, out of the blue, turned to Liz and winked before easing the hydraulic lever forward and lowering the boat slowly toward the water.

The blush that flooded her cheeks was instantaneous. After their last encounter she'd expected anything from burning looks to high-handed contempt—but not a wink. What the heck was a wink? What did it signify?

"Mommy? Why did Mr. Eastman wink at you?" asked Susy, who had eyes like radar scopes and ears like satellite dishes.

"He was just being friendly, honey. That's all." On balance, Liz decided, that's exactly what he was being: friendly. Not amorous, not hostile, just plain old friendly.

It was disappointing. Despite her careful attempt to seem in control of her emotions, Liz realized now that she'd been allowing herself to fantasize about the man. Why else had she run upstairs at the last minute for her cloisonné barrette? Did she really need a barrette to make her presentation?

The *Miss Betty* eased into the water like an old dowager into a hot bath. Yardhands unhooked the slings on one side while the boat bobbed gently in place, her new bottom-paint pristine and barnacle-free. The lobsterman, obviously relieved that the unnatural situation was over for another year, accepted a bow line from one of the men aboard and made it fast to the dock.

Jack climbed down the side rungs of the Travelift and exchanged a word or two with the owner, who shook his hand and tucked a cigar into the pocket of his shirt. Then Jack said something to one of his men, who scrambled monkey-quick up the rungs of the Travelift and began backing it away from the launch area.

It was an oddly touching ritual, done with a minimum of fuss and emotion: no hand-wringing, no screams, no cries of joy when it was over. Liz had been right in the first place—the shipyard was very male, very foreign terrain.

Except to Susy. "Wouldn't it be fun," she whispered in Liz's ear when Liz bent down to hear her wish, "if we could go for a ride on that boat?"

"Susy, it's a work boat," Liz explained. "It's not for rides."

She was giving her daughter only half her attention. The other half was being devoted to Jack Eastman, who was approaching them—then was stopped by a young man in canvas overalls.

"David!" Jack said, obviously surprised to see him. "Jeez, no one told you? The work's been put off for now. Customer got cold feet when he saw the estimate."

"I don't see how I can put in a new transom for less," the young man said with no apologies.

"You can't. It's a big job. I know that. Well, I'll keep

working on the guy. In the meantime, if something else comes up, Cynthia'll let you know.''

"Sure."

Jack shrugged and added, "You know, David, skilled carpentry like yours—well, it doesn't come cheap. Nor should it. But my customers aren't willing to pay nowadays. I've never seen anything like it.''

"I know. They all want fiberglass."

The young carpenter went on his way, and Jack came up to Liz and her daughter with a wink-friendly smile on his lips.

Why do I think of his eyes as sea-blue? Liz suddenly wondered. *I've never seen an ocean that blue. Not in New England, anyway.*

"I'm sorry to hold you up," he said graciously. "We had a little last-minute welding repair to do on *Miss Betty*'s rudder. And Mike's an old fussbutton—won't let anyone but the boss launch him.''

"A lot of bosses wouldn't be bothered," Liz said, matching his gracious tone. She was thinking, *How are your hands? Are you all right? There was so much blood.*

He saw her glance at the unbandaged red scratches. "I'm fine," he said briefly. "Well, hello there," he said with a friendly smile at Susy.

Liz introduced them, and Susy said with great solemnity, "I liked to see you put the boat into the water. You didn't even make it splash.''

"Well, thank you, ma'am," drawled Jack with an utterly irresistible smile. "That's a very nice compliment. How old are you, Susy?" he added, curious.

"Five."

He stared at her with grave suspicion. "Are you sure? You seem much older than that to me. I'd guess you were closer to six, at *least*.''

"Almost," Susy admitted modestly. It was obvious that she didn't like to brag about it.

Liz, caught up in a new round of sensations, smiled at them both. Here was a side of Jack she hadn't seen before. She wondered whether little Caroline had ever been as lucky as Susy, or whether Jack turned the charm of his attention on and off like a spigot.

"I'm sorry for the—complication," she told Jack, inclining her head toward Susy. "If your office has a waiting room . . ." She knew it did; she'd seen it earlier.

"Wel-l-l . . . sure," he said.

His hesitation said it all; he did not approve of working mommies. No doubt *his* wife—should he ever condescend to take one—would stay at home where she belonged, keeping an eye on the servants.

Jack said, "We'll drop your daughter off, and then I'll show you the shed we'll use in case it rains." His voice was less personal now; apparently the time for pleasantry had expired.

She nodded and let him lead them through the middle door of a row of doors in a long, low building that also housed a ship's brokerage and a rigging store. The office—really an assembly of half-walled cubicles—was modern and nondescript and, at the moment, empty except for a busy-looking secretary sitting at the front desk before a computer.

"Cynthia," Jack said to her, "Mrs. Coppersmith and I are going to go over the picnic plans. Would you mind keeping an eye on Susy, here, while we do?"

Cynthia, a vivacious young woman with an attractive figure, shot Susy a brief but friendly smile and said, "Okay. Would you like a pencil and paper, honey?"

Susy reached over her shoulder for her backpack and said politely, "No, thank you. I brought my own."

At the sound of their voices, Cornelius Eastman, who'd apparently been in the cubicle behind Cynthia's desk, came out to greet them all.

Jack said tersely, "I didn't know you were here, Dad."

"Just making a few calls," he said, returning his son's cool look. He noticed Susy and said jovially, "Hey there, sailor! Goin' out on the water today?"

Susy's eyes sparked with sudden hope at the stranger's words. The child, who'd insisted on dressing for sailing in red sneakers, dungarees, and a bright yellow windbreaker—just in case—smiled at Cornelius Eastman in shy confusion.

Jack, of course, was a familiar sight to Susy. She'd seen him in the distance while she ate breakfast, which was when Jack sometimes spent time outside training Snowball to fetch, sit, and lie down. Cornelius, however, was a new face. Susy looked up at her mother for permission to trust him.

Liz made the introductions. "This is Mr. Eastman's father, honey. He lives at East Gate, too."

Cornelius smiled and said, "Only during the summer. In the winter we live in Florida." With a wink at Liz, he added, "Much to Jack's relief."

Jack said impatiently, "We'd better get cracking," and began walking away, expecting Liz to fall behind in his wake.

Liz blew Susy a kiss and mouthed the words, "Be good," and hurried to catch up to Jack, who was holding the door for her.

Outside, he took such long, quick strides that she was forced into a near-jog to keep up with him.

"Any word about the stolen letters?" he asked her in that same impersonal tone.

"Not much," she answered, put off by his whole manner. "I found out from the detectives that Grant Dade is off hiking the White Mountains this weekend. He'd better come back before his hands heal," she said with sudden fierceness.

"You're just not gonna give up on that guy, are you?" Jack said, glancing at her with amazement.

"Not unless you have a better suspect."

"Hell, my father's a better suspect!" There was a bitterness in Jack's tone that he reserved exclusively for Cornelius Eastman.

"Meaning *what*," Liz demanded to know. She'd pretty o much had it up to there with Jack's snide references to the man.

Jack decided to answer her. "Meaning—I say this strictly for example—I ran into him behind the house after you called there. I asked him what he was doing outside at that hour. He gave me an evasive answer, something like, 'Getting my head clear.' "

Wide-eyed, she stopped, turned, and confronted him. "You suspect your own *father*? What kind of man *are* you?"

The sea-blue eyes froze over; she could've ice-skated across them. "The kind who prefers logic to intuition."

"You know what?" she said impulsively. "I think you're holding Caroline against your—her—father."

Immediately she regretted it.

Chapter 9

◆

"I didn't know you were intimately familiar with the branches of my family tree," he said in a calm, cold voice.

She turned and resumed walking at a nervous clip. "I'm not, but . . . Mr. Eastman dotes on her so much . . . and you resent her so obviously—and—and then, too—"

Liz didn't want to implicate Netta, so she finished with a lame, "I just had a feeling, that's all."

"Really. I thought it was Victoria who was the psychic over there."

It was Liz's turn to look surprised. "How did you know about Victoria?"

His voice was dry as toast. "She told Netta through the fence that she's the reincarnation of a nineteenth-century spiritualist who used to live in your house."

"No," said Liz, correcting him. "She's a walk-in."

He laughed contemptuously and said, "But we digress. The point is, your suspect isn't necessarily any more likely than my suspect. Can't you see that?"

"No, dammit. The comparison is absurd," she said, refusing to argue further.

They'd reached their destination: a huge corrugated-aluminum shed, not unlike an airplane hangar. This was it? She felt as if she'd been handed a lump of coal, with two weeks to turn it into a pear-shaped diamond. Her spirits sank lower and lower as he explained the traditional setup: a couple of folding tables with salads and grilled fish, burgers, whatever, that they could carry inside quickly if it began to rain. If she preferred, she could arrange a New England clambake, he told her, only without the hole in the sand, the heated rocks, or the seaweed. In short, without the New England.

"As a rule, the men end with a game of soccer while the women and kids watch," he finished up.

It sounded dismal. "But—but you said you wanted *magic*," she said, utterly dismayed.

"And so I do. What have you got in mind?"

He opened a door that was dwarfed by the height of the shed. Liz stepped through, and he followed her, letting the door swing shut behind them.

After the blinding light outside, the hangar-size shed seemed dark, despite the fiberglass upper walls that let in a limited amount of daylight. Without waiting for her eyes to adjust, Liz went trotting forward across the hard-packed dirt floor and instantly tripped on a block of wood that lay across her path.

With a yelp of pain, she stumbled sideways into Jack's arms. He caught her handily, just as he had when she fell from the ladder on her upstairs landing. But this time he wasn't inclined simply to stand her up straight again.

He let his hands linger on her upper arms, sliding them slowly up and then down. She felt his callused palms through the thin sleeves of her salmon-pink blouse. An odd, irrelevant thought popped into her mind: *Hardly the hands of an artist.* But she felt the power in them, a strength that she found almost intimidating.

"I say again," he murmured as he lowered his face closer to hers, "what did you have in mind?"

"M-magic," she repeated, aware of his warm breath wafting over her cheeks.

"Can you be more specific?" he asked, his voice low and amused, as he lowered his mouth gently onto hers, catching her lower lip in a soft, tantalizing caress.

Her eyes fluttered closed as she struggled against the temptation to enjoy what he was doing to her ... with her ... for her. *Specifics,* she told herself. He wants specifics.

"I—I wanted a fairy tale of a picnic," she whispered, turning her mouth a little away from his. "A ... castle," she said, catching her breath as he slid his mouth across the line of her jaw, dropping nibbly, exciting kisses along the curve of her neck.

Kiss me, she thought dizzily. *Kiss me and be done with it so that I can act hurt and outraged and we can get on with this—this—oh, God—magic.* His mouth was pure magic.

He lifted his head and caught her chin gently in one hand, turning her face back to his for the very kiss she desired and dreaded.

"I can't," she murmured, her mouth half a breath from his.

"Can't?"

"Make a castle out of a shed. No one can. This is all wrong."

She wasn't even sure she was talking about the picnic. But at least she was talking; her brain had begun functioning again on some minimal level. She lifted one shoulder in an attempt to ease out of his grip. Jack understood the signal, childish as it was, and let go of her instantly.

A gentleman, after all. Or not too terribly interested. Just her luck either way, she thought with a sad, wry smile.

In the meantime, he was taking her at her word. "So you don't think you can do something with cardboard turrets and an asphalt moat?"

"I thought I could," Liz admitted, "but now I see it would be idiotic to try."

She had a thought—she'd had the thought since the day

he'd first suggested the event—and now she threw it out to him, letting her words soar upward like barn swallows in the great, cavernous expanse of the nearly empty shed.

"Picnics are for *kids*," she said in an earnest, coaxing voice. "I don't want them to go away from this with some memory of a bunch of grown-ups playing soccer. I want them to take the memory of my picnic into their *own* adulthood; I want them to wonder why no one in the year 2010 knows how to throw a shipyard picnic as good as the ones in the good old days."

He laughed sardonically. "There may not be a shipyard, much less a picnic, in the year 2010."

"All the more reason!" she shot back.

"I can't afford to rent one of Newport's castles on a Saturday in July," he warned.

"Of course not," she said, detecting a certain responsiveness in his answer. "East Gate will do fine."

"East Gate!"

She could see he was scandalized by the idea. People like him simply didn't throw their doors open to—well, people like her.

"What if it rains? Where do you think I'm going to put a hundred people and a soccer net?" he asked incredulously.

He could probably put them all in his entry hall, if it came to that. But she didn't want him to feel cornered, so she said, "I absolutely, positively guarantee it's not going to rain. And if it does, we can empty your carriage house of vehicles and carry on there. Half the people wouldn't show, anyway."

She glanced around the empty shed. A couple of yachts sat forlornly in their cradles, like rich kids left behind at their boarding school for the holidays.

"Not here," she said at last. "I simply can't do it."

He hooked his thumbs in his front pockets and glanced at the roof, then at the dirt floor. "Just what I need," he said, half to himself. "A prima-donna party planner."

"*Events* coordinator." *Yes!* He was going to say yes!

"You'd better *damned* well pray for sun," he growled as he headed for the door.

Liz fell in beside him with a satisfied spring in her step. "You won't be sorry, Jack," she said with a sideways taunting look. "I'll probably end up working for free again."

He smiled at the memory, then took out the cigar he'd been given and began peeling away the cellophane. "Why do you do it, then?" he asked. "Just for the pleasure of my company?"

He bit off the tip of the cigar, pulled out a pack of matches, and turned away from the wind and from her, cupping his hands around the stogie as he made a couple of attempts to light it.

He couldn't see her face, which was just as well: Liz was blushing furiously. The *pleasure*! of his *company*! That was like saying she had a cavity fixed for the pleasure of the novocaine!

Jack turned back around, blue eyes squinting in the sun, cigar rolled jauntily to one side of his mouth. Amazingly, he seemed to be waiting for her to tell him just how much pleasure he did give her.

Plenty, dammit, she realized with a sinking heart. His kisses had left a white-hot trail on her neck that—now that the shock of the encounter in the shed had worn off—was beginning to throb in earnest. Involuntarily she raised her hand to the spot, as if she'd been scratched by a bramble.

"Thanks for taking the barbed wire down," she suddenly said, free-associating like crazy. "The view is so much prettier now."

"For me, too," he said with a smile that was oddly wistful.

He stroked her cheek lightly with his fingertips, then let them trail lazily along the scorched route of his kisses.

Yowch. Liz turned her cheek away, embarrassed by the low threshold of her pain. What was going *on* here?

"Well!" she said briskly. "That's it, then. Don't worry about a thing. It'll be a day to remember."

He gave her a wry look. "Didn't you say something along those lines about Caroline's birthday party?"

Liz was saved from having to come up with a smartalecky answer by the sight of Cornelius Eastman shepherding her daughter in their direction. Susy was skipping her happy-skip; the child-size life jacket she clutched in her hand probably had a lot to do with it.

"Where'd you get the life jacket, sweetie?" asked Liz when her daughter drew near.

"Mr. Eastman gave it to me," Susy said, hardly able to contain her joy. "He said that if it's all right with you, we can all go see his family's boat. Even you, Mommy! It's right over there! Not for a ride, though," she added in a stage whisper. "But sometime soon. He *promised*! It has a bathroom and a TV! And a kitchen—no, a galley! Isn't that right, Mr. Eastman?" she asked as Cornelius caught up to them. "The room with the stove is a galley, isn't it?"

"That's right, Susy," said Cornelius. "And the bedrooms are called staterooms. And the bathrooms are called heads."

Susy said, "I know. I remember from what you said!" and kept on happy-skipping in the direction of a stunning antique motor-yacht that was tied up to a dock not far from where they stood.

Liz, who thought she was beyond being impressed by Eastman status symbols, was impressed all over again. My God! A sixty-footer with all that varnish, all that brass— what must it cost to keep it up? Even if you *did* own the shipyard.

"Pretty snazzy," she conceded, repressing a surge of blue-collar resentment.

Cornelius said gruffly, "That old bucket of rot? She's been

around forever; more trouble than she's worth." But he complained in a voice that was deep with affection.

Even Jack was smiling. It was obvious that here, at last, was something the two men agreed on.

In the meantime Cornelius, with a good-natured grimace, was saying, "I didn't realize how enthusiastic Susy was about boats. I hope I haven't made things awkward for you by promising a tour."

"Not at all," Liz said with a smile of her own. "I'm sure she just took your hint and ran with it. I have no idea where she gets this love of the sea. Hardly anyone in the family is into boats," she explained, without adding that hardly anyone could afford to be. "The Portuguese side has always been heavily into agriculture, and as for the Irish side—no sailors there, either."

In other words, she descended from a line of farm help and houseworkers. Why couldn't she just say it?

Maybe because both Jack and Cornelius were looking so damned aristocratic, poised alongside their family yacht. There was no denying it: everything about the two, from their Waspy good looks to the offhand way they carried themselves, suggested that they were to the manner born.

"You strike me as a superconscientious mother," the older of the men ventured to say to Liz. "Which is why I fished out a life jacket. I assumed you wanted Susy wearing one for the tour."

"You assumed right; thanks," said Liz, fitting the orange vest over her daughter's head. It was a long way down from the deck to the water, and Susy couldn't swim. That was Liz's fault; she'd never really encouraged her to learn.

Cornelius unhitched a heavy nylon line that was roped across the gangplank and led them down it. The slope was steep—it was low tide—and Susy was forced to take little mincing steps. Liz hovered behind her, ready to grab her if she tripped or fell. She was aware, all too aware, of Jack behind *her,* obviously impatient to get down the darned thing. What did *he* know about children and drowning?

The gangplank led to a float to which the yacht was tied up. Between the rolling gangplank and the floating dock, Liz was feeling a little rubbery-legged. "Be careful, honey," she cautioned.

Susy, as sure-footed as a three-legged stool, laughed at her mother's warning and dashed up the five boarding steps through a cut-out gate in the side of the hull.

And there they were: aboard their first and probably last true yacht. It was a spectacular vessel: miles of teak decks with every seam in place; varnished cabinsides that gleamed in the midday sun; a small sailing dinghy hanging in davits, ready to be swung over the side and lowered into the water; an afterdeck with a built-in crescent of cushioned seats around a low round table topped with a crystal bowl filled with cut flowers. Cut flowers, for Pete's sake! On a boat!

Susy sat gingerly on one of the canvas-striped cushions, looked around briefly, then slid off, ready for the next feature on the tour. Cornelius said to her, "Wanna see the anchor? It weighs more than I do."

Susy said, "Yes!" and ran forward, despite her mother's warning to *"Walk, young lady!"* sounding in her ears.

"You listen to your mother," Cornelius said amiably.

He turned to Liz and said, "She's a doll. Reminds me of my—of Caroline. We'll have to have 'em out for a little cruise soon."

Jack gave his father a dry smile and said, "Caroline hated the boat, Dad."

"Because she had no one to talk to," his father said easily. He ambled up to the bow, where Susy was waiting, with little hops-in-place, for the tour to continue.

Spoiled forever, Liz thought as she fingered the name of the yacht, *Déjà Vu,* that was gold-leafed on the white life-ring hanging alongside one of the cabin doors. "This truly is a magnificent yacht," she said to Jack. "I always thought of wooden boats as old, smelly, and leaky."

"I prefer to think of her as 'seasoned,' " Jack murmured with a dangerous smile. "As for your other misconceptions: she smells clean and sweet—and she's real tight."

"Oh," said Liz, coloring deeply. "Then I guess I was wrong. Is—is the hull fiberglass?" she asked, just to have something to say. "It looked so smooth."

"Fiberglass wasn't invented then," he said, brushing her windblown hair away from her mouth with his fingertips. "The boat's over a hundred years old."

"Oh," she said faintly. "Wrong again."

"And contrary to what you're thinking, when it was built, it was regarded as a modest vessel for the time—especially considering the owner had a shipyard at his disposal."

She heard a loud thump and whipped her head around. "Susy!" she cried.

"It's all right, Mommy. I was just jumping down from the—the *capstan*!" Susy said proudly, glancing at Cornelius. "That's what holds the chain for the anchor!"

"Well, come back here by me," Liz said sharply. "We've taken far too much of these people's time as it is."

Looking chastised and sullen, Susy began dragging her steps toward the back of the yacht. She perked up when she reached the small dinghy hanging in its davits, however, and said to Jack, "Do you ever go for boat rides in this?"

Jack smiled and said, "I used to sail that when I was just about your age."

Susy's mouth fell a little open; she gave Liz a big brown-eyed look of reproach that said, "*You* won't even let me take lessons with a *grown-up*!"

They went through the wheelhouse and down the cabin steps and toured the sparkling galley, with its gleaming brass sinks, leaded-glass cupboards, and wood-paneled fridge, then made their way through the cozy staterooms and the main salon, with its varnished furnishings, built-in bookcases, and deep-green-velvet upholstery. It was all very stately and dignified, as masculine as East Gate itself. Liz wondered where, if anywhere, the Eastman women got to express the softer side of the empire. It was a silly thought; obviously the men ran the show in this family.

They came back up into the wheelhouse, and Cornelius sat Susy on the tufted leather helmsman's seat, where she pretended to steer the brass-bound varnished wheel. "When I grow up," she announced blithely, "I'm going to drive a ferry. Or maybe even a big ship."

"I thought you wanted to be president," Liz said, smiling.

"—if I don't get elected," Susy shot back.

They all laughed and retraced their steps through the boat, with Liz warning Susy at regular intervals to go slow, be careful, not touch, and leave it alone.

Jack murmured to Liz, out of Susy's earshot, "She's not going to be president *or* ferry captain if you keep such a tight rein on her. I mean, an untamed cub like Caroline is one thing, but don't you think—"

Surprised by his impertinence, Liz turned to him and said tersely, "Excuse me, but Susy is all I have." *All I'll* ever *have*, she thought, washed over by a complex wave of emotions. "*Naturally* I'm protective."

"Okay, okay," he said, throwing up his hands as if she'd pulled a gun on him. "None of my business."

"None at *all*," Liz agreed.

At the top of the gangplank she said to her daughter, "Go get your backpack, honey. I'll catch up to you. After Susy thanked Jack enthusiastically and set off for the office with Cornelius, Liz said to Jack, "I guess we're done for now—?"

"Look, I'm sorry if I stepped over some line you've drawn. After all, I'm not a parent—as far as I know. What do *I* know about childrearing?"

"Apology—such as it is—accepted," she said, annoyed by his flippancy.

"Prove it," he said suddenly. "I'm taking the boat out on a twilight cruise tonight with half a dozen friends. Cocktails, the usual thing. Join me."

"Um . . ."

Was it a date? It didn't sound like a date. It was a cocktail, with other people just like him. What did one wear on a yacht at twilight? What did one say when one was asked where one went to school, and what yacht clubs one belonged to, and what one thought of so-and-so, the new tennis instructor at the Casino?

And what did one tell one's daughter when one's daughter—who'd give her baby teeth to be able to go for a boat ride—learned that her mommy was going instead?

"Um . . ." Liz bit her lip and shook her head.

Jack gave her a level look. "I see."

No, he *didn't* see; but she let it pass. Let him think she was still angry over his bachelor-knows-best advice. Let him think anything except the ultimate rock-bottom truth: that she didn't want to end up being another notch in his gun. If he couldn't find a suitable match among the rich and the gorgeous, he sure as hell wasn't going to be swept away by a thirtysomething mom who couldn't even bear him the heir he would so obviously require.

Still, it would be nice if she could come up with another reason besides "um."

She gave him a carefully friendly smile and said, "I have other plans." (She didn't.) "I'm sorry." (She wasn't.) "It would've been fun." (It would've been agony.)

Jack was about to say something when an older, overweight man in a plaid sportshirt came hurrying up to them shouting, "Jack, Jack—my boat's been broken into!"

"What! Impossible, Jay!" Jack said automatically. Under his breath he murmured, *"Shit."*

Liz gave Jack a quick, sharp look; he seemed almost to be expecting the news.

"What'd they take?" Jack asked as the man got near.

"Can't tell," Jay said, winded from his sprint. "It looks like a hurricane went through belowdeck. Everything's in a heap. They even busted in some of the bulkheads, by God." He held his hand over his left ribs; he'd gotten a stitch from running. "Should I call the cops?"

"Absolutely. You can use my office. Was the *DeeJay* locked?"

"Well, no," Jay said sheepishly. "Dee and I came down for sundowners a coupla nights ago; we knew we'd be coming right back on the weekend, so . . ." He shrugged. "Who woulda thought? There's not a damned thing on the boat that's valuable. You know that."

"Yeah," said Jack vaguely. He turned to Liz, all business now, and said, "I'm sorry. Please excuse me."

"Of course," Liz said.

They were all headed for the same destination, so Liz hung back a moment, apparently to admire Jack's yacht a little longer. The men hurried on ahead while she walked slowly along the pier, studying the boat from stern to stern. No question, it was someone's labor of love. The thought popped into Liz's head from nowhere at all: *If he can cherish and protect a* yacht *his whole life, why can't he do the same to a* woman?

She shook off the question—a truly idle question—the way she'd shaken off the memory of his kisses earlier. *He can have anyone he wants,* she told herself, *and he doesn't want anyone—at least, not for long.* That's how bachelors stayed that way. Well, nuts to that; it wasn't how Liz did business. She had the wedding ring—and the divorce papers—to prove it.

She found herself staring in a daze at the afterdeck, with its deep cushions and fresh-cut flowers, imagining it as it would be at twilight . . . and after the sun went down . . . with no moon . . . only the amber glow of the kerosene lamps . . . and the faraway flicker of stars in the sky. What a setting for soft lies and faint promises. . . .

Suddenly the chime-sound—loud, rich, ringing in the air—shattered her reverie like a baseball through a window. Liz let out a muffled cry and jumped back, terrified. Why now? Why here? What was the pattern? Nighttime, noontime, his house, her house, here, there, everywhere—God! *Why?* It was making her wide-eyed, making her crazy. Liz whirled around, a cornered, haunted creature, ready to do battle with—what? *Who* are *you?*

The fact that she was cavorting alone on a pier in broad daylight bothered Liz not a whit. *Show yourself,* she demanded silently, stamping her foot.

The chime filled the air between her and the sun. She stared in the direction of the sound, blinded by sunlight, unwilling to look away, unable to keep it up, furious beyond fear now.

Dizzy from the effort to stare into the sun, Liz dropped her gaze, trying to blink away the dark spots that bobbled across her line of sight. What an *ass* she was being, blinding herself that way! She rubbed her eyes with her hands, which only made things worse, and began to panic, convinced that she'd ruined her sight forever. She closed her eyes and kept them closed, standing as still as a pilon, gathering what was left of her wits, trying desperately to stay calm.

She took a deep breath, held it, released it slowly, and then opened her eyes again.

And there he was, just as clear as could be, nothing vapory about him: on the afterdeck, standing in just about the same place where she'd been imagining—well, someone she shouldn't have been imagining at all.

He was wearing some kind of old-fashioned yachting get-up this time. *Sure. Why not? He's on a yacht,* Liz reminded herself with bizarre lucidity. He seemed shorter than when she'd seen him lounging against the grandfather clock in the hall at East Gate; but then, Liz was standing high on the pier, looking down on the *Déjà Vu*.

Navy slacks, elegantly cut; a long-sleeved white shirt with the sleeves rolled up; a dark tie (was it *really* fluttering in the wind?); and a yachting-cap trimmed in gold braid that glittered in the sun—

"No blazer," she muttered inconsequentially. It must have been hot out.

Then? Now?

His hands were hooked in his pockets, and his head was cocked a little to the right as he looked up at her, returning her stare with an insolent, arrogant one of his own.

Except for the insolent, arrogant part, he didn't look like an Eastman. His jaw was less squared, his face a little longer. She had no idea what color his eyes were, but his mouth— ah, she knew the Eastman mouth, and his was not the same. The upper lip was wider, perfect for a handlebar mustache. She wondered why he wasn't wearing one, since they were all the rage.

Then? Now?

God help me, she thought dizzily. *Have I gone back? Or has he come forward?*

There was no easy way to tell. With only him, her, and the antique yacht in her field of vision, Liz was unable to say which of their time zones was being breached. She tore her gaze away from him: the first thing she saw was a silver Lexus parked nearby. Liz was never so glad to see a status symbol in her life. It meant she might be hallucinatory, but at least she wasn't leaping freely through time and space.

She turned back to the vision, but it was gone.

She stood there, her head cocked attentively, listening for the chime-sound. But it was over. Feeling oddly desolate and more rubbery-legged than ever, Liz turned and retraced her footsteps to the office. Jack was gone, and so was Cornelius. Only Susy remained, backpack at her feet, under the watchful eye of the shipyard secretary.

"It's the sex. The sex is just . . . so . . . *good,*" Victoria told Liz after she got back from Block Island. Dr. Ben had been there, just as Liz suspected, and a truce between Victoria and him had been declared.

"Of course, we declared it in bed, so who knows how long it'll last? But he promised not to keep looking for the me behind the me," Victoria said. "He promised to accept me at face value."

Liz whacked off a stray sprig of privet with her hedge clippers and said, "If your Dr. Ben really does that, he's a better man than most."

"Tsk, tsk," said Victoria, bending over for a handful of cut branches to stuff in the recycle bag. "We're sounding bitter today."

"Yeah, well, blame it on the fact that you're getting some and I'm not," Liz said. Really, it was ridiculous, the hunger she was feeling. Where had it come from? She was as restless and irritable as a caged cat.

"Anyway, I meant what I said," Liz continued. "Men go at this mating thing differently from women. Women—most of us—have only the vaguest idea of what we want. We say, 'Okay, this guy's not perfect, but he's not a bad compromise, either. He'll do.'

"But a *man*—a man draws up a precise list: big boobs, blond hair, good dancer, flashy dresser, whatever. The sensitive ones maybe would like her to have an intellectual side—in other words, know a little about sports. So that they can share the Super Bowl together," Liz added with a dry smile. "Then, if the man doesn't find an exact match, he has an excuse for not making a commitment."

Victoria blinked and said, "Is that how you picked Keith? You said, 'He'll do'?"

"You bet," Liz said with brutal candor. "And he would've done, too, if he hadn't run away. But then, 'baby' wasn't on his list."

"You never loved him?"

"I guess not," Liz said grimly, moving her ladder to the next section of untrimmed privet. "Or I would've been able to keep him, baby and all."

"But you said yourself that 'baby' wasn't on his list. I mean, family just wasn't his thing. He was more selfish than that. He's probably standing guard over some marijuana patch in northern California, even as we speak!"

Liz laughed and said, "You think maybe that's why I couldn't trace him for child support? Because he's not paying tax on his income?"

"You *never* loved him?" Victoria repeated.

"I thought I did," Liz confessed in a whisper. "But I was so young."

"They're not all like him," Victoria said, hauling the brown bag out to the curb. "Jack Eastman isn't."

"Jack!" cried Liz after her. "He has the longest, most specific list of all! You're the one who told me he's already sampled everyone on Bellevue Avenue."

Victoria cringed and made a shushing sound. She came back and in a lowered voice said, "I think in his case it's a good thing, not a bad, that he hasn't married yet. Obviously he could find himself a gorgeous socialite who'd jump at the chance to be his wife. So he must be looking for love as well."

"Well, bless his heart. I hope he finds his perfect package."

"I've seen the way he looks at you," Victoria said evenly.

Liz blushed and said, "Yes. The same way I look at a hot fudge sundae." She whacked silently at the straggly privet for a minute or two, then climbed back down the ladder and folded it shut.

"There's definitely something there when we're alone," she admitted as she laid the ladder against the mud shed. "The trouble is, it's the wrong something."

"Love has to start *some*where," Victoria said, impatient now. "Give him a chance. You're letting one bad experience define your whole life!"

Liz turned to her friend with a sad, surprised look and said, "You aren't?"

The arrow hit its mark. Victoria colored a vivid pink. Liz had never done that before, thrown Victoria's amnesia in her face.

"Let's talk about something else," Victoria said, obviously hurt. "Any word about our graduate student?"

"Ah—I haven't told you!" said Liz, glad for the diversion. "Grant Dade came into the station, and yes, he *did* have scratches on his hands. But he claimed he got them hiking, which was plausible enough."

"Did he go hiking with anyone who could corroborate that?"

"Nope," said Liz. "I gather he was amazed and angered by the questioning. Apparently he charged a gas fill-up in New Hampshire, but he can't produce the Visa slip. They're looking into that now."

"So no lineup or anything?"

"Nobody mentioned that. It'll be just my luck that he's really innocent but pissed off enough to come back and make trouble for me."

"If he's innocent, then who stole the letters? And why?" Victoria mulled it over for a moment, then said, "For someone with no men in your life, you sure have a lot of men in your life."

Liz flashed to the afterdeck of the *Déjà Vu*. "Tori," she said, "you don't know the half of it."

Chapter 10

◈

"*R*-i-p-e-n? I'll look it up," said the official who answered Liz's call to the Adult Correctional Institute. He didn't even have to put her on hold; the computer was too fast to bother.

"Nope," he said, "he doesn't show up. He's either dead or discharged. I can find out for you, but the request will have to go through the archives in Providence. It'll be a couple of weeks."

It was a disappointment. Liz wanted to find out what happened to Victoria St. Onge's murderer, and she wanted to find out *now*. She wasn't sure why it mattered; maybe she wanted to know for poor Tori's sake. She declined the official's offer and decided, instead, to play a hunch.

It paid off. In the Newport City Clerk's office she learned that—however long he'd been at the state penitentiary— Johnny Ripen had ended up coming back to Newport. He died nine years ago, when he was seventy-one years old.

So the murdering gigolo had passed on. If Liz had had any wild ideas of finding out what he knew about the woman he'd conned and then killed over half a century ago, those hopes were dashed forever. Morbidly curious now, Liz drove the few short blocks back to the library and looked up the date of Johnny Ripen's death in the *Daily News* obituaries, half expecting to find out that he died in royal splendor in some big estate on Bellevue Avenue.

Wrong again. Johnny Ripen was found dead under a cherry tree in the Common Burying Ground, which was a favorite gathering place for drunks and disreputables. It was as good a choice as any: None of the colonists, Indians, and slaves who were buried there were likely to complain about rowdiness.

When she got home, Liz telephoned Victoria to tell her what she'd found.

"The police speculated that Johnny Ripen either cut his own wrist or got into a fight over the broken bottle of vodka they found lying in his lap."

"How horrible," Victoria said, truly shocked. "If he was drunk, and he probably was, he wouldn't even have known he was bleeding to death."

"I checked with Detective Gilbert. The police never did make a case for murder. I'm surprised I don't remember the episode. But I was living in Middletown then; I suppose it just got past me."

There was a thoughtful silence at the other end of the line. Then Victoria asked in a low and apprehensive voice, "Do we have any idea where Victoria St. Onge is buried?"

"Don't be theatrical," Liz said all too quickly. "There was nothing supernatural about Johnny Ripen's death. It was a predictable end to a wasted life."

"If so, it's the only predictable thing that's happened so far. I'm frightened, Liz. It was exciting at first, the letters and all—but now I'm scared."

"Well, don't be," Liz said with a reassurance she did not feel. "Come over tonight. We'll have a cookout. Bring along your Dr. Ben. It's high time I met the man."

Victoria agreed, and Liz hung up, more uneasy now than ever. *Were* these bizarre events connected? Was someone, somewhere administering a kind of rough justice every once in a while as the world went spinning around? Or was every-thing—the deaths, the visions, the box, the letters, the pin—simply the clutter and mess of life itself, with Liz desperately looking for a pattern, trying to impose some kind of order and meaning on it all.

It would be so nice if she knew.

In any case, that world was spinning plenty fast at the moment; Liz had no idea when she'd find the time to squeeze in a cookout. It wasn't as if Jack Eastman's company picnic were all arranged, or the back-to-back weddings over and done with. Tomorrow alone she had three meetings with po-tential clients. Not to mention, her new landlord had moved hell and high water to make her office ready for occupancy; the least she could do was to occupy it.

Liz spent the rest of the day on the phone with florists, bands, jugglers, mimes, and minstrels, then dashed out at five to pick up steaks and hot dogs and some ready-made salads. By the time Victoria arrived with her beloved internist, Liz was in a darn good mood: she'd mixed up a pitcher of rum punch and had helped herself to an icy tall glass of it. Sud-denly her life was seeming a lot more manageable. After all, it was a beautiful summer night in Newport. Thousands of people were in town expressly to have fun. Why shouldn't she be one of them?

Dr. Ben turned out to be a charmer. Shorter than Victoria, with dark, quizzical eyes and a self-deprecating wit, he had Liz in his corner in no time at all.

"So you're the lady with the letters," he said with a nudge at Victoria. "The letters that hold the key to my lady's heart. And soul. So to speak."

"Ben!" cried Victoria. "You promised!"

"Yeah, I know," he said, pulling up a chaise longue close to the barbecue. "But this way we don't spend the evening waiting for that particular shoe to drop. Madame?" he said to his belle with a flourish. "Will you sit?"

"I never should have told you," said Victoria, pouting prettily. She arranged herself in the chaise, a picture of other-worldly elegance in a longish white sundress trimmed in crochet. She wore a hat, of course: a small-brimmed affair of crushed linen with big silk cabbage roses sewn to the band. Liz, wearing dress jeans and a V-necked T-shirt of bright coral, felt positively frumpy.

And very much like a third wheel. Ben pulled a resin chair up close to Victoria and—when he wasn't making pleasant, amusing conversation about the trials and tribulations of his practice—was dropping light kisses on Victoria's shoulder or idly rubbing the back of her neck.

Now he *has the hands of an artist,* Liz thought ruefully. She thought of Jack Eastman's hands, callused from his work at the shipyard. But then, remembering his touch, she had to admit: Jack had the hands of an artist, too.

Suddenly she decided to wallow in her rum punch. Victoria had someone, a very nice someone indeed, while Liz had . . . no one. Where was the justice in it? Rich, pretty, tall Victoria had a whole new life ahead of her—but Liz? What did Liz have to look forward to? Making sure that other rich, pretty, tall people enjoyed happy birthdays, wonderful weddings, joyful holidays, and—if she ever got that far—successful fund-raisers.

Some entrepreneur. She was in *service,* plain and simple. Just like her laundress grandmother and her gardener father. Maybe it ran in the genes. There had to be *some* reason that she'd never gone into, say, banking. She stole another peek at Ben and Victoria. Yes. She could see them married, with children, shopping for a summer place on the Vineyard.

Oh, who cares? she thought, pouring herself another rum punch. She had a delightful house with a year-round view, enough money for the mortgage, and a daughter who made every minute of life worth living. She gazed through a fond, rum-soaked haze at Susy, sitting at her minitable with her waterpaints and her artist's pad, humming a happy, inane little tune.

Susy looked up just then and gave her mother a happy grin that was short one tooth. "Wait till you see what *I'm* making, Mommy. You'll like this one especially!"

Ben chuckled and sauntered over to her table for a preview. "Wow," he said, impressed. "That looks *exactly* like your house from the back. It even has a barbecue grill! But what's this over here, above the roof?"

"That's the *ghost*," said Susy gleefully. "He's trying to get down our chimney."

Victoria and Liz shot each other startled looks.

"Oooh," said Ben, falling in with Susy's tone. "Is your house haunted?"

Susy giggled and said, "No, of *course* not! Mr. *Eastman's* house is haunted. That one over there," she said, pointing through the fence at East Gate with her paintbrush. "I heard Mommy and Aunty Tori one time when they were talking about the ghost who lives there."

"Oh, Susy, we weren't talking about a real ghost," said Liz quickly. "That was just what-if talk. What if a real ghost lived there, we were saying. You must have misunderstood."

Susy drew her brows together in a puzzled look. "I *think* I understood. Aunty Tori said, 'What was it like?' and you said, 'It got very cold.' "

My God. She can hear us when she's up in bed. My God. "No, no, honey, what I said was—"

Liz was saved from coming up with yet another lie by the sight of their cat Toby flying across Jack Eastman's grounds with Snowball—who ran amazingly fast for a bouncing mop—in hot pursuit. Liz let out a cry and ran up to the chain-link fence with the others right behind her, but there was nothing anyone could do but watch in horror as fat old Toby did his best to outrun the fierce little canine.

Toby picked the maple nearest the fence to claw his way

up and didn't stop until he was out on a limb too narrow to perch on, at which point his hind legs slipped off, dropping him a foot closer to his tormentor.

They all held their breath as the cat scrambled to regain his footing, and then they burst into action. Ben began climbing the fence, Liz picked up a stick to throw at the dog, Victoria shouted *shoo-shoo-shoo* as loud as she could, and Susy yelled words of encouragement to her terrified cat.

Snowball refused to budge from the base of the tree, piercing the air with his relentless, high-pitched bark. The cat, embarrassed and unhappy with this arrangement, began wailing like a banshee. Then Ben dropped to the ground on the dog's side of the fence, and Snowball turned on him instead, locking onto the cuff of his slacks and growling ferociously as he tried to tear the doctor limb from limb.

Ben was trying to shake off the clinging dog without hurting him when Jack Eastman came running up with a look on his face that was more annoyed than not. He called the dog's name—once—and Snowball left off the attack and trotted meekly to his side.

For some reason, it was Liz who felt she should apologize. "Sorry about that," she said to Jack through the fence. "Our cat's in your tree. Ben was just trying to—" Liz shrugged; she didn't know *what* Ben was trying to do, other than to seem heroic.

Smiling away his act of trespass, Ben introduced himself to Jack with an extended hand. "I was a diversion tactic. Worked pretty well, don't you think?" He lifted his right leg and surveyed his shredded cuff. "Ah, well. Linen's too fancy for a cookout, anyway."

Jack sniffed the air that was carrying down to them. "Speaking of which, I'd say your cookout is just about cooked out."

"The steaks!" cried Liz.

Victoria ran to the grill and lifted the hood. The extra shot of oxygen was just what the steaks needed to burst the rest of the way into flame. "Too late," Victoria said as she speared the burning slabs and flung them on the grass. "We'll dash up to the A&P and get more. C'mon, Spider Man. Can you make it back over?"

Ben grinned and took the fence in three quick strides. Liz was reminded—and so, no doubt, was Jack—that without barbed wire, this sort of thing was bound to happen more often. Ben and Victoria were headed through the rose arbor when Liz impulsively turned to Jack and said, "Any chance that you can join us?"

"Sure."

"Bring extra!" she shouted after them, even as she wondered what the *hell* she was doing, asking Jack into her life. It made no sense. She'd worked it all out. This new signal would only confuse him.

So what? she decided. *Why should I be the only one who's off balance all the time?*

"Meanwhile," she said with a smile that she knew was more come-hither than it should be, "my cat's stuck in your tree."

Jack nodded, then said, "Go home," to the dog. Snowball skulked off dutifully toward the house.

"I'm impressed," she said to Jack. "Are you having as much luck training Caroline?" It was a provocative question, she knew. But he chose to parry it with a laugh, for which she was grateful.

"I'll get a ladder," he suggested.

"Wait," Liz told him. "Let me try something first." She left Susy and Jack trying to talk the cat down from the tree and went into the house for a knife and a sharpening stone.

When she came out, Susy was showing Jack her latest artwork through the fence and explaining, no doubt, how she hoped the East Gate ghost would come slumming over to *their* house every once in a while. Whatever Liz believed, whatever she hoped still to discover, she would have to wipe those thoughts out of Susy's head, and quickly.

"I've had Toby for thirteen years," Liz said to Jack, rudely interrupting her daughter. "We've developed quite a vocabulary during that time." She poised the knife over the sharpener. "These are the words for 'raw meat,' " she explained, and drew the blade down over the stone left to right, right to left.

Toby pricked up his ears and stared down gingerly at them from his perch. Liz kept at it, adding a few words of encouragement as the cat began backing awkwardly toward the trunk. *Raw meat, raw meat, raw meat, raw meat,* said the knife and stone.

Jack chuckled as he watched Toby's determined maneuvers. "Must be a bore when you have to sharpen the bread knife."

"Oh, no," said Liz blithely. "He knows the difference in the length of the blades, and between steel and stainless steel. This is the only knife that brings him running."

In less than a minute Toby was down from the tree, making a beeline for the hole under the fence that was a popular shortcut with the local wildlife—possums, coons, a tree shrew, skunks, maybe even the red fox that Liz had spotted on Jack's grounds.

"Unfortunately, now I have to find some raw meat to feed him," she said to Jack. "While I'm doing that, why don't you come on over—or under—or around," she said with an offhand smile that was betrayed by the pounding of her heart. "Whichever way you like."

"I'd like to come *through,* is what I'd like," Jack said with a frustrated look.

"You can't do that, Mr. Eastman," Susy piped up. "Only ghosts can do that."

"That's right," said Jack with a penetrating look at Liz. "Only ghosts."

Liz smiled lamely and beat a retreat to her kitchen. Why had he looked at her that way? Did he know something about the artist-ghost? Was it a fixture at East Gate? That the ghost was an Eastman, she had no doubt. Maybe it would take another Eastman to confirm its existence. Liz had assumed that *she* was the one who'd let the thing loose, that day in the locksmith's shop. But maybe it had been hanging around the mansion for the past hundred years, and she'd just happened on it at East Gate and later on the yacht.

What she didn't know was why it had chosen to appear to her. Twice.

Let me rephrase that, she told herself, her natural skepticism reasserting itself. *What I don't know is why I've convinced myself I've seen a ghost. Twice.*

Liz bought off Toby with a few minced pieces of frozen chicken livers and went back outside. Jack had cleaned up the steaks, poured himself a rum punch, and generally looked comfortable in the role of lord of her very small manor. Susy was working on another watercolor. It didn't surprise Liz at all to see that this one was a close-up of the ghost, a Caspar lookalike in a flowing white sheet.

"What's this stick in his hand?" asked Liz.

Susy frowned. "I don't know," she admitted. "I was going to make it a magic wand. But I think I'll make it a—*paintbrush*!" she said triumphantly. "Just like the one I'm using."

Liz felt the blood leave her face. This was too close for coincidence. Never mind Susy's logic; something was happening here, something that made the hair on the back of Liz's neck stand on end.

Jack, seeing Liz weave, put his drink down and took Liz by the arm. "What? What is it?" he asked, steadying her.

"Nothing," she said quickly. "This rum punch packs a punch, that's all." She sucked in a deep breath. "There. That's better. I'm fine now, thanks."

Liz had to say that, since Susy was watching her closely. The truth was, she felt anything but fine. Was it possible that whoever—whatever—it was had begun to communicate through her *daughter*? The thought chilled Liz's soul. Suddenly she was furious with herself for having had the drinks, for not staying completely in control. More than curiosity was involved now. Much more.

Jack said offhandedly, "When you were inside, I took a little tour around your house. Do you realize your south gutter is mounted to the house badly? No way it'll drain properly like that. I'll show you."

He led her, unprotesting, to the narrow strip of land on the south side of the cottage, the only place where they had a chance at privacy. Liz knew this, and so, of course, did Susy, who gave her mother one of her oh-you-grown-ups smiles as they walked away.

"What's going on?" Jack asked Liz as soon as they were out of earshot. "You turned white as a sheet when you saw Susy's watercolor."

"Not at all. I just get hypoglycemic if I eat late," Liz said briefly. She held out her hand. "Look how I shake."

"Bullshit. This isn't about food. This is about these chronic stops and starts of yours. I've known you only a few weeks, and yet this is the third time I've seen you behave as if—okay, I'll say it—you've seen a ghost."

"You saw the watercolor," Liz answered with a calmness she did not feel. "It *was* a ghost.

"You know what I mean, dammit! I saw you whirling around on the dock the other day. What were you doing? A rain dance? And the night of Caroline's birthday party: you fetched up short at the longcase clock in the entry hall, then broke into a sprint for the door. What the hell was *that* all about? I had a cat like you once—completely goofy. It didn't live too long."

Liz blushed down to her shoes. The good news was, he

really did seem aware of her. The bad news was, he really did seem aware of her. "I appreciate your concern," she said, trying not to sound huffy. "And I'll also grant that I haven't been myself."

"So you haven't always been this way?" He shook his head thoughtfully and let out a low, bemused laugh. "That's a relief—I guess."

Liz glanced around the corner, knowing full well that Susy had periscope ears. "Look, can we talk about this later?" she said, tilting her head in her daughter's direction. "I actually *do* have some things I'd like to ask you."

It seemed to satisfy him. He nodded, his deep blue eyes looking more troubled than she had seen before, and said simply, "Don't encourage your guests to stay."

By the time the meal was actually grilled, served, and eaten, everyone seemed tired and on the quiet side. It was a reasonable response, given the long gap between the alcohol and the food. Besides, Victoria and Ben could hardly wait to fall into each other's arms, that was obvious. And Susy was just plain tired; nine o'clock was well past her bedtime. As for Jack, he seemed to have fallen into a brooding, reflective mood that made Liz alternate between a desire to call him on it and a dread of what he might tell her.

When Liz stood to take her daughter up to bed, Victoria and Ben seized the moment to escape. Quick hugs and handshakes, and out they went.

Susy turned to Jack and said formally, "Goodnight, Mr. Eastman." Liz was too conservative a Yankee ever to encourage her daughter to kiss new guests good night, and Jack was no exception to her rule.

Jack nodded to Susy with a friendly smile but made no attempt to leave the chaise longue in which he sat. He was staying.

This was new, at least to Susy. She glanced back at him when she was on the porch and then sneaked a peek at him, sitting alone in the candlelit garden, from her bedroom window before being tucked in for prayers.

"Doesn't Mr. Eastman have to go to bed, too?" she asked innocently.

"He's just finishing his coffee, honey," Liz said, but she felt the familiar flush in her cheeks as she spoke of him.

The fact was, she'd never had to explain a man hanging around the house before; there simply hadn't been one. Liz had been so involved in keeping Susy and herself afloat that she'd had no time for anyone else. When well-meaning relations came up with what they considered suitable young men, she'd put the kibosh on their designs at once. Nor had the party-planning business yielded any real prospects: once or twice a single father had hit on her, but they were clearly on the rebound and she'd wanted no part of them.

And now Jack. He was far less likely a prospect than her mother's second cousin's son; far less likely than the airline pilot who was desperate for a woman to help him manage his three children on custody weekends. So why, oh why, did she insist on viewing him as a prospect at all—good or bad?

"And bless Gramma and bless Grampa and also bless Oliver."

"Oliver?" asked Liz, coming out of her daze. "Who's Oliver?"

"He's the ghost," Susy said, curling one arm around her dog-eared teddy bear. "I think Oliver is a good name for him."

"But he doesn't look anything like an—"

Good God, what was she *doing*, going on about what he looked like? One fleeting hallucination—okay, two—and suddenly the thing was being regarded as fact. This was how myths, legends, and wild stories that brought down presidents began.

Struck with an inspiration, Liz said gently, "I don't think you should call Oliver a ghost. I think you should call him your pretend-friend." God knew Susy needed one; she was never going to have any brothers or sisters.

Liz tucked her daughter in with a sweet-dreams kiss and was at the doorway when Susy said through a sleepy yawn, "I just think I don't know him good enough to call him my *friend,* Mommy. Maybe I'll just call him my pretend-ghost."

" '*Well* enough,' " Liz corrected in a weary cop-out. "You don't know him well enough. Good night, honey."

Outside, Liz dropped into a chaise longue with a tired sigh. The first words out of Jack's mouth were, "Is the front door locked?"

"*Oh* yeah. Ever since the burglary. It's too bad, really; my parents never had to lock their door. Oh, and I have news about my graduate student," she admitted, hating like hell to have to pass it along. "It turns out that the scratches on his hands *were* from hiking. The police got hold of the Visa record of his fill-up; he really was in New Hampshire. Or at least his car was," she said, not giving up entirely on her theory.

She glanced up automatically at Susy's bedroom window, listening for a possible summons.

"Should we go inside?" asked Jack politely.

"No, I'll be able to hear her through the window," Liz said. "By the same token," she warned, "she'll be able to hear us, too."

She heard the smile in his voice as he said, "In that case I won't spell out where I'd *really* like to spend the rest of the evening."

The words washed over Liz like warm honey. She felt caught by them, held by them, unwilling to work her way out of them. She should run. But she didn't want to.

"She's probably out like a light by now, anyway," Liz said, amazing herself. Apparently she was hoping that Jack would spell out exactly where and how he'd like to spend the evening.

Dangerous, she told herself. *This is getting dangerous.* But she hardly cared. She rolled her head lazily toward him and murmured, "I'm glad you were free for supper. It was fun."

Liz had turned off the kitchen lights on her way out, leaving the two of them in a deep, satisfying darkness broken only by a small citronella candle flickering in its red bowl on a nearby stepstone. Jack reached over and took her hand, threading his fingers through hers. "I hardly know anything about you," he said in a voice more wistful than before. He seemed surprised by the fact, as if he'd just found out she was a double agent. "Tell me who you are."

Liz laughed at the challenge of explaining herself in a phrase or two. "Single working mother," she said, defining the most elemental thing about herself.

"Right. Now tell me something I *don't* know," he said, absently rubbing the pulse point of her wrist with his thumb. "Tell me . . . oh, let's see . . . how did your marriage end?"

"Awkwardly," Liz said, sucking in her breath. Did he really have the right to know? It was such a humiliation; even her family hadn't been told the whole story.

"I'm sorry," he said after a pause. "You don't want to say."

Liz decided after all that she *did* want to say. She didn't know why. She wanted to make some sort of . . . gesture. Of trust. It was all, really, she could ever give him: a small, wrenchingly intimate piece of her history.

"When we got married," she said very softly, "it was with the understanding that we wouldn't rush into having children. Well, what can I say? In a couple of years I changed my mind. I suppose it had something to do with this *slew* of babies that were being born, all at once, into my family. We all joked about there being something in Newport's water. I was the only one, it seemed, who wasn't pregnant or nursing."

Liz stopped and listened for sounds through the upstairs window. Susy was asleep; she knew that. And yet she felt as if she were about to say something disloyal, and it made her hesitate.

She took a deep breath. "What began as theoretical discussions about the pros and cons of quitting my job to have a baby became . . . well, knock-down, drag-out fights. Keith was dead against it. I was dead for it. It became—I don't know—a power play between us. I don't think, now, that he was as against it as he said. And maybe I wasn't as ready as I'd insisted I was. Not that I'll ever know," she added with a small, pained laugh.

"Anyway, one day—without telling him—I just stopped taking my pills," she said, forcing herself to go on. "The maneuver was a grand success; I got pregnant almost instantly. If I'd had any second thoughts, they disappeared in the next round of arguments over whether to keep the baby or not. I suppose, if I'm going to be brutally honest about it, that was a power play, too."

The candle flickered more fitfully than ever; it was on its way to burning out. Liz fixed her attention on it, listening for sounds from Susy's bedroom, wondering whether Jack was going to interrupt. But he said nothing. He could have been asleep, for all she knew; only the gentle, idle caress of his thumb on her wrist told her he was not.

If the candle goes out, I'll stop the story. The end is obvious, anyway. But the candle flickered on, and Liz resumed.

"I had the baby," she said simply.

She wanted to say, "And suffered a postpartum infection," but he hadn't asked her how the delivery went, and she hadn't either the courage or the audacity to offer the information on her own.

"About a week after the baby—after Susy—was born, I came home from a visit to the pediatrician and found—" She bit her lip and told him what she'd found. "A note. From Keith. At least he took the time to say good-bye. We think he's in California, but nobody really knows. There was talk of an ashram in Iowa, but Keith's more of a loner than a commune type."

After a long pause, Jack said, "He can be tracked down, you know."

Liz blinked away the tear that had risen, Pavlov style, at the thought of the note, and then blinked away her disappointment at Jack's response. That was it? An offer to track Keith down? For this she'd split her heart open in front of him?

She slid her hand carefully out of his and sat up on the chaise. She, of all people, should've been able to predict that he, of all people, would cut right to the chase: the missed payments of child support. Everything with his kind was about money. Everything.

"Thanks all the same," she said, rubbing her arms against the chill that had come out of nowhere, "but I don't particularly want to find him anymore."

"You don't really mean that" came Jack's voice from behind her. He sat up, too, and swung his legs over the side of his chaise so that he could face her. "Look, this guy's got a responsibility here. He's Susy's *father*. He should be visiting; he should be writing; he should be paying for child support."

She laughed softly. "You don't get it, do you? But then, why should you?" she said, implicitly throwing his bachelor status back in his face.

"You're right," Jack said, coolly now. "I *don't* get it. Enlighten me. Tell me how a man can walk away from that kind of commitment."

Liz jumped up and rounded on him. "Are you kidding?

Because he thought Susy was a dirty trick I'd played on him! Because he never *committed* to having children! As far as he was concerned, *I* was the one who broke the commitment.''

"I guess I don't see it that way," Jack said, looking up at her. "I guess I see it as a case of your hurt pride getting in the way of your daughter's welfare.''

"That's—*outrageous*!" Liz said, stunned. She walked off to the far end of the yard, stifling the urge to scream and shout. Overhead, the branches of the huge copper beech on the other side of the fence began to sway in the steadily rising wind. Clouds were scuttling through, and the dark, starry night was turning into a seesaw affair between the threat of rain and the pledge of more fine weather.

Fine for what? Liz wondered while she waited for Jack to leave. Not for romance, which ten short minutes ago had been uppermost in her mind. What a fool she'd been, to think she could depend on his sympathy. God! He didn't even admire her spunk! *Everyone* who knew her admired her spunk.

"We can agree to disagree on this, you know," Jack said.

His hand was on her shoulder. She tried, not very hard, to shrug it away, but he turned her around to face him. "You're right," he said with that improbable melancholy that she associated with him. "In matters of family, I don't have much to go on. I've never been married, and my own father was— as you now know—a master of irresponsibility.''

She felt like arguing, so she said, "Is he? After all, he's taken in Caroline—and even her brother—when they needed someone.''

"A noble gesture. My mother doesn't think so.''

"She knows about this?''

"What do *you* think?" he snapped.

Liz said defensively, "I'm not the psychic around here, remember? All I know is that Netta said Mrs. Eastman had extended her visit in Italy. That could mean anything.''

"Sorry; sorry. The situation's been going on for weeks, but it's still very . . . raw." He sighed and said, "I don't know what the hell my father was thinking—that he'd get Stacey Stonebridge in and out of the clinic before my mother came back? That he'd just let the chips fall where they may? That we'd all live as one big happy family at East Gate? I have no idea how his mind works anymore.

"Anyway, in answer to your question, my mother may well not come back. No one knows. My mother, probably least of all."

Maybe it was the darkness; maybe it was the baffled, rueful tone of his voice. Whatever the reason, Liz felt like his equal for the first time. They were two lost souls, wandering through the swamp of human motivation together. It was reassuring that he was just as confused as she was.

"Your father knew Caroline existed?" she asked.   ·

"Oh, yeah. There was a generous settlement, all very proper and legal, when she was born. If my mother was aware of it at the time, she never told me. I guess Stacey went through all the money and came back for more. I'm not exactly in the loop on this one."

"I guess you can always give her the benefit of the doubt."

"Right."

Liz tried not to hear the irony in his voice, but it was hard to miss. It left her feeling dispirited; she didn't need any more evidence that he had a cynical view of women. "Stacey might really want to do right by Caroline," she ventured.

"You haven't met Stacey" was all he said. "Jeez," he said, laughing softly, "will you listen to me? All I've done is carp about the way people try to cope: my father, Stacey, Keith—I don't even know the guy!—and worst of all, you."

"Yes," she said lightly. "What a scoundrel you are."

"Well, I'm sure as hell no expert on relationships. Forgive me?" he asked.

"Forgive you for what? For being honest with me?" Liz shook her head, sad that he didn't find her spunky, glad that he was sorry about it. "In a weird way it's pretty flattering."

His chuckle, soft and low and sexy, lingered in the air around them like the scent of roses. "Forget your career in party planning," he said, tilting her chin up to him. "You should go into public relations."

The kiss, when it finally came, was as inevitable as a high tide. His mouth, warm and soft and interested, closed on hers. She was surprised at how familiar it seemed, as if it weren't their first kiss at all, but the kiss that came after they'd already made love. *It's supposed to be electric,* she thought, disappointed. *We've danced around this kiss for so long. . . .*

And then he probed her mouth further, and the touch of his tongue sliding over hers simply blew her away. She made a yielding sound low in her throat, and Jack Eastman, who probably knew that sound the way Toby knew knives, had to know that Liz was his for the taking.

Come and get me was what the sound said. *Oh, lord, here I am. I have waited so long for you; for this. And I am* ready.

All that, in one wordless sound.

He slid his hands down her back and, still kissing her, began inching her shirt out of the waistband of her jeans. In a flash she understood that the restlessness she'd been feeling for the past year had had nothing whatever to do with forging ahead with her career.

"Liz . . . Liz," he murmured, breaking off the kiss to nuzzle the curve of her neck, "if you don't want me to keep going . . ."

She made another sound, a moan, which obviously translated as "Are you *crazy*?"

He laughed then, a low, rich, utterly devilish sound that maybe should have frightened Liz but absolutely did not.

Instead, she found her hand on the zipper of his khakis, because she had an urgent, demonic need for him of her own.

Later, she thought she must have been possessed.

The cry that ripped through the night from the upstairs window sent shivers of terror hard on the heels of the pleasure she'd been feeling.

"Susy!" she cried in anguish.

She broke away from Jack and made a blind dash for the back steps. The candle had flickered out sometime during the kiss; in her haste Liz stumbled over the first step and sprawled forward, scraping her arm on the concrete risers. She rose and yanked the back door open, then raced like a madwoman up the varnished stairs to Susy's bedroom.

She found her daughter standing on the bed, her arms in front of her, warding off—Liz didn't know what.

Chapter 11

"Susy, honey, what's wrong, what's wrong?" Liz said, holding her daughter in her arms. The child was shivering violently and sobbing with fear; Liz lifted her up and then sat down on the side of the bed, cradling her.

"I s-saw something," Susy stammered between sobs. "Over *there*." She pointed to the closed louvred doors of the closet, averting her head from the sight, burrowing into her mother's breast. "Is it gone?" she asked in a muffled voice.

Liz turned on the lamp. "I don't see anything," she said, listening automatically for the chime-sound. She made reassuring murmurs while she rocked her daughter and stroked her hair reassuringly. *This has to end,* she thought. *I'll tear up the letters, burn the box, bury the pin—this has to end.*

"It was kind of pink," Susy finally managed to say. "And I could see right through it. It didn't look like anything," she admitted, "but it was as big as you." She began to sob again, then checked herself with a brave little effort. "It was—it was like the wrapping on my Easter basket."

Despite herself, Liz smiled. Cellophane? The image was so innocuous, so unlike what she feared Susy might have seen. "*That's* not a ghost," she said soothingly. "That's just color that was left over from your dreams. When you opened your eyes, it was still there. Probably you were dreaming of a big fuzzy toy rabbit, that's all."

Susy seemed persuaded by that, and let herself relax in her mother's arms, and finally lay back down to sleep.

Liz said softly, "Would you like the door open or closed?"

"Closed," Susy said, surprising her. "Because if the ghost comes in our house through the chimney," she explained in sleepy confusion, "then after it got up the stairs . . . I can keep it out."

Liz kissed her and said, "I'll be right in the kitchen."

Which was where she found Jack with his sleeves rolled up, washing dishes. He looked so impossibly domestic, so unlike the imperious businessman-bachelor with little time or patience for life's more mundane chores, that, again, she had to smile.

He glanced at her over his shoulder and caught her appraising look, then eyed her with a sudden burning one of his own. For one spark of an instant, some of the backyard electricity crackled again between them. But he knew, and she knew, that the moment had passed, at least for tonight.

He said amiably, "Nothing serious, I take it?"

"Depends who you ask. Susy thinks so," Liz said with a tired sigh. She felt like a racquetball after a hard game between two lawyers. Emotionally, she'd been batted all around the court tonight. And she still wasn't sure if the game was over.

"I used to have a recurring nightmare when I was a boy," Jack recollected as he rinsed the last of the cups. "There'd be some kind of emergency—usually medical—and I'd have to drive someone to the hospital, only I didn't have a license. Sometimes I tried driving without one, sometimes I couldn't find the car or the keys—but I always woke up in a cold sweat, feeling as if I'd desperately failed somebody. Oddly enough, the dreams stopped when I turned sixteen and got my license," he said, flashing her an all-male, all-modern grin.

When Liz didn't respond, he said, not without sympathy, "So she's in one of those monster-in-the-closet phases?"

Liz laughed bleakly and said, "You might say that—only the monster's a ghost."

"Ah." He wiped his hands on the dish towel and hung it back on the hook. "Well, lots of different things go bump in the night."

Instantly Liz pictured herself with him in bed, which she knew was not what he'd meant at all. "Speaking of ghosts," she said, recovering with an awkward laugh, "don't you think it's funny how only the mansions get haunted, never the three-bedroom ranches?"

"You've deduced this scientifically?" he asked with a wry smile.

"I've read stories," she said, riding roughshod over his irony. "Let's take East Gate. Just—for example. I'll bet that over the years there've been all manner of sightings and unexplained goings-on there."

"Nope," he said, leaning back on the counter and watching her with a sideways look. "Can't say as there have."

"Nothing at all? You never had a crazy aunt who saw, well, something going up or down the staircase or . . . maybe by the clock?" she finished in a tiny, failing voice.

"Nope."

"You never took a photograph and ended up with strange vapory columns in it that you couldn't explain?"

"Nope." The smile on his face was gradually settling into a straight line that ran parallel to the square set of his clefted jaw. Liz found herself getting distracted again, thinking how impossibly like an old-fashioned screen star he looked, when he said seriously, "What exactly have you been seeing, on and around the Eastman property?"

Liz couldn't quite face him for the answer. She turned and made a business of cleaning off the kitchen table, picking up a bottle of A•1 steak sauce with one hand, the pepper grinder

in the other. Suddenly, arbitrarily, she remembered that her
T-shirt was still half in, half out of the waistband of her jeans.
Very carefully, blushing furiously, she put the bottle of steak
sauce and the pepper grinder back on the table, then casually
began tucking her shirt back into her jeans. If she'd been a
cat, she could have hidden her embarrassment in a fit of
grooming.

But alas, she wasn't a cat. "I've been seeing an Eastman,
I think," she murmured, more embarrassed now than ever.
And yet, what else could she say? It was the truth, whether
or not it was stranger than fiction.

Jack made a wry, almost comical grimace and rubbed his
chin with his thumb and forefinger as he considered his response. "Which Eastman?" he merely asked.

"It's the artist who painted in the studio that used to be
on this property during the 1890s. I don't know his first
name. He was a younger brother, dashing, impulsive, somewhat scandalous in his behavior. But not for an artist," she
quickly added, amazing herself by defending her ghost. "For
a while he was in love with one of the servants at East Gate,"
she said to explain her last remark.

The half-amused expression on Jack's face disappeared. In
its place a puzzled look took over; then that, too, got lost
behind a curtain of scarcely veiled suspicion. "How do you
know all this?" he asked evenly, folding his arms across his
chest.

Liz didn't need a clinical psychologist to translate his body
language: he had assumed the role of defender of All That
Was Eastman. "It's in the letters I found," she said haplessly. She felt like a teenager caught smoking in the girls'
bathroom. But she wasn't guilty of anything.

Except, apparently, of having an overactive imagination.
She could see it in Jack's eyes: he thought she was impressionable at best, hysterical at worst. "The only one who even

remotely fits your description is Christopher Eastman," he said at last.

"Who is—?"

"My great-great-grandfather. As for his scandalous behavior, I know nothing of it," Jack added grimly. "He married a woman whose portrait hangs in the entry hall. As a matter of fact, he *painted* the portrait."

Liz went blank for a moment, calling up in her memory the various paintings that hung in strategic locations above the paneled wainscoting of East Gate's grand hall. Then it came to her. She knew exactly which one he meant. It wasn't the subject so much as the style of the artist that she remembered: it was different from all the rest, and yet—now that she thought about it—disturbingly familiar.

"The blond woman in the blue gown?" she asked.

"That's the one."

"Hmm. And his death wasn't . . . untimely?" she asked, grasping by now at straws.

"He lived a long and healthy life."

"As an artist?"

"No, he gave all that up to run the shipyard and to manage other scattered real estate the family owned at the time. A hundred years ago," Jack explained with a dark flush, "the Eastman empire was farther away from bankruptcy than it is now."

"Oh. I'm sorry," Liz said, fixating on the bankruptcy part. "These are such hard times."

He was just as glad to change the subject. "Our customers have been hit hard. Commercial fishermen are running out of fish, and mom-and-pop boaters are running out of leisure. The recession didn't help, and neither did the luxury tax, despite its repeal. Few have the money to keep boats for business *or* pleasure.

"The only real scandal in our family nowadays," he

added ironically, "is the amount of the shipyard's receivables."

Liz remembered seeing some very fine yachts when she visited the yard. "But surely," she argued, despite her reluctance to provoke him on such a sensitive matter, "the rich are still getting richer."

He arched one brow at the hostility in her manner, so predictable whenever she spoke of the wealthy. "Yeah, but they can cut better deals at other yards in less prime locations than ours, and they are. Look, it's getting late; I really ought to be going." He looked around the homey kitchen as if he were doing one last sweep of a hotel room before checking out. "Thanks for supper. I hope your cat's none the worse for wear."

"Not a snowball's chance in hell," she said with a wan smile. *Leaving? Just like that?*

He ignored the pun, passed on a kiss, and got out of there as fast as he could, leaving a hurt and puzzled Liz to wipe the dishes by herself.

One thing she knew: Jack had a wide choice of reasons to run from her. Tonight he'd got a close-up look of a woman who abandoned sex at the drop of a hat; who hallucinated regularly; and who didn't seem to care very much for people who had either servants or boats. Which of these sterling character traits had scared him the most?

All of the above, Liz decided glumly. She was a pretty frightening package.

Several days later Liz was glued to her television, watching the weather, when the doorbell rang.

"Who is it?" she yelled, unable to move away from the weather map that had her transfixed. *A hurricane. A frigging hurricane!*

It was Victoria, demanding to be let in. "In a minute!" said Liz, ignoring the summons and turning up the volume.

Wildly impatient by now, Victoria began alternately pounding on the door and cranking on the ear-splitting door-bell. "Dammit, Liz! Let me in! I know who he is!"

The hurricane had formed overnight west of Hatteras and was projected to follow a northerly path. "Too soon to call," Liz heard the weatherman say over her shoulder as she went at last to get the door. "We'll be watching this one closely."

Victoria was standing on the stoop, waving one of Victoria St. Onge's letters in Liz's face like an American flag at the summer Olympics. "I got it, I got it!" she cried, brushing past Liz into the living room.

"I promised Jack no rain for his picnic," Liz moaned—unnecessarily, since Victoria wasn't listening. "Wait'll he hears about *this*. A stupid *hurricane*. Of all the rotten, miserable breaks—"

Victoria was scanning her letter, searching for what was obviously the good part, oblivious to Liz's new problem. "Ah! Here it is. Listen!"

" 'Last week I attended an amusing affair—' "

"Oh, *please*," Liz said, interrupting her at once. "Not another amusing affair! I can't *take* any more. I've read through endless years of endless accounts of endless balls, fêtes, tennis matches, fox hunts, yachting parties, and soirées. God! How could they *stand* such nonstop idleness?"

Victoria shrugged and said without irony, "You know how it is: same old same old. You get used to it, like a job sorting mail. Are you sure you've made the right career choice?" she added. "Anyway, trust me—*this* event will be worth it," she promised.

She began over. " 'Last week I attended an amusing affair at *East Gate*,' " she read, glancing up at Liz with a look of triumph.

Liz became quiet. Not outwardly—outwardly, she was

leaning forward in the wing chair, breathless to hear this of
all the letters. But deep inside, in her soul—that's where she
became very, very still. She felt as if she were at the altar
of some great truth; that some impossibly difficult code was
about to be deciphered with the key that Victoria was holding
in her hand.

Victoria read on, in a deeply pleased voice:

The event was a fête champêtre, *hosted by John and Lavinia
Eastman, a coolly old-fashioned couple in this overheated
age. I have written before of their moody, reckless son, the
artist who so rudely removed me from his studio last year.
To this day, there is little love lost between Christopher Eastman and me; but his mother, who is anxious to communicate
with a recently departed aunt, has decided to take me up. To
that end, she invited me to the festivity of which I now write.*

*Lavinia Eastman had urged me to come early so that we
might make arrangements for a sitting later in the week. This
we did, and as we had time to spare before the arrival of
the first guests, she carried me off to the dining hall so that
I might admire the artful arrangement of the table.*

*It was charmingly done up in a seashore theme. Shells
and beach roses were scattered freely up and down the service. The centerpiece was a stunning tableau, rendered in
crystal, of a mermaid cavorting with dolphins amid roiling
seas.*

*At each place setting there was a small child's bucket,
filled with sand and with a shovel stuck into it. A nice bit of
whimsy, I thought, and remarked upon the fact—though I
could not help feeling that very soon we should all be tasting
sand in our soup. Lavinia was pleased with my enthusiasm
and boasted happily that she had hit upon the sand buckets
as an ideal way to present the guests with their party favors.*

*She told me that her son Christopher had been assigned
the pleasant task of inserting a semiprecious gemstone—*

tourmaline, amethyst, citrine, agate, topaz, and the like—into each of the buckets. Later, the guests would be instructed to take up their shovels and dig for their treasures. As I say: sand in the soup.

I thought no more about it—the favors were neither diamonds nor rubies, after all—until a few minutes later, when I returned to the room to fetch my spectacles, which I had left behind. I was about to leave when my nemesis came in to do his mother's bidding. He did not see me, and as I felt rather awkward about engaging him alone, I tucked myself behind a carved leather screen that stood nearby and waited for him to be done.

From the crevice between the panels I was able to observe his very odd behavior. The young man walked directly up to one of the settings and replaced the place card with one he had brought with him. Then he made a quick circuit of the table, carelessly pushing a gemstone into each of the buckets. When he returned to his original setting, the one with the new place card, he took a small pin from the pocket of his dinner jacket and, with a smile, stuck it, instead of a gemstone, into the sand.

Consumed with curiosity, I went directly to the altered place card after he left the room and read it. I did not recognize the last name, but I certainly knew the first: Ophelia, the servant with whom he had been having the affair! I had heard nothing about the matter lately and had assumed, if I thought about it at all, that the infatuation had passed. ''Apparently not,'' I murmured to myself. And then I had an inspiration.

Locating my own placecard, I carefully fished out my favor—a dull little citrine—and switched it with the pin in Ophelia's bucket. As of this writing, I still do not know why. It can hardly have been because I desired the pin, which was a small, quite humble little heart with an insignificant garnet set inside. So it must have been because I wished, purely and *simply, to make things as awkward for Christopher Eastman as he had for me that afternoon in his studio a year ago. (You know, dear sister, how I can be.)*

It was clear to me, as I left the dining room in haste, that this besotted man had every intention of forcing his paramour on Newport society. Perhaps, I thought, the pin was meant to be the catalyst to an announcement of his betrothal to Ophelia, or even a public proposal of marriage to her; the man was outrageous enough to do either. I had no doubt that Ophelia would present very well—in the nude paintings she had presented very well indeed—but I could not imagine how he dared risk his parents' wrath.

Still, it was obvious to all that his mother doted on him. She respected and trusted her older son, who had already assumed the responsibility of running the family's large holdings. But it was her younger son whom she loved, and dearly. As a consequence, he probably realized that the risk was not—

Victoria looked up through a mist of happy tears and folded the pages of the letter gently on her lap. "So now we know," she said with a limpid smile.

Liz was so thoroughly prepared to hear the end of the tale that she simply sat there, waiting for more. And yet it was clear that there was no more. She said stupidly, "You're not going to finish the letter?"

Victoria sighed, then leaned over and handed Liz the folded, heavy sheets. "This is all there is, this middle section. The pages weren't dated—they weren't even numbered—so I'd stuck them in one of the 'miscellaneous' shoeboxes. I guess they should've gone in the 1896 shoebox."

"But that *can't* be all," Liz wailed. "Did you look through everything else in the miscellaneous boxes?"

"I didn't read every word; but there were no other sheets with the same ink and nib. And you know how erratic her handwriting is; nothing else there matched this style, which is oddly legible—for her, anyway."

Victoria undid the clasp of the heart that was pinned to the lapel of her blouse. "So now we know," she repeated, studying the little bauble that lay in the palm of her hand. "Isn't it amazing? You see so many pins in flea markets—in antique shops—at yard sales—and you never have a clue how they got there. But we know exactly how this pin ended up in your red-lacquered box."

Liz wasn't as satisfied as her friend. In a fit of frustration she flung the pages into the fireplace, where they got hung up in a basket of dried flowers that she'd placed on the metal grate for the summer.

"Oh, I can't believe it!" she said, jumping up from her chair and pacing the three strides up and then down the length of the room. "I simply can't believe it! I'm going to go out of my mind if I don't resolve this soon."

Victoria, nestled in the down-filled cushions of the chintz sofa, was puzzled. "Resolve what?" she asked, clearly amazed by Liz's reaction. "We know now where the pin came from—"

"We know practically nothing!" Liz said angrily. "We know Victoria St. Onge stole the pin. We don't know why she stole it—*she* didn't know why—and we certainly don't know why she kept it."

"That's true, but—"

"And Christopher Eastman! Did he marry Ophelia or not? Obviously not," she said, answering her own question. "His wife was blond; Ophelia was a redhead. I don't understand; what could've happened? Oh, damn, damn, damn."

"How do *you* know his wife was a blonde?"

"Jack told me."

"Jack!"

"And why does he keep appearing to me, anyway? What does he want?"

"What! He's appeared more than once?"

"Twice. Where do I fit in? Where do *you* fit in?"

"*Twice!* But where—? No; tell me later. I can answer your last question, and I will!" said Victoria. She got up to retrieve the letter fragment from the fireplace grate, then carried the pages over to the cherry foyer table that stood, in lieu of a larger table, behind one end of the chintz-covered sofa. For a moment she stood quite still, with her back to Liz, as if she were composing herself before a difficult feat of acrobatics.

She turned and said, "Listen to me, Elizabeth!" in a voice that was shaking with excitement. "I know *exactly* where I fit in. *Finally*. Now that I've found the letter." Her eyes were deep green pools of liquid fire.

Liz, herself a jumble of conflicting impulses, took one look at Victoria and decided that each of them, in her own special way, had completely lost touch with reality.

Victoria took Liz by the hand and led her to the sofa. She laid the heart-shaped pin in Liz's hand, then placed her own hand over it and held it there. Lowering her voice to a breathy whisper, she said, "I'm here—I came back—to return the pin to its rightful owner."

"He's *dead*," said Liz. "Despite what I may have implied."

"Not Christopher. Jack. His heir." Victoria smiled dreamily and took the heart back, then pinned it to her blouse.

Liz watched her do it, hypnotized by the simple, ordinary act. "You honestly think that Christopher Eastman is haunting the area because he wants that dinky pin back?"

Without in the least taking offense, Victoria said, "The pin must've had some sentimental value. He could've afforded to give Ophelia a diamond necklace if he'd wanted to."

"Not necessarily. He was a younger son, remember."

"Even so. He could've done better than this," Victoria said, tapping the heart that lay across her own heart.

They became silent a moment, each of them caught up in her own thoughts. By now, there was little doubt in Liz's mind that some strange game was afoot, and that she had a role to play in it. The game was perhaps not so complex as chess, but neither was it as straightforward as Parcheesi. It fell, like life itself, somewhere in between. Victoria had figured out the rules—at least, as they applied to her—but Liz was still reading the back of the box, scratching her head and wondering what the ultimate goal was, and just how many players were allowed.

"What will you do?" Liz asked, suppressing a sigh.

"Return it, of course."

"I suppose that's reasonable," Liz allowed. "Technically the pin was stolen—although if it was special, I wonder why Christopher Eastman never bothered to get it back from Victoria St. Onge."

She tried to imagine a scenario but came up empty. "Damn," she added in a soft, sad voice. "I wish we had the rest of the letter."

"Why?" asked Victoria, shooting Liz a surprised look. "We don't need it." Clearly she felt none of Liz's sense of being adrift. "As soon as I sneak the pin back—"

"*Sneak* it back? Why wouldn't you just explain to Jack what happened and hand it over? Show him the letter if you like," Liz added with a shrug. "I don't care." She wouldn't allow herself to care—not where Jack was concerned. Not after the other night. She didn't dare; who knows how badly she'd get hurt?

Victoria shook her head, sending long red spirals of hair sailing back and forth. "The pin was sneaked out; it has to be sneaked back in. Into Jack's bedroom would be best. I'll do it when we're over there this weekend for the company picnic."

Liz tried to argue with her over taking such an unnecessary risk, but Victoria seemed to find a rough cosmic justice in

exposing herself to it. "It must be done my way," she said
simply. "This is why I'm here. This is what the last six years
have been leading up to: to return this pin. It must be done—
my way.

"So! Now that that's resolved," she said cheerfully to Liz,
changing the subject, "can we back up a little? When did
Christopher Eastman appear to you the second time?"

With considerable reluctance, Liz drew a brief, vague
sketch of the gentleman in yachting duds that she'd seen on
the deck of the *Déjà Vu.* "I suppose I was projecting like
mad," she said, admitting the obvious. "I was so impressed
by the boat: it was in such original pristine condition. No
Formica, no Ultrasuede. Stepping aboard was like stepping
back a hundred years; all it lacked was a Gilded Age owner."

"Which you conjured up?" asked Victoria, smiling. "I
don't think so. We know what we know," she said crypti-
cally. "I have to say—the boat does sound exceptional."

"You have no idea. I doubt that the yacht has suffered a
day of neglect in its life. I mean, there was another boat in
the yard of about the same vintage—the interior had been
vandalized, actually—and it was in just awful shape. It was
little more than a piece of flotsam: peeling paint, duct tape
around the portholes, a bilge pump that never stopped pump-
ing. What a contrast. All I can say is, I hope I look as good
at a hundred as the *Déjà Vu* does."

"I want to go out on it sometime," Victoria decided.

"You and Susy," said Liz. "She acted as if she owned
the thing. I can't get over the girl," she added, aware that
the only way her daughter was ever going to get a boat ride
was at Disney World with her grandparents. "Sometimes I
think she's a changeling."

Victoria's laughter had a surprisingly melancholy lilt to it.
"When you think about it," she said softly, "aren't we all,
at some point in our lives?"

Chapter 12

◆

The hurricane ended up veering off the coast and heading out to sea, and Netta, for one, was glad. They had enough on their minds without worrying where to find seventy or eighty umbrellas.

Such a week! Why, the old place hadn't seen such bustling since—"Well, I can't remember when," said the housekeeper to David Penny as he nailed a makeshift table together on the grounds at East Gate.

"I suppose it would be for Mr. Eastman's thirtieth wedding anniversary. You weren't working at the shipyard then, David. But take my word for it; it was quite the gala affair, even for Newport."

The carpenter, dripping wet from his efforts to hurry the project through before the guests arrived, wiped his forehead on his arm and said laconically, "No, that'd be before my time. Just like this here's after my time."

"I know, I know," Netta said, clucking sympathetically. "Any luck finding another job, dear?"

"Bits and pieces here and there," David said, sliding his hammer through his belt like Wyatt Earp would a six-shooter. "Keeps me busy."

"Is Cynthia coming?"

"She wouldn't miss it."

"I still think you should stay, David. You're perfectly entitled to."

"Nope," he said, throwing his shoulders back with proud resolve. "Got work to do."

Netta suspected that he'd feel embarrassed to be among his old co-workers. And really, it was a little awkward, with Cynthia getting her job at the shipyard just because of him, and now him out of his own job. Well, he shouldn't have got so full of himself and quit. Not before he had a better offer lined up, anyway. Still, Jack was trying to use him whenever he could for odd jobs; that was a nice thing. And Cynthia's medical covered them both. Things could be worse.

David picked up the scraps of lumber and hauled them out to his pickup, and Netta threw a gingham-checked tablecloth over the unpainted impromptu table. Lucky for them that they had extra plywood in the carriage house. Who would've thought that you couldn't rent a table in this town? Even if it *was* a weekend in July.

Netta hurried back to the house and was surprised to see Victoria and Elizabeth lollygagging in front of one of the ancestral portraits in the cavernous entry hall. There was no law against admiring the artwork, she supposed, but it did seem odd that they were finding the time to do it just now. The shipyard employees and their families would be arriving at any moment, and then who was to say what crises mightn't take place? Look what had happened at Caroline's birthday party, for pity's sake.

She slowed her steps as she approached the two women, not wishing to seem to be rushing them. Victoria With-No-Last-Name: now there was an odd, fey creature. Netta liked her, but she didn't understand her at all. The young woman seemed to have lots of enthusiasm, but Netta could never make out, at any given moment, what exactly the enthusiasm was *for*. Victoria had the look of someone who's won the lottery but hasn't yet picked up her money.

Look at her, thought Netta. *How wide-eyed and excited*

she is. And over—what? Lavinia Eastman's cleavage? Because that sure seemed to be what she was pointing at.

And Liz Coppersmith—so calm, so in control all week; but now she was just as wide-eyed as the other one. *For goodness' sake. Everyone knows that was the style back then. What prudes. And that Madonna woman running around in steel-pointed bras!*

Victoria suddenly looked up and spied Netta staring at them, which sent the two women scurrying back to the kitchen like scullery maids, exactly what Netta had wished to avoid. This was *their* event, not Netta's. In no way were they obliged to her. She was only there to point out where they kept the big pots.

The housekeeper paused before the painting of Lavinia Eastman, wondering what was so all-fired shocking about it. A nice buxom woman with thick dark curls and mischievous eyes: Lavinia was a favorite of Jack's, and Netta could see why. As for the gown, Netta had always rather liked it. It was a simple flowing affair in a pale, creamy color, unadorned except for the small heart-shaped pin at the low point of the bustline. All in all, a much more appealing package than Lavinia's more fetchingly painted daughter-in-law, whose portrait faced opposite.

Netta gave that one—Blue Brunhilde, she called it—her usual frown. Netta had always liked the skill of the painter more than the subject. Brunhilde was tall, blond, Teutonic. Better-looking than Lavinia by far, in a smashing blue gown—and yet, well, those eyes. How piercingly empty they were. How possibly cruel. Brunhilde was the kind of woman, Netta felt sure, who would run over your dog with her carriage if it meant avoiding a puddle in the road.

Beautiful, well-bred, with money enough to bring to the marriage: nowadays they'd call Brunhilde a trophy wife. But as far as Netta could make out, the lady in the blue gown had launched a line of unhappy marriages that continued to this day.

It's like a curse, Netta thought, shaking her head before the proud, imperious woman who hung above her in a gilded frame. *And this is the witch who's cast the spell.*

She shrugged off the unpleasant sensation and went on her way to the kitchen, which was humming like a medieval cooking room before a visit from the local king and queen. Netta looked around with satisfaction; the caterer and her two assistants seemed to have matters well in hand. Liz Coppersmith seemed to think so, anyway: she spooned into one of the salads, closed her eyes for the tasting, put the spoon down, and gave the caterer a high-five.

The steaks, the lobster, the sausage and steamers and corn, the potatoes, the salads, the carved-out watermelons filled with fruit—here was the plenitude of New England, piled high on every counter, every table.

Netta beamed with pride. It was a wonderful sight.

The shipyard people will know that Jack cares about them, she thought, pleased that the picnic was being held at East Gate this time. *They'll see all this and realize how grateful Jack is that they're trying as hard as he is to make a go of the yard.* She knew that Jack had just negotiated a difficult contract with the yard workers. True, a picnic was no ten percent raise; but it was a breaking of bread together between management and labor. It was a celebration of past success, and a toast to better times ahead.

She wondered whether any of the yard help knew that Jack had convinced his father to take out a sizable loan on East Gate and pour the money into the shipyard. Probably not. Probably they looked around East Gate and thought, there's plenty of money here for everyone. When in fact nothing could be farther from the truth. Still, what could you do? Jack would never try to get leverage by hinting to his men about the loan; he wasn't like that.

Jack came into the kitchen just then, and Netta thought he'd never looked better. Why, he'd dropped ten years just since breakfast. Netta had a theory about that, and it had to do with Liz Coppersmith. When Liz was around, Jack Eastman lost that haggard look he habitually wore nowadays. Of course, Netta had seen Jack snap to attention lots of times when a beautiful woman walked into view.

But Elizabeth, she was different. For one thing, though she was pretty, she wasn't really what you'd call Jack's type. True, her hair was wonderful—thick and shining in rich shades of brown and red and gold; and her hands were very well formed, very graceful. But her height and shape were more or less average. And those eyes! My goodness! Gypsy eyes, dark and unfathomable.

Her smile, though, was sunshine itself—when she chose to let you see it. Her teeth were very white, very straight, and when she grinned, a small, easily missed dimple showed up on the left side that gave her a lopsided cheerfulness: somehow you wanted one to show up on the right side, too. Yes. Very intriguing, she was.

Certainly Jack thought so. *Look at him,* Netta thought with affection. *The way he stares. One minute he's a man of the world on fire for her; the next, he's a boy who's come to school without his homework. He doesn't know what to make of her, and that's a fact.*

Netta smiled sympathetically. Jack had always, always had his way with women: the best, the brightest, the most beautiful of them had become meek as hens when he cornered them. And right away, he'd lose interest.

"What's wrong with that one?" Netta would ask him every once in a while. "She looks like she'd make a good wife."

And Jack would smile that dry smile of his and say, "You know the old saying, Netta: 'Marriage is a covered dish.' "

The man was raised in a bad marriage, of course; naturally

he'd think that way. So here he was, forty and still looking. Maybe *that* was his problem: he'd been looking so long that he'd forgotten what he was looking *for*.

Could it be Liz?

Ah, but when he catches her eye, she looks away, like right now, and not in a flirty kind of way, either. If she were flirting, there'd be a trace of a smile on those lips. And there most definitely wasn't. In fact, Liz was turning her back on him altogether, to talk with Victoria.

Jack couldn't see Liz's face where she stood beside the big Viking stove; but Netta could. Some faces—that face— didn't lie: the cheeks were flushed, the eyebrows pulled down in concern. The mouth was set in a determined line. But Netta was sure that none of it had anything to do with potato salad, which the conversation seemed to be about.

Well, well, well. Here was an interesting turn. Now, why would a woman like her reject the likes of a man like him? Netta—having raised Jack as she did—would be the first to admit that she might be biased in his favor, but it didn't take an Einstein to know that whether or not the shipyard made a go of it, Jack would still be a wonderful catch. True, he was forty-some and still a bachelor. But so what? Women seemed to dismiss bachelorhood as a temporary affliction— like flu season, or a heavy fog. Was Liz one of the exceptions?

Perhaps, Netta surmised, Liz Coppersmith simply lacked the confidence to take him on.

The doorbell rang, and Netta had to abandon her speculations to answer it. She was expecting their first guests, but what she got was someone—she supposed, a male—dressed in white shirt, white pants, white shoes, white face. He or she was smiling a simpleminded smile.

"Oh! You must be the, uh, whatchecallit, the mime," Netta said, startled. "Come in."

The mime did a little hop in place, then made as if to cross the threshold but seemed to run smack into a wall that wasn't there. Looking surprised, he began groping the imaginary plane with his white-gloved hands, then stood back, scratched his head, made a dash over the threshold, and crashed into the wall that wasn't there again.

He was about to not go through for the third time when Netta, thoroughly fed up with waiting, snapped, "Go straight around back, then. You can hang out with the fellow with the ukelele—mandolin," she said, correcting herself. "Can't you talk?"

The simple smile got simpler.

"Oh, never mind. Just go." Netta sent him off and closed the door on him, muttering dark things about sticking Renaissance themes where they didn't belong, in New England picnics. She was about to jump back into the kitchen fray when she heard, from the top of the carved mahogany staircase, a scandalized giggle from the new nanny, a pretty young Irish girl named Deirdre.

Netta knew that Jack's father was upstairs, supposedly catching a nap before the big event; he'd asked specifically not to be disturbed.

"We'll see about that," Netta said under her breath, and began stomping heavily up the stairs in her Naturalizers. As far as she was concerned, the nanny, sweet and charming as she was, had exactly two choices: mind her p's and q's, or take a job waitressing at one of Newport's thirty thousand restaurants. Bedding down with the old man was *not* an option, not with all the other complications at East Gate this summer.

She saw a flash of amber dress head quickly toward the nursery and heard the quiet click of a heavy door fall back into place down the hall from Caroline's room.

First, the nanny. Netta, still breathing heavily from her not-so-agile ascent, marched directly into the newly converted nursery, a sunny guest room papered over with roses and with casement windows opening onto the treelined street. Pretty black-haired Deirdre, still flustered, was making an artificial fuss over Caroline's new doll, which the child— fearing doll-abduction or worse—was clutching possessively to her breast.

Netta's intention was to warn Deirdre through Caroline. She said, more sharply than was necessary, "Caroline! I want you to be on your best behavior today. It's a very important day for young Mr. Eastman, who would be very upset if anything were to go wrong. All of us—*all* of us—must be on our best behavior today."

In a bored voice and without looking up, Caroline said, "Only today?"

"And every day," Netta said grimly. She gave Deirdre a pointed look which she hoped was enough to put the fear of God in her. Cornelius Eastman may have hired the girl, but it was Netta who could make or break her in a thousand different small ways, beginning with not bringing her tea.

Caroline tossed her blond curls back and said, "Is that Susy girl here yet?"

"Not yet."

"She can't play on my swing unless I say so," said the imperious child. "I hope someone told her that."

Poor Susy; there wasn't room in her own yard to swing a cat, much less to swing a swing. Frowning, Netta said, "I expect you to be nice to Susy and to all the other children, too."

Caroline surprised her by saying, "I know. Dada says that I'm the lady of the house now."

Mrs. Cornelius Eastman might have another opinion about that, but since she was holed up in Capri, she was hardly likely to argue the point. Acting as Mrs. Eastman's proxy, Netta said, "It's early days for that, young lady," and left Caroline in her nanny's care, such as it was, while she went on to Jack's father's room.

She knocked and entered and found Cornelius Eastman changing his lisle shirt for a silk one. He had a cool, innocent look under that silver brow that she knew well: tuck a piece of butter in that mouth, and it would still be a hard little patty one week later.

"Sir, I wanted to ask you if you've been in touch with Mrs. Eastman this week?"

"Is it important?"

"I would have to say yes," she said, returning his calm smile. "Mrs. Eastman had wanted her room done over by September, but so far as I know, she hasn't picked out the wallpaper from among the samples we sent her. It's a special order, and then, too, the decorators are working her in as a favor, seeing as she won't have anyone else than them, and—"

"You honestly expect her in September?" he asked bluntly.

"I do."

"Yes, all right; I'll call her," he said, not bothering to conceal his irritation. He perfectly understood Netta's little reminder that there was indeed a Mrs. Eastman alive and well somewhere and that East Gate was still her home.

"I would do it, sir, but you know how awkward it is not speaking Italian. If she isn't in, that is, and I had to relay the message to one of the help. But if you'd rather I gave it a shot—"

"I said I'd take care of it, Netta!"

"All right, sir," she said, satisfied that she had ruined his amorous mood, at least for today. She left him to complete his toilette.

Still, there was no sense in thinking he would change. Cornelius Eastman had always had a weakness for pretty women, both upstairs and down. When he was younger, that kind of thing was distressing to see; now it was mostly sad.

How long had it been since that time he'd groped her in

the nursery? Thirty-six, thirty-seven years? Netta had pushed him vigorously away without thinking; and give the man his due, he'd accepted that and had never tried any funny business with her again.

She caught her passing reflection in a hall mirror: old, fat, and gray. She grimaced automatically, then sighed resignedly. Cornelius Eastman was old and gray, too. But did he care? No. To the endless succession of Deirdres that were forever passing through Newport, he was not only charming but distinguished. Netta sighed and clucked softly under her breath: Mrs. Eastman would do well to come back home and mind her garden.

Downstairs, guests had begun arriving in force. A path leading from the portico directly to the grounds had been charmingly staked out with buckets of pink geraniums and, for later, bamboo-staked citronella torches; but some people naturally were bound to ignore the suggested route and head straight for the front door. It might have been awkward, but the to-ing and fro-ing of guests was being managed very deftly, thanks to Liz and Victoria.

And Jack! He was greeting the arrivals as if they were long-lost family. How pleased he was to greet the men and to see their wives and children again. Netta knew that Jack cared fiercely about the shipyard, but seeing him now put his devotion in a whole new light. Suddenly she understood: shipyards weren't about ships; they were about the people who worked on and sailed those vessels.

She was glad, very glad, to be part of the celebration.

Liz was aglow. Her Renaissance fair—despite Jack's and Netta's initial reservations—was a hit.

The juggler, a social sciences major dressed in a Harlequin outfit, had all the younger kids tossing oranges and potatoes up and down while he himself did amazing things with uncooked eggs. For teenagers, there was a marionette show featuring hip, anti-authority skits that kept the kids laughing and begging for more, and a smelly-feely guessing game that had them all screaming in delighted terror.

Every female there over the age of twelve had fallen head over heels in love with the minstrel who wandered among them singing romantic ballads in an achingly sweet tenor. As for the males: they were happy enough being offered hearty snacks and ice-cold ale by a couple of lusty-looking serving wenches. There was also a winsome maiden, dressed in a white gown edged in gold, whose only function was to give the troubador someone to sing to. The mime did what all mimes are supposed to do and did it very well: irritate.

It was everything a Renaissance fair should be, and probably nothing like a Renaissance fair at all. But even Jack had been forced to admit that the price was absolutely right. (The juggler owed Liz a favor, the maiden was his girlfriend, the barmaids were two of Liz's cousins, the puppeteers were dirt cheap, the minstrel—a member of an Irish band—was engaged to Netta's niece, and the mime? He came along for the food.)

Yes, Liz thought, jubilant with the results so far. The day was turning out very nearly perfect. Cornelius Eastman had made a point of telling her, twice, that the picnic was the most delightful event he'd ever attended, indoors or out. Would he make that up? Twice? If nothing else, she now had a solid reference in the father. *This* time she deserved a gold star.

She looked around for Susy and saw her tossing two small potatoes—at the same time—high over her head and then cringing as she waited for them to come back down. A juggler she wasn't; but somehow she'd cajoled Caroline's little brother Bradley into bringing back the potatoes for her, a trick that was a lot more useful in life than juggling.

Susy wouldn't be there if Jack hadn't asked specifically

for her to come. Liz couldn't begin to guess his motive—
she hoped the gesture was more generous than calculating—
but in any case, Susy was the icing on Liz's picnic cake. Her
daughter was having a ball. All the kids were.

Except, of course, Caroline. She seemed to have taken up
permanent residence under the chestnut tree—either to make
herself available should the kids beg for her company, or to
guard her swing; Liz couldn't be sure which.

Liz was on her way across the grounds to ask Jack whether
she should give the signal to throw on the steaks and drop
in the lobsters. She was halfway to him, her heart trip-
hammering as it always did at the sight of him, when she
was intercepted by Victoria. The redhead had a look of panic
under her white straw hat.

I knew it, Liz thought. Too confident, too soon. "What?"
she said. "What's happened?"

"The door to Jack's bedroom! It's locked!" whispered
Victoria.

"So what if the—? Oh, surely not the pin thing, Tori. Just
give it to him. Show him the portrait of Christopher's mother
Lavinia, and give it to him. What's the big deal? Do you
want me to do it?"

Victoria's chin came up. "I do it my way or not at all.
Don't you understand that? It's very, very important. How
many times do I—do you think Netta has keys?"

"Are you *crazy*?" Liz knew exactly what Victoria was
thinking of: the board of keys hanging in the pantry. "You
can't go fiddling around with rings of *keys*," she said in a
hiss. "You could get caught! You could get arrested!"

"If I'm caught," Victoria said with an infuriating shrug,
"it's because I was meant to be. I'm not afraid of my
karma."

She turned and was about to march off to her karma when
Liz grabbed her by the arm. "No, Tori! Not today!"

"Problem?"

Liz swung around. Jack was standing there, smiling and curious; but there was something about the set of his jaw that made Liz think the gold star wasn't—quite—hers for the taking yet. The memory of Caroline's party was all too fresh, apparently.

"Hi-i-i," she said in an overly spontaneous way. "We were just trying to decide whether—"

"—we could fit everyone in a group shot," Victoria blurted.

Jack looked at Liz. "And why 'not today'?"

"Because . . . I don't have my wide-angle lens," Liz explained. She turned to Victoria. "So *never mind,* Tori."

Victoria smiled prettily and said, "Whatever you say," which of course was a lie, and then began to saunter off toward the house to pick Jack's lock.

Liz had to try hard not to run after her and tackle her to the ground. With a fervent wish that was half-prayer, half-curse, she let Victoria go and said to Jack, "I was just on my way over to you—"

"I noticed," he admitted in a rueful voice that puzzled her. "For the simple reason that I haven't been able to take my eyes off you."

Smile politely and say thank you, Liz told herself. But instead she said flippantly, "After the last fiasco, who can blame you? You're probably worried I'm going to let a bunch of coyotes loose on your lawn."

Clearly he wasn't in the mood for humor. The smile settled into something more serious. Grim, almost. "Liz, the other night we left things hanging—"

So to speak. "Oh? Gee, I thought the evening wound down in the usual way. We did the dishes—"

"Before that part."

"You mean, when I told you about—" She cleared her throat. "Christopher Eastman?"

"Of course not," he said, brushing aside her offhand ref-

erence to being insane. "I meant, outside. When we kissed.
When you—"

Attacked his zipper; he was going to remind her that she
had actually begun to unzip the fly of his trousers. Mortified,
she said quickly, "That was the rum punch . . . an alcoholic
indiscretion—"

"The hell it was," he said with a blazing look. "Look,
you can't deny what happened between us. Whatever it
was—and I'm damned if I know, right now—you can't deny
it."

"Yes, I can," she said, amazed at his timing. "Watch
me."

There was just enough fantasy around them for Liz to
wonder whether she was being wooed by Prince Charming
himself. But that would surely be the biggest fantasy of all.
In real life princes like him didn't pay court to beggars like
her. Not unless they were on top of a haystack, anyway.

"We have to talk," he said, taking her by her arm. "I
didn't think it would come to this, but it has."

No. She'd gone around and around the attraction in her
mind and—no. "Ah, look," she said, brutally diverting him.
"There's your father," she said, waving to Cornelius. "*He*
seems like he's having a good time."

Jack scowled and let go of her arm—as if a gold chain
he'd picked up from the sidewalk had turned out to be only
gold-plated—and said, "Sure he's having a good time. He
reckons he'll never have to do this again."

"I'm sorry?" she said, puzzled.

"You must know that he'd like to sell the yard."

"I heard something to that effect," she said cautiously,
remembering the shouting match in the Great Room on the
day she met Jack.

"He's old, he's tired, he wants out."

"Can he do that?" Liz asked naïvely. After all, Jack acted

as if he pretty much owned the yard. "You don't have some say in that?"

"I have a forty-nine percent say."

"And he has fifty-one," she said, seeing at once what the problem was.

"No; he also has a forty-nine percent say."

"That leaves two percent—?"

"To my mother," said Jack with a thin smile.

"Ah."

Since Liz didn't know Jack's mother, she had no idea how she'd vote. Would she want to thwart her husband? Go for the big bucks and bail out of the marriage? Jack wasn't saying. Maybe he didn't know. Maybe *she* didn't know.

"I can see why things might be tense," Liz allowed.

"Tense?" Jack said sardonically. "Tense is when you're caught in traffic on your way to the airport. This is life and death!"

"Life and death seems strong," Liz said, put on the defensive by his vehemence. "People do sell businesses. People do sell properties." She got a little breezy. "What's the big deal?"

Without dropping his gaze from his father, Jack said in a menacing voice, "The big deal is, he's willing to sell the yard to an unsavory group who want to tear it down and stick a casino in its place. That's the big deal. God*damm*it. That's the big deal."

"Oh." Not good. She'd managed to bring his temper up to flash point. Fearing an explosion, Liz went on to say the most conciliatory thing she could think of: "Lots of people are for casinos—not just the mob. If that's who you meant."

Which, when she thought about it later, was a remarkably stupid thing to say. Jack didn't care who was for or who was against casinos. All he cared about was the shipyard and the employees who worked there. In an age of takeovers, mergers, and downsizing, Jack Eastman was one of a dying breed: a traditional, stubborn, utterly loyal business owner.

Liz winced under his scathing look and said placatingly, "But I suppose it *could* be the mob."

"Mob? What mob? What're you talking about?"

She was saved by the arrival of Cornelius, who'd been making his way toward them with a relaxed and mellow smile on his face.

"You did a damned good job here, Liz," he said for the third time, winning her over to his side in one sentence. "I hope we can count on you next year for the event."

"Thank you, Mr. Eastman. I tried really hard—"

"You hypocrite," said Jack in a voice of seething candor. "Who're you kidding? You just took a long call from them. Couldn't you put them off at least for the duration of the picnic?"

"Business is business, Jack," said his father amiably.

"This business stinks to high heaven!"

"You're being emotional, son. I always said you got that from your mother."

"I certainly didn't get it from you!" Jack said hotly. "This is the most cold-blooded sellout—"

"Jack, Jack—things change; learn to roll with it."

Liz should've been gone at the sound of the first shot Jack fired across his father's bow, but somehow she'd become trapped in the circle of their maneuvering. It was Cornelius's fault: he kept glancing at her with that half-smile of his, as if to say, "See the abuse I get?"

Now he said to Jack, with a benign and sorrowful shake of his head, "My job . . . is to look after my daughter's interests as well as your own."

It was an outrageously bold remark, shocking to make at any time but particularly in front of her. Liz sucked in her breath, expecting fisticuffs at best, a duel at worst, while at the same time feeling ridiculously flattered that she should be allowed to hear their exchange of insults.

She hardly dared look at Jack, who had as ugly, as combative an expression as she'd ever seen on a man. He seemed to be waiting for her to leave before he began swinging.

Suddenly tired of their turf war, she decided to oblige him. "I think I'd better see how the *other* children here are doing. Please excuse me."

"No, stay," Jack said with a sudden harsh laugh. "The two of you can chat about the bright future of the gaming industry in Rhode Island."

He turned on his heel and walked away, leaving Liz feeling like a co-conspirator at a racketeering trial. Dismayed that Jack seemed to think she wanted to see a casino replace his shipyard, she said to his father, "He counts me among the enemy."

"Anyone who disagrees with Jack is the enemy," Cornelius said. "He won't read the writing on the wall: the shipyard's doomed. The land it's on is too valuable. We could sell the damned thing for fifteen mil and make more in interest in a year doing nothing than we make in profit running the shipyard—far more."

He turned a cool, unruffled look on Liz. "The sooner my son accepts the idea that we're sitting on a gold mine," he added dryly, "the better."

"It seems to be going down like cod-liver oil," Liz said uneasily.

She excused herself. With a reassuring wave at Susy, she went straight to the long buffet tables that were set up on the north side of the house, under a tent and out of the sun, to tell the caterer to fire up the propane. To the satisfying sound of steaks being slapped on the grills, Liz made a last-minute circuit of the heavily laden tables, festive with centerpieces of summer-fresh fruit and big glass vases of daisies.

Immediately, her spirits improved. Jack and his father

could agree to disagree all they wanted; it wouldn't change the fact that the company picnic—her first bona-fide Bellevue Avenue *event*—was a smashing success. Even Snowball was cooperating, romping with the kids in a far corner, away from the food.

Was there enough food? Liz suffered the standard bout of last-minute panic, then reassured herself that they could probably feed most of Newport if they chose. Bread piled high . . . twenty pounds of melted butter . . . bowl after bowl of salads. . . .

She lifted lid after lid, reassuring herself with mounds of colorful rotini and artfully assembled pastas. But when she came to the Meissen bowl with its matching lid, she did a double-take. The serving bowl was part of East Gate's exquisite formal service and certainly didn't belong out here. Annoyed that someone would jeopardize her success—a tiny *chip* to the bowl would be a disaster—Liz lifted the lid of the china bowl and found: ants.

Millions and millions of ants.

Chapter 13

◆

*B*eating back an instant wave of nausea, Liz slammed the lid hard enough to break it in two. Some of the ants had already gotten out; she brushed them violently from the tablecloth, then set about tracking down the dozen fastest ones, crushing them mercilessly with her thumb.

Ants! God in heaven, whose idea of a sick joke was this? Liz picked up the serving bowl, nailing the lid to it with the palms of her hands, and marched it over to a remote corner of the grounds. To the three people who were bold enough to ask her what she was doing, her answers were brief: nothing, never mind, and what's it to you?

Behind the carriage house she dumped out the ants—swarming over a few wet pieces of hard candy that had been placed in the bowl as bait—at the base of a birch tree. Then she went back to the tool shed for a sprinkling can, rinsed out the bowl, and examined it for the dreaded crack she was sure would be there. But the precious Meissen was intact, even if Liz's nerves were not. Still shaky from the disgusting shock of her discovery, she found a small, tucked-away bench and sat down on it, trying to make sense of the wretched deed.

Why the ants, besides the obvious reason that no picnic was complete without them? It was such a simple question, and yet—because Liz had no answer to it—a profoundly unsettling one. Who was the butt of this prank, and who was behind it?

Since it was Jack's affair, the short answer seemed to be that someone wanted to spoil the picnic to get at him. Was it an isolated act, a nasty little statement by an employee who would've rather had a raise?

A less satisfying answer was that it was related, somehow, to the other, seemingly unconnected events that had been plaguing the shipyard recently—the toxic spill; the vandalized boat.

But the picnic was *her* affair, too. Was it possible that someone was trying to make her look bad? After the birthday party fiasco, it wouldn't take much. A few thousand ants drowning in vats of melted butter, and her name would end up a laughingstock on Bellevue Avenue. She'd be grist for the anecdote mill whenever the subject of events-planners came up—and in Newport society, that was sure to be often.

But who around here could possibly care whether she succeeded in the carriage trade or not? It wasn't as though she was even a remote threat to the competition. And in any case, the thought of party-planning saboteurs sneaking around with bowls of ants was ludicrous.

The graduate student. Grant Dade. The image of his angry, bitter face when Liz denied him access to the letters hovered in front of her, sending chills through her. Dade was a maniac, and whether or not he had scratched his hands hiking in the White Mountains was irrelevant: no one would ever convince her that he wasn't the one who'd stolen the packet of letters from her cottage and then escaped over the barbed-wire fence. He hated her, and he was certainly capable of a stunt like this. But could he have done it unnoticed?

And was he capable of worse?

A sharp crack behind Liz sent her bolting up from the little wooden bench. She spied a mop of blond curls behind an enormous, rotting tree trunk: Caroline Stonebridge was hiding there, and Liz wanted to know why.

"Are you looking for me, Caroline?" she asked in a sharp voice. "Or are you just playing hide-and-seek with yourself?"

The sarcasm was unkind; but Liz was jumpy and angry and—suddenly—suspicious of this selfish, manipulative child. *She* wouldn't have realized how valuable Meissen was; she'd see it as just another serving bowl in a cupboard filled with them.

Caroline stood up slowly, clutching a dandelion in her hand. She held it out silently to Liz—not as an offering, apparently, but as evidence of her purpose in crouching behind an old tree trunk on a remote, overgrown corner of a property that at that very moment was brimming with bright amusements and enchanting games.

I'm supposed to think she'd rather be picking weeds. Right.

"Come over here."

Caroline considered whether she should obey or not; then, with an indifferent shrug, she approached Liz.

"Don't you have an ant farm in your room?" Liz asked her.

The child let out a bored sigh and said, "I don't any-more."

"I'll bet," Liz said dryly. "Where is it?"

"I suppose, under your feet—and under *Susy's* feet—and under everyone's feet. I got tired of it."

Unsatisfied with her answer, Liz asked her directly, "What *are* you doing here?"

Caroline glanced at the Meissen bowl on the bench and said to Liz, "What are *you* doing here? Aren't you supposed to be getting things ready for people to eat?"

Very true. Liz didn't have time to be investigating snotty

five-year-olds. She made an impatient sound, picked up the covered bowl, and began walking away.

She heard the child's voice, high and brittle, ring out behind her: "Is my mother coming back or not?"

Liz stopped and turned and said, more softly now, "Of course she is, Caroline. I'm sure you know that."

"Because sometimes she doesn't, you know," the child said with a tremulous sneer in her voice. "She stays away. And when she comes back, my father yells, and she yells, too. And then Bradley always cries. But I never do."

"Your father—?"

"Not Dada," Caroline said dismissively with a flip of her little wrist. "The man who lives with her."

She sounded so world-weary. It was impossible for Liz to believe that the child was Susy's age. The sad irony was that neither girl seemed to have a clue what a real father was— and in that, they were more alike than not.

Liz said with gentle caution, "When your mother comes back from the clinic, it will all be fine, Caroline. Really."

But the child seemed to have jumped onto another track altogether. She folded her arms across her floral sundress; the dandelion, its stem bent in two, hung from her hand like a broken promise. "You want to live in East Gate, *don't* you," she said, clamping her lips in a tight grim line. "You and *Susy*."

Liz hesitated before she acted puzzled. "Why would I want to live at East Gate, Caroline? I have a pretty little house of my own."

Caroline gave her a shrewd look. "I knew you wouldn't tell me."

Flushing, Liz said, "I'm sorry, young lady; I'm very busy right now," and left her.

She had absolutely no idea what Caroline's game was. Was the child afraid that Liz was going to displace her mother—who was threatening to displace Jack's mother?

What an unholy mess! Didn't *anyone* believe in the nuclear family anymore?

It occurred to Liz, as she slipped the Meissen bowl back to its rightful place, that Caroline's cross-examination might have an element of wishful thinking in it. The girl seemed so jealous of Susy; was it possible that Caroline was simply fishing? That she was willing to take any mother she could get? Liz fervently hoped not—it was too distressing to imagine such open, aching need.

As for Caroline's suspicion that Liz had designs on East Gate: it was simply unfair. Certainly, Liz would like to live at East Gate. Who *wouldn't* want to live in a fairy-tale palace? It was a perfectly normal desire.

The question was, would she like to live there with the fairy-tale prince as well?

The lump of fear that had lodged in Liz's throat began to ease when no one actually dropped dead of food poisoning. She had worried, not unreasonably, that the ants might merely have been the warm-up act to the main event: salmonella or arsenic or worse. But the guests ate, and the guests survived, at least for today.

And at least for today, Victoria gave up on sneaking the heart-shaped pin into Jack's room. None of the keys on the first key ring had fit the lock, and when she'd approached his door the second time with the second ring of keys, she'd been intercepted by Cornelius Eastman himself.

"Y'know—I think he was coming on to me?" Victoria said to Liz in a bemused voice. "We stood in the hallway for a long time, and he said something about what an intense 'presence' I had. And he asked me if I'd ever—honest to God—been on the stage."

Liz rolled her eyes and said, "I suppose it's better than 'What's your sign?' "

"*I* thought it was cute. It was such an old-fashioned thing to say; he probably learned to hit on women before movies were even invented. He's charming, actually."

"He's married, actually."

"Liz! I wasn't taking Old Corny seriously. I think the guy was just on automatic, anyway. I mean, look at him now— flitting from pretty woman to pretty woman. He's like a bee in a flower bed."

The picnic was clearly winding down; guests were departing. From where they stood in the shadows of dusk, Liz and Victoria had a good view of Cornelius Eastman extracting a little bit of nectar from every female he chose to alight on.

"He's a man who loves women, no doubt about that," murmured Victoria, half in admiration.

"From what I've seen," Liz said, sighing, "it's a family curse."

Victoria laughed and said, "If you mean Jack, I'm not so sure anymore. Word on the street is, suddenly he's taken himself out of the action. He hasn't been seen holding up anyone's arm in a couple of weeks."

"Because he's preoccupied with the shipyard, I imagine," said Liz at once. But in fact she was imagining something else entirely, and it frightened her.

Don't start fantasizing, she warned herself. *Don't. Where can it lead? Nowhere*

Victoria was smiling her knowing smile. "Do you really think a man like Jack Eastman would give up women just to put in a few extra hours at the shop?"

"Why not? It's been done before."

"Get real, Liz. I mean, *look* at the guy."

Victoria took her by the shoulders and turned her ninety degrees. There was Jack, standing alongside a tall bamboo torchère, his hair glinting black in the amber glow of the citronella lamp that burned brightly in its hobnailed bowl.

He was laughing and saying good-bye to little Amy, whose father, a welder at the shipyard, lived on Liz's parents' street. Even from that distance, Liz could feel her body begin to hum in response to his sheer physical presence.

All day it had been this way, even though they'd scarcely had time to speak since the casino conversation. Liz would be doing her job, minding her own business, and suddenly her radar would lock onto him. She'd look up, and there he'd be, sometimes staring at her, sometimes not. But every time, it was a jolt to her system, a shock to her heart. And every time, she felt a little more consumed, a little more lost.

This couldn't go on. Either he'd have to sell his house, or she'd have to sell hers. Because it *couldn't* go on. She was falling in love with him, and it was the most pointless, time-consuming, heart-wrenching waste of time she'd ever spent.

"Yes," she said calmly. "I see him. So what?"

"So what? So buttons! He's rich—"

"He's not rich; it just looks that way. His money's tied up."

"He's handsome—"

"Not so handsome. I think his nose was broken once; it's a tiny bit off to the left."

"—and he's looking your way. Oh, Gawd." Victoria burst into nervous giggles and turned aside. "How can you *resist* him?"

Liz felt hot tears rush up and then recede. "I don't know," she admitted. It came out in a moan, not in a boast.

Victoria swung slowly around. Her head was cocked curiously to one side, like a cardinal checking out a new feeder. "Is something going on? Have you been—Liz, you *haven't* gone to bed with him! Not without telling me!"

Liz shook her head.

Victoria looked unconvinced. "I guess after seeing you two today, my next question is: Why the hell not?"

"He hasn't suggested it, for one thing," said Liz, hiding

behind a wry grimace. "And for another, it's none of your business, dammit."

"Aha! So you *are* planning to jump in the sack with him. Good for you! Heck, things are gonna close up down there if you don't use 'em soon."

"Tori!"

"Don't Tori me," Victoria said, undaunted. "How long has it been? Years, right? You understand how neurotic that is? Is that what you are at this point? Just plain old *afraid*?"

"Don't be dumb. Look, I've been raising Susy—"

"Oh, like you're the only single mother on the planet."

"And I've been trying to get a business up and running—"

"You think everyone else is on welfare?"

"And . . . and he's not my type—"

Victoria merely laughed out loud.

"And he *undoubtedly* wants children—"

"For goodness' sake, you'd just be bedding him, not marrying—*wait* a minute," said Victoria, touching her hand to her forehead in lieu of a smack. "That's what this is about? You won't do it without a wedding ring? Oh, sweetie, you *have* lost touch with reality. Ha. And they shake their heads over *me*."

Liz glanced around: the true reality was, they were having the kind of chat that belonged on a couch with pizza and video rentals. Not here.

"Thank you for the update on the dating game, Miss Landers," she said. "Now, will you kindly gather up my exhausted daughter and take her home? I'll be there just as soon as I've got my money."

"And well you deserve it, if I may say so, Liz. Great job. This one really did go perfectly."

"Pretty much," Liz said, brushing aside the revolting ant episode, about which she'd said nothing so far. "You didn't by any chance see Grant Dade skulking around?"

"The student nutcase? Good lord, no. Why?"

Liz frowned and said, "Somehow I don't think he's through with me."

"Ah, well, let's not think unpleasant thoughts. See you back at the ranch. Don't worry about Susy; I'll tuck her in."

"Mmmn. And thanks, Tori. For everything." Liz embraced her, then bundled her happy, weary daughter into Victoria's arms for the four-block spiral home.

After that there was nothing much to do but the final cleanup, most of which was the job of the caterers. Liz gathered up the chairs and umbrellas and resin tables and stacked them for pickup the next day. She bagged the linens and took down the banners and boxed the leftover souvenir glasses, each hand-painted by her with a ruby-red clematis and the year of her Renaissance picnic. She kept one of the glasses for herself, staring into it as if it were a crystal ball. Would there be another picnic, another theme, another year? If only she knew.

At about the time Liz snapped the last table shut, the last of the guests finally left and Jack came over to lend a hand.

"Oh, sure, now that all the dishes are done," she teased. He didn't have to offer his help; but she was inexpressibly pleased that he had.

The caterers, more proficient at breaking down a party than Liz, had done their job, gotten paid by her, and were long gone. Netta—if she had any sense—was in her room with her feet on a hassock and an ice bag on her head. Deirdre must've had Caroline and Bradley en route to their beds. As for Cornelius Eastman, he'd designated himself the driver of a perky female yardhand who'd had a bit too much to drink. That left just Liz and Jack, and a galaxy of stars overhead.

They walked side by side down the torchère-lined path, taking turns blowing out the candles as they passed. The smell of citronella and paraffin began mingling in the air

around them, adding a smoky, sultry ingredient to the heady
mix of roses and honeysuckle that were in bloom upwind of
the house. Beneath their steps the gentle crunch of pea-stone
echoed their ambling pace. It was a moment of almost magical seclusion, despite the traffic that ebbed and flowed a
mere hundred yards away under the nostalgic amber glow of
iron streetlamps on Bellevue Avenue.

They talked in random snatches about the day, and then
Jack said in a surprisingly fervent voice, "I don't know how
to thank you enough. It was—well, what can I say? It was
memorable. Just as you promised it would be."

Deeply pleased that he was so pleased, Liz smiled and
quipped, "Does that mean I'll be getting paid the whole
amount this time?"

"And then some," he said, which suggested a handsome
gratuity and also pounded home the fact—as if it needed
pounding—that she was a simple working girl and not one
of Newport's Four Hundred.

But it wasn't a socialite who was walking alongside Jack
among the roses and under the stars; it was Liz. And if he
was just now extinguishing the last of the lamps—if that part
of the spell was coming to an end—well, it wasn't a socialite
he was taking in his arms in the bewitching blindness of the
night. It was Liz.

He kissed her then, a deep, satisfying kiss quite unlike the
ones that had left her on fire the other night. This kiss was
filled with gratitude and something else: the sense, perhaps
best left unsaid, that they had come this far without their
attraction for one another having diminished in any way.

Oh yes, she told herself as she slid her arms around him
and slipped her hands across his broad back. *I am definitely
in love. I am apparently also a fool. So, Lizzie. Happy now?*

She *was* happy. Despite who she was, and despite who he
was, for as long as that kiss lasted—she was happy.

With a murmur of pleasure, he held her close and called

her "Elizabeth" and buried his face in the thickness of her hair.

Elizabeth. She loved to hear him say the name, every single syllable of it. When she was young she'd longed to be called something perkier, like Julie or Bonnie or Dawn. But that was then.

And this, she thought, closing her eyes to savor the caress of his lips on her throat, *is now*.

They kissed again, and it became clear that the moment for feeling grateful had passed. He kissed her harder now, his tongue probing more deeply, his body impressing hers with a sense of his urgency. His mouth, searing and hot, covered hers: again and again he returned to her lips—as if there were a drug there, and he was hooked. When he finally broke off, his breathing, like hers, was labored and unsteady.

"This is . . . ah . . . new, darlin' . . . ohboy . . . this is new," he said again with a ragged, baffled laugh.

He framed her face with his hands and kissed her, tenderly this time, and said in a half-groan, "You know what comes next . . . it *has* to come next—or I'm pretty sure we'll explode."

All of Liz's resolve, all of her good intentions, were going by the board. Part of her was still tracking her pointless descent into the quagmire of passion—but the other part was wondering, *his place or mine?*

It couldn't be her place—there simply was no way. It had to be East Gate . . . and yet . . . Cornelius? Netta? *Caroline?* It couldn't be his place, either—there simply was no way.

"I don't see how—"

The sentence got lost in a sharp intake of her breath as he skimmed the curve of her ear with his tongue, nibbling at her earlobe, teasing her, tasting her.

He solved her agony in half a dozen words. "The carriage house has an apartment," he whispered in her ear.

"Ah . . . I see."

What Liz also saw, perversely enough, was a line of beautiful women passing in and then out of that apartment. She shut her eyes against the vision; she did not want to know, did not want to see.

He sensed her hesitation and let go of her, as if he didn't want to be found guilty of applying undue pressure. But his voice was low and urgent as he said, "It's going to happen. Sooner or later—it's going to happen."

Sooner. She wanted it to happen sooner. "But I won't be able to stay long," she said in a soft wail. "Susy—"

With a hoarse laugh he said, "I'll take what I can get. If you only—"

Headlights from a car turning into the circular drive flashed across them, bathing them in a ghostly white light that blinded Liz and drew a swift curse from Jack.

The car pulled alongside, and Pete, the yard foreman, rolled down the window. "Bad news, Jack," he said glumly. "Do you want to go inside for it?"

The transformation in Jack was instantaneous. The hot-blooded lover vaporized and in his place appeared a two-hundred-pound businessman. He turned to Liz and said in a distant, formal voice, "If you don't mind waiting a few minutes, I'll make out that check for you."

Uncertain what signal he was sending, Liz agreed to come into the house with them. Jack left her in the smaller of a pair of reception rooms on the first floor, then took Pete down the paneled hall into the Great Room. Liz heard the double doors close, and that was all. She took it as a good sign that she couldn't hear Jack shouting, as she had the first time she was in the house.

She tiptoed out to the hall to listen more attentively for the sound of anger. It was quiet—ominously so, she now thought. Her imagination was all over the map of possibilities. More dirty tricks? Worse? Why was it that every time she found herself in Jack's arms, something got in the way?

Were they violating some divine order? Was it ordained somewhere that she could only mate with the middle of the middle class? *Damn* it!

She took a few steps farther down the eerily quiet, dimly lit hall. The longcase clock—Christopher Eastman's clock—chose that moment to signal the half-hour with a deep, resonant bong, sending her leaping out of her skin. Feeling snoopy and guilty, she went back to the reception room to wait for Jack.

The sound of the chime was still echoing in her ears when Liz was overwhelmed by the vivid memory of crawling, swarming ants. Shuddering, she closed her eyes, but still she saw them: horrid things, everywhere! Irrationally convinced that some of them had gotten inside her dress, she shook out the fabric of her hem, then began brushing her bare arms violently, feeling creeping things she could not see.

By the time Jack returned, Liz had turned on every lamp in the room and was standing in the one place from which she could keep watch on all three windows and the door. For ants? For the ghost of Christopher Eastman? She didn't know, and she hardly cared. All she wanted was to get out of there.

"Good lord—what's this?" Jack said, taking hold of one of her arms. It was covered in self-inflicted welts from her repeated efforts to brush away the sensation of crawling ants.

She stared at her arm, aghast at what she'd done. "I don't know," she mumbled. "Poison ivy?"

"We don't have poison ivy," he said flatly.

"I know," she said, reversing herself. "But I felt . . . itchy."

"An allergic reaction to the food?"

"Oh my god—I forgot about food poisoning."

"Food *allergy,* I said."

"*You're* all right?" she asked with sudden concern. "You don't look good."

"Nothing to do with the food, I assure you," he said caustically, and then more gently, "You'd better get some calamine lotion on that arm." He went to the one open window, shut and locked it, then said with bitter resolve, "I'm afraid I have to leave. The boat that Pete and Bobby launched this afternoon sank."

"Sank!"

"Yeah. Sank," he said, his eyes flashing. "They found a couple of hoses pulled off the head and engine intakes—and the rest, as they like to say, is history. Pete accepts all the blame, of course, but I trust him to have checked the through-hulls when they launched the boat. He always does."

Liz didn't understand all the boat jargon, but the word *sank* seemed perfectly clear. "No one noticed it happen?"

"The boat didn't go down completely—just enough to take out the engines, the electronics, and the wiring, and the furnishings," he said ironically. "Just enough to slap us with an insurance claim and maybe an emotional-distress suit. Just enough to make sure our premiums go sky high."

"How did Pete and Bobby manage to find out before you did?" Liz thought to ask.

"Netta took the call and told my father, who decided not to say anything; apparently no one wanted to spoil the picnic."

"And the owner?"

"—is furious. Can you blame him? Christ, one or two more stunts like this, and the yard'll be a joke up and down the whole damned coast."

His sentiments matched Liz's earlier feelings so closely that she decided to tell him about the ant episode.

It came out in a confusing, nervous jumble. When she was finished, she said, "I wasn't sure whether it was you or me that someone was trying to sabotage; but now it seems obvious that the prank was aimed at you."

If there *was* a connection, Jack certainly wasn't making it.

He was looking at her as if she'd just stepped out of a space ship. "So you think whoever sank the boat rushed back and—what? Filled our best serving bowl with ants?"

Liz stiffened and said, "I didn't put it that way. I said *someone* put sticky candy in the bowl and left it *somewhere* to attract ants before he—or she—put the bowl on the table. And anyway," she added, rallying, "*you're* the one who thinks your father's being duped by the mob."

Jack's laugh was harsh and ironic. "And if I'm right, they sure as hell aren't going to be rifling through the Meissen in the middle of a picnic. Give them a little credit, will you? *Ants?*"

"Fine," she said, hurt by Jack's condescending manner. She folded her arms defensively across her chest. "It was just a theory. Maybe you're right. Maybe the ants were intended to discredit me after all—in which case, I'd love to see a list of your suspects. Maybe I'll be able to figure out who's so determined to sink my career."

"Your *career*! For God's sake—it was a picnic! A pleasant afternoon; an amusing diversion! I'm talking about the fate of a hundred-year-old *shipyard*! Never mind its historic significance. Never mind the Eastman reputation. I have sixty-three employees, most of them with families to support, who're counting on me to stay in business. Maybe we're not as big a deal as AT&T—but *goddammit,* we're a damned sight more critical to society than a—a party planner!"

His vehemence was like a pan of ice-cold water over her. Shocked—and practically sputtering with rage—she began to say something; stopped; started; stopped; and then, with a final, furious, wordless gasp, swung around a hundred and eighty degrees and stormed out of the room.

Chapter 14

◆

The signal cannon at the Ida Lewis Yacht Club boomed across the harbor and up the hill to Liz's bedroom, rousing her from a sleep as profound as a state of coma: eight A.M. She squinted at her little quartz clock. Damn. The cannon was right.

She had to drag herself out of bed despite having slept solidly. It was catching up with her, she realized: all the unsolved mysteries—little, big, and in between—were having a cumulative effect. Either that, or being in love without sex was exhausting. Whatever the reason, Liz went through her morning routine like a zombie, grateful that Susy was even more tired from the picnic than she was, and still in bed.

Why *him*? How could she fall for someone who considered her frivolous? For that matter, how could *he*—the owner of a *yacht yard*—consider her frivolous? If the society column in the *Daily News* was anywhere near the mark, Jack Eastman hadn't exactly made a career out of dating Margaret Thatchers and Golda Meirs. What a self-important, condescending—okay—*pig* the man was.

She brushed her teeth with vicious abandon and spat out the toothpaste the way she would've liked to do to the memory of his kisses. Then she took a cold, hard look at herself in the mirror.

Thirty-six, mother of one, no pedigree, no fortune, no university, no fertility and—unless she had her taste buds removed and a pretty impressive makeover done—no possible hope of being either pencil-thin or blond and blue-eyed. She frowned, then smiled, then squinted at the mirror, tipping her chin this way and that. Nope: a Bellevue Wasp, she was not. Maybe if she sat behind the wheel of a Mercedes convertible? Would *that* make her eyes less brown, add inches to her height?

Nope.

She turned away from her image, blushing at the vanity of her dissatisfaction. This was absurd. Until she moved here—until she met *him*—she had been perfectly happy with how she looked and what she did. When Liz was a teenager, her mother had summed her up very well: her legs were straight, and she'd never robbed a bank. What more, Liz wondered wryly, could any man ask for?

That afternoon Liz asked her mother why she'd never been encouraged to go to college.

Patricia Pinhel, happy in her garden, filled the plastic sprinkling can for Susy, then adjusted the hose flow to "gentle shower" and hung the nozzle over a clump of thirsty pink gayfeather. "I don't know," she said, thinking back. "I suppose because you were the girl. Girls get married and have babies. Then what happens to all that schooling? Down the drain. Whereas with your brothers, everyone knew they'd have to be the breadwinners."

"As opposed to me, of course."

Her mother shrugged her shoulders. "Who knew? Besides, look how far you've come without one. Speaking of which: how was your medieval picnic?"

"Not medieval, Mom. Renaissance."

"Renaissance, schmenaissance," said her mother. "Did everyone have a good time is the important thing."

Liz took a pair of old barber shears out of her mother's tool basket and began snipping the tiny faded yellow stars in a mound of threadleaf coreopsis. "It sure seemed like it," she said. "In fact, Francie—she was the caterer—called me this morning to ask whether I can do the same theme for a garden party at Windrise in September."

"Windrise! Is that the one with the gargoyles? Around the corner from the Breakers? Oh, Lizzie! Just what you wanted, then: to design parties for those kind of people!"

"Yeah. Yippee," Liz said, snipping away.

"*Now* what's wrong? Didn't he pay you again?"

"Not at all. His housekeeper brought over the check with a big fat bonus first thing today. It's just that . . . I don't know . . . I thought it would be more—" She snipped off an entire stem by accident. "Fun."

"Fun! It's a *job,* Lizzie. It's not supposed to be fun," said her mother. "Do you think your father had fun being gardener to Mrs. Drake all those years? And her the type who wasn't satisfied with anything or anyone a day in her life? But he stuck it out, and he bit his tongue, and she ended up remembering him a bit in her will, which is about the best he could hope for. *He* didn't go into work every day expecting to have *fun*. And it helped that he wasn't above walking the dog or doing a dump run when Mrs. Drake needed it. My point being, it would never have done for your father to put on airs."

After this sharp little reprimand, Patricia Pinhel cast a baleful eye on the coreopsis and said to her daughter, "Just the dead flowers, please; not the whole plant."

Liz stared in surprise at the pile of stalks that she was methodically stacking on the grass.

Her mother added, "The worst thing you can do, Lizzie, is make the mistake of thinking you're a guest at one of your own affairs. That's like the chef sitting down at the table when the meal gets served."

"Okay, okay, I get it already," Liz said. She went back to deadheading, halfheartedly now, as she mulled over her mother's dismally practical advice.

Patricia Pinhel was a master at lowering expectations. She hated being disappointed, and she hated even more for those she loved to be disappointed, so she solved the problem by simply lowering everyone's expectations. Whether someone was hoping to get into college, qualify for a mortgage, find a parking space on Thames Street, or be the fifth caller in a radio contest, Patricia Pinhel's answer was always the same: "Don't get your hopes up."

Her response had become something of a family joke, amusing to just about everyone except Liz, who at the moment was less enchanted than ever by it. She gazed across her parents' jam-packed garden at her mother, short and sturdy and patient, who was on her knees next to Susy, showing her granddaughter how to thin her own tiny carrot crop in her own little special square of dirt.

The woman is so warm . . . so loving, Liz thought. *How can she be so defeatist?*

With a mother's instinct, Patricia Pinhel looked up and, over her half-glasses, bestowed a glowing smile on Liz that was anything but defeatist.

It's because gardens rarely disappoint, Liz decided. Her mother would say it was okay to get your hopes up with a garden: if you were good at it, it was good right back to you. Where else would an investment of love and time pay off so predictably? You couldn't count on people that way.

You couldn't count on Jack.

"Lizzie?" said her mother, breaking through her reverie of stinging disappointment. "Don't forget that lamp for Susy's room. Get it now, before the attic heats up much more."

"Oh, right," said Liz, rising up off her knees. She stretched and looked around admiringly, stalling a little before the trek into the superheated attic.

Her parents' garden had always been pretty, of course. But now that Liz and her two brothers were grown and gone, most of the grass in the backyard and all of the grass in the small front yard had been turned under to make room for flowers and vegetables, berry-bushes for both people and birds, a strawberry patch that was out of control, and half a dozen miniature fruit trees that bore life-size apples and cherries.

The result was a five-thousand-square-foot riot of charm and surprises, with garlic rubbing elbows with roses, and seven-foot tomato plants duking it out with clambering vines of flowering sweet peas. Touches of humor and tiny treasures were tucked everywhere, from the terra-cotta saucer filled with century-old shards of crockery uncovered in all the years of digging, to the tiny intact ceramic frog that Liz, no older than Susy, had uncovered when they were putting in the original perennial border.

It was all there, in whimsical counterpoint to the rigid formality of Mrs. Drake's estate. "Therapy for me," Liz's father liked to say. "I get so damned sick and tired of carving conifers into spirals all day."

Liz went into the house through the kitchen door, hanging her straw hat on a big peg-rack buried under three or four other hats, and passed through the carpeted hall and up the stairs to the second-floor landing. The house, a scale-shingled Victorian, was a bigger version of Liz's own, with three bedrooms instead of two upstairs, and a half bath squeezed between the kitchen and the dining room downstairs: an altogether typical Newport cottage.

The hall window, hung with lace, was open to the afternoon breeze. Liz threw it up the rest of the way, catching the scent of honeysuckle—now forever associated with Jack Eastman's kisses—and then pulled down the attic staircase, steeling herself for the ascent into hell.

It wasn't as bad as she'd feared. The windows at both ends

of the attic were open, allowing a fresh cross-current of air to pass through. Still, it was hot enough for Liz to want to retrieve the iron floor lamp and get out. She found it tucked in a corner alongside her banished bed, looking, like the bed, sad and embarrassed to be of so little use to anyone anymore.

Pleased to be giving the lamp a new lease on life, Liz wrestled it free from the surrounding clutter and took a good look at it. It was smaller, less heavy than she remembered from her own childhood; but the Very Special Switch on the base—installed there by her father when he realized that Liz couldn't reach the switch at the bulb—was what made her want the lamp for her own daughter. When Susy was a little bigger, Liz would be back for the bed as well.

She patted the headboard affectionately, then began an awkward stagger back to the stairs with the lamp in one hand and the shade, with its sepia-painted scenes of Paris, in the other. The electric cord—which had instantly come unwrapped from the shaft—dragged behind her. As cords always do, it found something to hook on: the treadle of her grandmother's old Singer. With a little curse of annoyance, Liz backtracked to the sewing machine to free the cord.

That was when she saw the huddle of prints and paintings wedged between the Singer and an old blond dresser.

And that was when she suddenly remembered one particular painting among them, one she hadn't thought about in twenty years or more.

She remembered it as vividly as if she'd just finished painting it herself; remembered everything about it, from the grand gold-leaf frame, chipped and scratched from a lifetime of being moved from one dusty corner to another, to the heavily applied brushstrokes, so surprisingly messy to an untutored child's eye.

Liz put down the lamp and began hastily shifting the stacked frames, wincing at the sound of breaking glass on an old print of Niagara Falls, until she was able to work loose from the others the ornate gold-leaf frame she sought. She lifted it—filthy, dusty, never once hung—and held it out in front of her. *Yes.* Without a doubt, a work of Christopher Eastman. She knew the style. Even more: she knew the subject.

It was a portrait of a woman reclining on a scroll-end daybed. There was a suggestion of a sloped roof with a skylight to the left, and a stack of sticks—framing material?— on the right; it might have been the artist's studio. The subject's back was to the viewer, but her face, with its pale complexion, was partly turned and visible. Her hair was waist-length and flowing, a rich, deep red; it hung down her back and over a paisley shawl, which seemed to be the only thing she was wearing. The pose was mildly erotic: the woman's tall, slender body was arranged to stunning advantage. It might have been a bit racy for its time, but that time had long passed.

If her hair were moved just a little to the left, I'd be able to see the dark-green ribbon around her neck, Liz thought. There was absolutely no doubt in her mind that the painting was one of the series that Christopher Eastman had done of the great love of his life, the mysterious Ophelia.

So this was the woman who'd so impressed Victoria St. Onge: the lover who'd scandalized Newport society, the servant who'd been dismissed from East Gate, and then— apparently—been forgotten by Christopher Eastman himself. This was the woman who'd been usurped by the imperious blue-gowned Brunhilde. How utterly tragic that Liz couldn't see more of her face! There was something quintessentially Irish about the delicate profile; in an intriguing way it reminded her of Victoria.

Liz blew away a generation's worth of dust, then walked with the painting over to the south window for better light. It was no use. The artist wanted the viewer to see only a hint of Ophelia's beauty and no more. Maddening!

And eerie. This latest link in the chain that seemed to bind
Liz to the fortunes of the Eastman family did not surprise
her; she had long since stopped blaming the events on coincidence. As with everything else, there was nothing
serendipitous about this discovery. The cord had gotten
jammed in the treadle because the cord had a job to do: prod
Liz into remembering the exiled painting. Okay, Liz accepted
that. But that didn't make it any less . . . eerie.

She wandered back from the bright light of the window
into the dusky shadows of the attic center. It seemed to her
that he was there, somewhere—the shade of Christopher
Eastman, pleased that she had stumbled onto this latest piece
of the jigsaw. Liz held her breath and stood absolutely still,
waiting for some manifestation of him: for the sound of the
chime, or—she desperately wished for it—an actual reap-
pearance.

But there was no sound, and there was no sighting.

So why did she feel such intense . . . satisfaction, almost
joy, holding the portrait in her hands? Was the painting itself
the manifestation? She peered at the reclining woman, murky
now in the attic's shadows. The tilt of her head had a sau-
ciness to it, the confidence of a woman loved and in love.
There was much intimacy in the portrait, and it had nothing
to do with Ophelia's state of dress.

The painting made Christopher Eastman more real than
either the chimes or the visions had done so far.

Leaving the iron floor lamp behind, Liz took the painting
downstairs and out to the garden. Her father had arrived,
direct from the local nursery, with a pair of tired-looking
Korean lilacs, balled and burlapped and ready to be squeezed
God only knew where.

"Planting time!" cried Susy to Liz from the inside of the
wheelbarrow. It was part of the ritual: a ride all around the
garden paths before the latest acquisitions were loaded into
the well-worn barrow from the station wagon.

While Susy urged her grandpa to giddyap, Liz sidled up to her mother with the painting. "Mom? You remember this?"

Her mother looked surprised. "Is *that* still around? I thought I got rid of it at a yard sale. I suppose your father dragged it back upstairs. He's so convinced an original oil painting—never mind that it's not signed—is worth something."

"I remember he was going to get it appraised sometime."

"Oh, sure," said her mother with a snort. "Right after he glues the old dining-room chairs together and just as soon as he rewires the toaster. Let's face it, Lizzie," she added with a resigned shake of her head in her husband's direction. "If it can't sprout, it doesn't stand a chance."

"Where did we get this, anyway? I remember it was considered too risqué to actually hang on a wall. As far as I can tell, it's never even had hardware attached for hanging," Liz said, turning the frame over for inspection.

Her mother frowned thoughtfully and said, "It must have come with all the stuff after your grandmother died. Your dad's aunt Mary might know more about it. But I wouldn't get your hopes up. She had first pick over her sister's things, after all; I suppose if this had any sentimental value, she'd have kept it."

Liz held the painting at arm's length. "I'll ask her," she said softly. "Can I have it?"

"Take it. Just don't let your father see it."

Later that day Liz dragged Susy, kicking and screaming, for a visit to the child's great-great-aunt Mary's house. Like all five-year-olds, Susy had an aversion to spending sunny hours in dark ill-smelling rooms surrounded by dying houseplants. Nothing Liz said could convince Susy that eight-legged bugs weren't going to drop in her hair from the spider plants hanging overhead, and that reptiles weren't going to slither out from under the neglected, forlorn leaves of the snake plants alongside.

Besides, Mary O'Neill-O'Reilly was hard of hearing. When Susy spoke in a normal voice, her great-great-aunt Mary demanded that the child SPEAK UP, CONFOUND IT! And when Susy got brave and shouted some pleasantry, the elderly woman silenced her with a warning that little girls should be seen and not heard. Poor Susy, batted this way and that by the contradictory demands of good manners, generally ended up staring at her shoelaces and heaving gently tragic sighs well-timed to the lulls in the conversation.

Well, it couldn't be helped. No one was around for babysitting duty, and Liz was beside herself with curiosity about the painting of the red-haired woman on the daybed. After an early supper with her parents, she bundled her daughter and the painting into the minivan and drove three blocks deeper into the Fifth Ward.

Mary O'Neill-O'Reilly had married and survived two different Irishmen, and at the age of eighty had begun dating a third: John O'Shaunessy. When Mr. O'Shaunessy, who'd been a tenant in Aunt Mary's second-floor apartment, got cold feet and backed down from the altar, the family breathed a sigh of relief: they had no wish to add another hyphen on their Christmas cards to Aunt Mary.

But Aunt Mary didn't see it that way. She never was the same after Mr. O'Shaunessy broke off the engagement and moved out. Some said Aunt Mary's heart was broken (which was why she was so cranky and stopped having the grass cut), while others said she was just bitter over the loss of the higher social security payments Mr. O'Shaunessy would've left behind (eventually).

Either way, a visit to her was an ordeal.

"Aunt Mary," Liz said in a high, clear voice, "I was just over at my mom's house, and she told me you might remember something about this painting."

She propped it on her knees facing her great-aunt. The elderly woman's response was odd, to say the least.

"Oh. Her. At least she's covered up in that one."

Liz's heart began to beat faster. "You know who this is?"

Aunt Mary bobbed her white-haired head toward Susy and said in shrill warning, "Little pitchers!"

The child, who knew the grown-up warning all too well, stood up and said, "I think I have to go to the bathroom, don't I, Mommy."

"And make sure you wash your hands! With soap!" said Aunt Mary. "And don't be throwing the towel on the floor!"

Susy, wincing under the weight of all the exclamation marks, went off dutifully, leaving her mother the privacy she sought. On an impulse, Liz handed the painting over to her reluctant great-aunt. The spare but feisty woman took a pair of wire-rimmed glasses out of the pocket of her smock, hooked them behind her ears, and peered at the work with nearsighted hostility.

"Foolish, foolish woman," Aunty Mary said primly, shaking her head over the portrait that lay in her lap. "She let her beauty go to her head."

"Who *is* she, Aunt Mary?"

"You don't know?" She handed the painting back to Liz. "Then maybe I shouldn't tell you."

"But that's why I'm here!" said Liz impatiently. "To find out. My mother said you'd tell me everything," she added in a shameless lie.

Aunt Mary frowned and said, "It doesn't surprise me. What would your mother care? It's not *her* side of the family."

"Family! This woman is family?"

Mary O'Neill-O'Reilly sighed. Liz could see that she was resigning herself to holding the closet door open so that Liz could peek at the skeleton inside.

The old woman unhooked her glasses from behind her ears and returned them to their pocket. Then she folded one blue-veined hand over the other in her lap and took a deep, purposeful breath.

She said crisply on the exhale, "This is a painting of Filly Ryan. She got off the boat from Ireland in 1867, got pregnant without benefit of the sacrament, and—remember, you wanted to know—was alone and two steps from the poorhouse when a Newport shoemaker took her in and, we assume, married her. Well? Are you shocked?"

Liz was more confused than shocked. "A shoemaker? But that must have been my great-great—or great-great-great, I don't even know—grandfather. Anton Pinhel? You're talking about Anton Pinhel?"

"How many shoemakers were there in our family?" snapped Aunt Mary.

Reeling from the information, Liz tapped the painting with her forefinger and said in a daze, "Oh. I thought this was someone *completely* else. So this is—this is a portrait of Phyllis Pinhel?"

"Phyllis? Who's Phyllis?"

"Filly. Phyllis. That was the shoemaker's wife's name, wasn't—?"

Later, when she thought about it, it seemed impossible to Liz that she could've been so dense. "Filly is for *Ophelia*?" she asked, her mouth agape. Without waiting for the obvious answer, she added, "I always thought Filly was short for Phyllis."

"This is what's wrong with these latest generations," said Aunt Mary with a look of disgust. "They don't care a tittle about the family history. They're too lazy to find out and too bored to listen when they're told it. You wait, young lady; when you're fifty, sixty, *then* you'll want to know about your ancestors. And then it'll be too late. All the facts will be six feet under.''

"No, I do care—if only you knew how much," Liz said softly. She was overwhelmed by the revelation that Christopher Eastman had been the lover of her great-great-grandmother. "*Ophelia*. I—"

"Hush," said Aunt Mary as Susy tiptoed timidly back into their presence. "Yes. Ophelia Ryan, she was. We *hope* she died Ophelia Pinhel. Well, good-bye."

Aunt Mary always ended her interviews cleanly and quickly; it did not do to linger. Nonetheless, on their way out the door, Liz ventured to say, "You implied there was another painting of Ophelia . . . ?"

"Dreadful. Shocking. I don't know what happened to it. Burned, I expect."

And that was that.

Chapter 15

◆

"Don't cry, Mommy," Susy warned. "I'll bring you back a Mickey Mouse hat."

"You promise?" said Liz, smiling at the bribe. "That would be great."

Her daughter's first real trip without her: Liz tried to act casual about it, but it was a milestone reached, and Liz—and her parents—knew it.

Her father, vigorous and purposeful as always, shifted his carry-on bag from one shoulder to the other and said, "C'mon c'mon c'mon. The overhead storage is going to be filled up. Susy! Let's go! All aboard for Disney World!"

Susy's face lit up as only a child's can at the mention of the Magic Kingdom. She took her grandfather's outstretched hand and, blowing one last kiss to Liz, trotted through the boarding tunnel to the waiting plane.

Liz waved and sighed and then said to her mother one last time, "You can't afford this, Mom. Let me at least—"

"Don't be dumb, Lizzie. We took the other grandchildren at her age; why wouldn't we take Susy?"

"Because I already owe you a million dollars in baby-sitting fees!"

"*Stop*. She's our only home-grown seedling. You know how special she is to us."

It was true; everyone knew that Susy was the favorite. Liz thought it was at least partly because Patricia Pinhel had never—quite—forgiven her two sons for taking jobs in other parts of New England. She'd never allowed herself to get her hopes up, of course—but when the boys did move on, she was twice as disappointed.

Mother and daughter shared a quick hug, and then Liz was alone in cozy Greene Airport, a place as alien to her as the inside of a space shuttle. Almost the only time she ever went to Greene was to pick someone up or drop someone off. Someday all that would change; someday she and Susy would take quick little trips here and there and everywhere.

But not today.

That night Liz felt alone and depressed. Hearing Susy's voice on the phone (and learning that earlier she'd burst into tears when it finally dawned on her that Mommy wouldn't be on the plane) had proved little consolation. Liz had to wonder why.

Her depression had nothing, nothing, *nothing* to do with Jack Eastman, she insisted to herself. The other night at East Gate he'd told her exactly what he thought. That was his prerogative. Liz had then stomped out of his house. That was her prerogative.

Yes, for a while she *had* waited breathlessly to see whether he'd phone, or come by, or—heck, he'd done it before— climb over the fence. But she wasn't Julia Roberts, and her life was not a movie.

Liz didn't even have the luxury of convincing herself that Jack was out of town: she'd seen him yesterday on the grounds of East Gate, hauling a broken limb that had fallen not twenty feet from the chain-link fence. In her kitchen, making supper, she was close enough to see the muscles bulging in his arms as he dragged away the heavy bough. But he never looked in her direction, and it made Liz wish, suddenly, that the chain-link fence was a wall of bricks.

After that, she decided that her mother was right after all: It was dumb ever to get your hopes up. Liz reminded herself, for the thousandth time, that a hundred years ago Christopher Eastman had seduced and then abandoned her great-great-grandmother. She asked herself, for the thousandth time, why she wanted to see history repeat itself. But it was no use: her hopes kept bubbling up, like oxygen from the bottom of a deep, deep lake.

By ten o'clock, when Jack didn't appear, Liz turned—for comfort? for answers?—to the shoeboxes. Somewhere there had to be an explanation for the failed love between Christopher and Ophelia. He loved her, and she loved him: it should have been enough. Liz wanted desperately for it to be enough.

She picked up one of the miscellaneous boxes that were stuffed with scraps of undated writing and began to read. Three hours later, she found what she was looking for. An incomplete page—one that began with a recipe for an herbal compress to relieve headache—was followed by a critical piece of gossip:

And that younger brother of whom you were so enamored? My temperamental artist, your mystery man in black? My dear Mercy, you never will guess: He has come back to the fold!

It came about in the most unexpected way. His older brother was killed in a riding accident not two days after the dinner party—the fête with the sand buckets—of which I wrote. It was a most devastating loss to the parents. Much as I hate to do it, I am forced to give our young man his due. He has put his infatuation aside, closed up his studio, and assumed the family mantle of responsibility. Some say he shuts himself up every evening to brood and to grieve. Others whisper that an engagement to an heiress is imminent. All, seemingly, overnight!

I must confess to feeling as if I have shared no small part of this man's destiny. Had I not switched the gemstone for the pin before that dinner party, who knows what might have happened? Our impulsive young artist might, for example, have had a falling-out with his parents and fled with Ophelia to Europe. Perhaps I foresaw the tragic accident that was about to occur to his brother and acted on that knowledge. Yes, that must have been my motive, I think. It explains

And that was all.

The writing was crabbed and ink-blotted. There were no margins. The paper was inferior. Maybe Victoria St. Onge was working on her last two sheets of stationery; maybe she was just in one of her moods. Whatever the case, Liz now had all the pieces to her historical mystery except one: Why was the ghost of Christopher Eastman choosing to appear to *her*?

There was only one way to find out, she decided, and that was simply to ask him.

He'd shown himself twice without the benefit of a go-between, so apparently Liz didn't need a medium or spirit guide or whoever people used to communicate with the beyond. On the other hand, she didn't have a clue how to initiate the process herself. *Could* she make contact?

Half an hour later, Liz had set her trap with herself as the cheese. She didn't have a crystal ball, and she didn't have a Ouija board. She didn't have a talisman, fairy ring, amulet, dowsing rod, tarot cards, trumpet, or pendulum. She had no mentor, training, or experience. All she had was a bedrock belief, deep inside her soul, that she shared a profound connection with the spirit of Christopher Eastman.

She'd chosen her bedroom, the most private room of the four, for the rendezvous. After closing the windows and hooking the shutters, she'd gone through the house and turned off all the lights. After that she'd put on a compact disc of New Age music—in part, to drown out the moans of the foghorns, which tonight sounded to her like grieving lovers. The dozen white votive candles that she'd placed around the bedroom floor and furnishings were flickering softly in their cut-glass holders, throwing fitful shadows over the muted yellow walls.

Ready.

She sat in the middle of her bed with her legs tucked under her and a paisley shawl of red and gold wrapped around her shoulders. Under the shawl she was wearing a waltz-length nightgown of white cotton—and a new pair of underpants, because if something happened and she died of fright, she wanted to be found properly, modestly dressed.

Smiling at the bizarreness of her priorities, she let herself drift off into a state that was at once unfocused and alert. Solemn thoughts floated before her like big, wobbly soap bubbles, and then burst, to be followed by other, sometimes smaller bubbles. . . .

Bit by bit, step by step . . . I am descending into an abyss. A year ago . . . a month ago . . . I would have been scandalized by this . . . and now . . . will Susy find a Mickey Mouse hat, I wonder? She'll feel she's let me down if she doesn't . . . she's so responsible . . . if she had brothers and sisters, would she be different? A brat? Like Caroline? Is a mother more critical to a daughter than a father? Caroline . . . does she suffer from the curse of illegitimacy? And what about me? Am I descended from Ophelia Ryan, or Ophelia Pinhel . . . impossible to know . . . yes . . . the curse of illegitimacy . . . the curse of lowered expectations. And yet . . . here I go, getting my hopes up . . . that he will show . . . before the candles burn out.

There was a sound, a ringing sound, from a great, great distance. Liz considered answering the summons, but it was so far away . . . she was so far away . . . lost in a trance . . . lost, and hopeful, and somehow, despite everything, serene. If only it could always be this way . . . this freedom from want . . . from disappointment and yearning . . . this simple, satisfying tranquillity. . . .

The ringing faded away, replaced by the more heavenly sound of a chimelike note filling the air around her. It was a sound that by now Liz knew well, the sound an angel must make when his wings bump against a cloud. The notion filled Liz with a piercing sense of happiness, more satisfying than anything she'd known since the birth of her child. A tear rolled out from under her closed eyelids, and her mouth curved in a smile of realized bliss.

When she opened her eyes, he was there, as she knew he would be. He was wearing his painter's smock, paint-dabbed and worn; the smile on his face was a smile of pure love. She wondered how she could ever have felt threatened by his presence; how she could ever have been puzzled by his mission. He was there, he must be there, to make her understand, once and for all, about love.

It seemed to her that he wanted to speak to her. He had an expression of fierce concentration on his face, as if life and death depended on his getting it right. He might have been painting her portrait. But it was more than that: He was coaxing a bit of her soul from her body, drawing it closer to heaven in a dance of sheer ecstasy.

In the blink of an eye, after a lifetime in the dark, Liz suddenly understood the transforming power of love. It was what made a painting immortal; a union, sublime. Time could not diminish it, and fate could not subdue it. Ultimately—eventually—love triumphed . . . love triumphed . . . love triumphed.

• • •

When Liz awoke, she was amazed to see afternoon sun shining through the shutters and even more amazed to realize that she had a pounding headache: ecstasy wasn't supposed to feel that way. She dragged herself into a sitting position, still wrapped in her shawl, and surveyed the burned-out candleholders.

My God, she thought. *I could've burned the house down.*

Was it all a dream? She couldn't have imagined it. She *had seen* him—he was there, as vivid, as real as the oak chest of drawers—and he had imparted to her some special wisdom, only she wasn't sure what. It had something to do with ecstasy.

Whatever had happened, it had taken its toll. Numb with pain, Liz headed straight for the aspirin. She had her hand on the mirrored door when she remembered that at four o'clock she was due at the local shelter for battered women; today was the day she donated her time to entertain the children there with her puppet show. She ran back to her bedroom and snatched up the small ticking clock. Four o'clock was . . . precisely twenty-six minutes away.

"Aaaghh!"

She was out of the house in less than five minutes, and the funny thing was, the headache left in a hurry, too. It didn't seem possible that two aspirin could make such a crushing hangover disappear so fast; Liz was forced to believe that higher forces were involved.

Did spirits relieve migraines, too?

The shelter, a rambling Victorian house called Anne's Place, held special significance for Liz. Her best friend in high school had married a man who beat her regularly; Liz had talked Marcia into fleeing to the shelter, where she'd gotten much needed support and counseling. Eventually Marcia started over in Phoenix, where she and her son were now thriving. Like Liz, Marcia had become leery of relationships. Unlike Liz, she was perfectly happy to live without one.

In any case, the warm feelings that Liz had for Anne's Place remained, and every so often she showed her appreciation by putting on a little show for the kids of the women in residence. It was the least she could do.

She was two acts into a light-hearted skit featuring Kris and Misha when she spied, through the peephole, someone who'd seen the play before—most of it, anyway. With a quirky, endearing smile, Jack waved from the doorway and then withdrew, leaving the children to enjoy their show in peace.

Seeing him was a staggering blow to Liz's presence of mind. After the other night . . . after *last* night—well, she needed time to sort it all out. Her emotions were a mess. She needed time!

The final act was an embarrassment of missed cues and dropped lines, but Liz's audience was too starved for joy to care. How glad they were to be able to laugh and feel safe— all of them, from the two-year-old who kept making mad dashes at the puppets to the little boy who sat in his mother's lap and kept his thumb in his mouth the whole time, even when he smiled.

After the puppets made their final bows, the children were shepherded away, and Liz began to break down the theater. She was interested to see that her hands were shaking as she did it. It wasn't surprising—she hadn't eaten for twenty-four hours—but she knew that low blood sugar wasn't the real problem.

One of us has to be sorry, she realized. *Why does it have to be me?*

Nonetheless, when Jack walked into the room, her first impulse had been to throw herself at him and beg for his forgiveness. She wanted him to take her back. She wanted to be in his arms again, before the anger, before the hurt.

Was she really so different from the women at Anne's Place?

"Hello," she said. She sounded cool and distant, which was the opposite of how she felt.

"Hi," said Jack in a surprisingly low-key greeting. It was as if some of the sadness of the shelter had worn off on both of them.

"How . . . did you know I was here?" Liz asked in a faltering voice.

"The note on your door to Victoria."

"Oh. Well, her answering machine's on the fritz. She was supposed to come by—"

"She did come by," Jack said, "at lunch. She called me afterward, looking for you. Your car was there, but I guess you'd gone off somewhere on foot."

"Oh, but I was—" Obviously Liz had spent the time in a brief but thorough coma. "Yes. I was out," she said, and then she changed the subject. "How were you able to get past the front desk?"

Jack grimaced and said, "I showed her my shipyard ID. I had no idea the security was so—"

"—necessary? It is. I have a friend with the mended bones to prove it."

He nodded thoughtfully. "I passed a woman. . . . Her face—it was black and blue—and cut." A look of pain came over him as he said, "You see it on TV. . . . It makes you want to turn away—but even then it's not the same as seeing it close. She was so—*battered*."

"They don't use the word loosely around here," Liz said.

"I heard her talking to another woman about life in the projects. Too much unemployment, too much stress—it's got to be hard."

Liz wanted to say, "You think rich men don't slap their

wives around, too?'' But it seemed gratuitous, so she settled for saying, ''The shelter is a lifeline for women like her.''

He said with a mixture of candor and bitterness, ''My mother, on the other hand, can escape to Capri.''

''You see a similarity?'' Liz said, surprised that he could be so perceptive.

He groped for an explanation. ''I don't know. I guess I see a connection between physical abuse and emotional abuse. Granted, my father never laid a hand on my mother or even raised his voice to her,'' he said musingly. ''But his constant philandering showed such contempt, caused her such pain. It's a form of abuse, isn't it? Only without the marks?''

''I see what you mean,'' Liz said softly. ''Well, since Capri is not an option for these women, I'm glad there's Anne's Place. It does so much with so little.''

Jack seemed to mull over what Liz said as she packed away the puppets. ''How *does* the shelter get by?'' he said at last, coloring. It was obvious that he thought he should know.

Liz shrugged and said, ''With a lick and a prayer: donations, mostly. From fund-raisers, gifts, mailings—''

''I see.''

He was silent another long moment. ''All right,'' he said matter-of-factly. ''Then that's what we'll do.''

Liz looked up from her carryall. ''Excuse me? Do what?''

''Whatever will bring in the most cash. You're the events coordinator, not me. What do you think? An auction? A food festival? Maybe a raffle? Dessert-and-dance? A direct-mailing appeal sounds pretty ho-hum to me, but—''

''Hold it, hold it!'' she said. His naïveté was mind-boggling. ''Number one, I'm not a fund-raising consultant. And number two—minor detail—the shelter hasn't asked us.''

Jack seemed genuinely surprised by both objections. ''The shipyard will underwrite a chunk of it,'' he said, lifting the folded puppet-theater from its table. "What's not to like? So: Will you do it?"

"Oh. Well. In that case. Of course I will," Liz said. She followed him out of the room, still shaking her head over him. "But I don't get it. This shelter has been here for years. Why you? Why now?"

"I've never been here before," he said simply. "Come on. We've got work to do."

They settled on an impromptu working supper at Liz's house. The proper place for such discussions obviously was her office. But Jack was going to be tied up in meetings with a couple of investors the next day, and Liz had no free time the day after that. Since Jack was determined to stage the event before the annual flight of Newport's summer colonists to Palm Beach, speed was critical.

They called ahead from the shelter for Chinese takeout, and Jack went to pick it up before continuing on to meet Liz. In the meantime, Liz drove like a madwoman, short-cutting through Newport's maze of one-way streets so that she could beat him to the mess she'd left behind.

Letters! Clothes! Dishes! Everything's on the damned floor again. . . . I haven't showered—oh, God, candles all over the bedroom . . . did I ever turn off that mindless New Age tape?

Why on earth hadn't they gone to *his* place? Plenty of room, plenty of food . . .

And plenty of people. Neither one of them had alluded to the fact that at Liz's place they'd be alone, but it was on both their minds as Liz murmured something about a little peace and quiet and Jack said how nice it would be to be able to hear themselves think.

Liars! thought Liz with brutal honesty. They could brainstorm anywhere—under a tree, in a coffee shop, at Netta's kitchen table—but they couldn't take off all their clothes and make wild abandoned love in any of those places. The carriage house apartment might do, but after the other night— well, the carriage house had sexual connotations that her own innocent house did not. Yet.

"So we're backing into this affair accidentally on purpose," Liz murmured, suddenly weary from the agony of thinking about it.

It was no use resisting; making love with Jack Eastman was absolutely inevitable. If there was a lesson to be learned from Ophelia's example, Liz hadn't learned it. Even after last night—maybe *because* of last night—Liz wanted desperately to be in Jack's arms. Victoria was right: Liz had gone way, way too long without making love.

Jack arrived close on her heels. Liz had barely had time to sweep a jumble of clothes and candles under her bed and dash down to the living room when she heard him knock and then try the handle of the front door. She ran to open it.

"Glad to see you're locking up at last," he said with a protective smile that made her heart wobble like a top.

She thought of the night she was burglarized, the night he climbed over the barbed wire. *It's true,* she realized. *We have been through a lot together. It's not as though I've just picked the man up in a bar.*

"You bet I'm locking up," she admitted. "Grant Dade's going to have to break the door down next time."

Jack shot her an amused look and said, "Still haven't given up on that graduate student?" Without waiting for her answer, he added, "In the kitchen, or out here?"

Liz had no idea why, but she assumed he was asking her where they were going to make love. "Oh—well . . . I hadn't considered . . . on the floor?"

"Hey, whatever turns you on," he said amiably. He plopped the heavy bag of food on the seaman's trunk in front of the chintz sofa and then sat down on the rug and began taking out the paper cartons. "Hope you like Szechuan."

He meant where to eat.

Clearly, Liz had sex on the brain. Embarrassed to be so gung-ho when he was not, she said, "Why don't we just sit at the kitchen table?"

He looked up with a relieved grin and said, "Thank God. My knees are killing me down here."

The phone rang as they were relocating to the kitchen: Susy was calling, with her grandparents' help, from the motel where the three of them had set up camp. Susy, thrilled and exhausted from the first day of her adventure, was too tired to sleep, too tired to talk. It was an unsatisfying conversation, made worse by the fact that the two of them weren't used to talking about Important Matters without laps and hugs. Still, Susy was happy and secure in her grandparents' care and just homesick enough to satisfy Liz.

"Is she getting plenty of boat rides?" asked Jack when Liz hung up.

"You bet. She's been through the Pirates of the Caribbean; on the jungle cruise; on the ferry to Tom Sawyer's Island. Tomorrow comes something called Mike Fink's Keelboats," Liz said, smiling.

"Sounds promising," Jack said. "Come and sit."

Jack had arranged the half-dozen white cartons on the table like a small village of food and had set out plates and silverware. He took a pencil and pad from her desk and tossed them on the table, then popped the tabs on the two cans of Budweiser he'd hunted down in the back of the fridge.

"Okay," he announced cheerfully. "First, food. Then work."

Then sex? she wondered. Was she the only one wondering it? How could he be this way—so casual, when nothing about their relationship was casual? Could he honestly have forgotten about their fight?

"Before we go any further, I want to apologize for the

way I stalked out of your house," she said briskly. "I over-reacted."

He was midsip in his beer. Putting the can down carefully, he said, "No, Liz, you didn't overreact. You behaved with a lot more dignity than I would have done. I'm the one who owes the apology," he said, coloring, "which is why I came looking for you. To say how sorry I am. I was—truly—an ass."

"Apology accepted," Liz said simply. His words sounded sweet in her ear; it occurred to her that neither her father nor her ex-husband had ever said them. She smiled to herself, thinking, *It's nice when a man can admit he's an ass.*

He misunderstood her smile. Laying his hand on her wrist for emphasis, he said softly, "I mean it. I had no right to trivialize what you do for a living. In the first place, it's not trivial: look at today, in the shelter. And in the second place, who am I to criticize?" he said ironically. "I launch rich men's toys for a living."

"You *know* that's not all you—" Liz stopped herself. "You're right," she said with a good-natured laugh. "Neither one of us is ever gonna get a Nobel Prize. Let's eat."

The air had cleared; suddenly it seemed easier to breathe. Liz put aside her will-we, won't-we agony and concentrated on the food and the fund-raiser. They attacked the meal with gusto and began throwing ideas back and forth with abandon.

"Okay," Jack started out by saying. "First question: How much of your time will an event take?"

"A biggish one? Half my time for the next three months."

"Too much time. We'll scale down. What are some min-imum-manpower events?"

"Who do we want to attract? An older crowd brings money; a younger crowd brings enthusiasm for the cause."

"Anne's Place needs both. What've you got? Talk to me, talk to me," he said comically, stabbing his Lo Mein.

"A dinner dance is one way to go. We'd need two bands for wide appeal, though: swing and rock."

"Nah. What about a walkathon? I see those all the time."

"Overdone. *Wow*. This Kung Bo Chicken's great. We could do an auction. No—no time for that."

"What if I produced a celebrity? Schwarzenegger likes Newport."

She was impressed. "You know *Arnold*?"

Jack smiled. "I know he likes Newport, is what I actually know. But say, someone like him."

She thought about it, then put the thought aside. "I don't have the experience to handle a celebrity event," she admitted ruefully.

"Beach party? Amplified music, big barbecue?" he suggested.

She cringed. "Just what the locals need—someone stealing their beach and playing loud music as they do it. You want to be run out of town on a rail?"

She stole a spicy shrimp from his plate, bit into it, started choking, and washed down the fire with beer. "Ha-a-hht," she said, gasping, as the tears flowed freely.

"Serves you right," he said with satisfaction. "This sounds a little decadent, but I've heard of something called Cow Pie Bingo. What you do is mark off a field into squares, then 'sell' each square for, say, twenty bucks. Then you let an overfed cow wander around, and where she drops her—"

"Yeah, yeah, I read about that," she said, laughing through her tears. "Did you know a ministry in Canada refused to grant some charity a lottery license to do it because they thought the cow could be influenced into where to drop her—droppings? In any case, it's gambling. Besides, we don't have a cow."

"There's always Snowball," he said helpfully.

The infamous Snowball incident sent them into a round of comfortable laughter, and she thought, *He's so easy to get along with. I am having such a good time here. I'd love to make it last.*

"That's the trouble with Newport," Liz said at last. "It's such a great place to stage a charitable event. We've got mansions, historic homes, gardens, galleries, restaurants, beaches, an ocean, a bay, superb architecture, an international reputation." She sighed in frustration and said, "We photograph well, dammit. *Everything*'s been done here."

"Garden tour?"

"Done."

"Cruise party?"

"Done."

"Food festival? Dine-around? Cook-off?"

"Done, done, done."

"Jumble? White elephant sale?"

"Not enough money. Look, Jack, maybe we should just make this a friend-raiser instead of a fund-raiser. We'll make sure everyone learns about Anne's Place, what it does, how important it is to the community. Then next year——"

"No," Jack said. "I want the money for them *this* year. I know you think I'm a Jack-come-lately to this. But something about the women there touched me in a—well—a really profound way," he said, almost embarrassed about it. "I want to do this. That's all."

"Sure," said Liz softly. "It's just a question of finding the right fit. Let me think."

She avoided the hot food and picked at the Moo Shu veggies, mulling her options. Jack respected her frown of concentration and busied himself with his Peking ribs. The silence went on for a while; but it was a comfortable, easy silence.

"Costume party," Liz said at last. "We'll have a costume party. It cuts across all age groups and income levels. It lets old people feel young and young people feel old. If someone doesn't have the money to rent an expensive costume, he can use imagination to design a clever one."

"Sounds good to me," Jack said, his blue eyes dancing with appreciation. "Will it have a theme?"

She had an inspiration. "How about 'From the Gilded Age to the New Age'?" she suggested, stealing shamelessly from Grant Dade's doctoral thesis."

"Fine. We're talking about a costume *ball,* right?"

Liz wrinkled her nose and said, "Too expensive. I don't know what the entertainment will be. But it'll be cheap. We want maximum bang for our buck."

The glitter in Jack's eyes faded. "I don't want this to look like some Spartan affair," he said diplomatically.

"I suppose you mean thrown together," Liz said, trying to decide whether to be offended. With a dangerous smile, she asked, "Have I failed to meet your high standards so far?"

"Obviously not," he said, retreating. "But we want real money to come to this thing. Are you sure we don't want a ball?" he asked, almost plaintively. "At least I know about balls."

"*Mis*-ter Eastman. This will not be an extravaganza. This will not be some private bash for you and your pals. This is going to be a cost-effective *event.* You can stack the honorary committee with every socialite you know. But I absolutely, positively have to have the final say on everything. Are we agreed or not?"

"Agreed," Jack said, disarming her with a smile. Then, resting on his forearms, he leaned toward her and said, "Kiss me."

"Kiss you!" She laughed uncertainly and looked away. "Why should I kiss you?"

"Because somehow I feel like a frog," he said with a rueful smile in his voice. "If you kiss me, I'm hoping I turn into your prince."

She shook her head at his antic. *If only you knew,* she thought.

When she turned back to him, he was still smiling: a sexy, beguiling, depressingly confident smile. It was in his genes—handed straight down, with the rest of his good looks and charm, from his womanizing father. The only difference between the two men was that Jack Eastman had too much integrity to marry some woman and then put her through hell.

I know this, and I love him anyway. Dammit, dammit, dammit. I love him anyway.

She sighed in distress—as if she were truly going to kiss some ugly toad—and leaned her face toward his for the kiss. *Stupid woman,* she told herself as she did it. *He's not a prince. He's not even a frog.*

He's a bachelor.

Chapter 16

She brushed her lips dutifully against his, then began to pull away.

"Hold it," Jack said in protest, slipping his hand behind her head. "That's not enough to break the spell." He pulled her back for another kiss.

This one was longer, warmer, deeper. His voice was rich and insinuating as he said, "Hmm . . . I think . . . I *do* feel . . . a change coming on."

"Don't," she said, shying away. "Don't make fun of enchantments."

That surprised him. His breath came in a soft, laughing exhale. "Don't tell me you're going to change into a *frog* after this!"

"Jack—don't tease," she begged. She was thinking of last night, of the apparition. She was remembering the intense, unforgettable expression on Christopher Eastman's face. Why couldn't Jack look at her that way?

"Madame, forgive me," Jack said in a tone that was only slightly more serious than before. "I've never had to deal with a real princess before."

She stiffened. "What's that supposed to mean?"

He gave her a lopsided smile and said candidly, "It means I feel totally inadequate around you. I can't seem to strike the right note."

The right note. The right note was the sound of a chime.

"I guess idle banter makes me nervous," she said.

"Idle banter! Is that what this is? I thought it was your idea of foreplay."

"Foreplay!" she said, astonished. "This is what makes all those socialites fall at your feet? I don't believe it!"

"I give up!" Jack let out a frustrated laugh and pushed his chair away from the table. He stood over her, angry and bemused at the same time, and rubbed the back of his neck in frustration. "You're so god-blessed . . . prickly. It's like trying to grab hold of a porcupine."

"Is that so?" she said coolly, looking up at him. "So much for the princess, then. Is there a fairy tale that covers frogs and porcupines?"

"Yeah," he said, a dangerous glitter in his deep blue eyes. He took her by the wrists and pulled her up out of her chair. "The story goes like this: the pretty little porcupine is real stuck-up, even though it's the frog who has the big house on the shore. One day the frog is singing his heart out for the porcupine—he's wildly attracted to her because she's different from all the frogs he's known—and what does the porcupine do?

He dropped his voice to an ominous whisper. "She shoots one of her quills right through his voice box. Because automatically she sees him as an enemy. She doesn't understand his song. She doesn't even try."

They were standing a breath apart in the shadows of a golden dusk that beamed through the kitchen windows. Liz dropped her own voice to a whisper. "What happens to the frog? Does he—you know—croak?"

"Not anymore," Jack said, smiling at her pun.

She let herself be seduced by his whimsical humor. "How does the story end, then?" she asked.

"How do you think?" said Jack, holding her by her shoulders, taking small, nibbling tastes of her mouth. "The porcupine takes the frog home, sticks him in her bed, and makes him her sex-slave.''

''The Brothers Grimm say that?''

''Well, words to that effect.''

''Jack—''

''Let me make love to you,'' he said suddenly. ''*Please* let me make love to you. I've asked you every way I know how. My God, Elizabeth. I feel like I've been thrown back into the Victorian age. I feel like your father's in the next room, shotgun on the wall. This is weird . . . this shouldn't have to be so hard—''

He cut off a groan deep in his throat and said, ''Ah, the hell with it,'' and yanked her against his chest, trapping her hands flat against him and covering her mouth with his in a hard, frustrated kiss. Liz opened her mouth to say something, to protest or to agree, she never did know which, and he thrust his tongue into it, filling it, beating back her words, beating back her thoughts.

He kissed her until she was breathless, until her ears rang and she had to jerk her mouth away, gasping for breath. His hands slid down the length of her back, coming to rest under the curve of her buttocks. Pressing her close, he held her fast against him, making her feel the heat. He kissed her again, holding her fast, making her want him, making her love him despite all her pointless resolve not to.

She pulled away in a last-ditch effort to avoid the agony that she knew lay ahead if she went on with this. To love him and not have it returned . . .

Panting, she said, ''*No;* don't you see? I—''

She raised her gaze to his. If she looked him in the eye and told him that she loved him, the affair would end right then, right there; no one feared commitment more than a bachelor.

His look was dark and burning, a mirror of her own hunger

as he began to interrupt, then wisely bit off the words. He waited.

In that fraction of a second Liz reversed herself completely. "Oh, dammit, Jack—*yes*," she said in a small, helpless wail. She slid her arms around his broad back and lifted her mouth, wet and swollen, to his. "I do want you—more than anyone."

It was so much less scary than admitting she loved him and risking his walking away.

He looked more relieved than triumphant as he lowered his mouth to hers in a perfect caress that moved her nearly to tears. His kiss turned into a sliding nuzzle at the curve of her neck. His voice was low, almost puzzled, as he said, "I feel as if I've wanted you all my life—and yet—where have you *been*, all my life?"

She arched her neck in offering, relishing the warmth of his lips on her skin, and said, "Right across the tracks— funny you never noticed."

That brought a low warning chuckle from him. "Nay, madame, I beg of you: Put down your arms this once."

He was right, of course. She was being a porcupine again. On an impulse, she raised her hands high above her head. "How about if I put my arms . . . up . . . instead?" she asked innocently.

He lifted his head. A slow, knowing smile played on his face, a smile that brought high, rich color to Liz's cheekbones. "Boldness becomes you," he said, impressed. He took the hem of her cotton top in his hands and slid it as high as her bra. "Especially considering there are no curtains on those windows."

"Oh!" Down came her arms, down came the shirt.

He laughed softly, then slipped one arm around her waist and said, "Come, fair porcupine. Bedrooms were made for times like these."

They began going upstairs. He was handling her with just

the right mix of pressure and tenderness. She felt like a skittish colt. Or worse: a virgin.

She wanted to ask, "Is anyone nervous besides me?" But he'd say no, and then she'd feel more nervous than ever.

What if she didn't meet his standards in bed? God knew, they must be high. What if Victoria was right—what if everything down there was closing up? What if—oh, God— people in his set made love altogether differently? Maybe they had some secret, illogical way of doing it—like the way they insisted on wearing long-sleeved shirts to weddings in August.

They were hand in hand at the bedroom door. Jack said, "You seem edgy."

"No kidding." Her voice was grim.

Turning to her, he cradled her cheeks in his hands, then slid his hands through the silkiness of her hair. "I want you to know—before we go in there—that this is different," he murmured. "Before, the bedroom has always been the end of the line. But with you . . . I don't know. It's someplace where maybe we can hide, while we figure it all out."

She put her fingers to Jack's lips to silence him and said, "No promises necessary. I'm not fragile. I won't break."

His brows drew together in a little frown of worry. "Everyone's fragile," he said.

If he ends up hurting me, at least he'll feel bad about it, she decided. It was such small comfort, but it was all she had.

She lifted her chin and, with her eyes closed, parted her mouth slightly for the kiss she knew would come. When he kissed her this time, there was a solemnity about it, as if they'd made a pact. But a pact to do what? To hide in the bedroom together?

He released her. "We've come full circle," he said softly. "This is where we met."

She remembered it well. She had been upside down and

covered in plaster dust when she first set eyes on him. Even then, she must have known that he was the one. The day she met him was the day the magic began. The day the magic began was the day she met him. "Full circle," she repeated, awed by the mystery of it all.

They went into her bedroom then, and Liz turned on a little rose-shaded lamp and sat on the foot of her bed, and Jack looked around as if he were in a make-believe room of a child's playhouse.

She didn't mind: he looked so beguiled by the humble, crowded coziness of it all. The small-print wallpaper; the painted shutters; the rag rug and the vase of black-eyed Susans edging the lamp off the nightstand—all of it seemed to charm him, all of it seemed to please. He peered out at the view of the harbor, its navigation lights blinking in reassuring harmony on the calm black water.

Liz jumped up from the bed and said, "But it's so much better in the daytime! You can see ships trafficking up and down the bay. You can see sailboats—"

"I've seen enough boats to last me a lifetime," he said, closing the shutters on the scene. He turned to her. The warmth in his look was unmistakable. He reached out his hand and trailed his fingers lightly on the wide-scooped neck of her cotton top.

She was thinking, *This would have been much easier if he'd just taken me on the kitchen table.*

"I'm sorry about the bed," she said, bursting into another round of babble. "It's not a king—"

"Neither am I."

"It's not even a queen—"

"Neither are you."

"That's right, I forgot. I'm a princess."

No response.

"Porcupine?" she corrected meekly.

He gave her a wry smile and said, "If the quill fits . . ."

"I'm sorry, I'm sorry," she moaned, all but wringing her hands. "It's been so long. Maybe I need a sexual therapist."

"Let's see what we can do on our own first." He sat down on the bed and patted the space next to him; Liz, feeling like the last kid to show up for the sex-ed class, sat down beside him.

"Now. Since I seem to have a bit more experience than you," he said in a mind-bending understatement, "I'll make a few suggestions. The first is—"

He kissed her lips lightly and then touched his finger to the spot. "—don't talk. The second suggestion—and mind you, it's only a suggestion—is, maybe you'd like to close your eyes and pretend that mine are closed, too."

"All right," she said, and did as he said. He was being just whimsical enough to arouse her curiosity. It remained to be seen whether the rest of her would follow.

Her lips were slightly apart with concentration; she felt him press his mouth to hers, then run his tongue along the shape of her lips, moistening them. It was a delicately erotic act, suggestive without being overbearing. *More to come,* it promised.

Eyes closed, she waited.

She felt him shift his attention to her ear, nibbling the lobe, tugging it gently. She held her breath as he trailed a gossamer line of kisses along the curve of her neck, murmuring her name, stringing out the syllables like pearls on a necklace. She felt him slide her cotton top down from one shoulder, exposing cool, unkissed flesh. He dropped soft kisses there, while she remembered finally to breathe, letting out the air in a rush.

After that, he surprised her by cupping her chin in his hands, then tracing the curves and hollows of her face with his fingertips. It was the act of a sightless person; it made her wonder whether he really *was* keeping his eyes closed.

If so, it added another, intriguing dimension to their home-made therapy session.

I love the way he touches me, she thought. *As if my cheeks were made of butterflies' wings.* She found herself sliding under his spell: more relaxed, and at the same time, more expectant. Impulsively she lifted her own hands to his face, skimming his high cheekbones, his wiry eyebrows, the first stubble of a beard.

It will scratch, she thought. *But not so much.* The thought made her cheeks warm with anticipation. She took a deep breath and was filled with the indefinable scent that made him Jack Eastman and no one else. No cologne, no hair treatment: just salt and sea air, a rugged all-male, all-Jack smell.

She felt him take her wrist and gently kiss the open palm of her hand, a gesture as courtly as it was romantic. No one had ever kissed the palm of her hand before.

For someone who's not a virgin, she thought, amazed, *I sure have lots of virgin territory.*

He laid his hands on her hips, then eased the knit fabric of her top upward, his hands echoing the line of her torso. She felt curves she never knew she had, simply through his touch. Automatically her arms went up as he peeled away the top; she heard it land on the floor in a hush. After that, she folded her hands in her lap and waited for the next step in his gentle, tantalizing disrobing of her.

She heard the snap of plastic as her bra fell away in the front, and she felt cool air wash over her unbound breasts.

"You are beautiful," he murmured, breaking the silence at last.

She sucked in her breath as she felt his fingers lightly circle the tip of her breast, and then, irrepressibly, she said, "How can you tell? Your eyes are closed, remember?"

"Ah . . . right," he said. "I forgot." She sensed his head lowering. "And anyway," he murmured, the words muffled in a wet stroking caress of her nipple, "You're not supposed to talk."

"Ah-h-h . . . right," she said, putting one arm on the white quilt to brace herself. "I forgot." The touch of his tongue was absolutely electric: her breath began coming in small, tight gasps, and her head began to droop, bringing the scent of him closer. She threaded the fingers of her free hand lightly through his hair, encouraging him as he moved from one breast to the other, wondering how it was she could've gone so long without this, without *him*.

He paused—she made a low, whimpering protest—and eased her back down on the coverlet. The bed was still made from two nights ago; she hadn't pulled the covers back on the previous night, the night she'd wrapped herself in the paisley shawl, the night of the apparition.

Lying full length, one knee up, she permitted herself to open her eyes for a peek.

"Wow," she said softly. "That was nice."

He was sliding one hand idly up and down the curve of her torso and was studying her intently, as if he'd just seen her across a crowded room and was trying to place her face.

"Shhh," he told her with a small, crooked smile. "Do you want to break the spell?"

She shook her head slowly, then closed her eyes again, trying to control a kind of giddy fear that it might not go on. What if this, too, were all a dream?

The next barricade to fall was her skirt, a cotton drift of summer pastels that she'd sewn herself. It had hooks and eyes at the waist instead of a button; the buttonhole attachment on her machine had been broken at the time she'd made the outfit. She began to warn him, but he knew all about hooks and eyes.

He knows too much, she thought, suddenly dismayed. *He's undressed too many women.*

But then he slid the skirt, and her panties, off in one fluid motion, leaving her skin rippling with goosebumps, and she found that the other women—however many there were—were as irrelevant as her ex-husband. What did it matter, really, how much experience he had or how little she had? He was a man; she was a woman. It didn't get much simpler than that.

Still, she felt obliged to state the obvious. She opened her eyes and gave him a steady look.

"Before you, there was only Keith," she confessed as he was about to kiss her. It was so embarrassing: only one man in thirty-six years. In her mind, it explained everything.

The look on Jack's face was heartachingly tender. "In that case, I feel sorry for every other male on earth right now."

She fingered the top button of his shirt and indulged in a tiny naked shrug. "I just wanted you to know."

"And now I do," he said, kissing her on her brow. "And I don't care." His mouth came to rest on hers—more to shut her up, she thought, than anything else—and his tongue sought hers in a taunting kiss that soon turned into a deeper, hungrier probe than anything before it. She hadn't been kissed like that since—well, she'd never been kissed like that.

He left her moaning, sighing, arching her hips skyward as he trailed a hot blaze of kisses up and down her body, coming back to her breasts again and again, each time ratcheting up the heat; each time, leaving her more fever-struck.

Secret places she never knew she had—inside her elbow, and halfway between her belly button and the downy clump of hair below it—these places were thoroughly mapped out and explored. She had never in her life been the focus of such relentless, attentive, concentrated *stimulation*.

She was on fire.

And she wanted Jack to catch up. When she said that to him, he laughed out loud in a kind of groaning whoop of sheer male enthusiasm. ''I'm ready!'' he said. ''Willing! *Bursting,* my love!''

Whether he was bursting or not, Liz loved the ''my love'' part. Between them they had already fumbled through the buttons of his shirt and peeled it away. Now she shrugged off his T-shirt, and he yanked off his trousers and then his shorts and tossed them on the floor.

She watched him undress with furtive curiosity. He was solid and fit, but hardly the washboard-of-muscles type: his strength had a more natural look than that. She couldn't imagine him displaying himself in a volleyball game at Easton's Beach, any more than she could picture herself Roller-blading down Thames Street in short shorts and a tube top.

He went back, suddenly, to retrieve his pants: bending over to pick them up, he slipped his wallet out from a back pocket. With a sheepish look he opened the wallet and said, ''My emergency stash—something tells me you don't have a drawer full of these.''

Protection! She'd forgotten all about it! Somehow the knowledge that she couldn't get pregnant, not to mention the fact that she'd been out of circulation for the past hundred years . . . she hadn't seen a condom this close up since her senior year in high school. The packet looked almost quaint.

She sat up. ''Wait,'' she said, after he tore off the top of the foil. She bit her lower lip. ''Are you planning to stay the night?'' she ventured to ask.

''If you let me,'' he said. He gave her a quizzical look.

''And you only have one of these?''

''This is it,'' he said, more tentative than ever.

''Then I suggest,'' she said with a demure half-smile, ''that we get a little creative.''

He quirked one eyebrow upward. ''What, pray, did you have in mind?''

Without a word, she took the half-opened foil from him and tossed it on the bedside stand. ''Hmm. Well, it's been a while,'' she said with a considering frown. ''But it seems to me that if I do . . . this,'' she said, trailing her fingers lightly across his very male, very responsive member, ''yes . . . that's what I recall used to happen. And then, if I do . . . this,'' she murmured, stroking him more boldly now, ''. . . yep. I guess men are all the same.''

He was standing next to her, hands on his hips, completely at ease in his nakedness—but maybe not so at ease as when he first undressed. ''Witch,'' he said in a sexy, shaky voice. ''If you think I'm going to stand idly by—you're absolutely right.''

She increased the pace, surprised at the ease with which she'd taken control from him, thrilled to be giving him pleasure. His breathing came more deeply now; she looked up and saw his face, tense with concentration, and thought, *How can I make him stay? I don't want him ever to leave.*

Suddenly he took her by the wrist and shook his head. ''No . . . dammit, no,'' he said hoarsely. ''I want us together. We'll worry about later, later.''

He sat on the side of the bed, took up the packet, and sheathed himself. She opened her arms to him, and he came on top of her, supporting his weight above her on his forearms.

''My eyes are open, as you can tell,'' he said softly, his voice slurred with desire, ''and I was right the first time: You're very beautiful, Elizabeth.''

''Shhh,'' she said, because it was impossible for her to believe he could find her beautiful.

She slid her arms around him. She realized in a profound way that he was broader, heavier, an altogether different person from the one she'd been with for a decade. He smelled different, he kissed different, he sighed different. *I have a new man in my life,* she thought, dizzy with wonder as she parted herself to him. *It truly is like being a virgin. Only better.*

He was gentle and slow coming into her. She'd been so long without someone; and yet in one slow wave of entry, it seemed as if she'd never been without at all. *Full circle,* she thought. *I have come full circle.*

They lay motionless for a long, long moment, savoring the heat, unwilling, after all this, for it to end. He threaded both of his hands through her hair, burying his face in it, taking deep, hungry breaths of her. "I'm crazy about you, Elizabeth. You know that," he said in an aching voice.

The words seemed to echo like a drumbeat through the chambers of her heart. "And I . . . am crazy, too," she murmured in response. What she wanted to say was: *I love you with all my heart, and I would do anything to spend the rest of my days on earth with you. I would do anything to be your wife.*

But she knew—after Keith—that talk like that scared men, and so she simply repeated, in her own soft echo of despair, "Crazy . . . crazy . . . crazy," as he pulled slowly back, and then began an easy, rhythmic ripple through her. She lifted herself to meet the rhythm, moved by him, moving him, she hardly knew which. It was all so right, so new, so old.

It seemed to her that they began to be surrounded by a kind of ringing lightness: and then, in the final, frenetic thrusts, the lightness around them entered into her soul, filling her, driving out despair, flooding her with a crazy hope that Jack wanted a wife, and not merely someone to bear his children. *Crazy . . . crazy . . . crazy.*

She heard Jack groan and felt his climax, and then she felt herself shudder in an overwhelming release. Marveling, she thought: *Both of us, at the same time. It never happens at the same time.*

Jack sank onto her breast; she held him close, cherishing him, and sighed heavily, feeling his weight rise and fall with the act. And then, in a slowly dissipating haze of passion, she opened her eyes and saw: Christopher Eastman.

Chapter 17

◆

*H*e was standing in front of the shuttered window, an artist's palette in one hand, a paintbrush in the other. An easel—an easel, for pity's sake!—was now standing alongside the wicker chair in front of the window. Perched on the easel was a large canvas, apparently a work in progress.

The ghost was wearing the same paint-dabbed smock that he wore the first time Liz had seen him at East Gate; his face had the same fierce frown of concentration that she'd seen in her vision the night before. He seemed more substantial than ever.

Liz absorbed it all in half a second and caught her breath in a sharp gasp of panic.

"What?" Jack said quickly. "Am I hurting you? Pinching somewhere?" He began to lift himself off her.

"No!" she cried. "Don't move." She yanked him back down over her and held him fast. Ghost or no ghost, she was naked and not taking any chances.

Jack nuzzled her neck and said, "Hey, love—these things aren't reusable, you know."

"Don't be silly," she said, distracted. "My husband could be back in business in two minutes when he wanted to."

"Not *that* thing," Jack said with a chuckle. "The condom. Unless . . . do you want me to run out to the drugstore—?"

"No! Stay right over me!"

"That's an odd way to put it, but—"

"Oh, God—I must be going crazy. I *have* gone crazy."

In the meantime Jack's great-great-grandfather, younger than Jack and just as handsome, had turned his attention back to his canvas and was laying down a brushstroke or two. He seemed to have settled in nicely. God only knew what he was painting.

Liz, utterly paralyzed by this turn of events, stared at the apparition in wide-eyed horror.

"My God, Liz—what's wrong?" Jack said, swiveling his head to see what she was seeing.

"Never mind, never mind!" she said, turning him to face her. "*Nothing's* wrong. I—I remembered something, that's all. I left the sink on. I mean, the stove."

Jack untangled her hand from his hair and began lifting himself off her. "We didn't use the stove. But I'll check—"

She grabbed his arm. "No! Dammit! Why won't you stay where you're told?"

He stared coolly at her hand gripping his arm, then gave her a level look. "Aren't you mixing me up with your five-year-old?"

"No, I'm sorry, never mind, yes, check the stove, please, yes, while I—well! Will you just go *away*?" she demanded, turning her attention back to the apparition.

Jack practically leaped out of the bed, which made her say, "Please, please don't go."

"Liz, for chrissake—this isn't funny! What's wrong with you?"

I knew it. I knew it. He thinks I'm Glenn Close.

"Absolutely nothing's wrong with me. This is *not* a Fatal Attraction. Get *out* of here!" she said, interrupting herself to yell at the artist.

Christopher Eastman was frowning thoughtfully as he glanced first at her, then at his canvas, apparently checking the likeness. Then he stuck the end of the paintbrush in his mouth, switched a small spatula from his palette hand to his right, and began blending two blobs of paint together on the flat surface. He seemed thoroughly unbothered by the chaos he was creating, perfectly content to be part of the weird ménage à trois.

Very gently, Jack said, "You know what I think? I think a nice cup of tea—"

"Oh, right!" said Liz, furious that the apparition wouldn't evaporate the way it had the other times. "As if a cup of tea can bring an end to this—this *nonsense*," she said, waving her arms in the direction of the easel.

Exasperated, Jack said with a dark look, "Do you want me out of here or not, goddammit?"

She was forced to divide her attention between Jack and the apparition. "No, no, it's not you, Jack, really," she said as her glance darted from man to ghost and back again. "You're just an innocent bystander—"

"Thank you very much," he said, unflattered.

"I mean, it's not your fault that you happened to be here right now—"

"I'd like to think I had *something* to do with it," he said, offended now. "What're you, the spider woman?"

"Stop miscontruing what I say!" she snapped. "All right. There is a connection: you're an Eastman, which—no, no," she said, after considering it. "That has nothing to do with it. I bought the house and found the box, and you had nothing to do with that. I was right the first time. You're irrelevant."

"Jesus," he said, watching her mind play Ping-Pong with itself.

"I'm sorry," she repeated, completely wrung out at this point. "The stove—?"

"Right," said Jack, unable to keep wary hostility out of his voice. "I'll check on it."

He pulled on his khakis and, with a puzzled glance at the

shuttered windows, walked out of the bedroom. They both understood that Liz had totally lost it; that she needed time to put herself back together again.

Not a chance, she thought. *Not if I had all the king's horses and all the king's men.*

She jumped out of bed and yanked the white quilt off it, wrapping the spread around herself and muttering, "This is what happens when you go too long without sex. The hormones overflow and go straight to your brain."

She turned, ready to do battle with the phantom interloper.

But there was nothing in front of the shuttered windows. No artist, no easel, no nothing. No snotty smile, no fierce look of concentration. Liz had a radarlike ability to pick up arrogance in a room. There was none there now.

Clutching the quilt at her breast with one hand, she sliced through the air with the other, feeling for—she didn't know what. Some kind of ghastly coldness, maybe. She listened for the chime-sound, but the room was silent. *Definitely gone,* she decided, relieved.

She staggered weak-kneed to the bed and collapsed on the edge of it, then pulled her longish cotton top over her head, wearing it like a nightshirt. *You've got to tell Jack what you've been seeing,* she decided. *If he walks, he walks.* Heck, after this fiasco, he'd walk if she *didn't* tell him.

What a bizarre form of misery. It was one thing to chat casually about haunted estates; but to have a haunting in the middle of sex, ending with the man you love backing away from you with a fearful look on his face—well, that had to stop.

She buried her head in her hands at the mortifying recollection of what she must have looked like, flailing her arms and screaming at walls. She stayed that way a long time, with one thought uppermost: *How did I ever get* into *this mess?*

She never heard Jack—barefoot, of course—walk up the

steps. He simply appeared in the room as magically as his great-great-grandfather had done moments earlier. In his hands Jack cradled a cup of tea.

"For you," he said, offering Liz a flower-bedecked china cup. It was her prettiest one, and for some reason it made the tears that had been hanging back come rolling out.

"Hey," he said in gentle alarm as he sat on the bed beside her, "I didn't think the sex was *that* bad."

She smiled, despite her pain and embarrassment, and said, "I don't suppose there's any way in hell—on earth, I mean—that you saw him."

" 'Him.' " Jack pressed his lips together thoughtfully, then made a tisking sound of regret. "No, I would have to say not."

Liz nodded and sipped from her tea, searching for a discreet way to explain what had happened.

Another sip.

And another.

"Okay, here's the problem," she blurted at last. "Christopher Eastman keeps appearing to me, and I don't know how to get rid of him. As you were able to tell," she added dryly, "yelling doesn't work."

Jack opened his mouth to say something, but nothing came out.

She waited.

"My great-great-*grandfather*? You, ah, saw him?"

"Yep."

He fluttered his hand toward the windows. "Over there?"

"Uh-huh."

"So you're saying, what, that you saw him. In this room. While we were—hmm. Let me ask you *this*," he said, weighing his words. "When—exactly?—did he appear?"

She chewed on her lower lip. "I can't say *exactly*. Naturally I didn't open my eyes and look around until, well, we were through," she added, coloring. "Naturally."

"*Oh* boy. Oh boy oh boy . . . *oh* boy." Jack dropped his gaze and began rubbing his middle finger back and forth across his forehead. Without looking at Liz, he said, "You've seen him before, I take it?"

Relieved to be knocking down at least one barrier of secrecy between them, Liz ticked off the occasions: "I saw him by the longcase clock in your hall the first time I was at East Gate. I saw him on the afterdeck of the *Déjà Vu,* the day I came to the shipyard to discuss the picnic. I saw him last night, right here—I think. And of course, just now."

She smiled and added wanly, "But that's really all."

"Oh, good," Jack said. "Just so long as he's not a nuisance."

Unable to sit still any longer, Jack got up and began to pace. There was nowhere to pace, of course, so he stopped and leaned against the wall; something about him reminded her of the artist, lounging by the clock.

"And what makes you think this apparition is Christopher Eastman?"

She shrugged. "Well, the way you're holding up that wall, for one thing. He does it just like you."

Taking that for flippancy, Jack gave her a sharp look. She added quickly, "But besides that, there are the letters written by Victoria St. Onge. Some of them refer directly to him."

"You never told me that."

"You never asked."

"How the hell—!"

He brought himself back under control and said with a lawyer's precision, "I'm asking you now. What exactly did you learn about Christopher Eastman . . . in the cache of letters . . . you found in the trunk . . . in your attic . . . shortly after you purchased this house?"

Liz put aside her teacup and folded her hands in her lap, like someone in a courtroom witness box. Alas, she was partly naked; but she felt sure that Jack wasn't aware of it. He was completely focused on hearing her answer.

As clearly as she could, Liz recounted the bits and pieces about Christopher Eastman that she and Victoria had gleaned from Victoria St. Onge's lifetime of ramblings.

Beginning with the artist's dashing appearance at the Black and White Ball (where Mercy St. Onge had fallen so hard for him), Liz went on to recount the story of his confrontation with Victoria St. Onge in the studio that used to exist where Liz's house now stood. Liz told Jack why his great-great-grandfather had thrown Victoria St. Onge out of his workplace: because the psychic had been snooping at some paintings he'd made of a beautiful auburn-haired nude who turned out to be a servant named Ophelia.

Jack said nothing, but a dark flush passed over his cheeks. Liz interpreted the look to mean, "Like great-great-grandfather, like great-great-grandson."

She went on to explain how at another date Victoria St. Onge, peeping through a folding screen in the dining hall at East Gate, had watched as Christopher Eastman replaced a place card at his mother's grandly set dinner table with one that had Ophelia's name on it, and then stuck a small heart-shaped pin in Ophelia's sand bucket instead of a gemstone favor like everyone else got.

Jack, arms folded across his bare chest, had been staring at the little rag rug as Liz went through her paces. At the mention of the pin, he jerked his head up.

"That's all she said? A heart-shaped pin?"

Damn. He must've remembered the pin from the painting of Christopher's mother Lavinia in his entry hall.

Liz had no desire to ruin Victoria's cosmic scheme to return the pin and redeem herself with the powers that be, so she answered Jack's question as narrowly as she could. After all, Jack didn't know that she'd found the pin in the red-lacquered box.

"Victoria St. Onge only wrote that the pin had a small garnet in it and that it wasn't worth very much."

Jack frowned and went back to studying the rag rug. "I see. Go on."

Liz said, "After Christopher left the dining room, Victoria St. Onge switched the small gemstone party favor in her own sand bucket with the heart-shaped pin in Ophelia's bucket."

"What? Why? She said herself it wasn't worth much."

Liz shrugged vaguely and said, "She had a history of doing stuff like that—taking things out of spite. She admitted that she wanted to get back at Christopher for embarrassing her in front of her friends. I think she was also a bit of a kleptomaniac. Often she had no idea why she stole something."

"This woman sounds damned unpleasant. Why the hell did your friend Tori assume *her* identity? Surely there were other ones available," Jack said, not bothering to hide his disbelief.

"It's a long story," Liz said wearily. "Let me tell it to you some other time." The night was catching up with her. She wanted desperately to sleep, to be done with this waking dream turned nightmare.

But no. Jack wasn't finished with her yet. "What else do you know," he said quietly, "about this Ophelia?"

This Ophelia. Fairly or not, Liz heard condescension in Jack's voice, and she resented it.

"Two days after that dinner party, Christopher's older brother was killed in a riding accident," she said. "Your wild artist-ancestor was forced to grow up overnight and take control of the family empire. His love affair with Ophelia was put aside. As you know, eventually he married Brunhilde. Did Brunhilde bring a minor fiefdom to the union? I often wonder."

Ignoring her sarcasm, he stayed focused on the story. "Where does Victoria St. Onge fit in?"

Liz shrugged and took a swallow of her tea. "She felt that by interfering in Christopher's party plans, she'd manipulated his destiny. She was a spiritualist, don't forget. She dabbled."

"Okay, fair enough," he allowed "But where do *you* fit in? Why is Christopher Eastman appearing to you and not, say, me?"

Was he being sarcastic? This time she couldn't tell.

Liz wasn't ready to confess that she was Ophelia's great-great-granddaughter, and so she simply said, "I'm the one who found the letters."

"Yes, you did find them, didn't you?" said Jack, obviously seizing on a new line of reasoning. "And they sound like damned lively reading."

"Some of it."

"With lots of detail. Sure. It makes sense. You're a creative, imaginative woman, Liz. How hard could it be for you to conjure up the ghost of Christopher Eastman on the basis of those letters?"

She let out a caustic laugh. "*There's* a left-handed compliment if I ever heard one. Anyway, don't you think I've thought of that possibility? But I saw Christopher Eastman by your grandfather clock before I read a single letter. It's true that Tori had discovered them and was reading through them at the very moment I saw him—but unless she and I shared the information telepathically, I don't see how I could have conjured up an artist—"

"How could you tell he was an artist, anyway?"

Liz described the stained, loose-fitting shirt he wore: how at first she thought the stains were blood but later realized that the shirt was a smock and the smears were paint.

Jack wasn't convinced. He went up to the windows, threw open the painted shutters, and stared out at the harbor, working through the problem. "You were in the grand entry hall of an old dark house with a Gothic interior," he mused, thinking aloud. "You were *ready* to see a ghost. The ghost of choice is of a murderer; everyone knows that. So you saw blood; you inferred evil."

He turned around to Liz with a look of obvious relief on his face. "Later, when you found out about Christopher Eastman and that he was artist, you tweaked your vision to fit the new information. Your so-called ghost wasn't a murderer at all; he was an artist. Simple!"

"Simple! *You're* the one who's simple!" she said, exploding. "Do you think I *like* believing what I'm seeing, Jack? I'm telling you: Christopher Eastman *exists*! In some way, in some form, for some reason! There are two many facts, too many coincidences—*dammit*!"

She slammed her teacup on the nightstand, spilling tea on the appliquéd linen, then stood up and stepped into her skirt, still lying like a nest on the rag rug. As far as she was concerned, this party was *over*.

Jack let out an exasperated curse and said, "Don't you get it? Don't you see that I'm trying to come up with a plausible theory to prove that—"

"I'm not crazy? Forget it, Jack," she said, her cheeks hot with anger. "That ship has *sailed*."

She fumbled with the hooks and eyes on the skirt with no success whatever, then was forced to go through the minor humiliation of stepping back out of the skirt, walking over to the bureau, opening a drawer, taking out a pair of shorts, and slipping into them instead. All of this was done in stony silence in a room too small to contain two people in love, much less two people at war.

When she was finished, she picked up Jack's discarded clothes and handed them to him.

"What're these?" he said, snorting. "My marching orders?"

She didn't know. She honestly didn't know. All she knew

was that Susy was in Disney World and that they were blowing the best damned opportunity she'd had in five years.

"Is the fund-raiser still on?" she asked, ignoring his question for one of her own.

He looked bewildered by her detour. "Of course it's on," he said, pulling the T-shirt over his head. "The fund-raiser is *business*. This is—"

"Pleasure?" she said sorrowfully. "I don't think so."

Something in her tone of voice made his anger melt visibly. "Okay, what we're doing *now* isn't much fun," he said, taking her in his arms. "But we can deal with this, Elizabeth. Truly. You're not the first impressionable person who's seen something she can't explain," he said softly into her ear. "The good news is, there's no logical reason for Christopher Eastman to be appearing to you."

He pulled his head back and looked down at her, anticipating her next crack. "Or is that the bad news?"

Liz sighed and said, "Neither. It's just not true. There *is* a logical reason for him to be appearing to me."

She hadn't wanted to tell him about Ophelia, but now she saw she had no choice. Her credibility—such as it was— was on the line. She led him silently downstairs where the oil portrait of Ophelia Ryan Pinhel stood leaning against the side of the sofa.

"I haven't figured out where to hang it yet," Liz said, handing him the ornately framed painting.

Jack accepted it with a puzzled look that disappeared at once when he saw the portrait. "This was painted by Christopher Eastman," he said quietly. "Ophelia?"

"Yes. She was my great-great-grandmother."

"My God."

Obviously stunned, he seemed to take refuge in the portrait, studying it closely as he gathered his thoughts. "You're nothing alike," he said at last.

He was the expert, she thought, blushing at the memory

of their lovemaking; he ought to know. "Ophelia was pure
Irish. I have more Portuguese blood than I do Irish."

"Where did you get the painting?"

"It came down through my family and ended up in my
parents' attic. I remember it from when I was a child. It was
the first racy picture I'd ever seen."

Jack smiled at that, then returned to an examination of the
reclining nude swathed in a paisley shawl. Liz could see that
he was practically willing it to speak to him. He seemed to
be racking his memory for mentions of Ophelia in the family
history, but it was clear that he was coming up dry.

"So tell me about this Ophelia."

This Ophelia. Again!

"Her affair with Christopher Eastman caused a great scandal in my family. After he abandoned her," Liz said, choosing the brutal verb deliberately, "a Portuguese shoemaker
named Pinhel took pity on her and made an honest woman
of her. We think."

"God in heaven," Jack muttered. He let out a short, bleak
laugh of disgust. "History repeats itself."

Liz was thinking of her ex-husband: of the note he left on
the kitchen table; of his flight from commitment. "I'm perfectly aware that history repeats itself," she said coldly.
"You don't have to remind me of it."

Jack looked up, puzzled. Then it dawned on him that they
were on different wavelengths. Coloring, he said, "I was
talking about myself, Liz. And my father. And his father.
And now Christopher Eastman. About our amazing inability
to stick with one woman. The Eastman curse," he said, more
to himself than to her.

"Curse? What curse? You sound like a vampire," Liz said
impatiently as she took the painting back. "I've got news
for you, Jack: That particular men's club has a very large
membership."

She laid the painting up against the side of the sofa, sorry that she'd let her bitterness show. He was who he was. They all were.

When she turned around, more composed now, Jack said gently, "This is a painful subject—for each of us. Why don't we put it aside for now?"

"True," she said, her voice catching in her throat. "We have so many other painful things we can talk about."

"Stop, Liz. Painful or not, they need to be talked about. What we need now is—"

"Some space. Please, Jack. I need to be by myself. For now, anyway." She looked at him with tense, pleading eyes.

"I understand."

Liz wondered if he was thinking, *Hell, I don't have a condom anyway.* She was appalled by her own cynicism; it was getting worse, not better.

Jack touched his fingertips to her lips, still puffy from their lovemaking, and smiled an almost unbearably kind smile. "You'll be all right here alone?"

"For sure," she said in a carefree lie. It was an impossible situation: She couldn't sleep with him, she wouldn't sleep without him. But she looked at the clock and feigned a yawn, trying to make it easy for him to leave. "Ten-thirty. Where does the time go?"

They walked to the door together, carefully avoiding the subject of his people and hers, and discussed the fund-raiser instead. They decided that it would be Liz who would approach the executive director of Anne's Place; Jack would be available by phone if needed. It was all very businesslike, all very free of emotion. It set the tone for his farewell at the threshold.

"Good night, Elizabeth," he said as she stood inside with her hand on the doorknob. He turned to go, then suddenly turned back and gave her a fleeting, almost furtive kiss. "Good night."

After that, Liz showered, then went to bed, utterly exhausted, unable to think, unable, almost, to feel. She was dropping off to sleep when a forgotten sensation slid like a snake through the clutter of her thoughts: she remembered that when she and Jack were saying good night, she'd had the distinct and entirely creepy sense that there was someone in the shadows, watching them.

Chapter 18

◆

*L*iz rose at dawn. She was restless, almost punchy, from the events of the day before. There was much to plan, much to think about. And she wanted to do it on Cliff Walk, with the sound of the ocean in her ears and the taste of salt on her lips.

Cliff Walk—a thin asphalt path between the mansions and the ocean, scarred and battered by countless storms and hurricanes—was so much a part of her life that Liz scarcely thought about it, any more than she thought about the air in her lungs or the blood in her veins.

Liz was a Newporter, and Cliff Walk belonged to Newporters—*all* Newporters. Centuries of trekking along the rocky cliffs had made the path theirs, never mind what the deeds to the mansions said. (Every once in a while over the last century or so, some mansion owner would try a little funny business by extending his fence across the path, sparking a hue and cry second only to the Boston Tea Party. The rich got away with a lot in Newport, but not with highway robbery.)

Liz walked along the path almost alone, every one of her senses alive to the profound beauty of the place. A robin pierced the air with its absurdly upbeat call of *cheer-up-cheerily,* while the sea—older, wiser, sadder—answered with a slow, mournful sigh as it ebbed and flowed over the rocky shore below. To the north of her, half a dozen sea gulls wheeled and darted in a midair brawl over a half-eaten fish.

Through a break in the brush growing along a stretch of chain-link fence, Liz was startled to see a fox standing bold and alert in the middle of a mansion's lawn.

Lucky you, she thought. *A hundred years ago they would've hunted you down here for fun.*

The fox became aware of her. With a flick of his red bushy tail, he trotted off.

How did he pick up my scent over the rugosa? she wondered. The smell of the bright pink blossoms was intense, driving out even the briny tang of the sea.

She walked on, leaving the fox, the roses, the sea gulls behind, wishing she wasn't walking alone.

Did Jack ever stroll on Cliff Walk? Probably not. Why would he, when he could be invited to any one of the estates and gaze at the sea from a higher vantage? No, Cliff Walk was strictly for the hoi polloi like her.

She came to the legendary Forty Steps, recently restored after a generation of neglect, and stopped to peer over the low stone wall at the forty granite slabs that led to the rocky shore below. In the old days, she knew, the spot was a popular rendezvous for the lower-tier servants of the nearby mansions. Vanderbilt maids and Astor footmen once dallied and danced to concertinas here in their rare free time.

Ophelia Ryan had no doubt dallied and danced here, too.

Why hadn't she married some nice young footman, or maybe a valet? What was the point of setting her sights on Christopher Eastman? Liz thought about her own kindred stupidity and smiled wryly. *History repeats itself,* Jack had said. And by golly if he wasn't right.

Her heart was so full. Her emotions seemed to be equal parts of pain and happiness; they weighed so heavily on her that there was no room for the strange unease she'd felt, the night before, of being watched and in danger. On a bright new morning she found it impossible to feel anything like fear.

She only had room for love. She missed Susy terribly; she longed for Jack even more. And Christopher Eastman? Ghost or fantasy, he'd become as much a part of her life as Susy and now Jack. What did he want? What did he need? If only she knew, she could take care of it and set his soul free.

"If you don't tell me, Christopher," she said, staring at the swirling sea below, "how can I help you?"

She sighed, and shook her head, and straightened up to go. When she turned, there he was, leaning against the sea wall not ten feet away from her. This time she was hardly surprised.

He was nattily dressed in a blue, almost black flannel blazer that was topped off with a straw boater banded in crimson and gold. His arms were folded across his chest in a manner she knew well; his foot was braced against the granite wall. It was a casual pose, elegantly struck. He looked exactly like what he was: the well-born son of American aristocrats.

She stared at him, wishing desperately that he could speak—willing him, with all her soul, to say something.

"Good morning," he said pleasantly. "Do you come here often?"

Liz gasped and jumped back, struck dumb by his fluency. She waited, wide-eyed, for the apparition to speak again; but he seemed to be expecting her to respond to his opener.

After a fearful hesitation, she decided to answer him.

"Gee, I knew that w-was an old line," she stammered, "b-but I didn't think it was *that* old."

"I beg your pardon?" he said, not getting it at all.

"Wh-what you said about coming here often: it sounded like a come-on."

"Come on? Are we going somewhere?"

"No, no—never mind," she croaked. She glanced up and

then down the path—no one around, thank God—then turned back to the apparition and cleared her throat, still searching for her normal voice. "I'm . . . I'm having trouble . . . seeing your face," she said, squinting at him more closely now.

"It could be the hat," he said. He took it off and flung it like a Frisbee into the air over the ocean below; she followed its path, then lost it in the sun.

"Is this better?" he asked, turning back to face her.

She shook her head. "You've always been clearer than this."

"Conversing with you takes a great deal of energy."

"I like to think I'm easy to talk to!" she said, a little offended.

He seemed to smile. "I mean to say, I have a limited amount of energy with which to manifest myself. I can appear to you, or I can speak to you. If I do both at once, the quality of each suffers."

In fact, his voice was faint.

"Tell me . . . please . . . why haven't you spoken to me before now?" she begged to know.

Christopher Eastman seemed amused by the question. She couldn't really tell, because he was becoming hazier, which she blamed at least partly on the sun shining behind him— or through him.

"There are rules of conduct," he said. "We do not speak unless we're asked to."

"We? There are more of you?"

"Oh, yes."

Oh, great. "Will I be seeing them, too?"

"I cannot imagine why. Your concern is with me."

As she thought. "It was the lacquered box, wasn't it? You got out when I opened it in the locksmith's shop."

"If you prefer to believe that, by all means do," he said. "But the truth is hardly as picturesque."

"Tell me the truth, then," she begged in a whisper.

"The truth, my dear lady, is that you are in danger of committing the same fatal mistake in your affair of the heart as I did."

"You mean, of falling in love with someone I have nothing in common with—with whom I have nothing in common . . . with?" she said in confusion.

His laugh sounded sad and empty. "No, I mean the opposite. I mean this: You love Jack Eastman, and you hope that he loves you; yet you are unwilling to believe that a match between you can thrive."

"Aren't you putting the cart before the horse?" she asked, her natural skepticism reasserting itself. "Your great-great-grandson seems in no hurry to marry."

"He will be," Christopher Eastman said. "Jack is of an age when a man begins to recognize a void in his life. He longs for something more, something deeper. . . . Ah, well. You will have to accept the declaration on faith. You're a woman, after all; you cannot be expected to understand."

"I see," Liz said, her feminine hackles rising up. "It's one of those guy-things, is it?"

"I beg your pardon?"

"Never mind. Anyway, even supposing he does love me and may someday be willing to marry me—even supposing all that, which I do not—the match could hardly thrive. I don't know how much you know about modern marriage, but one out of two of them ends in divorce."

"Ah. I was not aware of that."

"You should have done your homework, then," she said with some asperity. "Before you went scaring people out of their wits."

"I *have* done what you call my home-work," he shot back. "I know that barriers between men and women that were insurmountable a hundred years ago no longer exist. Anyone, I see, can marry anyone these days."

"Yeah, well, maybe that's why one in two ends in divorce," Liz cracked.

Out of the corner of her eye, she saw an early morning jogger approaching them on the path. In a panic she turned her back on the ghost, reasoning that if she couldn't see Christopher Eastman, maybe the jogger wouldn't notice him either.

As it turned out, the jogger didn't see either one of them; he just shot on by, totally focused on his pain.

"Should you not set the police on that fellow?" asked Christopher, alarmed.

"Good lord, why?" asked Liz. "For exercising?"

"Exercising what?"

"His muscles. What else?"

"He puts himself in a lather for no practical purpose? He is not delivering an urgent message, or flying to his mother's deathbed? He's doing that for . . . ?" He was at a loss for words.

"For *tone,*" said Liz. "Never mind. How—what—oh God—where do I start?" Frustrated, she buried her face in her hands, trying to center her thoughts, then looked up.

Still there. But for how long?

"Why didn't you marry Ophelia?" It was the question that burned the hottest in her mind.

Christopher bowed his head in an eloquent expression of regret. For a long time he said nothing. When he looked up, Liz was surprised to see that he had become more real, as if she'd finally gotten him tuned in, somehow. His face, so clear, so handsome, was the picture of pain.

"I *wanted* to marry Ophelia," he said. "I loved no other woman, ever, besides her. But two things happened—one of them trivial, the other significant."

Liz said softly, "Someone took the pin. And your brother was killed."

"Yes. Of course you know all that. My plan to announce

our betrothal—thwarted the first time by that meddlesome, disagreeable St. Onge woman—became postponed again in the grief and chaos that resulted from my brother's sudden death.''

'' 'Postponed'? I *guess* it became postponed. For eternity, as far as I can tell,'' Liz said before she could stop herself.

He averted his face, as if she'd slapped it.

"I begged Ophelia to be patient," he said, obviously in agony after the brutal reminder. "She would not. I needed only a few months to put my family's affairs back on course. My father was ailing, my brother gone; there was no one else.''

He turned away from Liz to look at the sea. "It took me a long time to understand that Ophelia was dismayed by my priorities. Who can blame her? Overnight, I had turned into a dutiful son and become a faithless lover.''

He added bitterly, "I did my job well. But without Ophelia the Eastman fortune became nothing more than cold, cruel comfort.''

Liz said to him, amazed, "Is it possible you don't know? Ophelia never told you she was *pregnant* by you?''

Christopher turned back sharply, then went very still. Clearly he did not know. Liz had no idea what the risks were for revealing secrets to long-departed souls, but she'd just taken a huge one. She watched, trembling, as a hundred years of regret fused into a single moment of horror.

"This cannot be true!" Christopher said angrily—and the sea itself seemed to rise up in indignation. Suddenly it sounded louder, closer. Unconsciously, Liz stepped away from the sea wall.

It was impossible for her to see Christopher Eastman's face, to understand what was happening to him. He seemed to pulsate and shimmer in place, a concentration of energy unlike anything she'd ever known. She looked away—it was too much like looking at the sun—but then she was compelled to look back at him, despite her terror. The hair on her skin stood up, and it was suddenly harder to breathe. She began shivering violently. Nothing in her life had prepared her for this. She had to bite her lip to keep herself from whimpering; to hug herself, to reassure herself of her own physicality. She was afraid to stay, unable to go.

"God in heaven!" he cried in anguish. "I see it now! She was too proud to throw her condition in my face; if I would not marry her for herself, she had no use for me. Ah, that pride of hers! That overbearing, self-destructive pride! It made her refuse to play the trump card that all women possess."

Not all of us, thought Liz, flinching.

"She tested me, and I failed the test utterly! Ophelia!" He turned away from Liz toward the sea and threw his head back. "Oh, *God* . . . Ophelia," he said in a broken voice.

His pain ripped through Liz like a blade. Ignorant of ghostly conventions, she had no idea how to console him. She could only try in human ways, on human terms.

"Please—please don't do this to yourself," she begged him. "If it's any comfort to you, I can tell you that Ophelia was cared for by a good man—a shoemaker in town, Anton Pinhel. I've been to see her grave. She lived a long life."

"Without me, without me," Christopher moaned. "And I without her. What *waste*. What *pain*."

"I'm so sorry," said Liz awkwardly. "Maybe I shouldn't have told you any of this. I—I can't believe you didn't know."

"She married very quickly," he said dully. "I assumed it was to hurt me. Whatever the reason, it would have been dishonorable to pursue her after that."

"Excuse me," Liz dared to say. "But . . . from what I've read in the letters, you were a bit of a—"

"Not with married women!" he flashed. "Never, with a married woman!"

He reminded her, just then, of Jack: a man who'd devised a strict moral code of his own and who didn't give much of a damn what society had to say about it.

"Can I—can I ask you something?" she ventured.

"Ask," he said in a flat, dead voice. He was standing against the sea wall, arms limp at his side, head bowed in sorrow. He was hard to see, harder to hear. Whatever he'd just gone through, it had consumed him.

"How does that work? I mean, don't you learn all the answers to things after you—?"

"Pass on?" he said, using the grim euphemism.

Liz winced and said, "Yes. After you die. Shouldn't you be able to look all this up somewhere?"

"I see. You assume that there is a City Hall in Heaven, is that it?" he said with a flash of Jack's wryness.

"Is that so very funny?" Liz asked. "I should think that enlightenment is the least we can expect for giving up everything we have on earth. We ought to be able to know exactly where we screwed up—failed, I mean—and where we did well."

"Some may have been given that satisfaction," he said quietly. "I was not. I know what I knew on earth, just enough to get me started on this mission. Which, I may say, you are not making any easier," he said, annoyance creeping into his manner.

He folded his arms across his chest in a way that, again, reminded Liz of Jack. "Are you as contentious with Jack as you are with me?" he asked. "You remind me more than a little of—" He laughed softly and finished his thought. "Of Ophelia. Of course you would. You have her blood in you."

"Obviously. She was my great-great-grandmother just as—"

"—I am your great-great-grandfather!" he cried, as it dawned on him for the first time. A look of utter amazement seemed to pass over the hazy features of his face as he considered Liz in this new light.

"*There* is your answer as to why I stand before you!" he said, astonished. "You are *my* flesh and blood as well as Ophelia's. You are the product, however distant, of a love so . . . so . . ."

The memory of that love seemed to bring home to him, again, how carelessly he'd thrown it all away. He seemed unable to trust himself to speak for a while.

Then he said, in the softest, most melancholy voice, "I wish I knew where she is now."

Trying to comfort him, Liz splayed one hand over the other on her breast. "Here, Christopher. Ophelia is here. At least you know that."

For one brief second he came into crisp focus for her. She saw his face as clearly as she'd seen Jack's the night before. He was not Jack: his chin was less square, his eyes a much paler blue. His hair was browner, finer, the sideburns thick, as the fashion dictated. But there was Eastman in him, and Liz responded to it in a way so complex, so unfathomable, that it made her heart hurt.

He said nothing, only continued to stare at her, as if he'd just seen her for the first time.

Liz felt the blood rush up as she said, "We should have had this talk several apparitions ago."

He smiled bleakly and shrugged. "Last night I did everything I could to provoke you. I was waiting for you to say, just once, 'What are you doing here?' "

"And instead I just ranted. I remember it well. But at least now that's all behind us. We simply have to agree to a system for communicating that's—"

Behind her, she heard voices on the path; they were raised in anger, and one of them she knew as well as her own.

"Judy Maroney is *dead,* Ben! She died in a car crash with her husband and two children! Accept it!"

Liz swung around and saw Victoria racing ahead of her Dr. Ben, gesturing vehemently with her hands. Victoria was in a state of high agitation. She didn't see Ben, she didn't see Liz, she certainly didn't see the ghost of Christopher Eastman. She was completely intent on making her point. "I am *not* Judy Maroney. Stop trying to *make* me Judy Maroney!"

"Tori, you're being unfair!" said Ben behind her. "All I said was, I've met a psychiatrist in Boston who's extremely interested in your case."

"I am not a case!" she tossed back angrily.

"Fine! Neither are the Cambodian women with healthy eyes who became blind after watching the horrors of the Khmer Rouge! There's nothing wrong with any of you! You're all fine!"

She rounded on him. "Stop it! Stop lumping me in with clinical hysterics! Stop it!"

She burst into tears, turned, and ran away from the path toward Bellevue Avenue, leaving Ben standing alone and frustrated just a little way from where Liz had been conversing calmly with her ghost.

Liz jerked her head around: Christopher was gone. She turned back to Ben and greeted him, confident that he'd been too caught up in his own trauma to eavesdrop on hers.

"Hi," he said glumly, coming up to Liz. "Who were *you* talking to?"

Reddening, she said, "Just thinking aloud. This is a good place to do it." None of which, strictly speaking, was actually a lie.

Ben jerked his head in the direction of Victoria's flight. "I've pushed her too far again. Hell, what do *I* know?" he said remorsefully. "I repair bodies, not souls."

"Tori's not really crazy, you know," said Liz with a last glance where Christopher had been. "Any more than I am," she added. That was for Christopher's amusement, just in case he was still hanging around.

Ben, still upset by the argument, said, "I left my car at the beach. Are you going that way?"

He wanted to talk; they fell in together on the path. Ben rubbed his dark beard with a slender hand; his brown eyes settled into their usual thoughtful, slightly cynical expression.

"What a fey little creature she is," he said, hopelessly bewildered. "I remember the day they brought her into emergency. . . . She was just a bundle of broken bones—so fragile—so near death. No one thought she'd make it. And yet look at her today: leading me on this merry damned chase."

Liz smiled and said, "You two do seem meant for each other. In your own strange way."

"I love her madly," Ben confessed. "But this fixation of hers—needless to say, we can't seem to get past it."

There were quiet for a bit as they strolled along the path, and then Liz said, "I have a question for you."

She had a personal reason for asking it. "What if Victoria *never* gets over her—situation? What if she refuses to—or can't—be any different for the rest of her life? Can a man accept a woman like that completely on her terms?"

Ben thought about it. "Some men can. I can, if I have to," he said quietly. "Not that it matters," he added in a sad-sack voice. "She won't even listen to talk of marriage until she's done her fateful deed."

"Which would be—?"

"Sneaking the pin back into East Gate."

"There's a certain order? I didn't know that."

"Yeah," Ben said, plunging his hands into the pockets of his shorts. "She won't commit to me because she's afraid Victoria St. Onge may only be using Judy Maroney's body temporarily. It's something called a walk-in. After the deed is done, Victoria St. Onge supposedly returns to some plane—fifth or sixth, I don't remember," he said dryly.

"Anyway, that's where Tori's a little fuzzy. Apparently this isn't a textbook walk-in. Tori assumes that she'll return to this plane of existence, leaving, well—the remains of Judy Maroney."

"Tori thinks she may *die* if she sneaks the pin back?" said Liz, shocked.

"She's convinced Judy Maroney's already dead—or if not dead, then just a heartbeat away from it. I guess that's because Judy and Victoria haven't been communicating in the usual way for a walk-in."

He laughed a pained, skeptical laugh. "I can't believe I listened carefully enough to repeat this stuff."

"Ben—*is* she in danger? I mean, judging from what you know about cases like these. If she really returns the pin— if she really believes she's fulfilled some kind of karma—"

Ben stroked his beard nervously. "Stranger things have happened," he admitted in a hapless tone. "The mind is a powerful instrument."

"Yes," said Liz. She felt the blood drain from her face. Her mind—the small part of it that was still rational—was telling her that she was afraid. Afraid for Victoria. Afraid for herself. Afraid for all of them.

Christopher wasn't waiting for Liz when she returned home. She had to remind herself that he wasn't a homing pigeon but a form of energy: a ghost, an angel, or—for all she knew—a projection of her own theories about Ophelia and Christopher. Maybe Jack was right. After all, she'd learned virtually nothing from her encounter with Christopher on Cliff Walk that she didn't know or couldn't easily imagine.

As for the ghost's stated purpose—to make sure that she and Jack didn't blow it the way he had with Ophelia—well, that could easily be chalked up to wishful thinking on her part. When you came right down to it, what the heck was he appearing to her for, anyway? *Jack* was the one who could use a swift little kick in the psyche.

Convinced that she was as deluded as Victoria and the Cambodian women Ben spoke of, Liz changed and drove to her office. It was time, past time, to focus on the task at hand, the benefit for Anne's Place. It wasn't that hard to throw a fund-raiser. The hard part was throwing a fund-raiser that actually raised funds.

Jack had promised to come up with a stellar honorary committee, which left Liz with the task of appointing the working committees. By nine o'clock she had roughed out the working-committee list:

> *Decorations*: me
> *Entertainment*: me
> *Ticket sales*: Victoria?
> *Publicity*: me
> *Invitations*: me
> *Food*: Who?
> *Program book*:
>   Yowch.
> *Check-in*: Mom and
>   Dad?

There it was before her, in plain black and white: Elizabeth Coppersmith was in over her head. The committee for the program book alone would have to be substantial. Someone would have to be savvy enough to sell the ads, write the copy, look after the printing, and collect the money from the advertisers. The trouble was, she didn't know the someones who could do that. She simply did not move in that kind of circle.

Unless . . . ? There was always Mikey. A fellow graduate at Rogers High, Mikey was an insurance agent nowadays; Liz had bought her house insurance through him and had thrown in her car for the extra discount. Mikey could sell sand to a Sultan.

It was a start. She got out her Rolodex.

• • •

Her office phone rang as soon as it was free. Jack, sounding pleasantly frantic, said, "Godamighty, I've been trying
to call you for two and a half hours. Was your phone off the
hook?"

Liz laughed and said in an intimate voice, "You could say
that. It's been glued to my ear since I got in, and all because
of your fund-raiser."

"*Our* fund-raiser."

"Whatever. I'm pleased to report that things are moving
right along," she said in a gross exaggeration. "The director
was thrilled that you're willing to underwrite the event,
though she seemed skeptical that we could pull it off in
time."

"So she's in. Good. Make her head a committee."

"I already have: as it happens, Katherine is married to a
computer wizard who's willing to produce something smart
in an invitation and may even produce the program itself. He
has a thermal-wax printer, whatever that is."

"Great. Nor have I been idle, m'dear. I've got Meredith
Kinney to jump in and chair the honorary committee. In fact,
she's damned enthusiastic about the idea."

He was waiting, apparently, for applause. "Oh, how very
nice," said Liz. All she knew about Meredith Kinney was
what she'd read in the social column: big house, big parties.
Presumably, big guest list.

"It *is* nice," Jack said a little dryly. "She's a woman of
some standing, and if she wants people to come—they'll
come."

"Exactly what we need, then," Liz chirped, feigning enthusiasm. But would this social lioness stay out of Liz's way?

Jack dropped the subject of the honorary committee, and
they chatted awhile about the search for worker bees to staff
the real committees. After that, Jack seemed to hesitate be-

fore he said casually, "So what's new on the metaphysical front?"

Liz had absolutely no idea how—or even whether—to answer that. So she stalled by saying, "Oh, nothing that can't wait."

"Tonight, then. Same time, same place?" he said in a voice rich with meaning.

"Um . . . I guess." And if Christopher decided to crash the party again?

"Gee, I was hoping for something like enthusiasm," said Jack, disappointed.

"I *am*—it's just that—anyway, don't compare me, please. I don't like being compared."

"To what? To whom, for chrissake? All I said was—"

"I *am* enthusiastic, Jack. I just show it differently from your . . . Merediths."

"Aw, I knew it. I could hear it in your voice. Here we go again."

"No, you're misreading me," she said hurriedly. "I just— someone just walked in, that's all," she lied. "I'll see you later," she said, and rang off.

Okay, she thought. *No need to panic. Tonight can't possibly resemble last night's train wreck.* Christopher said he didn't speak unless he was spoken to. So: mum would be the word this evening. If he decided to show up and provoke her by acting goofy, well, she'd ignore him, that's all.

She could do that.

Chapter 19

◈

*H*er first date with planned sex in over a decade: Liz had forgotten what it was like to feel single and sexy. She decided that she liked it—a lot. The feeling stayed with her as she rummaged through her drawer for a bra with a little more lace and a top with a little more plunge.

The feeling went away when her parents called and she spoke to Susy, who was tired and cranky and getting more homesick by the minute.

The feeling came right back when she heard the crazy *br-r-r-ring* of her hand-cranked doorbell.

She opened the door, and there was Jack, tucked behind a huge bouquet of warm pink roses. No box, no tissue; just big cupped blooms with a heavenly fragrance.

"Bourbons, Netta tells me," Jack said, handing them over in a smiling, awkward gesture. "Watch for thorns. I don't usually go rummaging through our garden. But these looked especially fine this year."

Touched by the homeness in his gesture, Liz said, "Maybe it was our wet spring."

"Netta says it was the deer we had last year," Jack said as he came inside. "It ate the rosebuds as fast as they formed. Netta has this theory that the plants finished up the year with energy left over."

"You had a *deer* on your property? In the middle of Newport? I don't believe it," Liz said flatly. But even as she said it, she was flashing back to the first time she saw the grounds at East Gate through the barbed-wire fence: *a deer park,* she had mused, *only without the deer.* She'd been closer to the truth than she knew.

Hands in his pockets, Jack strolled into the kitchen after her, seeming to take pleasure in her pleasure at arranging the roses in a simple clear vase. "Oh, we had a deer, all right," he said, smiling at the recollection. "A beautiful young doe, all legs and ears. We figure it swam across the Bay from Jamestown or even Little Compton. It must've wandered straight up Bellevue Avenue early one morning; I doubt that it could've come up from the harbor through your dense neighborhood.

"Anyway, for three weeks we more or less stayed inside and walked around on tiptoe, praying it would leave and give us back our lives, yet hoping it would stay."

"In Newport?" Liz asked incredulously. "How could it possibly?"

"I know, I know," Jack said, sighing. "For three weeks I listened with the deer's ears to the summer noise of this city: to the the groundskeepers' machines—which never seem to stop—and to the garbage trucks, recycle trucks, fire trucks, rescue wagons, Harley-Davisons, planes buzzing the harbor, helicopters delivering VIP's; to the Fourth of July fireworks, the marauding drunks, the noisy parties, the loud music, the police sirens, the dogs barking nonstop at all of it—it was stressful to *me,* a rational human being; I can't imagine what it must've sounded like to a lost and disoriented wild animal."

Jack seemed to want to talk about the experience. In an oddly emotional voice, he said, "We all had trouble sleeping at night. We jumped at every loud noise, putting ourselves in the deer's place, wondering which corner of the property she was cowering in as she waited for each dawn; waited for peace and quiet."

Moved and distressed by his story, Liz said, "I never read about a deer in the paper."

Jack shook his head. "None of us said a word; we didn't want kids—or worse, some drunken yahoos—chasing her down."

"Couldn't you get someone to tranquilize her? To relocate her?"

"No. We called everywhere; no one was set up for it. Maybe by now they are. We were told to open our gates and leave her alone, that eventually she would make her way."

"And . . . did she?" whispered Liz, almost afraid to ask.

Jack said pensively, "One day she was gone. We never heard anything more." He shrugged off his seriousness and added, "I've convinced myself that either she's happily munching rosebuds on one of the bigger estates to the south, or she got so fed up with the summer scene here that she swam back to wherever she came from."

He went up to Liz's long kitchen windows, with their old wobbly-glassed panes, and stared out at the deer park—his deer park—that no longer had a deer in it. "I wonder," he said softly, "where she is now."

Liz jerked her head up. Something about his voice—something about the very question—reminded her . . .

Christopher, wondering about Ophelia. It shouldn't have surprised Liz, this dizzying sense of déjà vu that she seemed to experience almost daily now. The forces at play were far, far beyond the reckoning of a simple mortal like her. Did the doe have a significance that Liz couldn't understand? Or was this just another tale of a wild creature caught in a hostile world?

Liz said softly, "I've lived in Newport all my life. I think that if I ever saw a deer in my backyard, I'd feel truly blessed."

"Yeah, it was like that. I have to admit, the doe did seem at ease here, as if she'd found a sanctuary. I don't suppose there are many more beautiful experiences than watching a deer graze peacefully in a patch of sunlight.''

Jack gave Liz a self-conscious smile and said, "Funny what a void she left in our lives. Of course, it was nice to be able to have guests on the veranda again and not feel guilty if someone laughed out loud; but ..." His voice trailed off in a sigh.

"Maybe she'll come back," Liz said, profoundly hopeful.

"I still scan the thicket for her when I'm in my bathroom shaving," Jack confessed. "It's automatic. She was here for less than three weeks, and I've looked for her every day for a year. Go figure."

"Gosh," Liz said lightly. "I wish *I* could make an impression on you like that."

Jack's laugh was rueful. "Oh, lady. If only you knew."

He walked back to where she stood holding the vase of roses, took the flowers from her and placed them back on the counter, and cradled her face between his hands.

"The fact is, every morning before I scan the thicket looking for the doe, I scan the fence between us looking for you. When I see you puttering in your garden or taking out the trash, my heart does this funny little tap dance of joy." He kissed her softly on her lips. "I don't remember my heart ever tap-dancing before," he said. "Not even for the doe."

Liz's heart was doing a little jig of its own as she smiled and said, "Ah—now *you're* making an impression on *me*."

"Darling, I sincerely hope so," he said, kissing her again, and then again, a little longer ... and then again.

His small, nibbling tastes turned to wet devouring kisses that left Liz feeling wonderfully, wantonly in love. He slid his hands around her hips and pulled her toward him; her arms were around his neck, pulling him close. This is what she needed, this is what she wanted: the solid, warm, electric feel of him tight against her body. Yesterday's reticence was long gone. Tonight she wanted to be with him, under him, around him; tonight she wanted simply to be part of him.

She dragged her mouth away from his. "Upstairs . . . ," she said, gasping. "Do you . . . want . . . upstairs . . . ?"

"Do I," he said in a shaky voice. "Let me think. . . . "

His droll response made Liz laugh, a rich, sexy sound that was filled with confidence: a lover's laugh.

They went upstairs to the tiny bedroom tucked under the house's eave, and there they undressed each other with a kind of gleeful abandon, making up for all the hesitant twists and turns of the night before. Liz lay down on the bed first, expecting Jack to be right behind her.

He had one knee on the bed when he said, "Hold on," and got back out. "While I still have a smidgeon of reason left in my brain, I should—"

He plucked his pants from the pile of clothing on the floor and began groping for the back pocket.

"Hold on, yourself," said Liz. She reached lazily over to the small worktable that served as a nightstand and pulled open the top drawer: it was filled with an almost comical variety of condoms, from understated skin-toned latex to a perky glow-in-the-dark number guaranteed to scare the dickens out of anyone who wasn't a party to the proceedings.

"I didn't know what kind you liked," Liz said with an innocent smile.

Jack surprised her by putting his hands on his hips and whistling. "Wow. That's quite a commitment," he said in an odd voice.

God, she hadn't thought of it that way! She blushed and said, "You're under no obligation to stick around for them all. They were a joke."

They were also her own secret way of saying, *I love you so much that I'm going along with your farcical idea that you're saving me from pregnancy. I love you so much that I'm terrified to tell you the truth.*

Jack sat down on the bed next to her and smoothed her hair away from her face in a gesture that was as tender as it was unexpected.

"I'm sticking around," he said seriously. "But I'm not so sure about the condoms. For now, yes. But—you have to feel this, too, Liz, I know you do—they're a barrier between us. Between us and . . . and all that could be. Have you thought about it? Am I being wildly presumptuous? Am I jumping the gun?"

For one split second—no more than that—Liz saw the image of Christopher Eastman hovering next to them with a "See? Told you!" look on his face.

Liz blinked away the vision and focused on Jack with a squinty look of concentration. "You're saying . . . ?" But who could tell what he was saying? The words *baby* and *marriage* weren't part of his vocabulary. *Was* that what he was talking about? What else *could* he be talking about?

Her wildest fantasy had suddenly become her wildest nightmare.

"I—I don't understand," she said, in an effort to stall further talk about babies.

Jack smiled a sad, tight-lipped smile. "I was right, then. Too soon. Okay."

She began to protest weakly—at that moment she was both the happiest and the saddest that she'd ever been—but he said, "Shhh . . . never mind. It can wait."

He slid his hand from her shoulder, along her arm, into the dip of her waist, and out again at her hip. "Something about you," he said, still struggling to express his thoughts. "The way you look, the way you are with Susy—with all kids, really. Something about you . . . fills me with such . . . *longing*."

"Shhh," she said to Jack, mimicking his own suggestion. She shook her head and forced back a glistening of tears behind a tremulous smile. "Not today."

There *was* something about her, she knew; but it wasn't the something Jack thought he saw in her. She was no goddess of fertility, no empress for his empire. She had no qualifications at all to be his wife. All she could ever be was an inspired lover to him.

In an unbearably ironic gesture of homage, Jack bent over just then and kissed the small scar that remained from the emergency C-section she'd undergone when Susy was born. It was too much for Liz: blinking back tears was as impossible as forcing rainwater back up the downspout of her house.

Tell him, someone hiding deep inside her begged. *Tell him now.*

"Jack—"

Her breath came in shallow useless pants from the effort to unburden herself.

"Make love to me," she whispered as she felt his hand slip between her thighs. "Make love to me now."

He stayed all night. In the morning they had coffee in the kitchen and wondered about where the deer went, and whether Susy should take swimming lessons, and whatever became of the stolen letters; and then Jack walked back to East Gate to shower and change in time to catch the early tide needed to launch a deep-water boat.

After he left, Liz lingered over Cheerios. Her time with Jack had seemed so wonderfully normal. They were behaving just like any other couple in the early stages of a love affair: laughing, teasing, finding excuses to touch one another, slipping easily into everyday intimacies. She'd brushed Snowball's hairs from his navy shirt; he'd blown his nose on a paper towel and complained about being allergic to cats. She'd made his coffee strong, the way she knew he liked it; he'd remembered which drawer held the can opener for Toby's food.

Little by little, step by step, they were building a relationship. They came from different worlds and moved in different circles, but to Liz those considerations were minor details now. The truly big obstacle—not counting the ghost who kept popping in and out of her life—was the fact that Liz was misrepresenting herself.

Jack had been sending strong, almost urgent signals to her about a possible future together, and Liz had chosen to ignore them. It was too ironic for words: Ophelia had refused to tell Christopher Eastman that she was pregnant; and Liz was refusing to tell Jack Eastman that she couldn't *get* pregnant. Each woman wanted to be loved for herself.

But Liz should've come clean. She *would* come clean. The very next chance she got.

By the end of the day, Liz was punchy. Sailing through the crowded waters of late-August fund-raisers took all her wits and nerves of steel. The gala-competition for the weekend Jack wanted was fierce: two cruise party benefits, two balls, a champagne tasting, a dedication, a rededication, an antique yacht race, a visit by a tall ship, and a benefit film premiere. Add to that the usual blistering pace of noncharity parties, and Liz had to wonder who the heck in the state was left to invite.

Still, by the time Jack called her at home, she was feeling pretty good and winding down with a glass of wine while she tossed a salad big enough for two to go with the pizza she planned to order.

"Hel-*lo*," she said in warmly shy greeting at the sound of his voice. It was their third phone call that day. "I have good news, sir: I think we'll be able to get Katie's Katerers for the costume party. And Victoria tells me she knows a four-piece band that's loud and cheap."

"Not *too* loud," Jack said with a grimace in his voice. "Not if we're having the event at East Gate. I have a neighbor I'm trying to impress."

Liz laughed and said, "Anyway, what I need from you now is a proposal outlining the terms of the shipyard's sponsorship, and then I'll get the director of Anne's Place to send you a letter of confirmation on their stationery."

"Sure. It'll go off tomorrow. Meanwhile, I should be at your house in, oh, half an hour."

"I'll order the pizza for then. How's the round of meetings going?"

She knew they were important: Jack was courting a couple of venture capitalists, hoping to get them to back the manufacture of a small but seaworthy powerboat at the shipyard. It was all part of Jack's plan to hold on to the help. If he could keep the yardhands doing paying work in the off-season, he could keep the yard turning a steady profit—and his father would be less inclined to entertain offers from ambitious developers of uncertain morals.

Jack seemed to think that the talks with the investors were going well. The yard had a lot of things going for it, he told Liz, not the least of which was a location in Rhode Island, a state that was trying hard to attract the boat-building industry.

"We've got the men, and we've got the space, and we've got a generally friendly bureaucracy and a recent tax break going for us. In the meantime this dude is faxing stuff like crazy to his partner from the other office. I guess that's a good sign."

"Great. Maybe we can really celebrate tonight."

"I plan to do that," Jack said softly, "in any event."

An hour later, however, they still hadn't begun their celebration. The pizza was cold, the salad was warm, and the bottle of wine Liz had opened to breathe was about to give up the ghost.

And speaking of ghosts, Liz thought, petulant now, *where the hell is he?* When things were going well, there he was, making a pest of himself. But now, when she could use a little divine intervention . . .

"Christopher?" she said aloud, feeling foolish. He'd told her he didn't speak unless he was asked to. Maybe the same held true for simply showing up.

She waited. "Fine," she said at last when no one appeared. "Two peas in a pod." This was what happened when you began to count on someone. When you allowed yourself to look forward to things. When you . . .

In a fit of pique she took the pizza box—still with the pizza in it—and folded it over in two.

Which of course was when the phone rang.

It was Jack, repentant. "We got into a conference call with the partner, and I couldn't break away to call you," he said.

"I understand."

"I'll be there as soon as I can. Hopefully in about an hour. Maybe a little more."

"I understand."

"Liz—this is a good development. A *great* development," he said in a confidential voice, obviously not wishing to be overheard. "I think they're gonna go for it."

"Jack, really, I'm delighted for you. Honest. It's just that—" It was just that she had only one more free night before Susy would be back. But how could Jack possibly understand? *All* his nights were free. "It's just that I miss you, that's all. And I'm being a dope. And I'm sorry."

"Wait up for me. Please. There's no one in the world I'd rather share this with than you. No one."

"I'll wait," she said in a startled, pleased voice. "Of course I'll wait."

"And if for some reason I'm held up—say, to get something down on paper—"

"I'll leave the key under the back-door mat."

"Not under the mat! That's the first place they look!"

She laughed. "Okay, in the bird feeder, then. But I'll be up, Jack," she said reassuringly. "Count on it."

By eleven o'clock and despite a shower, Liz couldn't keep her eyes open. She was like Susy on New Year's Eve: the spirit was willing, but the flesh was sleepy. The TV sounded unbearably loud to her, and the lights hurt her eyes. She put the key in the bird feeder, locked up, turned everything off, and curled up on the down-filled sofa to catnap until Jack came in.

It's the stupid wine, she told herself. The euphoria part never lasted as long as the tired part. *What a dumb aphrodisiac.*

She meant only to rest her eyes. But the night was cool—one of those July cold fronts had whizzed through that evening—and it was perfect for sound sleeping. In a few minutes she dropped off into deep, untroubled slumber, the kind that usually left her refreshed and raring to go.

If only this had been one of those times.

Chapter 20

◆

*W*hen Liz woke up, it was by force: a hand—rough, foul-smelling, horrific in its strangeness—was clamped over her mouth.

"One word and you die," a voice growled in her ear.

His breath stank: drink, rot, tobacco, she couldn't begin to guess what else. She'd been dropped into some pit of hell. Her mind shut down completely except for one thought— *does he have a gun, a knife, a gun, a knife*—playing over and over.

All of this took no more than a second.

"Where are they? Where the *fuck* are they now?"

Her eyes were wide open. The streetlight outside filtered through the shutters, throwing him into dim relief. He was a tall man, and not a young one. His hand, gross and filthy, still held her pinned to the sofa, leaving her unable to speak. She shook her head, trying to convey that to him.

He misinterpreted her. Lifting his hand away, he brought it back down in a vicious swing. Liz averted her face, but he caught the side of her jaw. She let out a stifled cry of pain—if she screamed, she was sure he *would* kill her—and tried to rally her senses.

"Where's what?" she said desperately. "You mean the—"

"—*letters*, bitch. The shoeboxes."

"Upstairs . . . I hid them."

He stood up, grabbed her wrist, and grunting like an animal, yanked her upright. "Let's go."

This isn't happening . . . this can't be happening. . . .

The one place she didn't want to go was into her bedroom. Not with him. *Stall,* she told herself. *Jack will be here. Jack will be here.*

"You can have them—all of them," she said as she stumbled over her own furniture toward the stairs. "But please—please don't hurt me."

"Shut up!" he said, grabbing her by the back of the neck and forcing her forward.

Something about his action triggered resistance in her. It was repugnant, an act of domination; he was treating her like a dog or a cat. Involuntarily she began digging in her heels. She was thinking of the women in the shelter, the ones who became all quiet and meek and got beaten up anyway.

She twisted her head back toward him. "Why do you want them?" she said. She was trying to engage him on some level, to get him to remember that he was a human being and so was she.

"What do you care?" he said in a low growl. At the same time he brought something out of his pocket. She heard a click. He had something long in his hand.

"I—" *Oh, shit.* He *did* have a knife. Briefly she closed her eyes against the sight, then opened them again when she felt the its cold, hard edge on her warm, soft neck. Nothing in her life had prepared Liz for this moment. It was all she could do not to pass out.

"We'll talk upstairs. *Move.*"

Despite her terror, the question remained: *why.* Why did he want the letters so badly that he'd risk her life for them?

He'd let go of her and was nudging her up the steps with the knife poking the small of her back. The prod kept her moving at a quick ascent while she racked her brain for a way out of her horror.

Mace. It was her only hope. But how to get at it?

At the landing he said, "Which way?" and she pointed weakly into her room.

"Where in the room?"

"They're . . . in the closet . . . in two cardboard boxes. . . . Under the photographs," she said, amazing herself by her reluctance to tell him.

The shutters were still open to the view. She could see the silhouettes of her neighbors' houses, and the harbor with its twinkling lights below them: serenity, downhill from terror.

He dragged Liz over the threshold and shoved her across her bed, then backed up to the windows and began closing the shutters top and bottom behind him. She saw the knife clearly, poised and ready to go.

"Turn on a light," he commanded as he closed the last pair.

Liz had one and only one chance to elude him; and that meant *not* turning on a light.

"Okay . . . just . . . let me do it," she said. She made a big deal of crawling back to the nightstand-side of her bed, then reached down for the canister of Mace that she now kept alongside.

He saw that she was up to something and lunged for her. At the same time she began spraying wildly in his direction. Somehow, some way, she got him. He screamed much louder than she had and dropped the knife. Liz scrambled out of bed and went flying down the stairs, still gripping her canister, with him screaming in agony behind her. But she stubbed her toe—on a rearranged table—so violently that she went hurtling to the floor.

The intruder fell on top of her.

New horror! She felt as if she were trapped under some writhing, putrid snake. With cries of disgust she shoved and pushed at him, infuriating him still more. He was still making ghastly sounds of pain, animal sounds; he sat on her, then grabbed her hair with one hand and slammed her head to the floor.

She was knocked nearly unconscious from the blow. She groped half-heartedly at the floor around her, searching for the canister. No use: it must've rolled out of reach. She felt like a swimmer going down for the third time. *Jack, Jack, Jack,* she thought, as if by invoking his name she could invoke his presence.

What happened next was as bizarre as it was abrupt: the intruder suddenly leaped up from her and clapped his hands on his ears, then began bending over in more excruciating agony than before. Liz was only semiconscious and it was mostly dark, but that was what she saw: the man was covering his ears—not his eyes—and howling with pain.

Only then did she become aware of the chime-sound, louder than usual, clearer than ever, a sound of awesome power and phenomenal beauty. If an archangel had a sword of heavenly tempered steel and he slammed that sword against the gates of hell, that was what it would sound like.

Christopher, she thought, slipping further into a stupor, more deeply into confusion. *Not Jack, then.*

Another surprise: she heard the back door burst open—explode, really—and heard Jack yell out her name. She wanted to answer him, to say, "*You* took your sweet time," but that was so many words . . . so many syllables . . . so many vowels. . . .

When she opened her eyes, the lights were on, the police were at the open door, Jack was holding her, and the intruder—a filthy-looking derelict—was lying, out cold, on the living-room floor.

"God," she said to Jack, "you must've really clobbered him."

"You're the one who got clobbered," said Jack in a shaky voice. He helped her to her feet. "How do you feel?"

She rubbed the back of her head. "Ow-ow," she said, wincing. "Okay, I guess." She was alive. That was all she cared about. But why did her jaw hurt?

The paramedics were there now, too, although she hadn't seen them come in. They looked Liz over and asked her questions. Liz knew her name, the day of the week, and how to count backward from ten, but they wanted to take her to the emergency room anyway.

"No!" she said impatiently. "Absolutely not. I'm fine. I'm just—*pissed,* that's all."

She watched with loathing as the police cuffed the dere- lict—whom they obviously knew—and read him his rights before they took him and the recovered knife away. The de- tective from the Grant Dade case arrived before they left and talked in the street with the arresting officers, then came and asked Liz if she felt in shape to come to the station and make a statement.

"Whatever it takes to keep him behind bars," she said grimly.

Detective Gilbert nodded in agreement, then hesitated and said, "Here's something you might find interesting, Mrs. Coppersmith. The perpetrator has scars on his hands and forearms that appear to be recent."

"*Does* he?" said Liz. She looked at Jack and sighed. "Okay, so it wasn't Grant Dade the other time. So sue me."

Jack gave her a complex look that made her heart, tired as it was, beat a little bit faster.

Eventually the professionals left, the neighbors retreated, and Liz, who'd been doing her best to look spunky for eve- ryone, collapsed on the sofa before her legs gave out alto- gether. She closed her eyes, then opened them again instantly. There was no peace in darkness. Perhaps there never would be again.

Jack came in from outside and sat down next to her. "How did I not see this coming?" he said in a voice of bitter self-reproach. "Obviously—once the grad student was cleared—I should have figured out that someone was still running around with an uncompleted agenda."

Liz said tiredly, "What does he want with the letters? That's what I want to know." But she didn't want to know, not really. She never wanted to think about him or his motives again. She shuddered at the recollection of him on top of her. "I have to take a shower first," she said in numb tones. "Then we can go."

"Oh, sweetheart, oh, Liz," said Jack, embracing her.

She pulled violently away. "No! He made me so—filthy. I don't want him to be passed on to you."

"But I don't care—"

"Jack!" she said, nearing hysteria. "Just let me do this! Let me get him *off* me!"

"Okay, I'm sorry . . . darling, I'm so, so sorry."

"I know, I know; I'll be fine. It's going to take a little while, that's all," she said stoically. She stood up and began heading for the bathroom, then turned and said to Jack, "Who is he? Obviously they know him."

"Eddy Wragg? Yeah. He's a vagrant. He's been in and out of Newport over the last few years. They had a warrant out for him for breaking and entering. There's more. I'll tell you later, if you want."

"I'm not sure I will," she confessed. "Will you stay tonight after we get back?" she added. "I'd rather not be alone."

"Do you think wild horses could tear me away?"

It occurred to her that if he had gotten there on time, none of this would've happened. It wasn't a kind thought, but life was looking a little unkind to Liz just then. She said with pointed politeness, "How did things work out with your investors?"

"Oh, them," he said. "They ended up lost in the shuffle. We had a fire."

"*What?*"

"A small one. It looks like arson. *That* sent chills up their spines, I can tell you. Everything's on hold for the moment. Anyway, go shower. We'll talk afterward."

She threw her arms out, palms up, in a gesture of bewilderment. "Are the planets out of kilter or something?" she asked plaintively.

Then she mounted the stairs to the bathroom, reliving every single step of her trauma as she did it.

After a shower and two shampoos, Liz felt decent enough to get on with the process of putting away Eddy Wragg. She dressed in jeans and a shirt, then went downstairs where Jack was waiting for her.

"All set?" he asked, watching her with a certain wariness.

"Almost." She dropped to her knees, flattened her cheek to the floor, and began looking under all the furniture. "Ah. There it is," she said, reaching under the skirted slipper-chair for her canister of Mace.

She tucked it into her purse. "Until I get a burglar alarm installed," she said in a steely voice, "and a gun, and Mace for every room, *this* stays by my side."

Jack had a simple four-word response to all that: "You have a child."

It pricked her resolve like a pin in a balloon. "Oh, God, that's right. I can't surround my daughter with weapons."

"You don't have to surround your daughter with weapons, Liz. Wragg's in jail," Jack reminded her. He watched her lock the front door, then check it twice. "You're safe now."

"But for how long?" she said as they walked to his car. "He knows I have the letters. He wants the letters." She could feel her voice rising, her throat constricting. "Sooner or later, he'll be *back*," she said shrilly.

She heard an upstairs window slam in a neighbor's house. It was pretty obvious that she was wearing out her welcome on the quiet, tucked-away street.

"He *won't* be back," Jack said firmly. "He's going to do time. And we'll make sure he knows that you've donated the letters, or given them to me for safekeeping, or any of a dozen scenarios. He will not be back, Elizabeth."

They were in his car now. Jack turned the key; the Mercedes sprang discreetly to life. Reassured by Jack's tone, Liz leaned back on the leather headrest, grateful to be in his care. She hadn't done that for a long time—given herself up for safekeeping to someone else. It felt good.

"What did you learn about Wragg?" she asked reluctantly.

"You remember that research you did on the guy who murdered Victoria St. Onge? The young gigolo who lived with her, then killed her and got sent up for manslaughter?"

"Johnny Ripen? Sure I remember. After he got out of ACI, he came back to Newport. He died about ten years ago; I think he was seventysomething at the time. The police found him, bled to death, under a cherry tree in the Burying Ground."

"Right. You told me his wrist was cut open on a broken vodka bottle and that the cops never made a case for it being a murder."

"I can see why," she said, reflecting on the scene. "The obvious clue—fingerprints on the bottle—would be no clue at all if the victim happened to be a derelict sitting in a graveyard and passing around a bottle to other—"

The little light bulb went on at last. "Eddy Wragg? Eddy Wragg knew Johnny Ripen?"

"Bingo," said Jack. "Detective Gilbert told me that for a while the two were as thick as thieves get. The cops knew both men well. Johnny Ripen used to be arrested routinely for petty stuff—drunk and disorderly, urinating in public, that kind of thing. But Wragg was a younger, more ambitious bum. He got caught at bigger crimes: breaking and entering, assault, and a mugging.''

"And yet here he is, right back out on the street. Oh, boy. I'd better donate those letters to someone real quick," Liz said nervously.

Jack reached over and took her hand in his. "We'll work this through. I promise. Anyway," he said, "until tonight Detective Gilbert never was able to figure out why someone like Wragg would have bothered with an old geezer like Johnny Ripen."

"Victoria St. Onge?" Liz ventured.

"Exactly. Gilbert remembered her name from when he investigated Johnny Ripen's death."

"It does seem more than coincidental."

"When you were showering, I got to thinking: By the time Johnny Ripen—still a good-looking gigolo, presumably—latched on to Victoria St. Onge, she would've been pretty old, probably senile if she let him under her roof. She would've had money, jewelry, securities. Maybe it was all buried in her backyard somewhere. She had a big place by then on Kay Street. Maybe Johnny Ripen got sent away before he could dig any of it up."

"Maybe pigs can fly," Liz said dolefully. "Okay, for the sake of argument, let's say Johnny Ripen reminisced in his old age to Eddy Wragg about Victoria St. Onge. Ripen tells Wragg how he was *this close* to getting his hands on Victoria's money," she said, pressing her forefinger to her thumb. "And then, one dark night in the graveyard, they argue about something stupid, and Wragg kills the old man."

"And then suppose, ten years later, Wragg sees the article in the paper about the trunk of St. Onge's letters that you found in your attic."

"So? What does Wragg think is in her letters? A treasure map?"

Liz could see, by the dim lights of the dashboard, that Jack was smiling. "Damned straight. Why not?"

"I've read all of the letters, except for some of the ones Wragg stole. There is no treasure map."

"Maybe it's in code."

"Oh, come on." She closed her eyes—saw her attacker—and opened them again. "I don't get it. I do not get it."

Her thoughts ebbed and flowed around the night's events. Suddenly she felt a surge of adrenaline.

What if Susy had been home tonight? My God. What if she'd been home?

She wanted desperately to think about something else.

"The fire! Good lord, Jack, you haven't said anything about it!"

"Lady, lady," he said, laughing softly. "One crisis at a time. Anyway, we're here," he said, turning left off Broadway and parking in front of the red-brick station.

"Should I tell Detective Gilbert about out theory? Or will he think it's too goofy?"

"Yes, and yes," said Jack. "If he doesn't want to take notes, he doesn't have to."

By the time they got back from the station, there wasn't a whole lot left to their third and last night together. Not that it mattered. The last thing in the world Liz wanted was to have someone on top of her.

"I guess your disasters and my disasters aren't related," she said in a dull, used-up voice.

"Not unless Wragg is evil incarnate."

That's just what she thought he was. "Jack . . . oh, Jack," she murmured into his shoulder as they sat in the dark in the engulfing softness of her prized down-cushioned sofa. "I was terrified. If I wasn't so exhausted, I still would be terrified."

"I know," he said soothingly as he smoothed her hair away from her face. "I know."

"What will I do? How will I get over this?" she asked in a voice that was bleak with despair.

"Time . . . give it time," he murmured, holding her close.

"But Susy comes home tomorrow," she protested in a tired, aching voice.

"Exactly. Susy comes home tomorrow."

The next morning, Liz learned from Detective Gilbert that the police were getting a warrant to search the room Wragg was staying in at the local shelter. They expected to find the stolen letters and hopefully some clue to Eddy Wragg's deadly interest in the ones that Liz possessed.

"Can I have the stolen letters back after you look at them?" she asked the detective, knowing full well what the answer would be.

He apologized and said they'd be kept for evidence.

"Can I at least read through them myself? I never got the chance, before they were stolen. I'd be willing to stay under someone's watchful eye."

"I'll see what I can do, Mrs. Coppersmith," the detective said. "But don't worry. You'll get them back safe and sound."

So that was that. In the meantime, Liz had a fund-raiser to launch. She had taken advantage of a completely unexpected lull (back-to-back broken-off weddings) to draft the working committees to handle decorations, publicity, and tickets.

Victoria had, with her usual enthusiasm, volunteered to be on all three committees, but Liz managed to confine her to what she did best—decorations, which included helping design the invitations. Dr. Ben, who'd been shanghaied for various charity events from time to time, was willing to write and distribute the press releases. (Liz agreed to sign him up on condition that he absolutely, positively avoided the subject of psychotherapy until after the event was over.)

Jack, with his widespread connections, was the obvious choice to head up the ticket committee; he promised, with two or three others, to come up with the ultimate list of guests to invite. Netta, Deirdre—the current nanny—and Liz's parents agreed to do the follow-up phone calls. Jack's father agreed to let his name be included in the honorary committee.

It was turning out to be a regular family affair.

On her way to the airport, Liz stopped by at East Gate to drop off some mailing lists she'd had on file. Cornelius Eastman, obviously on his way out, answered the door.

She hadn't seen him since the day of the picnic. Did he know about her and Jack? If so, he wasn't letting on. He greeted her in his usual formal way, then added in a surprising, gentle pun, "Taking it on the chin lately?"

Automatically Liz's hand went up to the bruise on her jaw. "It seems like it," she replied with careful good humor.

Apparently Jack hadn't filled his father in on the previous night's events. Good. Liz had no desire for this man's sympathy.

Jack came out of the Great Room just then. His face lit up when he saw her, which made Liz herself want to burst into a refrain from *The Sound of Music*.

Hopeless, she thought, amazed at herself. *I've become hopeless.*

"Hey," he said in greeting. "On your way to the airport?"

"Yes. But I wanted to drop off this list for you to collate into your master. You may already have one; it's from the Chamber of Commerce."

"Great. How about if I tag along with you? No, on second thought, Susy will want you all to herself. If I stop by after she's in bed? How about that?"

If Jack's father had been in the dark about them, he wasn't any longer. It didn't take a Supreme Court Justice to decide that she and Jack had something going.

Liz forced herself not to look at Cornelius Eastman for his reaction. "That . . . would be nice," she said, coloring.

It crossed her mind that Jack was showing off. Then it crossed her mind that she wasn't exactly a trophy date. Then it crossed her mind that she didn't have a clue what Jack was up to.

Jack's father said blandly, "Should I leave the alarm on or off?"

Jack answered just as blandly, "On."

Liz had a sneaky suspicion that the question was a rich man's version of "Should I wait up?"

Feeling once again caught in the middle, she said quickly, "I've got to be going. Nice to see you again, Mr. Eastman."

Cornelius narrowed his eyes almost imperceptibly and smiled. "Please. Call me Neal."

"Mommy! Mommy, Mommy, Mommy!"

Was there a better word in the English language? Liz felt her heart leap up in simple joy at the sight of Susy breaking away from her grandfather's hand and making a mad dash for her. She crouched down and opened her arms wide for her daughter, then caught her and held her tight.

She still smells like Susy, clean and sweet and innocent. . . . My little girl . . . three days . . . three lifetimes. . . .

And suddenly it had never happened.

"I love your T-shirt," Liz said, outlining the Mickey Mouse ears on her daughter's chest. "Was that a present from Gramma and Grampa?"

"Yes, and Grampa gave me—*this,*" Susy said, whipping her wrist up in front of her mother's nose. "It's *quartz!*"

"A Mickey Mouse watch as well! My goodness, Grampa," said Liz with a scolding look above her daughter's head.

"Not only that! I got Mickey Mouse pajamas, too!"

"We did it for the others," said Liz's mother, cutting off her protest.

Liz rose and gave each of her parents a quick hug, then turned her attention back to Susy.

"What happened to your chin, Mommy?" Susy asked with a puzzled look.

Liz was ready with her answer. "I slipped off the ladder when I was trimming the roses. I should have been more careful," she said gravely, turning the lie into a lesson.

"And I got you a Mickey Mouse hat!" said Susy, returning to her adventure. "I hope it fits. It's way big on me. That's how I tested it. But if it doesn't fit, we can't take it back. I don't want to go on the plane right away," she said with a wary look in her brown eyes.

Liz glanced up at her father, who made up-and-down movements with his arm. "Oh, it was bumpy, huh? Sometimes they're like that. But my goodness, after all those rides at Disney World, I'm surprised you even noticed!"

Liz, her mother, and Susy fell in behind Liz's father, who was hell-bent for the luggage carousel. "Tell me what you liked the best," Liz asked her child, relishing the feel of the small hand in hers. "Tell me everything, every little thing."

Susy talked nonstop, right through the drive home, right through her bath. Tired as she was, the child was still too wound up to sleep. Dressed in her new Mickey Mouse pajamas, she cuddled in her mother's arms, listening to her favorite dinosaur tape as Liz rocked her for longer than the usual time.

Out of the blue, Susy said in a sleepy voice, "Are you going to marry Mr. Eastman, Mommy?"

Liz was unprepared for that one. "No, sweetie. I only said Mr. Eastman is coming by later to help me plan the costume party benefit."

After a moment of rocking, Liz couldn't resist a question of her own. "Susy? What made you think I was going to marry him?"

"Just because," Susy said with a shrug of her small shoulders. Then she added, "Is my real daddy ever coming back?"

"Maybe he'll come someday for a visit," Liz said vaguely. How she hated this particular conversation.

"I mean to *live*."

"No, honey. Not to live."

"Well . . . in that case . . . I think Mr. Eastman would make a pretty good dad."

"You do, do you," Liz murmured, rubbing her chin in her daughter's hair. "You know what? I think you could be right."

There wasn't a doubt in Liz's mind.

In a distressing display of perception, Susy said, "But he probb'ly wants baby kids, not bigger ones, huh."

Her voice was so forlorn, so resigned. She deserved a father so much. It broke Liz's heart to think that the sum total of Keith's contribution to Susy's existence was one spermatozoon.

"I think if Mr. Eastman ever gets married," Liz said to her daughter, "he'll love *all*-sized kids: babies and older ones, too. But—he hasn't asked me, Susabella."

Big, big yawn. "But if he did?"

"He hasn't asked."

"If he did?"

"Hasn't."

Another yawn. "If?"

They played the game back and forth until Susy nodded off in her mother's arms.

Liz tucked her daughter in bed and moved the night-light so that its halo fell over her sleeping form. It didn't seem possible to love a child as much as she did at that moment. Liz would do anything—give up her life—to protect Susy from harm. She would do anything; but she couldn't manufacture a daddy out of thin air.

Jack came later, knocking softly. Liz stood on her side of the door and whispered "Who is it?" which made her feel like a bouncer at a speakeasy.

He identified himself, and she let him in, and he wrapped his arms around her in a long, silent embrace. "I missed you," he said simply.

"Yes. Me too."

Words were either unnecessary or inadequate, Liz couldn't decide which. All she knew was that when he had his arms around her, it felt as right as when she had hers around Susy.

"All locked up?" he asked unnecessarily as they sat down in what Liz now considered "their" spot on the sofa.

He was freshly showered, soapy clean and with damp hair clinging to the back of his neck. She loved that he was trying his damnedest to present a contrast to the filthy intruder who'd terrorized her the night before.

She curled up against his chest. "I think I'm going to change the lock on the back door," she said, drawing idle circles around a button of his polo shirt. "It bothers me that a key to my house is sitting in an evidence room somewhere."

She shuddered to think how stupid she'd been to announce, near an open window, where she was hiding the spare. "I can't shake the feeling that Wragg's going to get out, steal it, and come back."

"Change the lock, then; get rid of the feeling. I'll change it for you."

"And, Jack?" she said, gaining confidence from his support. "I wanted to say something else. About last night. There's something I can't explain. Or—I can explain it, all right, just not to the police. Not even to Victoria."

She told Jack how at the height of the assault, after Wragg had nearly knocked her out—how he suddenly jumped off her and clapped his hands over his ears and was bent over in two from the pain. "I don't think Mace, even if it got in his ears, would cause that reaction," she said, trying to put a light touch on it. "It *had* to be the chime-sound."

Jack knew all about the chime-sound by now. "But the chiming didn't hurt you at all?"

She lifted her head from his chest and looked at him. "Oh, not at all. Just the opposite. It sounded like the cavalry." She laughed wryly and added, "Between the two of you, Wragg must not have known what hit him."

There. It was out. Let him call her crazy.

But Jack took another tack altogether. "Don't sell yourself short, ma'am. I can't think of many women who would've had your presence of mind. I'm not sure I can think of any."

So that was how he was choosing to handle the subject of Christopher Eastman: he was choosing not to handle it at all. Well, whatever worked for him. She could live with that.

"He was *there*, Jack. I felt him."

Or not. The encounter on Cliff Walk—had that really happened? She was far less sure that Christopher had chatted with her than she was that he'd defended her.

After a thoughtful silence, Jack said, "I read somewhere that nearly three-quarters of people believe in guardian angels."

"But you don't?"

Jack rubbed her back in reassuring circles. " 'Fraid not," he said with a sigh of regret.

She could tell he wanted to. Somehow, that was good enough for her. In a world where it got harder every day to believe in anything at all, the fact that a man of Jack's experience was actually sorry that angels did not inhabit his realm—well, that was good enough for her.

She turned her face up to Jack's, and they kissed, gently at first, and then more deeply. Liz had been afraid, up until now, that the assault by Wragg might have wrecked her responsiveness forever: how wrong she was. Despite last night—because of last night—she wanted Jack more than ever. He was the beacon in the foggy uncertainties of her life; he was the deep-water harbor for her to sail home to.

He was Jack.

In utter silence they went up the stairs, then paused at Susy's room where, with Jack watching over her shoulder, Liz quietly eased the door the rest of the way shut. Then they treaded softly into Liz's bedroom, and each of them undressed, still without saying a word, and they lay down, side by side, on Liz's mercifully unsqueaky bed.

They made love, then: carefully; quietly; with breathtaking intensity.

And when they were finished, Jack murmured in her ear, "I want a Susy with you."

It was the knife she'd dreaded, a day late.

For a long, infinitely long moment, Liz said nothing. When her answer came out, it came in a whisper—because she couldn't have said the words aloud even if her daughter weren't in the next room.

"You can't have a Susy with me."

Chapter 21

There was another long pause—Liz was sure, afterward, that both their hearts had stopped beating for the length of it—and then Jack said simply, "Tell me why."

Her "shhh" was as quiet as a slow leak in a bicycle tire. "I can't, now," she whispered in his ear. "Not with Susy here."

"But—"

"Shhh."

"Can we talk downst—?"

"Shhh."

The next sound Liz heard was a short quick exhale of defeat. Jack shook his head slowly; in the dark she felt the thickness of his hair brush against her temple.

"Okay," he murmured.

He rolled off her and swung his legs over the side of the bed and sat with his forearms leaning on his thighs—a looming, brooding presence in the unlit room. He stayed that way for a long time. Liz began to feel ill at ease: Jack's silence was even more thundering than his speech.

Wrong, wrong response, she realized. Why hadn't she just given him the same answer she'd given Susy earlier—"You do, do you?" He would've had to accept that, and he'd be in her arms still. Instead he was standing up; lifting his clothes from the back of the chair; walking back to the side of the bed.

"Tomorrow. We'll talk," he said, still unable to keep his voice within the range of a whisper.

Some men were like that, she knew. They'd never learned to whisper because they never had anything to hide.

"Yes," she whispered.

Tomorrow came and nearly went without the summit taking place. Liz was tied up in the morning; Jack wasn't free in the afternoon. She was reluctant to see him at the shipyard; he was reluctant to have Susy sent off for his sake. It was obvious to both that they wanted to meet on neutral territory, and yet when Jack suggested that they have dinner at the Cooke House, Liz declined: she wanted something more downscale. She suggested Burger King. He thought that was funny.

They agreed, finally, to meet at a middle-of-the-road restaurant on downtown Thames Street called Mean Cuisine, one of the summer's bumper crop of new eateries. It hadn't been given either the seal of approval or the kiss of death by Newport's locals—that would have to wait until fall—but in the meantime it would be filled with nice, anonymous tourists.

Liz was late: it was hot, it was Friday, and everyone on the planet seemed to think the place to cool down was along Newport's waterfront. Liz had to weave her way through, around, and sometimes over a crush of strolling, aimless tourists; by the time she fetched up at Jack's table, she was in no mood to confess to anything but her irritation that he hadn't agreed to come to her house.

He was on his second glass of wine. She thought he looked melancholy, but his greeting was mild enough: "You look hot. Did you walk?"

Liz took that to mean she looked like hell. She excused herself with a tight little smile and went to freshen up. The ladies' room was lit by soft, flattering lights—but even they weren't enough to hide her sweat-dampened hair and flushed face.

Dammit! So much for the trendy, sophisticated look. Her rayon dress felt hot and clingy, and if she wasn't mistaken, that was a blister throbbing against her brand-new shoes. She touched up her lipstick and marched back out in a grim frame of mind. The point of it all was to end it all, so what did it matter how she looked as she did it?

Jack, on the other hand, looked as cool and confident as ever. Yes, indeed. The man had some awfully good genes to pass down. Too bad he wouldn't be passing them down through her. *Well, that's life,* she decided, letting him pull out her chair for her. Although that was the whole problem, wasn't it? That she couldn't give what he had, life? *Too bad, too bad,* she thought, her mind racing through the scenario that was about to be played out. *No little Susies for you, fella, not from me. Sorry I can't oblige.*

"Hi," she allowed herself to say.

His smile was as edgy as her mood. "I wish you looked happier to be here," he confessed, filling her wineglass for her.

"I'm just exhausted from all our pretrial negotiations," she quipped.

He called her on that. "Who's on trial?"

"I suppose," she said faintly, "our relationship."

He nodded once. "Maybe it is."

Too soon! They were cutting to the chase too soon! She couldn't bear to have this discussion, not right off the bat like this. She did a wrenching emotional somersault and said cheerfully, "This looks like a pretty nice place. Care to lay odds on whether it makes it through the winter?"

"Let's wait till we've tasted the food," he said, opening his menu.

It'll taste like cardboard, all of it, she thought, but aloud she said, "Southwestern cuisine is all the rage."

"I guess."

While Jack surveyed the menu half-heartedly, Liz launched into a monologue on how *won*derfully plans were proceeding for the costume-party benefit. She was *so* pleased to be working with Meredith (who actually was turning out to be pretty damned helpful). As for the other members of the honorary committee—Diana and Johanna and Cuddie and Bebe and Hope—well, no doubt they would prove indispensable, in due course.

Liz lied about other things, too. She told Jack that the fund-raiser would cost less than her original rough estimate (which could only happen if she charged nothing for her time, something she was prepared to do). She told him that advertising for the program book was going amazingly well. And she told him that considering how late they'd jumped into the benefit, early interest was extremely encouraging.

"So we're hoping to sell up to two hundred tickets at forty dollars each. Are you sure that East Gate can accommodate two hundred people, even with the tents?"

"It won't be the first time," he said.

"Okay, because we print the tickets tomorrow. And you're absolutely, positively sure you have no objections to the dinner party for thirty that precedes the general event?"

"Not if Meredith is convinced she can move the meal tickets for two hundred bucks a pop," he said, picking over his broiled lobster. "It amounts to a nice piece of change for Anne's Place."

"I always wonder why some high roller doesn't just write out a check for the target amount," Liz confessed with a sigh. "It seems so much more efficient."

"That's called a will, darlin'. While the high rollers are still alive and kicking, benefits are how it's done."

"Of course. What was I thinking?" she said, betraying

just a little bit of attitude. She smiled a brisk smile and said, "Well! Now we can take a tax deduction for this dinner."

He wasn't amused. "Liz—"

"Oh, and what about the *fire*?" she said quickly, rerouting his thoughts once again. "Any more news?"

His face darkened. "Not so far. It's hard to prove it was arson. Spontaneous combustion in a paint shed isn't unheard of—which is why we have big vents, and a long list of rules about disposing paint-soaked rags. No one's come forward to take credit, if that's what you mean."

"Do you think it *could* be—" She looked around them and lowered her voice. "You know—the developers?"

"You know my feelings on that. I think it's someone who's hell-bent on taking down the yard, and the list of suspects is damned short. All I can do is increase our security and warn the help to be on the watch."

"Any sign of your venture capitalists? Or have they fled forever?"

"I don't think they're coming back," he said with no apparent regret. "I've begun to pin my hopes on the international race the New York Yacht Club's decided to start up. Eventually it could be as big as the America's Cup. The question is, can I can hold on that long?"

He topped off his glass, and hers, and said, "Liz—"

"No! Boy, this really is—just—delicious!" she said, with no idea what she was putting into her mouth.

"Don't," he said quietly. "Don't put this off any longer. It's no way to run a relationship. I hate double-talk; I thought you did, too."

When she said nothing, he took the initiative. "I . . . look . . . I'll admit it, Liz: I don't know why I said that about wanting a . . . Susy . . . last night. It just came out," he admitted with a baffled look. "You couldn't have been any more astonished than I was. It was as if someone else were saying the words."

Liz took that to mean he was sorry he'd said anything; that it had all been a mistake. But the relief she felt was tempered by the onset of a deep, dull ache. "I'm glad to hear that," she said, her voice catching. "Because it really did seem too—too—"

"Soon?"

"Yes. I mean, we're only just getting to know one another . . . and . . . and, well, you have to admit: a relationship goes through a level or two before it reaches the let's-have-a-baby stage."

It was so ironic. Her own relationship with Keith never did reach that last wonderful stage. She sighed nervously, hoping she'd put an end to the discussion.

Jack nodded, almost solemnly. "You're right, of course. But I seem in a fierce hurry about life lately. I suppose it has something to do with having reached forty. A man starts to look around—to wonder, has he missed the boat? But it's not just that, Liz. Truly, it's not."

His eyes burned brightly as he said, "You know I'm crazy about you, Liz. You *know* that. And I'd have to be a damned fool not to realize that you—you do care for me?"

"Yes," she murmured.

"Deeply?" he asked in a guileless follow-up.

"Yes," she said again.

He pushed his plate away from the table's edge and folded his forearms there, leaning closer, ready to read her lips if need be. "Then tell me why I can't—someday, if all goes well—have a Susy with you."

It was such a simple request. He wasn't asking her why she believed in ghosts, or what she thought was the best way to lower long-term interest rates. He wanted to know why they couldn't have a baby together. Someday. If all went well. He deserved a straight answer.

And she couldn't give it. "Why you can't, is—" She

shook her head and tried again. "It's because I, ah, really am done with that phase of my life."

He was trying not to look disappointed. "But you're only—what, thirty-six? I know you have a pretty wonderful kid—Susy's great—but . . . doesn't she make you want another?" he asked softly.

Liz said, "Not necessarily."

"Is this because I didn't take your career seriously? Because you know that's not true anymore." He gave her a lopsided, heart-melting smile. "You know I'm a reformed chauvinist."

"No, that's not it," Liz said in a strained voice.

His own voice was tight with emotion as he said, "Is it because you could never care for me enough to overcome the agony of Keith?"

She looked out the window at a pair of young lovers stopping, hand in hand, to read the menu posted outside. "I was devastated," she admitted without looking at Jack. "But that's not the problem."

He reached out across the table to take her hand. "Then *what*? You *know* that I'm not after a fling with you. You've probably known that since day one. It's not as if I've been any good at hiding it."

She turned back to face him. "You were *pretty* good," she said as an unwanted, infuriating tear rolled out.

"Hey, what's this?" he said softly, wiping the tear away from her cheek. "I thought the problem was when one person was serious and the other one wasn't," he said, surprised.

No doubt he'd seen plenty of that—not to mention plenty of tears. She tried a feeble smile of reassurance. "No problem there."

He didn't really look encouraged, but he plowed on anyway. "And . . . if you care deeply about me, and if I'm crazy about you . . . then presumably . . . this relationship could go somewhere? Somewhere I've never been before?''

"I don't know," she said, squirming in pain. "I don't.''

"Ah." It was a blow, a shock to his system, she could see that. His cheeks flushed to a dark shade. For a moment he said nothing, composing himself behind a sip of wine. Then he said in a low, careful voice, "I guess I assumed that women cared about things like—like love, and marriage."

"And a baby carriage? Isn't that a little old-fashioned?" she asked out of sheer desperation.

He laughed awkwardly, obviously out of his element on the whole subject. "You know me," he said, tight-lipped. "Just a simple, old-fashioned kind of guy."

"I'm sorry, I'm sorry, Jack," she said, withdrawing her hand from his—because it seemed the height of hypocrisy to treat their confrontation as a romantic interlude anymore. "But you're *rushing* everything," she wailed.

"Rushing?" He looked genuinely astonished. "I've waited all my life for you. *Rushing?* I've wandered through a *wilderness* of women looking for you. And now that I've finally found you—" He laughed again, apparently amazed that she could be so dense. "No; if anything, I wish I could turn back the clock a decade or so. I want you so much, Liz. I can't imagine letting you slip through my fingers."

It was a dream come true: the prince was at her door, glass slipper in his hand. All she had to do was . . .

Lie. "I want to concentrate on my daughter and my career, at least for now," she murmured, cracking the door open to him.

His face lit up with renewed hope. "Oh, understood," he said, holding his hands palms up in agreement. "I didn't mean we had to start tonight. I just thought . . . somehow you sounded so final . . . huh! See that? You're not the only one with a flair for melodrama. God, was I off base. What an ego. C'mon," he said with an utterly relieved grin, "let's eat. The food *is* pretty damned good here."

Somehow Liz managed to work through the courses and make it through the conversation without cluing Jack in on the magnitude of her deceit. It was a first-rate acting job, and it used up every atom of energy that she possessed. By the time the meal was over, even the cappuccino couldn't revive her.

Jack ignored her insistence on sharing the tab and dropped his Visa card on the bill. Smiling sympathetically, he said, "Let's go, droopy. I'll take you home."

"No, maybe not," she said suddenly. "I think I should just walk back. I could use the air. I still have lots of work to do tonight. Is that all right?" she asked humbly. "Would you mind?"

He gave her a baffled look. "No, sure, if you'd rather." But it was clear that he did mind. Still, what could he do? She knew he didn't dare act like a chauvinist, not after his self-assured little speech earlier.

She stood up abruptly, unable to stay with him a split second longer, and said, "Good night, then. And thank you so much. Don't forget to tell your secretary that I'll need a master of the mailing list by next Tuesday."

She fled outside, leaving him waiting to square up the bill. Less than fifty yards away, she was suddenly overcome with revulsion at her own cowardice. She closed her eyes tightly and bit her lip till it hurt; then, turning on her blistered heel, she limped back to the restaurant and intercepted Jack as he was rising to leave their table.

"I lied," she said in a whisper. "I can't have a Susy. I can't have anyone, ever. It's not that I won't. I *can't*. So now you know."

She had no idea how he'd react, but she wasn't expecting stillness. His handsome face settled into an expression so dangerously discreet, so devoid of shock or anger or even disappointment, that she was forced to look away.

"Shall we go somewhere and talk?" he asked quietly.

"No. There's nothing more to say."

"But . . . why didn't you say it earlier?" he asked, obviously rethinking everything she'd said so far. "When you told me about Keith, for example."

She stared at the flickering candle on the table between them. "I didn't know you."

"Or when you pulled out your drawer of . . . supplies?"

"I didn't know you."

"Or last *night*."

"I was afraid," she whispered. She lifted her gaze to his and said, "I'm still afraid."

And then she left him for the second time, knowing full well he would not follow.

"You told him?"

"I told him."

"What did he say?"

"What could he say? Nothing. Thanks for baby-sitting, Tori. Now, go home. I can't share this one with you.

That night Liz dreamed of Christopher Eastman. It wasn't a vision; there was nothing supernatural about it. It was a plain, ordinary, everyday dream. In it, Liz and Christopher were sitting on one of the ledges of Cliff Walk, high above the sea that crashed on the rocks below. They were drinking Cokes and eating Burger King Whoppers and sharing a large order of fries. Behind them on the Walk, Susy and a young playmate were laughing and running around. Liz—for once—had no fears for Susy's safety, because Susy had taken swimming lessons from Mickey Mouse at Disney World.

Liz was having trouble explaining to Christopher how it was now possible for a human heart to be transplanted from someone who had just died into someone whose heart still beat, only badly. Christopher was frankly astonished and had deep misgivings about surgeons who played God; he wanted to meet this Dr. Ben.

"Sure," said Liz, and she stood up. "Let's go. I'll take you home."

Suddenly someone in the dream—either Liz, or Christopher, or Susy, or her playmate—slipped on the rocky ledge and went hurtling down the side of the cliff, sending Liz bolting up from her pillow with a half-muffled scream.

After that she cried, on and off, until dawn.

The phone rang early, as Liz thought it might. It was Jack, sounding as haggard as she felt.

"I followed you last night."

"I asked you not to."

"But I lost you in the crowd."

"Easy to do."

"I went back for my car and drove to your house, but I saw Tori through the front window. I felt like a stalker, so I went home. Do you want to talk now?"

"No."

"When?"

"I don't know when. This is way, way too painful for me, Jack. Can't you *tell* that? God!"

She shuddered, then sighed and said, "Please. Not now. *Please*."

"All right," he said soothingly. "Not now, then. I'll leave you some room."

But beneath the gentleness of his words, Liz thought she heard something else: the first faint sound of wariness.

The next few days were the longest of Liz's life. During the day she pretended to work, and during the night she pretended to sleep. But all she was doing, day and night, was waiting. It occurred to her that before she fell in love with Jack, the days flew by in a satisfying way. Now they crawled to a close, empty and meaningless.

This is what happens when you give up control, she realized.

She'd never do it again.

Eventually—finally—Tuesday rolled around. Liz waited, bleary-eyed, until three in the afternoon before putting in a call to the shipyard. But she needed the master list today, and she had no choice but to call and try to get it.

Cynthia, the shipyard secretary who'd baby-sat Susy briefly the first time Liz had gone there, was completely enthusiastic about the yard's sponsorship of the benefit; Liz had no trouble getting her cooperation.

"Mr. Eastman won't be in today," Cynthia volunteered. "He's in New York, wooing those investors of his."

He sure wasn't wooing Liz. "That's all right," Liz said in a voice of false cheer. "I didn't need to talk to him. Can I come by around five for the addresses?"

"Come by sooner if you like. All the stuff's in the computer; I just have to set them up to be collated. Nothing could be—oh. Here comes Mr. Eastman."

Liz felt her heart automatically slam up against her chest at the sound of his name. In a faltering voice she said, "He must've got through sooner than he expected in New York—"

"No, not that Mr. Eastman," said Cynthia, obviously disappointed. "His father. Cornelius Eastman."

"I'll let you go, then," said Liz, somehow relieved that Jack still had an excuse for not calling her. She hung up, not at all surprised that Cynthia, married or not, had a little crush on Jack. Was there anyone in the world who didn't?

Liz had intended to go directly from her office to her parents' house to pick up Susy; but in between those two points was her sweet little cottage with its own little answering machine, its red light possibly blinking.

She had to know.

She left the car running as she ran inside and up the stairs to her bedroom, where she'd relocated the answering machine out of Susy's earshot. Considering the agony of the last few nights; considering that Liz was in the thick of planning a last-minute benefit; considering how much she plain *wanted* there to be a message—it didn't seem possible that the little red light wasn't doing a damned thing.

With a moan of disappointment Liz threw herself on her bed, facedown and arms outstretched, like a tired butterfly basking in the summer sun that poured through the west windows. Hoping somehow to be recharged, she fell, instead, into a weary sleep.

"Elizabeth. Wake up."

"Uh!" she said, instantly alert.

He was sitting on the side of her bed, just the way Jack liked to do, watching her with a look that was more disappointed than bemused. "This isn't going very well, is it," he said, dispirited.

He was close enough to touch. She considered trying it, then backed away from the idea. He looked too young, too real, too altogether attractive in his loose-fitting shirt and tight-fitting pants.

"How come you're here?" she asked, lapsing back to a groggy state. She rubbed her nose with the back of her hand and said sleepily, "I thought I had to summon you."

"You did," he said, smiling. "In your dream just now."

"My dream? I'm *never* going to get the rules straight. What was I dreaming? I don't remember." She wanted to sit up, but her limbs felt extraordinarily heavy, as if she'd been drugged.

In a gentle rebuke, he said, "You took your time telling him, don't you think?"

She buried her face in the coverlet. "Like great-great-grandmother, like great-great-granddaughter," she said in a muffled voice. "With a twist, of course."

"I tell you, it doesn't matter about your condition."

"To Jack it does."

"It shouldn't."

She turned to face him. "Were you there when we were together last?" she asked Christopher. When he nodded reluctantly, she said, "Then you saw the look on his face."

"It should not matter," he repeated.

"Why are you telling *me* this?" she asked, suddenly aware of what a rotten job he was doing as intermediary. "Why aren't you convincing *him*? Why aren't you appearing to *him*?"

Christopher shrugged. "You need me more than he does."

"The hell I do!—ah, sorry," she said tiredly. "You probably don't like that kind of talk." She tried to raise herself up, but she was positively immobilized. "Okay, tell me why I need to be worked on more than he does," she said, sighing. "I'm curious."

Christopher was succinct: "You're afraid of him. Of his wealth. Of his position."

Defensive now, she managed to drag herself up on one elbow. "*Afraid* of him? I don't *think* so. I'm a working mother, mister. I'm not intimidated by Jack Eastman."

"Good. Go to him as his equal, then. Not with your head bent low in apology."

She fell back down on her nose. "Fine," she said, yawning and drifting off again. "Fine . . . fine . . . fine." She turned her face onto one cheek and gave him a dopey little smile. "Are you my guardian angel?"

"No, sweet one," he said in a voice that was low and oddly melancholy. "Not technically."

"Just a ghost, then. Well . . . whatever."

"But do I care about your destiny?" His voice was rich with emotion as he added, "Oh, yes, dear lady. Be certain of it."

She watched him for a long time, puzzled by his tone and yet deeply stirred by it. Something was happening here, something she felt rather than understood. "Thank you for that night," she said, her eyelids beginning to droop once more. "You saved my life."

"Not so," he said softly. "You saved your own life. And you still can."

He stood up then and held his arms in the air over her prone body. Warm, golden light fell over her, engulfing her like a halo, wrapping her in a warm caress. "Now sleep, Elizabeth . . . sleep."

When Liz woke up she felt terrific. Dream? Vision? Who could tell anymore? What was a vision, anyway, but a waking dream?

Whatever it was that he infused in me, she thought, *I wish I could bottle it*. She washed her face and combed her hair and went out to her car with a new spring in her step.

The van was still running.

Embarrassed by how thoroughly she was losing it, she jumped back in, drove down to her parents' house to gather up Susy, and then raced with her out to the shipyard before Cynthia closed up the office.

There were wooden horses blocking the front of the shipyard office—no doubt to keep the area free for moving a boat—so Liz was forced to park around the side of the building. Reluctant to leave her daughter alone, she hauled Susy inside with her.

The glass entry door was open, but Cynthia wasn't at her desk. Liz assumed that the secretary had stepped out; she motioned her daughter to take a seat while they waited for her to come back.

The next voice she heard was Cynthia's, high and agitated, at the far end of the aisle of cubicles. "He'll kill me if he finds out! I know he will! He gets so jealous—"

And then the one voice that Liz was not prepared to hear: "He won't find out, Cyn. Don't worry."

Instantly Liz went over to Susy and yanked her out of her chair. "We're going," she said to her startled daughter.

"But, Mommy! I hear Cynthia—"

"Liz!"

The word went through Liz like a long, thin blade. She turned, proud that she wasn't staggering, and said in a flat tone, "Jack. How're you?"

Jack was clearly embarrassed and angry; Cynthia, embarrassed and scared. Between them they looked caught, as the church so delicately liked to put it, pretty damned *in flagrante*.

"Oh, you want your list," the young secretary said, rifling red-faced through a stack of papers on her desk. "I almost forgot."

Jack made himself smile at Susy and then said to Liz in a voice of pure steel, "How's the fund-raiser coming?"

"Wonderfully well," Liz said with a faint smile. "We've sold so many tickets, we may not even *need* this mailing list."

They'd sold eleven, but who was counting?

Liz was saved from the impossible task of making chitchat by the arrival of Cornelius Eastman with his daughter Caroline and the child's lovely Irish nanny, Deirdre. Cornelius took one look at the assembly and broke into a wide, engaging grin.

"Well, for goodness' sake," he said, singling out Liz and Susy, "here's perfect timing. We were just about to take the *Déjà Vu* for an evening spin. Won't you join us?"

Liz said at once, "Thanks for the offer, but we haven't eat—"

Susy squeezed her hand in a signal that, roughly translated, meant: *If you say no, I'll pout until I'm eighteen.*

Meanwhile, Cornelius was pooh-poohing Liz's excuse with a hearty, "Oh, come on along. Netta's packed a cold supper for us—anything to get us out of her hair. What about it, Susy? Want to go for that boat ride at last?"

Little blond Caroline was giving Susy the same kind of look a cat gives a mouse. Susy knew it and—gutsy kid— said "Yes, please" anyway. Liz was working herself into a thorough snit over being put on the spot when Jack decided to put in *his* two cents.

"If Liz doesn't want to go, Dad, I don't think we should force her."

We? Since when was he part of the equation? And in any case, what right had he to disinvite her in his father's name? Liz remembered the first time she'd turned Jack down, certain she couldn't meet his standards. Well, to hell with his standards.

"Actually, Susy and I don't have anything special planned this evening. Thanks for the offer . . . Neal," she said, passing over Jack with a sweet and vengeful smile.

"Excellent. Let's go, then. Catch you later, Jack."

Oh—Jack wasn't coming?

"Maybe I'll tag along with you, Dad," Jack said with a fairly grim smile of his own.

He *was* coming.

"Cynthia?" said Cornelius to Jack's secretary. "The more the merrier!"

Shit. *She* was coming?

"Oh, no, Mr. Eastman," Cynthia said, blushing probably down to her toes. "I have to get home, really. David will be waiting for his supper."

She wasn't coming. So. The sailing party consisted of a married philanderer, a single philanderer, an old chick, a young chick, and two kids. What could come of *that* combination, Liz had no idea.

They stopped at Cornelius's Lexus to take out a wicker basket which probably contained pâté and smoked salmon and other things Susy wouldn't eat, and then they boarded the superbly exquisite *Déjà Vu*. Liz had been in a fair number of mansions—all of them tourist attractions charging admission—but she'd never sailed aboard a real yacht, for money or for free.

She liked it. It was impossible not to feel like a Susy-in-Disney-World when Jack threw off the heavy nylon dock lines and his father began backing the boat expertly out of its slip. The low blub-blub of the engine echoed discreetly through the water, nothing at all like the ear-piercing high-speed boats she sometimes heard racing up and down the bay. By the time she had Susy strapped into her life jacket, the *Déjà Vu* was quietly threading its way past the docked boats heading down the bay.

Newport, her little City by the Sea, looked even more charming from the deck of a boat: a collection of white and stone steeples sprinkled among ancient trees and gambrel roofs. The scale was surprisingly intimate and cozy; it was hard to believe that a town so small could have been a major seaport during the Revolutionary era. It gave Liz great satisfaction to be living in what was basically the same colonial town—give or take a few awful condo projects—that had graced the side of the hill for centuries.

Liz had Susy next to her on the semicircle of cushioned seating on the afterdeck. "Look for our house, honey," she said, pointing up the hill. "See the big square steeple that looks like a castle? Look up behind it. Oops—too late; it's gone behind a tree."

Susy slipped out of her mother's reach and sidled up to the rail where Caroline, also in a life jacket, was standing. The two girls—one as dark as the other was fair—watched as the piers and condos fell away and the yacht, bearing right, began to steam out the channel.

Liz had to force herself not to tuck Susy somewhere safe in the middle of the boat, because she knew her daughter would never forgive the humiliation of it. But the *Déjà Vu* wasn't Disney World: there were no seat belts or safety bars here. Their only protection from all that water was a hundred-year-old wooden hull and the expertise of two men who were barely on speaking terms.

She looked for Deirdre and found the black-haired beauty draped over Cornelius's shoulder, pointing to various instruments and asking questions in her enchanting Irish accent. *So much for the nanny,* thought Liz. She resolved to keep an eye on Caroline, too. As for Jack—where *was* Jack?

She peeked around the starboard—or was it the port?— deck; but he surprised her by approaching her on the port— or was it the starboard?—side.

"Can I get you or the kids anything?" he asked in a depressingly polite tone.

"I think we're all set for now, thanks," she said, still without taking her eyes off Susy and Caroline.

Jack followed her gaze. "Don't worry, they're fine there. As soon as we hit the chop around Fort Adams and catch a little spray aft, they'll come running for cover."

He left her to go below deck. Liz wondered why—since he'd invited himself along—he was staying so removed from the party.

But in the meantime the boat was bobbing through the wake of a much-too-fast sport fisherman that passed them in the opposite direction. The *Déjà Vu* ended up taking some spray aboard and—Jack was right—the girls got washed with a fine mist of salt water. They squealed in surprise and ran back to Liz with hunched shoulders and arms pulled in tight. That lasted ten seconds. Then Susy went right back to the rail, and Caroline, not to be outdone, took up a position next to her. Clearly they were hoping for a hurricane.

The varnish-framed cabin windows behind Liz were slid open, allowing her to hear some, but not all, of the exchanges between Deirdre and Cornelius in the wheelhouse. Their talk was innocent enough, but their flirty tone made Liz uncomfortable. Deirdre's laugh was just a little too eager, a little too shrill.

Cornelius began to turn the yacht north, up the calm water of Narragansett Bay.

Deirdre cried out gaily, "Beggin' your pardon, sir, not that way! The other way! Toward *Ireland,* we should be goin'!"

Cornelius laughed and said, "Ireland it is, then!" and turned the helm sharply to the left. The *Déjà Vu* began heading out the bay, toward open water.

Chapter 22

❖

*A*lmost at once Jack appeared. "What the hell's going on?" he said, not bothering to hide his annoyance.

His father, who'd fallen into the spirit of Deirdre's whimsy, said affably, "We're sailing to Ireland, that's all. Don't worry, son; we'll have you back at the yard by the time the whistle blows in the morning."

Ignoring his father's flip tone, Jack said, "I just monitored the weather. There's an advisory posted until nine o'clock tonight. A line of thunderstorms is moving through Connecticut."

"Was it a watch or a warning?"

"A watch."

"No problem, then," his father said with a wink at Deirdre. "We'll hold our course for Ireland."

"We've got a couple of kids—"

"Hey, we'll take 'em along," Cornelius said with a laugh.

"For God's sake, Dad! Give it a rest!"

The look in his father's eyes turned suddenly cold. "Something bugging you, Jack?"

Jack turned on his heel and went back below.

More uncomfortable than ever now, and nervous to boot, Liz walked up to the rail, expecting to see a dangerous sky to the west. But what she saw was a benign and reassuring summer sunset. As long as they didn't actually try to make

Ireland tonight, they should be back before any weather rolled through.

Meanwhile it was Susy's suppertime, and Liz didn't dare go rummaging through the wicker basket, wherever it was, because she was a guest. Who the hell was the host? She turned her back on the western shore and, gripping the rail behind her, watched Susy and Caroline carefully ignoring one another as they stood at the rail opposite. It wasn't the ride Liz thought it would be: she had the profound sense that nobody liked anybody on this boat except the two people who had no business liking one another at all.

"Deirdre, dear," she heard Cornelius say in the wheel-house, "why don't you bring up another bottle of wine? Jack will show you where they are."

Oh, great. Sailing under the influence. Liz had declined a glass, and she hadn't seen Jack take anything; that left the daddy and the nanny responsible for any empties.

She felt so trapped. How did you get off a boat? You could walk out of a party, step off at a train station; even airplane flights could only last so long. But a *boat*! This could go on until Ireland.

She almost jumped for joy when she saw Jack come out from the wheelhouse with the wicker basket. He put the basket down on the low round table and said simply, "C'mon, kids, have something to eat."

He began spreading out the contents. Just as Liz feared: everything was way too fancy to stick to the stomach. Marinated mushrooms; an assortment of cheeses; *pâté de foie;* caviar (naturally); thin, thin crackers; and last but not least, the predictable smoked salmon.

"Whaddya think of *that*?" Jack said proudly to Susy, who was eyeing it all with intense dismay.

I was right the first time, Liz decided. *The man knows nothing about being a parent.*

Jack was peering into the picnic basket. "Oops, how did

that stuff get in here? Cookies? Peanut butter and jelly sandwich? Netta must've put that in for the sea gulls.''

Susy's eyes got wider. "No, *I'll* eat the sandwich—if no one wants it, I mean."

She looked at Caroline, who said loftily, "*I'd* rather have the pâté."

Jack glanced at Liz with easy humor and then handed Susy the sandwich. "Here you go," he said to her, "if you're sure you don't mind eating something so boring. Actually, you'd be doing me a big favor."

He tucked a napkin under cach of the girls' chins, and in that simple, nurturing gesture, Liz was lost completely and forever to the possibility of loving any other man. She could've watched him with the children all the way to Ireland.

Caroline spread the goose-liver pâté on a wafer, which broke in half. She said quickly, "I did that on purpose."

Liz watched, impressed, as Caroline popped one of the halves into her mouth, took one chew of the goose liver, narrowed her eyes, stifled a look of surprise and disgust, glanced around in a bored fashion, got up, wandered over to the rail, and spat out the mess when she thought no one was looking.

As for Susy, she was in love. Jack could do no wrong. Once he found out that Susy liked riddles, he kept them coming one after another—surprising Liz yet again—and seemed genuinely eager to add Susy's own repertoire to his collection.

Eventually Caroline sat back down, and Susy offered her half of the peanut butter sandwich, making Liz absurdly proud of her. Caroline actually accepted it, making Liz absurdly proud of her, too.

In the meantime the *Déjà Vu* had passed through most of the fleet of boats and yachts that were returning to their home port. Cornelius put the boat on autopilot, and he and Deirdre joined the others in what was turning out to be, after all, a very nice boat ride.

The problem was the wine. It was flowing too freely. The fairly innocent gaiety between Cornelius and Deirdre was escalating into something else. They were taking over the show, and nobody much wanted to watch the performance. Not Liz: she began to wish they'd go back into the wheel-house.

And not Jack. He was becoming quieter and angrier by the minute. When Deirdre, laughing hysterically at some-thing unfunny, spilled wine over herself and Cornelius rushed to her bosom with a napkin, it was the last straw for Jack.

"Dad, I need to talk to you in private," he said through gritted teeth. "Can we go below for a minute?"

"Heck, no," said his dad jovially. "We're all friends. Say it on deck."

"Oblige me this once, please."

"Oh, all right."

Jack scanned the horizon for boats, then turned to Liz and said, "Keep an eye out, would you?"

Cornelius stood up unsteadily—though the sea was flat as a mirror—and followed his son into the wheelhouse and then down the ladder steps to the cabin. That left four nonsailing females alone in deepening twilight on the afterdeck of a sixty-foot boat that no one was steering.

To Liz it seemed downright surreal. Torn between Susy and the assignment, she said to her daughter, "Sit right here, and don't you dare move from this place. You, too, Caro-line."

Deirdre, not so drunk that she couldn't feel repentant, said, "I'll watch them, don't worry."

Liz took up a position just inside the wheelhouse where she could see both the horizon and her daughter, and yet stay out of earshot of the conversation below.

That, it turned out, was hard to do. Jack was angry and his father was high. Every loud word funneled up the cabin stairs into the wheelhouse.

"God*dam*mit, Dad, the older you get, the bigger the fool! What's wrong, the last one wasn't young enough? Deirdre's a *kid,* for chrissake!"

"You bet. And a damned good-looking one."

"You're embarrassing everyone! You're embarrassing yourself!"

"No-o-o, not me, son. I feel just fine."

"Don't push it, Dad!"

"Well, well, this is new. Since when do you give a damn what I do and who I do it with?"

"Knock it off, I said!"

"Or else what? You're going to tell your mother? You think she cares?"

"Yeah, I think she cares! *You're* the only one who can't see that!"

"Where've you been all your life? She hasn't cared since you were born."

"What the hell are you talking about? She's always loved you, God only knows why."

"Get with it, Jack. Why do you think you're an only child? She's ignored me for years."

"That's a goddamned lie!"

"Maybe an exaggeration. Not a lie. I bore her."

"Your running around bores her. And *hurts* her. Don't you see that? You're rationalizing your idiotic behavior!"

"You see it your way. I see it mine."

"Divorce her, then! Why make a mockery of your marriage with kids like Deirdre?"

"Oh-h, come on . . . Deirdre's nothing—we're just horsing around."

"I'm warning you, Dad: If you go up there and pick up where you left off—"

"—you'll what? Lock me below? Keelhaul me? Come on, son. We're both adults."

"*One* of us, maybe!"

"Don't pull that bullshit! You're the one who's made it to the halfway point of his life *alone*. At least I gave marriage a shot. I had you. I had Caroline. It may not be a perfect family, but at least I was willing to step up to the plate. Now let me pass. I'm your *father*. I deserve more respect than you're giving me."

Whether Jack was going to let his father pass or not, nobody ever found out, because at that moment an alarm went off on the instrument panel, and Jack came flying up the companionway steps.

"Now what?" he muttered, scanning the gauges. "Damn! Overheating! Dad! Get up here!"

No need to tell Cornelius; he was right behind his son.

"Let me look over the engine quick," Jack said to him. "You shut it off when I tell you."

Jack dropped down the steps in one leap and disappeared into the cabin below. Over the dramatic pulsing of the alarm, Cornelius said sheepishly, "I never went in for that engine stuff. That's why God invented mechanics."

They waited an agonizing number of seconds and then heard Jack's voice from the belly of the boat: "Okay! Shut it off!"

Cornelius did. The boat fell strangely, perilously silent. There they were, well offshore, floating as aimlessly as a sixty-foot piece of driftwood. It was confirmation of Liz's deepest dread.

Susy and Caroline were standing on the semicircle of cushioned seats, noses pressed against the aft windows of the wheelhouse, as curious as two bear cubs eyeing a cherry pie. Deirdre was standing behind them, looking oddly tentative. Liz motioned the girls to sit back down—they ignored her—

and then she waited, with all the others, for Jack to reappear with a diagnosis of the problem.

Liz knew little about engines, even less about boats, but she had absolutely no doubt that Jack could fix whatever it was that needed fixing. It was an act of pure blind faith, an homage to her regard for him—and it surprised the heck out of her. Here she was, despite a lifetime of warnings by her mother—allowing herself to get her hopes up.

At last Jack emerged, holding what even Liz knew was a broken fan belt in his hand.

"It's been cut," he said without preamble. "Three-quarters of the belt's diameter is razor-smooth," he said, showing it to his father. "Only the last quarter shows signs of fatigue. Obviously the uncut portion couldn't carry the load, and it broke apart. As it was meant to do."

Cornelius looked as guilty as if he'd cut the belt himself. "Jesus. This time they've gone too far. What're they trying to do? Get someone killed?"

"Think about it," his son said tersely.

"Well, put on a spare and let's get out of here," Cornelius said, casting a wary eye to the west. "Who knows what other booby traps they've set? What if—?"

Jack looked quickly at Liz. "No need for hysteria," he said, cutting his father's speculations short. "If the pattern holds true, then this is all the wake-up call we'll be getting tonight."

If. Liz didn't like that *if*. She waited with Cornelius in the wheelhouse, saying little, reluctant to move an inch farther away from news of a repair than she had to. The yacht sat uneasily on the calm water, rising and falling gradually with the swell. In the meantime Susy and Caroline, tired of waiting for something to happen, decided to try on each other's shoes.

Deirdre began repacking the wicker basket with unsteady hands and then, halfway through her task, suddenly dropped everything and made a sprint for the stern rail. The wrenching, wracking sounds of her seasickness sent a surge of queasiness through Liz. But she couldn't get sick; she didn't *dare* get sick.

Caroline, watching Deirdre furtively, looked a little green around the gills as well. Susy seemed to be holding up fine, which hardly surprised Liz. The child was so clearly in her element out here.

Half of us are sailors, thought Liz with an edgy sigh. *But half of us are not.*

At last Jack came back up the companionway, but the black look on his face told Liz that once again she had placed her trust where it didn't belong.

"There are no fan belts—not a one—in the spare-parts locker or anywhere else," he said with unnerving calm. He looked at his father and said, "So it looks as if I was wrong: this one's a two-parter."

"What do we do now?"

It was Liz, trying to keep the fear out of her voice but not succeeding. Maybe no one else was watching out to the west, but she sure was. And what she saw was hardly reassuring: a black line of clouds, with some depressingly vertical buildup among them.

Jack said, "One of the pulleys has a double fan belt on it. I'm going to try refitting the second one as a replacement; I may have enough adjustability—but enough with the gory details," he said to Liz with a flash of humor. "The short answer is, I'm going to try a jury rig."

He glanced out at the sky impassively, which made Liz feel better, and then said to his father, "Flip on the running lights, Dad. It's getting dark," which made her feel worse.

"Won't we run down our charge?" asked Cornelius.

"We don't have much choice," Jack said, and went back below.

A couple of minutes later, he was back in the wheelhouse.

"The nuts on the pulley are frozen; it's going to take a little while." For some reason, he looked to the east, not to the west, this time. "We're going to have to anchor."

He went up to the bow of the boat and undid the lashings of a big Popeye-style anchor that was secured to the rail. He worked some mechanism that released the anchor, which fell into the sea with a thunk, and what seemed like miles of chain went roaring out behind it. So now they were no longer a piece of floating driftwood. They were a sitting duck.

Jack went back below, and Liz, tired herself of waiting, brought Susy and Caroline inside the wheelhouse where it was warm. She sat on the settee with Susy in her lap and an arm around Caroline, who was propped up sleepily against her side. Deirdre collapsed on the cushioned semicircle of the afterdeck, and Cornelius joined his son below, to hold a flashlight for Jack to work by.

So this is yachting, Liz mused, watching the spooky red sky with its dull red glow and distant, pulsating flashes of lightning. *All in all, I guess I can live without it.*

She had a moment of hope. About twenty minutes later, Jack's father came up and started the engine again. It rumbled to life and she thought, *Finally. We're on our way again.*

And then Jack's voice, up from the cabin: "No good! Shut it down, Dad!"

He came back up, looking disheartened now, and said, "The belt's too big; it keeps slipping. We can wait to flag down someone for a tow, but with the kids on board—I'm going to call the Coast Guard."

It was obvious to Liz that he hated to have to do it. "Don't worry about us," she said quickly. "Everyone's fine."

"Baloney," he said, and picked up the transmitter to his marine radio. "This is the *Déjà Vu, Déjà Vu, Déjà Vu,* whiskey-yankee-sierra-one-zero-zero calling the Point Judith Coast Guard, Point Judith Coast Guard."

"*Déjà Vu*, this is the Point Judith Coast Guard; switch and answer twenty-two."

"Switching two-two."

Jack punched in the digits on his radio and then calmly, but with some embarrassment, explained the plight they were in.

"I roger that," said a young voice at the other end. "Cap'n, are you in any danger right now?"

"No, sir," said Jack. "We have an anchor down."

"Roger that. We have all boats out on an emergency call, so if you could just sit tight and monitor this station, we'll get back to you as quick as we can."

Jack acknowledged the response and signed off. He came back to where Liz sat with the sleeping kids and took a seat beside her.

"Look, I'm really sorry about this."

"It's not your fault, Jack," Liz said wearily. "It's the fault of—of whoever these *monster* saboteurs are," she said, trying to suppress her outrage. Still, the word *monster* made Susy stir in her sleep.

"Let's put these two to bed," Jack said softly. He lifted Caroline up in his arms, and Liz, carrying Susy, followed him carefully down the bronze cabin steps to a guest stateroom below. Jack tucked Caroline, life jacket and all, into a narrow berth that was secured by a beautifully carved bunkboard; Liz tucked Susy into the berth opposite.

"You just nap here for a while, honey," whispered Liz, pulling up a blue cotton blanket with a big gold anchor on it. "We'll be home before you know it."

Susy roused from her sleep enough to take it all in. "Mommy?" she said. "I like this bed."

With a bemused shake of her head, Liz went back to the wheelhouse. She was determined to monitor both the weather and the Coast Guard radio frequency. She saw Cornelius on the afterdeck with a drink in his hand, keeping his own silent vigil over demons that she, for one, would never be able to see.

The old man—right now, standing at the stern with shoulders bent, he looked very old indeed—had found a blanket and covered Deirdre with it, which made Liz melt a little toward him.

Maybe there are no real villains in his marriage, she thought. *Just as there were none in mine.* It was the first time since the day Keith walked out that she was able to admit it. The realization made her a little bit older, a little bit sadder, a little bit freer.

She stood in the dark wheelhouse, staring at the radio's red "22" as if it were a ghost, willing it to say something. The boat was bobbing up and down a little more now; a chill, damp breeze was blowing through the open windows of the wheelhouse. The flashes of lightning were brighter; the thunder seemed less distant. The front was coming closer.

Come and save us, she pleaded to the silent radio. *Save us now.*

She saw Jack's dark shadow emerge from below. He stood alongside her, staring at she didn't know what, absorbing something she didn't understand from the sea around them.

"I've got one more thing I want to try," he said in a voice more taut than before. "Would you mind sacrificing your pantyhose for it?"

She had to laugh; how could she not? "Anything for the *Déjà Vu,*" she said. Without asking for details, she hiked up her skirt and peeled away the hose, then handed them to him. "Good luck—Cap'n."

"I'll need every bit of it. And I'll need you, to hold the flashlight while my dad monitors things up here." He called his father in from the afterdeck and said to him, "I just listened to the weather. The watch has been upgraded to a warning. If the boat goes beam-to, yell."

"Won't be much we can do about it, son."

Here was a detail Liz preferred to know. "What does it mean if the boat goes beam-to?" she asked as they headed for the engine-room.

"It means we're dragging the anchor," Jack said tersely.

"Does that really matter out here?" Liz asked him.

"It does if you're upwind of a rocky ledge."

"A ledge, way out here?"

"Check the chart," Jack snapped.

Liz left it at that. Even she could see that the stakes were escalating with each new roll of thunder.

Ducking her head low, she followed him into the cramped and narrow area alongside the exposed engine. It was a brute of a thing, much bigger than the little mass of efficiency that powered her van. Jack flashed the light over it, focusing on an obviously unbelted pulley.

He adjusted the beam of the flashlight to spread wide and said, "Keep it aimed at my hands."

She did as she was told, watching with skeptical fascination as he measured off her pantyhose against the broken belt, then cut off one of the legs and began fitting it around the two pulleys.

"Boy, suddenly I wish my legs were an extralong," she said fervently as she hovered above him with the flashlight.

He laughed softly and said, "Your legs are perfect the way they are."

Ridiculous, to feel a thrill shoot through her at a time like this, but there it was: goosebumps.

"Have you done this sort of thing before?" she dared to ask. It was bad enough that he knew about hooks and eyes; it would be terrible if he knew about pantyhose fan belts.

"Hmm?" He was concentrating on his task, pulling the pantyhose as tight around the pulleys as he could before removing it and tying a knot in it. "No, I've never tried this. But I thought to myself—what would MacGyver do in this situation?"

She smiled at his self-deprecating humor and said, "He'd probably string together paper clips and a bobby pin."

"You don't use bobby pins in your hair."

True; too true. He knew everything about her, inside and out now. If only he knew how much she loved him. Why hadn't she beaten him over the head with it? Instead she'd let him drift away—back to the old life, back to the Cynthias in it.

No. Not to Cynthia. Whatever Liz thought she'd overheard at the shipyard office earlier, she'd heard wrong. There was simply no way Jack would make a move on a married woman, any more than his great-great-grandfather would have done. So she must've heard wrong.

Jack was finished. He blew air through puffed cheeks and said, "Let's give it a shot. Stand at the bottom of the cabin steps where I can see you and where you can see my father. Tell him to start it up when I give you the signal."

Liz took up her post and waited. She could see Jack's elongated shadow on the engine-room walls, and the slanting beams of his flashlight as he checked over the engine one last time. "Okay," he said to her.

Worried that Susy would go jumping out of her berth from the noise, Liz nonetheless passed the signal to Cornelius. She heard the uncovered engine roar to life and waited one minute—two, three—for Jack to signal her to have the engine shut down again. When he let it keep on running, her heart soared. Fixed! They could go!

"Shut it down!"

Shit. Shit shit shit! She passed Jack's disheartening command up to his father and then, struggling awkwardly now, climbed the steps to the wheelhouse to check the sky.

After the quiet below, she was shocked by the change on deck: the wind was howling now, and rain pounded against the windows of the wheelhouse, reducing visibility nearly to zero. The dull red glow of the running light to her left and the even duller green glow to her right seemed pitifully inadequate to warn off approaching ships. A white light high above the wheelhouse threw a bleary halo over the *Déjà Vu,* just enough to let her see that she could see nothing. But she knew the sound of breaking seas; and she could hear seas breaking all around her. The yacht was pitching much more than before; she had to grab things in the dark to keep herself from hurtling off balance.

Why hadn't Cornelius lit the kerosene lamps?

She turned on her heel, impelled by a loud crack of thunder, intending to warn Jack and to check on Susy; but Cornelius, whom she'd scarcely noticed, called her back to him.

"Liz . . . Liz . . . get Deirdre inside . . . and I . . . can't breathe . . . tell Jack. . . . '' He staggered back and collapsed in a sitting position onto the settee behind him, abandoning his post at the helm.

For one endless pinpoint in time, Liz's mind simply shut down: too many people needed her at once. Then she snapped out of it, prioritizing the demands. *"Jack!"* she cried. "Come up here!"

She staggered through the door that led to the afterdeck and tried to rouse Deirdre, but the girl was in too much physical agony to move. Soaking wet from the rain that slanted under the open roof of the afterdeck, Deirdre clung to the cushions, resisting Liz's efforts to help her up.

"Oh, *God,*" she moaned, "I want to die . . . get me off this thing . . . please . . . oh, God . . . just let me die."

Wine, fear, and seasickness: it was a deadly combination. Liz had no time to cajole. Rain-soaked herself now, she hauled Deirdre forcibly up from the cushions and stood weaving with her on the pitching deck, trying to regain her balance. She was reaching for the handle on the aft door to the wheelhouse when it slammed shut after an especially violent lurch of the boat.

It wouldn't open. Liz could see the shadowy form of Jack

bending over his ailing father. No help there. She decided to go around to one of the side doors of the wheelhouse. She staggered with her burden to the left deck, closest to where Jack and his father were. The rain, cold and sharp, stung her face and her eyes, making her blind, forcing her back. She bent her head and plowed forward with her moaning burden.

The *Déjà Vu* had been rearing up higher, it seemed, with each oncoming wave. Now it rose to a frightening angle and fell off to its side with a shudder, like a horse taking a bullet in a western movie.

Instantly, horribly, Liz understood the meaning of *beam-to*. The *Déjà Vu* had ripped out its anchor from the bottom of the sea and was dragging it along uselessly as the boat faced the wind and the seas broadside.

Liz and Deirdre happened to be on that side. *The port side,* she realized irrelevantly. *Port means left in their godforsaken lingo.*

A sea, higher, wetter, colder than everything that had preceded it, rose up and came crashing down on Deirdre and her, sending them both skidding and falling on the watery deck.

"*Get up.* Get *up!*" Liz screamed in Deirdre's ear.

By sheer force of her own strength and will, Liz pulled Deirdre's dead weight off the deck and got her moving forward again. When she got to the cabin door, it flung open wide to receive them. Jack was there, pulling them both into the relative safety of the wheelhouse. A small mountain of water followed them in, making a headlong rush for the cabin steps and below.

Liz felt no comfort from being inside: *Out of the fire, into the frying pan* was her only thought.

"I have to go to Susy!" she cried, furious now that Deirdre had used up her time and energy. The boat was lying at a ghastly angle; Susy wouldn't understand.

Jack grabbed her arm. "Not now!" he said loudly over

the din of the storm. "My father may be having a heart attack. You've got to stay here, responding to the Coast Guard, while I try one more time on the engine."

"*What!* With that stupid pantyhose? It'll never work, Jack! Let me go!"

She tried to bolt past him, but he dragged her to the radio. "*Watch me.* Watch what to do!" he said, picking up the transmitter. "Press it when you talk, let go when you listen. *Don't leave it pressed after you talk,* or you won't be able to hear them."

He pressed the button. "Point Judith Coast Guard, the *Djà Vu*!" he said, reducing the distress call to its essence.

The Coast Guard came back immediately, and Jack, in half a dozen sentences, conveyed the emergency, gave them the coordinates of their position, and handed the job of further communications over to Liz.

God only knew how close they were to the rocks by now. Liz accepted the transmitter with a trembling hand, and Jack jumped down below, leaving Deirdre and Cornelius slumped on the settee like casualties in a MASH unit.

And what about Susy and Caroline? Where were they? Knocked out cold? Screaming in panic? How would Liz know? Above the horrendous, fearful noise, how would she know? It took every ounce of discipline she possessed to stay with the radio, ignoring her child.

Susy's safe; safe below, she told herself. But another big wave broadsided the boat, forcing its way through the wheelhouse windows, the doors, through every possible seam and cranny, and she realized that boats could sink from above, not just from below. She resolved to run down to the stateroom, just to see, just to know, just to . . .

Trust him, Elizabeth.

The words vibrated through her, cutting through the howl and crash of wind and sea. No need to ask who spoke them. Liz stopped in her tracks, waiting for more.

The radio crackled. "*Déjà Vu, Déjà Vu,* this is the Point Judith Coast Guard, Point Judith Coast Guard."

Liz pressed the button the way Jack showed her. "Yes? This is the *Déjà Vu.*" She remembered, barely, to release her death-grip on the button.

"*Déjà Vu,* Point Judith Coast Guard. Ma'am, can you repeat the coordinates that your captain gave us just now? Over."

What're you, deaf? she thought. Aloud she said, "He's not here—" Then she remembered to press the button, and in that split second she also remembered the latitude and longitude that Jack had given them. "Point Judith Coast Guard, this is the *Déjà Vu,*" she said clearly. "The coordinates are: 41 23.5 north; 71 28.5 west. Over."

The young man at the other end of the radio signal repeated the numbers, then said, "I have a vessel en route to your position, making the best possible speed at this time. At this time I would advise you to be sure that everyone is wearing a life jacket. I'll check with you again in a few minutes to see how your situation is. Please stand by on this channel; over."

She pressed the button and said, "Point Judith Coast Guard, this is the *Déjà Vu.* Yes. We'll stand by."

She staggered back to check on Jack's father, leaning at the same cockeyed angle as everything and everyone else. "How are you holding up?" she said, unable to tell on her own.

"Ah . . . hanging in there . . . ," he said with what she thought was extraordinary bravery.

"A rescue boat is on the way."

"Yes . . . I heard."

"They want us to put on life jackets," she suggested as calmly as she could.

"No . . . no . . . Won't be needing 'em."

And in the meantime the *Déjà Vu* was being lifted and

thrown, lifted and thrown, ever closer to its destiny. She thought of the *Titanic*; she thought of the *Mary Deare*.

She thought of the life jackets. Would Susy and Caroline have dared take them off? Suddenly she wanted the girls in the wheelhouse, ready to hand over to their rescuers. She groped her way down the cabin steps and stumbled into Jack.

"Back to the helm," he commanded. "We're ready to try again. I want you to count to five. Then turn the key. Then press the ignition button and hold it till you hear the engine catch. I'll be up after I've made sure the fix works."

Mentally, Liz was already abandoning ship. She marveled at Jack's can-do spirit, but she was in no mood to join in. She was about to tell him that, when she heard—*felt*, really—Christopher urging her again.

Trust him. Trust him.

"All right," she said. They were the hardest two words she'd ever spoken.

She turned and made her way back up the steps and took up her position at the helm.

One potato. Two potato. Three potato. Four potato. Five potato. She turned the key. Pressed the ignition button. Held it until the engine caught.

And then she waited.

Chapter 23

$\diamond$

The boat continued to lift and fall, lift and fall, in an interminable dance of death. The horror Liz felt turned to agony and then, as the minutes ticked by, to something like dreadful hope. This time . . . this time . . . maybe.

In the meantime the wind, which had swung so viciously into the black northeast, showed no signs of abating, and the seas were worse than ever. Wind and sea: two thugs as old as time itself, brutalizing the pitifully fragile *Déjà Vu* and her mortal cargo.

It made Liz want to fall to her knees and weep.

But there was no time to feel humbled. Jack rushed up the cabin steps, his voice tight with urgency. "All right! Next, we get the anchor back aboard!"

She was afraid it meant he'd have to go on deck and brave the storm, but that wasn't necessary: "The engine's charging again," he said. "We'll use the windlass."

He headed the boat directly into the wind; immediately the boat became upright again. Liz couldn't see the anchor-chain being hauled aboard, but she could feel the ratcheting action echo through the hull. *Clackety-clackety-clackety-clackety:* link by link, they were regaining control of their destiny. She wanted to sing for joy.

"Now let's get the hell out of here," Jack said, and he altered course away from the perilous ledge.

354 Antoinette Stockenberg

The *Déjà Vu* was still struggling, still thrashing, but even Liz could feel that it was doing so with purpose now.

Liz left Jack in communication with the Coast Guard rescue vessel and rushed below to check on Susy and Caroline. Amazingly, Susy was sound asleep. Liz had to lay her hand on Susy's chest to convince herself of it. *You angel, you,* she thought, inexpressibly relieved.

Caroline, however, was awake and scared. She sat huddled in the farthest corner of her berth like a small wet cat, shivering and trying hard to hide her sobs. Liz hugged her and comforted her and suggested that she tuck in with Susy. Once that was done, Liz returned to the wheelhouse, expecting to see Cornelius preparing to be offloaded to the Coast Guard vessel.

She was surprised—and yet hardly surprised at all—to find Jack and his father arguing about it.

"I'm telling you, I feel better!" Cornelius was insisting. "I don't need to be rushed to any hospital, goddammit. Stop treating me like an old man!"

"Christ, Dad, you're not a young one!"

"It was indigestion, I tell you! Too much wine, too much everything."

"You're crazy, you know that? Their forty-one-footer could get you into Newport two, three times faster than the *Déjà Vu.*"

"You're the crazy one, Jack!" his father said angrily. "You know how dangerous it would be for them to come alongside in these seas? You'd put everyone in jeopardy— and it'd be hell on the *Déjà*'s topsides."

"We're talking about your *life,* not a paint job!"

"My life's just fine, thanks. Butt out of it!"

Cornelius brushed past his son and took up the transmitter. In a voice not unlike Jack's, he raised the Coast Guard and called off the rescue mission. Only then did Liz notice a brightly lit vessel astern of them, obviously the forty-one-footer. The rescue boat offered to accompany the *Déjà Vu* and, indeed, did so until it was called away on another mission.

Then the forty-one-footer peeled away from the formation like a fighter jet, leaving Liz feeling oddly bereft.

"Busy night," muttered Cornelius to his son.

"Yeah. Reminds me of that nor'easter that hit us out of nowhere in Nantucket that time."

"Mmm. I remember. Incredible damage in the harbor. Was that the one where the sloop burned to the waterline?"

"Yep."

And so it went, with Liz, wrapped in one of Jack's sweaters, listening in amazement to the two men chatting quietly, almost nostalgically, about various disasters while all hell broke loose around them and the *Déjà Vu* inched its way through it, courtesy of half a pair of pantyhose.

Cornelius apparently felt well enough to take the helm a couple of times and let Jack duck into the engine room to check his handiwork. When he came back up, his voice was almost bemused as he said, "She's holding, by golly."

Eventually they slipped into smoother water under the lee of Brenton Point and Castle Hill; and then finally, miraculously, the granite bulkhead of Fort Adams hove into view. The harbor, secure and welcoming and wonderfully calm, lay to port.

They were home.

Within fifteen minutes the *Déjà Vu* was tied up snugly at its berth, and Liz and Jack were carrying two wiped-out five-year-olds like sacks of grain over their shoulders. Deirdre recovered almost spontaneously the minute she stepped on land. It didn't surprise anyone: she had so damned much youth in her favor. Under the docklights Liz thought Cornelius looked a little ashen. But she felt a little washed out herself, so she could hardly blame him.

Jack, with Caroline in his arms, was leading the tired party to his father's Lexus; Deirdre had already volunteered to do the driving back to East Gate. Liz was behind them, carrying Susy.

"Mommy," Susy murmured sleepily in her mother's ear, "I have to go potty."

Liz sighed and said, "Jack, I'm going to take Susy to the bathroom."

"Use the one in the office," he suggested.

"No, that's okay; the yard one's closer." She didn't want Jack to have to detour with his keys to the office for their sake.

She put Susy down, and the two of them split away from the rest of the bedraggled party and headed for the neat and shiny-clean set of bathrooms that were housed in a permanent trailer on the shipyard grounds.

"How come you didn't use the bathroom on the boat?" she asked her daughter in a gentle chide; at this point all Liz wanted to do was go home.

"It's not a bathroom, mommy; it's a *head*," said Susy with nautical precision. "And anyway, Caroline told me they're hard to use. She plugged it up one time just with toilet paper."

"Oh. Okay."

She and Susy threaded their way through the hauled-out boats, virtually all of them for sale, that stood high and dry near the trailer of bathrooms. Liz was grateful for the bright new lighting that Jack had had installed since the sabotage began: it made it easier for them to see around the obstacles.

They detoured around a carpenter's wooden tool caddy that was sitting on the ground in their path, and Liz thought, *It can't be too unsafe around here if someone's willing to leave valuable tools out all night*. But then, she reminded herself, theft was not what any of the incidents were about.

Mother and daughter went up the two steps into the trailer, and Susy made a beeline for the middle of the three stalls.

Liz took the time to wash her face and hands, trying to wake up for the short drive home. She stared at herself in the mirror: wet flattened hair; dark hollows under her eyes; and—worst of all—a sweater that was navy blue, a color that made her look old.

She was turning away from her own dreariness when she caught sight of maroon fabric in the slit along the closed door in the end stall behind her. She looked down at the floor of the stall: *no feet.*

Her heart rammed up against her chest. *Again!* Oh no oh no oh no . . .

In pure blind terror she whipped open the door to Susy's stall.

Susy, surprised, said, "Mommy, wait—I'm not finished yet."

"Shh. I'll help," Liz said in a deathly whisper. Automatically she closed the door behind her to shield them.

"No, Mommy—I'm not a baby!"

"Never mind, I said."

Liz yanked up the child's underpants and turned to flee.

Outside their stall she saw the pair of feet at last. Men's feet, shod in hiking boots.

Oh no.

No time to think, no time to weigh decisions. She put both hands up against the door. With a sudden, instinctive, infuriated cry of *"Enough!"* she slammed the door outward as hard as she could.

She heard a scream of pain—a broken nose, at the least— and then a hand reached out and caught her arm as she tried to escape with her child.

"Run, Susy! Get Jack!" she cried.

Wide-eyed, Susy did as she was told and took off while Liz struggled with yet another assailant in her life. This time, the encounter was brief and far more violent on her part than his: she pushed, she fought, she scratched, she screamed. She was a wild thing, enraged and furious and protective.

It wasn't long before David Penny, blood still streaming from his nose, broke away and fled from the trailer into the night, leaving his carpenter's tools behind him. Liz ran out after him, terrified that he'd find Susy and make her his hostage. It was only when she saw Jack running in her direction that she knew Susy must be safe.

That was when she stopped to think: *Was it possible that David got caught using the wrong bathroom and was just trying to tiptoe past them?*

No. It was not.

Jack arrived in a state of breathless alarm. "Are you okay?"

When she nodded, he said, "Did you see who it was?"

Liz, winded herself, had no words for him. She pointed to the capenter's tool caddy on the ground.

"That's Penny's toolbox," Jack said. "What're his tools—?"

"That's—who it was: David Penny."

"Oh . . . *shit,*" said Jack in a black, black voice. "That's who it was."

"Unless he was perfectly innocent and I've just broken his nose by mistake—"

"No," Jack said with a sense of finality. "He's the one. Of course he is. It all fits."

"What fits?" she said, her fear easing nicely into a fit of anger. "Will you *please* tell me what—?"

Susy came running up at that moment with Deirdre and Caroline right behind and Cornelius bringing up the rear. Liz dropped down nose to nose with her daughter and said, "All a big silly mistake, honey. The man was in the wrong bathroom, and when I bumped him with the door, he got a little upset. But we worked it all out. Now you just wait here with

Deirdre. I have to talk to Mr. Eastman. I'll only be a minute.''

She walked a little away from the group; Jack followed.

"What the hell's going on?" she asked in an undertone. "Why would David Penny want to bring down the yard? He quit here on his own; Netta told me that, on the day of the picnic. Besides, you throw him work whenever you can. What would he have against *you*?"

"My father, that's what," Jack said bitterly. "After David got a job here, he brought in Cynthia when he heard we had an opening for a secretary. Right after that, he quit, hoping to free-lance. But the timing was bad; he couldn't find work. So they needed Cynthia's job more than ever."

"And your father—?"

"—couldn't pass her up," Jack said, his voice filled with disgust. "Cynthia didn't say anything for a while, but eventually my father made the job unbearable for her; she told her husband about it. David came here in a jealous rage. We cooled things down with a lot of reassurances—my father was getting out of the business by then, anyway—and a healthy raise for Cynthia."

"Why didn't Cynthia bring a lawsuit instead?" said Liz, surprised. "Isn't that how it's usually done?"

"They needed the medical that came with her job," Jack said without irony. "Also, my father had evidence of employee theft by David and—I hate to admit this—was willing to use it. Anyway, we had an uneasy truce going—I thought. Obviously I thought wrong."

Liz remembered Cynthia's state of distress earlier. "Did your father try to start something up with her this afternoon? Is that why David was here tonight?"

"Who knows?" Jack said wearily. "From what Cynthia told me, it didn't sound like it, frankly. But David walked in on them and must've thought so. Ah, Christ, I'm sick of all this!"

He glanced again at the droopy huddle of people a few feet away and said to Liz, "I'm sorry you got caught in the cross fire; and look—don't worry about any of it. I'll take care of David—I'll take care of my father and the others. . . . I'll—"

"Am I going to be in trouble over this?" she asked, suddenly aware that she was the one who'd done all the actual assaulting.

"No. David has no proof, any more than we do. David's the one I'm going to—"

"Jack!" cried Deirdre.

Jack and Liz turned to see Deirdre helping Cornelius stagger over to a small pile of blocking timbers and sit down on them.

Everyone gathered around him. Cornelius said thickly, "It feels like someone's . . . sitting on my chest."

It never ends, Liz thought, shocked, as she circled Susy with one arm. "Should I call an—?"

"No," said Jack, making a decision on the spot. "I can get him there in five minutes. Don't move, Dad," he ordered his father, who didn't argue this time. "I'll get the car." He turned to Liz. "You can get home okay?"

"Of course," she said. "Go!"

Jack ran and got his car, and they helped Cornelius into it. Liz saw Jack punching a number into his car phone as he pulled away. Then she and Deirdre, obviously feeling vulnerable despite the presence of a security guard at the entry gate, got into their respective cars and drove their respective charges home.

As it turned out, the proof against David Penny came at dawn.

That was when a half-million-dollar sailboat, propped up on boat stands while it awaited work at Jack's shipyard, fell over onto the asphalt, crushing in its starboard side. Besides the hull damage, the boat's extensive, sophisticated electronics got zapped into oblivion when the boat's aluminum mast, crashing through a power line on its way down, caused a massive power surge.

Liz found out about it because, like a fair number of Newporters, she woke up to discover her power was out. After it was restored, she heard a report on the radio that said the sailboat, buffeted by high winds all night, had wriggled its boat stands loose and had fallen over.

Sure, she thought. *With a little help from a friend.* But how would Jack ever prove it?

Truly, the night before had been the night from hell. Her mind refused to dwell on any of it for the simple reason that there was too much to dwell on. She felt just like the electronics on the sabotaged sailboat: zapped into oblivion.

She poured the last of the hazelnut coffee into the last of the clean mugs and dragged herself over to the kitchen table, waiting for the caffeine to jump-start her brain. Despite her exhaustion—maybe because of it—she found herself mesmerized by the beauty of the view through her kitchen screens. The nor'easter had roared through, leaving a crystal-clear morning in its wake.

Fall was on the way. Everything about the scene in front of her suggested it—from the bright pink impatiens that were making their final headlong spurt to eternity, to the gang of finches fighting over the sunflower seeds, trying to fatten up for hard times ahead.

It seemed too soon. She wasn't ready. She eyed the scattering of dried leaves on the lawn with dismay. Once Fall came to Newport, the rich went south. Maybe for a month, maybe for the season. But they didn't stay north. They didn't stick around to work things out.

Snowbirds, they were called. Newport had a lot of them.

The phone rang. Liz answered it, as always, with her heart in her throat until she learned, as usual, that it wasn't Jack.

This time it was Tori. "That was really tough luck about the boat falling over," she said. "Naturally you've heard."

"On the radio," Liz said dully. "Not from Jack."

"Uh-oh. So you haven't seen him since—you know. Since the restaurant?"

Liz laughed a weary, ironic laugh. "Oh, I saw him, all right. We went out on the *Déjà Vu* for an evening cruise yesterday."

"Wow! That's *great*. So it doesn't matter to him. I *told* you it wouldn't. That's great, Liz. I'm so happy for you both—"

"Your happiness is somewhat premature," Liz said in the same flat voice. "It wasn't that kind of cruise." She gave Victoria a brief summary of the nonstop run of horrors they'd all been through.

By the time she finished, it was a much more sober and subdued Victoria who said, "Is Susy okay with all of it?"

"Susy was amazing. I'm much more worried about Caroline. She didn't handle the storm well, and later she must have realized that there was something badly wrong with her father. As far as I can tell, the girl has absolutely no one she can count on now. No one at all."

"There's her mother."

"Wherever she is." Liz sighed and said, "Any tally on ticket sales? Tell me we've sold more than eleven."

"Okay. We've sold more than eleven. Two more than eleven."

"My god. Well, this is just perfect. What're we going to—? Oh! Tori, let me call you back. I see Jack out there. I want to find out how his father is."

Liz hung up and went flying out her back door before Jack got out of shouting distance; she knew by now not to expect him to stroll too close to the chain-link fence.

Respecting my privacy, no doubt, she told herself with a grimly ironic smile.

She flagged him down with a whistle and a wave of her arms, and he came over, with Snowball bouncing along behind him. He was wearing the same clothes he had had on the night before. It didn't bode well.

"How is he?" Liz said through the fence.

Jack looked terrible. His eyes were rimmed and bloodshot; his voice was taut with fatigue as he said, "Doing okay. It *was* a heart attack. They're doing some tests on him now. They seem guardedly optimistic. He'll have to stop smoking, of course. But he's always watched his weight, and he's fairly regular in his exercise."

"That's good news, then," Liz said—especially considering that Jack looked as if his father had just died. "Will your mother cut her stay in Italy short?" she ventured to ask.

The look of pain on Jack's face etched itself more deeply. "Hard to say. Before this, she'd pretty much made up her mind not to come back to him at all. But besides everything else, now we've had some other news—bad news—for Caroline, anyway. Her mother—Stacey Stonebridge, you never met her—is dead."

"What?"

"Three days ago. Pills and alcohol. They've only just found her. Apparently she checked herself out of that clinic and . . . it's just incredible, that's all. It's not surprising, really; just . . . incredible."

"But what about Caroline? What about Bradley?" Liz asked, overwhelmed with sympathy for the children. She wrapped her fingers around the chain links of the fence, like some internee in a camp. She felt so separated from Jack, from his problems; so powerless to help.

Jack shook his head, obviously not sure himself what would happen. "The kids have an aunt—Stacey's sister—in Phoenix. She's the one who called. She sounds a little flaky, but maybe I was misreading her over the phone. I'm flying out there with Caroline today. There'll be a memorial service in a couple of days.''

''But . . . what about your father?'' asked Liz, unable to comprehend it all. ''Does he know? Will you be able to leave him?''

''He knows. As for leaving him—I'm not about to stick Caroline on a plane with a note pinned to her collar. That's why my mother becomes so—'' He sighed and said, ''Netta's a better nurse than I am, anyway.''

''And . . . David Penny?'' Selfish, she may have sounded; but she had to know about David Penny. He might well have a score to settle with her.

An echo of an ironic smile played on Jack's lips and then died away. ''There, at least, we have closure. Cynthia took him to the emergency room sometime before dawn. The police were there on another matter; David saw them, panicked, and tried to bolt. After that, with Cynthia's prodding, he confessed to everything—even the ants were his inspiration. But it came too late to save the boat from falling over. You know about the boat?''

Her smile was a pale echo of his own. ''Everyone in your power grid knows about the boat.''

He nodded. ''The electricity. I forgot.''

It wasn't surprising. He did look shell-shocked. Liz wanted desperately to put her arms around him, to comfort him. But he wasn't making any effort to scale the fence; and though she would've done it gladly if he'd asked her to— he wasn't asking her to.

''You haven't been to bed,'' she said in a gentle, beaten voice.

He snorted and said tiredly, ''Bed? I'm not sure I'll ever be in one again.''

If the moment hadn't been so sad; if their relationship hadn't been so far along; if the fence between them hadn't been so high and wide and deep—she might've come back with a quip and a promise. *Oh, you'll be in a bed, all right,* she might've said with a saucy smile. *Trust me.*

But this was not the moment, and theirs was not the relationship.

"Well . . ." Jack plunged his hands into his pockets and shrugged haplessly, then turned and stared for a long, strained moment at his ancestral home, brooding and dark under its canopy of ancient trees. "I guess I'll go tell Caroline."

"I'm so sorry, Jack," Liz said, still holding on to the fence.

She wanted, despite everything, to say, "But what about us? What about *us*?" But she might just as well have bayed at the moon.

He smiled in bleak acknowledgment and walked a few steps away. Then, on an impulse, he turned back and said, "You were great in the storm last night. If you hadn't been there, I hate to think what might've happened."

She knew it was a high compliment, coming from him. She flushed all over with pleasure and said, "Then it's true what they say?"

He gave her a puzzled look. "What's true?"

"That gentlemen prefer Hanes?"

He laughed out loud at that, and shook his head in despair, and smiled, and laughed more softly.

"Good-bye, Liz," he whispered, and then he walked away.

Chapter 24

◆

For a while Liz considered the disasters to be plain bad luck.

"But bad luck," she told Victoria, "is when you're walking down a street minding your own business and a flower pot falls on your head. These tragedies are beyond bad luck. These are—"

"—retribution," said Tori. "For the sins of the great-great-grandfather." She punched in the next phone number on her list. While she let the phone ring, she added, "How *is* the great-great-grandfather, by the way? Have you had any sense of him being around?"

Liz shook her head. "Nothing. Maybe he flew off to Phoenix with Jack and Caroline."

"You do like your little jokes, don't—ah, good morning! Is this Mrs. Vauquiez? Hello; my name is Victoria, and I'm calling on behalf of Anne's Place, the home for battered women here in Newport? I'd like to personally invite you to a benefit that promises to be a magical evening to all who—"

Victoria winced and looked at Liz. "Hung up." She made a note next to the name on the list and punched in the next number. "Good morning! Is this Ms. Viera? Hello; my name is Victoria, and I'm calling on behalf of Anne's Place . . ."

Liz watched with deepening dismay as Victoria worked her way through the V's. Ticket sales so far had been dismal, despite the posters, the mailing, the radio announcements, and the lovely write-up in the paper. Obviously there were too many worthy causes running after too few subscribers. She was right: they should've waited for Halloween to hold the event.

But then they would've missed the snowbirds. And without Meredith Kinney, one of the richest snowbirds in town, there would be no two-hundred-dollar-a-plate dinner. It was as simple as that. Not only was Meredith the honorary chairwoman—not only had she already gotten commitments from over two dozen dinner guests—but she'd completely taken over running that part of the benefit herself. There was nothing honorary about her; she was a full-fledged working chairperson.

Which was just fine with Liz. She had neither the time, the experience, nor the heart to design an intimate, glittering dinner in Jack's house for Jack's friends. It would've been awkward at best, painful at worst. This way she could stay outside, under the tent with the rest of the common folk, and concentrate on managing the second half of the fund-raiser. And if inside East Gate the entrée wound up overcooked or the floral arrangements too big to see around—it would be Meredith's fault, not hers.

Liz's job was to sell two hundred tickets. So far they'd sold thirty-one. A hundred and sixty-nine to go.

Victoria hung up again and spun around in her desk chair to face Liz. "*Sold!* Two tickets!" she said, interrupting the meandering gloom of Liz's thoughts.

Liz perked up. "For sure? Or: She'll think about it?"

"She's sending the check today. The benefit falls on her anniversary, and Mrs. Young thinks this'll be a memorable way to celebrate."

"*Young?* Oh, God; you're on the *Y's* already?"

Victoria laughed and gathered up a handful of her long red corkscrew curls for binding in a comb.

"Cheer up," she said. "I still have four more Youngs to go."

"But there are no Z's! I thought we'd get well over a hundred sales from the list. Can you believe this? Meredith Kinney probably made thirty phone calls in one day and hauled in six thousand dollars' worth of contributions, while *we*—"

Victoria gave her a sheepish look. "Actually, Meredith didn't even have to make thirty calls: I bought some tickets myself. Oh, don't look at me like I'm some traitor, Liz. The buzz around Newport is that it's a very exclusive event. Everyone knows Jack Eastman doesn't entertain."

Liz said with lofty irony, "I don't blame you at all, Tori. But after you've dined in regal splendor, I do hope you'll join the rest of us under the tent for the cocktail reception. All thirty-four of us. I shouldn't be hard to find: I'll be the one clutching a hundred and sixty-six unsold tickets in my hand."

"Don't be silly; we'll sell them," Tori said with her usual breeziness.

"You're damned right we will," said Liz, grimly determined now. "I'll put 'em on Visa if I have to and hand them out free on Thames Street. Meredith Kinney, bless her well-born soul, is *not* going to outperform me at this event."

She got up from her desk and walked over to one of the multipaned windows of her office, housed in a colonial building overlooking Washington Square. The octagonal fountain in the small grassy oasis that separated the Broadway district from the waterfront shops was bubbling cheerfully away, but for once Liz took no pleasure in the sight.

Her mind was picturing a full dining room and an empty tent.

"Dammit," she said in a soft, heartfelt curse. "I'm not going to fail at this. I need an angle, that's all. I need something to bring them in—some*one* to bring them in. I need a

celebrity. I need royalty. I need . . . Princess Diana. That's who I need," she said, almost wistfully.

She thought for a while, then said over her shoulder, "You remember how crazy people went when Charles came to Newport a couple of years ago? Even Prince Andrew—he was here before your time—sent everyone a-titter. Think what *Diana* would do."

Victoria laughed as she punched in the next number on her list. "Hey, why not? Even as we speak, she's rumored to be aboard a yacht on Martha's Vineyard. We could fly a plane overhead trailing an invitation—"

Liz stared unseeing at the ebb and flow of lawyers, tourists, and court employees on the street below. "That's just it," she said thoughtfully. "She's *rumored*. No one's actually seen her, despite the media crawling all over the place."

She turned to Victoria with a calculating look. "How many royal-watchers so you suppose have jumped on ferries to the Vineyard, hoping to get a glimpse of her?"

"Probably a—Mrs. Young? Good morning. My name is Victoria and I'm calling on behalf . . ."

Liz had never actually started a rumor before; but Victoria had no qualms about doing it. Some idle speculation at just the right time in just the right circles—and almost immediately the calls began coming in.

As it happened, Tori took the call from their first Diana-watcher.

"Good *morning,* Mrs. Tewhitt," she said as she motioned frantically for Liz to pick up the extension. "I enjoyed talking to you the other afternoon. I'm still considering that marble-topped plant stand."

Liz lifted the receiver carefully and heard Mrs. Tewhitt, an antiques dealer who was herself many, many removes from royalty, say, "I'm *so* upset that I couldn't get tickets for the dinner. Only thirty? Are you certain you can't squeeze two more at the table?''

"Oh, I'm afraid not, Mrs. Tewhitt. And in any case, Meredith Kinney has complete control over the earlier part of the benefit. Our office is handling ticket sales for the costume party afterward—and to tell the truth, I'm not certain how many tickets to *that* are left, either.''

Mrs. Tewhitt gasped. Her voice became conspiratorial. "How many will you let me have?''

"I'm afraid we've had to limit sales to four tickets per person.''

"I'll take them. Can you drop them off at the shop?''

"You're right on my way home.''

Victoria hung up, and Liz pounced on her. "Four? Are you crazy? Why didn't you let her have ten? Twenty? *Fifty?*''

"She wouldn't have bought any, in that case. Liz, Liz—don't you see how it works? We all want what we can't have. That's what makes whatever it is so desirable.''

"True,'' said Liz with sudden penetrating sadness. She was somewhere else in time as she said it. *We all want what we can't have.* Dammit, dammit, dammit. Blindsided again. She'd done so well this week, keeping focused, shutting him out. And now, just like that, she could hardly keep the tears from rolling out.

"I do understand,'' she whispered. "I understand exactly.''

Victoria took two other calls in rapid succession, selling four tickets to each of the callers. "Friends of Elena Tewhitt,'' she explained to Liz. "One of them is in real estate; the other's an ex-councilman's wife. Excellent. They'll spread the word.''

"What exactly did you tell Mrs. Tewhitt that day in her shop?''

"Nothing that wasn't true. I said that Jack has a friend

who knows Princess Diana—okay, so it's a friend of a friend—and that we all had high hopes, *very* high hopes, that she'd take advantage of the anonymity our costume party offers. And then I speculated a little over whether she'd dress in Gilded Age or New Age costume."

"Tori, you have no scruples at *all*."

Victoria shrugged and said, "It's not against the law to speculate."

Liz began to think that maybe Tori *was* an embodiment of Victoria St. Onge. It took her breath away to think that they were getting people to buy tickets to a main event without a main event. She resolved to have no part of it.

When the phone rang while Victoria was out getting them lunch, Liz answered it with the very noblest of intentions.

"I'm so very excited that—*she*—is going to be there," said Andrea Lexim, a gallery owner. "How clever of her to come in disguise."

"Oh, but you mustn't just assume—"

"Well, of course, one doesn't *assume,* dear. One merely hopes. Obviously one can't say, can one? But then, one knows what one knows."

Gibberish!

"In that case, how many tickets may I put you down for?" asked Liz in a silky voice.

"Oh, the maximum, certainly. Six, I believe?"

"I'm so sorry. Four."

By the end of the week they'd sold an amazing hundred and forty tickets; but the Diana thing had been pretty much milked for all it was worth.

"Short of taking an ad in the paper actually advertising the fraud, I'm not sure what we can do," said Liz, putting her feet up on the desk.

It was late—Susy was staying overnight at her grandparents'—and Liz and Victoria were lingering in the office over design sketches and cold pizza. Liz picked off a mushroom from an uneaten slice and said, "Know any stunning blondes with Roman noses we could hire?"

"I try not to hang around stunning blondes," said Victoria, rolling her green eyes heavenward. She took a long, noisy suck on her straw, then shook an ice-cube from the paper cup into her mouth.

"You're kidding," said Liz. "Why would *you* be intimidated by a gorgeous blonde? You're a gorgeous redhead."

Victoria pulled her knees up to her chin and wrapped her arms around her cobalt-blue, star-spangled skirt. "I'm way too tall for anything but a model's runway," she said, sucking on the ice cube. "I'm taller than Ben, and I don't like that. I wish I was normal height. Like you."

"And your hair," Liz said, ignoring her friend's lament. "Who has hair like that except heroines in novels?"

Victoria bit down on the ice, then swallowed it. "It's just one more thing that makes me stick out from everyone else. I wish I had thick straight hair. Like yours. And smooth tawny skin without one freckle. Like you. I've always thought you're better-looking than I am," she added.

"Wow," said Liz, staring at her friend incredulously. "Of all the things I know about you, *that* amazes me the most."

Victoria shrugged and said, "Okay, fine. Don't believe me. Ask Jack."

Liz felt the color come flowing over her cheeks. "I've told you, Jack is out of my life. I haven't heard from him since we said good-bye through the chain-link fence. Obviously he knows how to pick his locations," she added, trying to make her bitterness sound droll. "With the fence between us, I couldn't very well throw my arms around him and beg him to keep me."

"Give him the benefit of the doubt, Liz," said Victoria with a sympathetic smile. "He's in Phoenix, trying to find a life for Caroline."

"And when he gets back, he'll have only poor Bradley to

place, and then he'll be free again. Well, bully for him. Anyway," Liz couldn't resist saying, "You notice he found the time to call Meredith from Phoenix? You notice he calls Netta?"

"He called Meredith to reassure her about going through with the dinner at East Gate. He called Netta to—well, *naturally* he calls Netta. She's nursing his father, for pity's sake. How is Cornelius, by the way?" she asked, steering the subject away from Jack.

Liz shook her head. "Not good. Netta says he's holed himself up in the carriage-house apartment and won't come out. He won't see anyone. Won't do anything. She says he looks twenty years older."

"He's scared."

"I can understand him being scared," said Liz, vividly recalling the brush with death her own father had suffered years earlier. "But I can't understand him being timid."

Her father's heart attack had been more serious than Cornelius Eastman's. But Frank Pinhel's reaction to it was: "The hell with it; the yews need trimming."

"What about Jack's mother?" Victoria asked—because she was as curious as Liz about the phantom mistress of East Gate. "Is she coming?"

"Nobody knows."

"Oh, well. Maybe the benefit will draw him out. It should be a magical evening." Victoria smiled impishly and added, "Even if the princess *is* unavoidably detained."

Liz winced at the reminder and said, "Have you decided what to wear? Gilded Age or New?"

The impish smile turned somber. "The question is more apt for me than for most, isn't it? I don't know, yet, what I'll wear. But it's my big night, the biggest of my life—the night I pay my karmic debt and return the pin," Victoria said softly. "I should dress for it."

She really does believe she may die once the pin's re-

turned, Liz thought, amazed. It was obvious in the way Victoria held herself, arms around her shins, chin propped on her knees, the picture of apprehension. It was obvious in the way she stared at the middle distance between them, seeing . . . what? The split second before—after?—the car crash? Or was she back a hundred years, staring at two lives gone awry because of one woman's mean-spirited meddling in their destinies?

"Victoria?"

"Hmm?" Victoria looked up, then smiled. "Well!" she said more briskly. "One thing I know. The costume's going to be as sexy as I can make it. I want Ben to be on his *knees* with desire."

The hundred and forty-first ticket sale was made despite Liz's best advice. The purchaser was a middle-aged woman who was dressed, despite the heat, in an ill-fitting lilac pantsuit. She was a heavy-set woman with red, rough hands and hair that clung damply to her flushed face.

"I had to park a ways away," she said, breathing heavily from her exertions. "I never come downtown in summer if I can help it. But I saw one of your posters in Jo-Jo's Fabric Shop that said I could buy a ticket here. For the costume party, I mean." With some hesitation she said, "Can anybody buy one?"

"Yes, you can, but—you could've mailed a check and saved yourself a trip downtown," said Liz with a friendly smile. "The traffic's really horrible today, isn't it?"

The woman shook her head in disgust. *"August,"* she said. "What do you expect? But I wanted to ask—because I heard two ladies in the A&P talking about this benefit thing. I've never been to something like it, but I heard them say that Princess *Diana* is coming?"

"Oh . . . no, she's not coming," said Liz, coloring deeply

now. "If that's why you want a ticket—save your money. Really."

"Oh?" The woman's face fell. "Are you sure?"

Washed over with guilt, Liz said, "Yes. I'm sure."

"That's too bad," the woman in lilac said. "Because they sounded so positive. . . . Oh, well. Thank you."

She turned away and headed for the narrow spiral steps that led to the reception area downstairs. At the top of the spiral, she reversed herself and came back.

Plunking her white plastic handbag down on Liz's desk, the woman snapped it open and began rummaging in it. "You know what? I want a ticket anyway. It's for a good cause. And I think I can talk a couple of my lady friends into going. And anyway, this is Newport; who's to say she won't show up? She's *so* pretty. And if she doesn't, well, forty dollars won't break me. That's why I buy lottery tickets. Just to dream. I don't *really* think I'll win."

With an irresistible smile, she handed Liz four hard-earned ten-dollar bills.

Liz wanted to hug her. She had exactly the right spirit for a benefit: generous, open, curious, and hopeful.

"You'll have a wonderful time," Liz said warmly. "We're going to have a palmist for the New Agers and a phrenologist for the Gilded Agers."

"Oh? That's nice," said the woman uncertainly.

Liz laughed and explained, "A phrenologist tells your personality by analyzing the contours of your skull; they were very popular during the Gilded Age. By the way, if you come in costume, make it as outlandish as you like. There'll be a prize at the end for the best one."

"I'll do that," the woman promised with an air of courage. She plunged her wallet back to the bottom of her purse, then looked up with a timid smile. "There's just one thing," she said. "What's a Gilded Age? And what do they mean by the New Age?"

• • •

Ten days after Jack went off to Phoenix with Caroline, he came back—with Caroline.

Liz was making Sunday pancakes, and Susy was in the yard, sailing a new boat in her wading pool. Through the kitchen screen Liz heard Caroline call Susy's name. Surprised, Liz peeked out and saw the child, pretty as a picture in pale pink and apple green, talking to Susy through the chain-link fence.

"I didn't see you for a long time," said Susy, who had always spurned pink in favor of rich reds, the color she wore now.

Caroline hooked her Velcro-fastened shoes into the chain links of the fence, but she couldn't hang on and fell back to the ground. "I was in Phoenix with Jack."

"Who's Jack?" asked Susy naïvely.

"*You* know Jack," Caroline said with an impatient laugh. "You always call him Mr. Eastman. He's my brother. He said I should call him Jack now."

"I never knew he was your brother!" said Susy, clearly bewildered by this new turn of events. She added, "He's old, for a brother."

"Not as old as my father. Dada said his hair was gray when I was born. Now it's white. Since the boat ride, it even got whiter."

"Is your mother so old, too?" Susy asked artlessly.

Caroline turned grave. "No. She was younger than your mom, I think." Her voice faltered as she said, "But she—she died. Jack said she's in heaven now, watching over me. And Bradley, too. But Bradley doesn't even know it."

"Do you miss her?"

"Yes. . . ."

"Do you want to play with me? I have a new boat. Sometimes when the wind is blowing, it can sail right across my pool. All by itself."

"Can I bring my doll over?"

"Yes, but you better watch her. Toby likes to scratch his claws on my doll's stomach. My doll's a Raggedy Ann. They're good for scratching on, I guess.

"My doll's a Madame Alexander. I don't think Toby would do anything to her."

He wouldn't dare, thought Liz, smiling at the scene before her.

She saw Netta coming up behind the children, so she popped the pancakes into the just-heated oven, then ran out to find out more about Caroline's return.

After the two women agreed that the girls could play together in Susy's yard—a first, of sorts—Netta hit on a short-cut method of getting there. Huffing and puffing, she dragged a heavy wooden staging ladder belonging to the shipyard over to the fence. Between her and Liz, they managed to set the thing up so that one set of rungs was on each property: a jungle-gym shortcut for the girls to commute back and forth.

Caroline ran to get Madame, and Susy went off to fetch Raggedy. Liz took advantage of the lull by asking Netta outright why Jack had brought his half-sister back to Newport.

The portly housewife glanced behind her, then said, "He didn't like the setup, is what he told me. Stacey's sister is sharing an apartment with two other women, all of 'em young and dating. He said they looked on Caroline like some pet cat. Besides," she said, lowering her voice, "it's the wrong environment, if you know what I mean."

"So Cornelius decided to have Jack bring her back to East Gate? Well, that's good news. It means—"

"Oh, no, Mr. Eastman did no such thing. Jack made the decision on his own. Mr. Eastman, he's still acting like he's got one foot in the grave. What that man needs," she added sharply, "is a good shaking."

"Will Mrs. Eastman be the one to give it to him?"

"I wish I knew."

After a couple of hours, Caroline climbed over the jungle-gym ladder back to her mansion. Liz cleaned up the breakfast dishes, put on a high-cut bathing suit, and went out to read the Sunday papers. She told herself that she was giving Susy some quality time. She told herself that she needed a little down-time herself. She told herself everything except the one obvious, unalterable truth: Despite all her previous resolve, she was hoping that Jack, if he was home, would notice her and stroll over to the chain-link fence.

But an hour went by, and the only one who noticed her was Susy. The child, wearing a Kelly-green bathing suit, came over to Liz and stood on the frame of the plastic-strapped chaise longue, showing off her balancing act.

"Are you going in the pool now, Mommy?"

"I'm still reading, honey," said Liz absently.

"Mommy? Are you old?"

Liz put her paper down. She knew exactly what was on Susy's mind, so she said with extra emphasis, "For goodness sake—no! I'm pretty young. I'll be around for a long, long time."

Susy jumped backward off the chaise onto the grass. "Forever?"

Liz held out one arm and pulled her daughter close. "Almost forever," she said, drinking in the sweet summer smell of her daughter.

But oh, how I wish it could be forever—for you if for no one else.

• • •

That night Liz dreamed about—or saw, or dreamed she dreamed about—Christopher Eastman again. But this time it was different; this time, he held her in his arms.

It felt so shockingly physical, so shockingly right. She buried her face in his shoulder and, with tears falling freely, said, "How can I make him love me enough? How can I?"

And Christopher, warm and solid, nuzzled his chin in her hair and said, "I do love you. I love you very, very much. Someday you will know that."

She said, "Someday! Will I live forever?"

And he answered, "There is only one way you can live forever, and that is through those who love you. Remember that. Now sleep, Elizabeth . . . sleep."

On Monday, Liz was in her office, working through lunch, when she heard someone taking the narrow spiral of stairs two at a time. She looked up, and there he was: Jack Eastman, in a thunderous mood.

He marched up to her desk and, flattening his hands on it, bent over it toward her at a frightening angle—the better, she thought, to grab her by the throat. She leaned her chair away from him.

"What the *hell* are you doing, telling everyone Princess Diana plans to come? Are you *nuts*?"

"We didn't . . . really say that," Liz said, cringing behind a placating smile. "We said you were friends with someone who was friends with her. Or something like that."

"Who are you talking about? The senator?"

She didn't have a clue. She took a shot. "Yes. Aren't you a friend of his?"

"I'm a friend of the senator's *son*. Not that it matters—the senator doesn't know her either! They met at a charity function. She said how do you do. He said I'm pleased to meet you. Jesus! It wasn't exactly a bonding moment!"

"Oh. We must've gotten that wrong, then," she said, still winging it. The one thing she didn't want him to know was that the whole thing was a fabrication from the start.

He spun away from her, slamming his fist on the side of the desk as he did it. She'd never seen him so angry. He ran his hand through his unruly hair and said, "I'll be a laughingstock—or an object of pity. I can't believe this!"

"I don't see why you should be either one," she ventured timidly. "You're just underwriting the event, not starring in it."

He turned back to her. His mouth, pressed tight in a thin line of fury, cracked a little into a contemptuous smile. "Really. Did I forget to mention that the society editor of *The New York Times* called me? That she wanted to know, was it true that I was Princess Diana's *date*?"

Aiii. "I don't know why she'd think tha-at," Liz said, bleating like a lamb.

"Could it be because one of you two dingbats *told* her?"

"Please. Give us *some* credit," Liz said, stung.

He wasn't listening. He was staring at the wide-board floor, hand on the back of his neck, clearly envisioning the night of the benefit. "Is there anything more *absurd,*" he said, seething, "than being stood up by the future Queen of England?"

Liz said lightly, "We don't know that she's going to be queen. The monarchy's in trouble over there."

Jack's head came up. His blue eyes locked on her in anger. He stood there, simmering in place, while she watched him with the same impatience with which she waited for her teapot to come to a boil.

Come on, she thought. *Get it over with. You've been looking for an excuse; this is it.*

"Do you," he asked in a barely controlled voice, "have any idea what a faux pas you've committed?"

Liz laughed out loud. "Faux pas? Excuse me? Does that

mean like, I goofed? Would you mind translating that for me? Because as we know, I was born in a cave and raised in a barn.''

"I *knew* it," he said, slamming his hand back down on the desk. "It always comes back to this, doesn't it—this *obsession* of yours with class.''

Liz jumped up, aching to do battle with him. She stood with feet apart, hands on her hips: the position of challenge.

"Class!'' she said. "*Class?* Listen, pal, I know class when I see it, and so far during this project I ain't seen it! All I've seen are a bunch of cloying, fawning, oozing, name-dropping princess-wannabes who'd do anything—anything!—to be photographed next to some poor skinny blonde whose life, pathetic as it is, is no longer her own!''

She took a breath; she wasn't done. "*One* woman—beautifully dressed; I hear you once dated her—stood right there, *demanding* a ticket to the dinner. When I told her, over and over, that I couldn't sell her one, she actually stamped her foot! Class? I don't *think* so!''

She thought she'd beaten him down, but he came back strong. "Never mind who they are, and never mind what they do! This isn't about them—it's about you, Liz! What were you thinking of? You're supposed to be a professional! You're running a charity event, not a con game!''

"Okay, things did get a little out of hand," she said, reddening. "But I warned all the real people—*my* people—that Diana wouldn't be there. They're not going to feel gypped. And as for the others—frankly? I don't *care* if they bought the tickets under false pretenses.''

"You *should* care, Liz!'' he said hotly. "You should grow up, goddammit! Because—frankly—that blue-collar routine of yours has become a real bore.''

She felt as if he'd slapped her. "Fine! Since we're being frank, this is what *I* think: *I* think your anger has as much to do with Princess Diana as it has to do with the Queen of Sheba!''

His look got more dangerous. "Meaning?"

"Meaning the *real* faux pas here—the one you'll never forgive me for—is the fact that I didn't fall to my knees on the day we met and declare my infertility."

The blue eyes got wide. "What are you—insane? That has *nothing* to with this. I've got kids coming out of my *ears*," he added irrelevantly.

"*Don't* deny it! I saw that look on your face when I told you I couldn't have children. You looked absolutely betrayed. Anyone would've thought I was a man dressed in women's clothing or something."

"And *I'm* telling you you're *wrong*. In the first place, you've hardly said a damned thing about it, except that you 'can't.' What does that mean, you 'can't'? In this age of high-tech, with all of science at your beck and call—"

"*Don't* lecture me about technology. My doctor said—"

"Is he a specialist? Did you get a second opinion? A third? A ninth?"

"All right, all right, all right!" she shouted. "If it's not about that, what *is* it about? Why have you been avoiding me since that conversation?"

"You said you wanted some space!" he said instantly.

"*That's* not what this is about. Let's face it: You got carried away in the heat of sex, and later you regretted it!"

"*What?*"

"I was right in the first place! Deep down, you're afraid of commitment!"

"My God! I practically *proposed*—"

"But you didn't *quite*, did you? You left yourself a little breathing room!"

"I left *you* a little breathing room, goddammit!"

"Baloney! If you really loved me—"

And that's when she remembered that he hadn't yet said

he loved her. Three simple words: *I. Love. You.* How much effort did it take?

Too much. She could see it in his eyes, the hesitation. In a blinding revelation, Liz knew the reason: to Jack Eastman, the words meant something so sacred, so inviolable, that he had to be one hundred percent certain before saying them. But Liz knew, and every married person knew, that hundred percent certainty wasn't possible. You had to take a chance.

And so her words hung in the churchlike silence like an unanswered chant: *If you loved me . . .*

His smile was bleak as he said, "We need to take a step back. We've gone too far, too fast. You were right."

Right or wrong, Liz had no choice now but to do exactly that: to step back from him emotionally. She'd been a breath away from telling him that she loved him.

Instead, she smiled a smile as bleak as his own and said, "The spiral steps are very steep. Be careful on your way down, Jack."

Chapter 25

$\mathcal{D}$uring the weeks that followed, Liz had no time either to mourn her shattered heart or to mend it: she simply put the pieces aside, like the broken fragments of the botanical plate, the stoneware jug, and the potpourri jar that were lying on a shelf in her basement, waiting.

There were other advantages to having an impossible schedule. Meetings with Jack—meetings with everyone—were kept to a minimum. There simply was no time. Between coordinating the music, the decorations, and the caterers; the press releases, program sponsors, and door prizes; the security, the volunteers, the vendors, and the press—between juggling all of it and a thousand small details besides, Liz was able to put every sleepless night to good use.

Though she was ashamed to admit it, one detail nagged at her more than any other: what to wear to the benefit. In the last several weeks, she'd seen too many well-dressed women to continue thinking she could get by in her old little black dress. So at the last minute she ran out and blew three hundred dollars on a new little black dress. It wasn't up to Meredith's standards, maybe, but it would certainly do.

On the night before the fund-raiser, Liz laid out the dress and was pinning an envelope filled with checks onto it when the doorbell rang.

It was Victoria, with a long, white, coat-size box in her

arms. "*Wait* till you see," she said, brushing past Liz into her living room.

"Tori, for cryin' out loud," Liz moaned. "It's almost midnight, and I've still got things to do."

Victoria ignored her whimpering. "I was poking through Sarah's Vintage Clothing on Thames Street again. Just *look* what came in this morning," she said, laying the box on the sofa. "Someone was cleaning out an estate . . . it's in wonderful condition. . . . I bought it instantly. Tell me if this isn't fate."

Victoria removed the lid to the box as if there were hummingbirds inside. Then, smiling radiantly, she folded back the white tissue and lifted up a gown of creamy satin, wrapped in tiers of fine lace, with a plunging, structured bodice that fell away into off-the-shoulder, short puffy sleeves.

She held the dress against herself. "I love the tiny seed pearls on the lace. Isn't it just perfect for tomorrow?"

Despite herself, Liz was enchanted. "Oh, Tori, yes. It *is* the Gilded Age. But I thought you were going as New Age."

"I am," Victoria said. She held out the gown to Liz. "This is for you."

"Oh, no, Tori," Liz said, shocked by her friend's generosity. "I can't. Really."

"You can. You must. Because—there's more."

Liz's eyes were shining. "More? A whalebone corset, maybe, so that I can squeeze into the thing?"

"It won't be much of a squeeze," Tori allowed, pinning the gown against Liz. "You've lost weight these last weeks. Look at the pants you're wearing. They hang on you."

"Do they?" Liz asked absently. "No, really, I can't," she decided all over again. "I've already bought a nice black dress."

"It's a *costume* party. Take the dress back."

"I've cut off the tags."

"Idiot! *Never* cut off the tags until ten minutes before you go. Now try this on."

Netta adjusted the heavy folds of the long black servant's dress that—somehow—that fey creature Victoria had talked her into wearing. At the time, it seemed like a good idea. What were they thinking of? It was too blessed hot for worsted. She patted her glistening brow with a linen handkerchief and tucked the folded square back into the pocket of her starched apron, then pushed a straying hairpin into her neatly arranged bun.

She'd drawn the line at the little granny glasses, and a good thing, too: she was blind as a bat without her prescription lenses. If faux-tortoiseshell frames weren't Victorian enough for Victoria, well, that couldn't be helped.

Netta opened the door to the tiny closet of her third-floor quarters and surveyed herself in the full-length mirror. The dress put ten extra pounds on her—one more sacrifice to satisfy Victoria's whim. Ah, well. The creature *had* worked hard all week, flitting like Tinker Bell from Meredith to Liz and back again.

"Everything has to be perfect," Victoria had said more than once. *"Perfect."*

Well, why wouldn't it be, with Meredith running the dinner and Liz running the costume party after? Both women were perfectionists, each in her own way. True, Meredith Kinney liked to delegate; but then, she had a staff that she could trust to do everything. Since she was donating the entire expense of the dinner, no one minded in the least that she was hardly around.

Liz, on the other hand, watched every penny and did a lot of her own legwork. No more than two hours ago, the girl was hauling potted palms around in Caroline's wagon, lifting them in and out as she rearranged the entrance to the big tent. Liz had noticed what everyone else had not: that the palms blocked the view of the palmist, if you entered the tent from the left.

Two different women, two different ways of doing business. Well, Anne's Place could only benefit, and that was a fact.

Netta stood for a moment in front of the small fan on her bureau, then impulsively hiked up her dress and yanked off the long, very full muslin underskirt that was part of her costume. Who the dickens would know if she was wearing an underskirt or not? She took a little cotton half-slip out of her drawer and slipped it on instead. Enough was enough.

On the second-floor landing she bumped into Jack, who waved a length of black tie in her face.

"Suddenly I can't tie a knot," he said in irritation. "Do it for me, would you, Netta?"

She obliged him, looping the tie under the collar of his white shirt and shaping it into a formal bow.

"God, I'll be glad when this evening's over," Jack muttered as he stood before her. "I want my life back."

"I hope you're planning to wear the waistcoat under the dinner jacket," Netta said in a grim reminder. "Victoria went through lots of trouble to find one for you."

"Oh, come on, Netta. The thing is old and moth-eaten."

"Too bad. You put it on. There—all done." She stepped back to survey her handiwork. Jack Eastman: her darling; her utterly beloved Jack. If she had gotten married and had a son, she'd want him to be Jack Eastman, never mind that Jack had gone to Harvard and she couldn't possibly have paid for it.

He gave her a mocking look. "Well? Will I pass muster?"

"You look very handsome, Master Jack," she said, as proud of him as if she had borne him. "Like a proper Victorian gentleman."

"And you, Miss Simmons, look exactly like the kind of

woman I might try to fool around with if I were,'' said Jack with a half-lift of his eyebrows.

The remark was too close to the reality; Netta brushed it aside with a ''Don't be fresh.''

She glanced automatically at the door to Cornelius East- man's room, though she knew he was holed up in the car- riage-house apartment. ''It'd be so nice if your father made an appearance later. Did you try him one more time?''

''Tried and failed. To tell the truth, I envy him; he has an ironclad excuse. Of course, I'll only have to suffer through the dinner; but even that'll seem endless.

''Oh, I *know,* poor thing,'' Netta said in a deadpan voice.

She turned on her heel and began walking down the stairs.

''Hey—what's *that* supposed to mean?'' said Jack behind her.

''Put the rest of your clothes on, dear,'' she said without turning around. ''The guests will start arriving any minute.''

''Netta,'' Jack said in a dangerous voice. ''Come back here, please. I'd like an explanation.''

She sighed and decided that maybe he deserved one. She retraced her steps to the landing, then took Jack by the shirt- sleeve and hauled him over to the eight-foot-tall cathedral window, intricately paned in clear leaded glass, that over- looked the grounds. Together they looked down at the huge tent, bedecked with thousands and thousands of white lights, that hovered over the lawn like a fairy castle at twilight.

''You see that?'' she asked Jack.

''It'd be hard to miss,'' he said dryly. ''I didn't have to turn on the bathroom lights when I shaved just now.''

''That tent is the result of a lot of hard work by a lot of good people. Everyone—even Deirdre—put in long hours. Now, I'm not saying that you haven't been generous with your house or quick to write a check. But that's about it, Jack. The rest of the time you hide behind closed doors, away from us all. Between you and your father—well, I don't know. It's very disappointing."

"You needn't be disappointed, Netta," Jack said, flushing with anger. "After tonight I'll probably come back out."

"Jack, Jack," she said, shaking her head in sorrow. "What're you afraid of? No—let me put that another way. *Why* are you afraid of her? Things were going so well between you."

Jack said nothing, only stared down at the tent. The caterers were moving about, making last-minute adjustments.

"She did a great job," Jack said curtly.

"Have you told her that? I haven't seen you say boo to her lately. And don't tell me you got tired of her, because I won't believe it."

Jack scowled ferociously. "She's not the kind of woman a man gets tired of. Her husband must have been the world's biggest ass," he added.

Emboldened, Netta said, "She could've dumped *you,* I guess, but that would be a first, and I don't suppose it happened."

"Not that it's *any* of your business, Miss Simmons, but the fact is, we've decided on a cooling-off period," Jack said in a lifeless voice as he scanned the tent and the grounds.

"And what would the point of *that* be?" asked Netta. "To keep from doing bodily harm to one another?"

"It's to—to reassess. Things were getting out of hand. I needed time to think."

"You think much longer, you're going to die of old age, dear," said Netta in a voice of sweet reason. "Do you love her or not?"

Jack's smile was noncommittal. "You know me better than that, Netta," he said ambiguously, and headed back to his room.

So. He wasn't going to confide in her. It wasn't surprising. Jack had grown up among people who believed that spilling your own guts was the worst form of barbarity. She sighed, then checked the time.

The creature had better know what she's doing, Netta thought as she went to answer the first summons of the evening.

It was the creature herself, in the same odd, fierce mood that she'd been in all week. Victoria was dressed in what Netta supposed was New Age style: her gown was of slinky silver lamé fabric that rippled and glittered when she moved. Her shoulders were bare, though the bodice reached up and encircled her neck in a seductively modest way. Her hair was piled high on her head and woven through with silver stars. She wore no real jewelry—unless you counted the stars— but over her heart was pinned what looked like airline wings, the kind pilots give little kids on long flights. What a curious sense of style she had.

"Oh, Netta, you look exactly right," Victoria cried.

"I look hot," Netta said, dismissing her enthusiasm. "Where's Liz?" she added, surprised. Victoria was supposed to have her in tow.

"She went right to the tent with a box of Sterno for the dipping chocolate. She won't come into the house; you know that."

Netta knew it very well. "And yet you think you'll be able to get her in here when you have to?"

"I got her into the gown, didn't I? You should see her, Netta. She fought the idea, same as you, but once she saw herself in it—well, I think she knows it was made for her. It fit like a glove. I put her hair up in a French braid; she looks breathtaking. It's all coming together. I *knew* it would. Is Meredith here yet?"

"She just called to say she's on her way."

"Isn't this fun, Netta? Isn't it?" Victoria sighed happily, then swayed in place. "God—I'm light-headed from it all!"

"Dear, dear—you have to calm down a little. Now: you have the pin?"

Victoria opened the drawstring on the little silver bag that was looped over her wrist and pulled out a tiny open heart of gold. "Okay, Netta" she said, her cheeks flushed with excitement. "Let's do it!"

She and Netta slipped off to the dining room. The table, Netta had to admit, was a tour de force. Meredith Kinney's staff had done a wonderful job, although it was Victoria who was the guiding light behind it.

Netta had been told about the old letter describing a dinner that John and Lavinia Eastman had given a hundred years ago, the letter that Victoria had used to persuade Meredith Kinney into using the same seashore theme for tonight's table. Netta had seen the letter—which Victoria was using like a recipe—but hadn't been able to make hide nor hair of the writing. So Victoria had read some of it aloud to her.

Netta was thoroughly impressed with the part about sand in the soup. Because with those silly little sand pails at every place—well, it was bound to be a mess, that's all. The party favors—bits of amber and other such stones—were already in the buckets, waiting to be dug out. Netta had been careful to put them in not too deep. No matter. There'd still be sand everywhere. Still, for now it was very pretty. They'd gotten everything right, from the dozens of candles intertwined with beach roses to the seashells that were scattered up and down the table.

The original crystal mermaid and dolphins, though, no longer existed. For maybe two minutes, Victoria had been stumped. Then she hit on the idea of an ice sculpture, and Meredith Kinney, a good sport, agreed to pay, and now the iceman was in the basement, chiseling away, and if the dumbwaiter decided to break down again, Netta didn't know *how* they'd get the blessed thing upstairs.

"It's nice to see the Meissen out again," she murmured

to herself, tucking a dinner plate a sixteenth of an inch to the right.

"Yes. . . . " Victoria was deep in a frown, staring at the seating arrangement. "No. This is wrong. I can't put her on Jack's right. She'll freak out if she sees she's in the place of honor."

"Meredith Kinney might not take kindly to your having fiddled with her seating arrangement, either," said Netta.

Victoria hardly heard. "I have to make it seem more casual than that. I'll put her four down, on his right. With Jack at the head—yes, he can still see the pin pretty well."

She moved quickly between the first and the fourth places, switching placecards. Then she took a chunk of amber out of the fourth-place bucket and put it in the sand pail at the place next to Jack. And after that, she took the heart-shaped pin, so small, so easily missed, and tucked it just beneath the surface of the fourth-place pail.

Suddenly she gasped and looked up, her face as pale as the damask cloth that covered the fully extended table. "Oh, Netta—do you see what I'm doing—*again*? I'm switching things—again! What if this is all wrong—again?"

"Whatever," said Netta, completely bewildered by the girl's manner. Why Lavinia Eastman's pin had to be returned in this roundabout way, Netta had no idea. She was willing to indulge the child in her whimsical secret plan. But now that the event was about to begin, it was time to put an end to all this.

"Time to go," she said, cradling one arm around Victoria's slender waist and ushering her firmly out of the dining room. "That will be Mrs. Kinney at the door."

Elizabeth Coppersmith stood in the middle of the still-empty tent and turned slowly around, taking it all in. This was her moment to enjoy the magic. Her Gilded Age to New

Age theme had lent itself irresistibly to a treatment in white lights and shimmering surfaces, and she had pulled out all the stops—within a strict budget, of course.

But the beauty of the theme was that she didn't need gold; she only needed gilding. Gold leaf, gold foil, gold paint— and lots of it—all contributed to the sense that when you stepped into this tent, you stepped into a magical place.

Gold-sprayed boughs of long-needled evergreens, pinned by huge bows of foot-wide cascading gold French wire-ribbon, lined the inside rim of the tent and led the eye upward to a cluster of fat, gold-leaf cherubs (on loan from a local church) that hung suspended from the peak, hovering be-nignly over the scene below.

Bright stars and gold suns, a leitmotif of the New Age, were everywhere, even hand-painted on the tablecloths and on the funky tiny tent that enclosed the palmist, who had agreed to donate half her reading fees from the night. (The "phrenologist," in reality a professor of Victorian literature, would read heads for free, of course: after all, he didn't know a bump on the head from a hole in the head.)

In any case, no cash would be used, only gold "coins"— little sun-disks that Liz had bought ridiculously cheap from a novelty shop. The first two sun-disks were complimentary; the rest, the guests would pay for.

Liz hoped that many paid-for discs would end up as wishes at the bottom of the marbelized fountain that stood, in a reasonable facsimile of majesty, in the middle of the tent. If not, then quarters and dimes would do just fine. Anne's Place would take whatever it could get.

Had she brought in too many palms and ferns? Could you *have* too many palms and ferns in a Victorian setting? She considered moving one last palm one last time—but her gown seemed to think not.

Feeling exquisitely feminine, exquisitely useless in her tight sheath of satin, Liz sighed a sigh of contradictory feelings. If only the guests got into the spirit of the night. If only Jack would peek in—and some of his dinner guests—at least to see what she had wrought. But who needed them, really?

"Lizzie!" hissed Victoria behind her.

Liz swung around, panicked by the tone in her friend's voice. It had to be the pin. "Oh, don't tell me his bedroom is locked again!"

"Nope, nope," said Victoria, "the pin's all set. I wanted to know—is everything all right? No last-minute, um, crises or anything?"

"Everything's fine," Liz said. *"Why?"*

"Just making sure. Well, I've got to get back inside. We're almost done with cocktails and about to go in and chow down. 'Bye."

"Have fun," she said to Victoria's retreating, shimmering figure. She pushed away the thought of Jack seated at the head of the table, playing host to his own. Thank God she'd begged off when Meredith asked her yesterday to come see the decorations; it made it easier not to picture Jack now.

I'm acting like a rival warlord, she admitted, which was too bad, because she respected Meredith very much. Meredith had dropped in when the tent was nearly finished and was generous with her compliments. No doubt she was disappointed that Liz hadn't reciprocated.

Five minutes later, Victoria was back. "Lizzie, Lizzie," she wailed. "You're going to kill me. . . . I don't know what to do. . . . Please, please don't be mad."

"My God, Tori, what? Tell me!"

Eyes glistening, Victoria said, "I did an awful thing. I put you down on the guest list for dinner—"

"Tori, are you *crazy*?"

"—and I didn't have the courage to tell you, and now it's too late to change it—because Jack has probably seen the place card, and if you don't go—he'll think you're being petty and stuck-up—won't he?—and I know I shouldn't have done it, and it's *all* my fault . . . but if the chair is empty, it'll be so embarrassing for everyone, especially after the fights over the tickets, and if you could just come, maybe through the main course? Because you said yourself you're in good shape here. . . . Oh, what was I thinking? I'm *such* a fool.''

And she burst into tears.

"No, wait, Tori, don't cry. For goodness' sake, it's not worth that. You'll ruin your dress. But you have to understand that I can't just up and leave here. There'll be things for me to do.''

"What things?" asked Tori between sniffles. "Everything's done.''

"Tori, I'm manager of the event," said Liz patiently. "I have to manage.''

"Well, Meredith is honorary chairman. You don't see that stopping her," Victoria said with a trembling lip.

"They aren't the same thing. You know that.''

"Why are you being so difficult?''

"Me? *You're* the one who's on the edge of—''

"You can leave the table the minute you have to," Victoria said in desperation. "I promise!''

"Okay, fine!" Liz said, exasperated. The plain fact was, she'd organized her part of the fund-raiser so well that she felt a little silly, standing around with nothing to do. "I'll stay for one course.''

"Cool!" Victoria said in a lightning shift of mood.

Feeling vaguely manipulated, Liz left word with the others and allowed Victoria to drag her into East Gate for what amounted to a fifty-dollar bowl of soup.

They caught the small and very select tide of humanity flowing from the Great Room to the ballroom. She could see Jack, head above the rest, leading the company in. Who was on his arm? She'd soon find out.

Behind them all was Meredith Kinney, bringing up the

rear. Liz went up to her with greetings and apologies in advance.

Meredith, a fiftysomething woman of intimidating poise, smiled a blue-eyed smile and said, "I'm pleased that you have any time at all for us. You've worked so hard. And how wonderful you look!"

Liz returned the compliment, aware that Meredith's gown of pale blue silk was simply classic, not historic. But the dog-choker she wore of pearls and diamonds—*that* was the real thing, something that might've graced the neck of Alva Vanderbilt Belmont herself.

They were swept into the once-empty ballroom on the hems of acres of jewel-toned taffetas (the favored fabric of nineteenth-century socialites) and beaded, sequined silks, the favored fabric of their descendants. Some of the men and women wore small masks, while others held more elaborate versions, feathered and jeweled, attached to ivory wands. It was a glittering display of wealth and whimsy, made all the more impressive by everyone's high spirits. Liz found it all fascinating, if slightly irrelevant to the life she lived.

She heard the oohs and ahs over the decorated table before she actually saw it. When she did, she was stunned: it was a replica of the setting that Victoria St. Onge had meddled with to such disastrous effect. Liz felt her cheeks flush with high color as she sought out Tori, obviously the mastermind behind it. But Tori was busy ooh-ing and ah-ing over the centerpiece, an exquisite ice sculpture of a mermaid cavorting among dolphins.

Ice, in August. It added to the sense of unreality that had been steadily mounting since Liz stepped inside the doors of East Gate minutes earlier. Fantasy was one thing—everyone loved a fantasy—but *this*. It was . . . unreal. She felt instinctively that neither she nor the mermaid would make it through the first course.

The guests were left to seek out their own seats. Liz

searched, like everyone else, for the place card that bore her name and found it several chairs to the right of Jack's.

Despite what Victoria had implied, Jack had no idea that Liz was one of the guests; she felt sure of it. He looked too disengaged, too bored, as he chatted politely with an elderly distinguished-looking woman. The smile on his face as he pulled out the woman's chair looked sewn on.

If he knew Liz was there, he'd be upset—even annoyed. After all, he'd kept a resolute distance from her since their final explosive showdown. True, they'd been forced to communicate several times over preparation plans. When that happened, he'd been polite, gracious, and remote. Just like Meredith. It was their way.

Liz was being attended to by her dinner partner, a party animal who looked as if he weren't above howling at midnight if the moon was right. But the alcohol hadn't kicked in yet; for now he was cheerful, mindless, and way too young to be interesting. Who had placed these cards, anyway?

She tried again to catch Victoria's eye, but Tori was chatting away with two or three people as they all settled in. Where was Dr. Ben? Way, way at the other end. She managed to catch *his* eye, anyway; smiling limply, she flapped four fingers up and down at him. Sooner or later, though, Liz was going to have to acknowledge her host, at least with a glance. To do anything less would be rude.

With a sense of reluctance that bordered on dread, she turned to look at him.

Chapter 26

$\mathcal{S}$he was wrong. He was aware of her.

When exactly he'd noticed her, she wasn't certain. But the look he gave her now was so scorching that she felt singed around the edges, even though she was four places away.

She lifted her chin. Her lips trembled as she formed them into a smile that couldn't begin to express the welter of emotions she was feeling: pride; hunger; fear; yearning; jealousy; anger; hurt—and pain. Mostly pain.

I love you so much, her look said to him. *I love you for who you are, not for what you can do for me. Damn you. I love you more than you love me.*

He looked inexpressibly handsome to her. Who else could wear a perfectly tailored tuxedo jacket over such an oddly shabby waistcoat? Who else could have such barely tamed hair—wild hair, really—and yet preside at a formal dinner with such offhand elegance? Who else could make every cell in her body respond with such complete, abject *willingness*?

She became aware that everyone at the table was looking at her. She thought they might be taking their cue from their host, but it wasn't that at all. It was because Meredith, in a short, pretty speech, was encouraging them all to attend the second part—Liz's part—of the fund-raiser.

Meredith added that the table motif was based on one that an East Gate hostess had come up with a century ago. "With that in mind," she told them, "take up your shovels and—dig in!"

Naturally the guests were wildly curious about the contents of their sand pails. Cautiously at first, and then more recklessly, they began poking around with their shovels. Squeals and exclamations filled the air.

"Amber! With dinosaur DNA, I assume!"

"Ooh, a gold nugget. Fool's gold?"

"Wait, wait, I had it . . . something blue—uh! Lost it again."

"Pooh—I don't have anything."

"Dig deeper. Shall I do it?"

"I'll trade my quartz for your amethyst."

"Beach glass! I *love* the color!"

"If I'm not mistaken, this looks like a crystal of copper sulfate."

"Liz?" said the party animal, handing her her little tin shovel. "Aren't you going to play?"

Liz, who had been trying desperately and unsuccessfully not to look at Jack, turned back to her dinner partner with a blank look. "I'm sorry? Oh—I don't think so. It's a bit messy, isn't it."

"Hey, it's not *our* rug," the party animal said, grinning.

Liz sighed in distress and looked away. *This was stupid and wrong,* she realized, *and now it's too late.*

"Elizabeth!" cried Victoria from half a table away. "Do it! *For God's sake, do it!*"

Startled by the hysteria in her friend's command, Liz accepted the shovel from her neighbor. Almost without thinking, she plunged it into the pail and came up with her treasure. Not until she saw the round bit of gold sticking out of the sand did she understand why Tori was so adamant about making her join in.

The pin. She's giving me *back the pin.* Baffled, Liz looked up at Victoria and said, "Wrong bucket, Tori."

Meanwhile the party animal had snatched the pin from Liz and held it up over his head. "Hey, everyone. She's got real jewelry!"

Those who hadn't yet found their favors searched more frantically, while someone wailed, "No fair! How come *she* gets something real?"

"Because," said Tori in a shrill voice of triumph, "life isn't fair! That's the beauty of it! *Anything* can happen to *anyone*."

"Put it on, put it on!" said someone, and the party animal handed the pin back to Liz.

Liz didn't know what to do. She turned to Jack, intending to pass the pin back to him.

He recognized the pin; she was sure of it. And yet he seemed to be somewhere else, despite the fact that he was following the general merriment that surrounded Liz and her treasure. He was squinting and leaning his head a little to the side—as if he were listening intently, trying to recall where he'd heard some song before. Liz watched him, almost with alarm, as his face became ruddy, then pale, by turns.

His eyes opened in recognition, as if he'd remembered the tune at last. And then Liz caught her breath, as she watched, amazed, while golden light from the dozen candles in front of Jack coalesced into one shimmering column, and the column became a form, and the form became Christopher Eastman.

The shape—still shimmering and insubstantial—seemed to float to a position alongside Jack and lean over him, as if Christopher had something to confide in his great-great-grandson's ear. Liz watched the scene, not daring, not even thinking to breathe, deeply convinced that it was last time in her life that she would see her on-again, off-again phantom.

Her eyes glazed over with sudden tears; it was too painful a prospect to consider. The golden light intensified into a burst of radiance that seemed to rain down on Jack like drops of sunlight.

And then her tears overflowed and ran down her cheeks, and it was over.

The whole time, she'd been surrounded by silence. If the guests had been keeping up their predinner chatter, Liz never heard them. She'd been somewhere else in time, someplace where spirits hung out and told jokes about humans.

And Jack? She knew that he'd been there with her. Together they'd been allowed a finite moment of infinite understanding: to know that they *had* loved; that they still loved; and best of all, that they would love again.

A dozen conversations took over the ballroom again. Jack stood up amid the noisy clamor. He looked at Liz. His smile was wise, his voice warm as he said, "I'd like to make an announcement."

Instant silence. "I'd *like* to, but I can't, until I finish a conversation I started in a restaurant with a goofy name I can't possibly remember. I remember the conversation, though, and so I'll pick up where I left off: Will you marry me?"

Little gasps, up and down the table.

And one fierce, jubilant, fist-in-the-air *"yes!"*

Jack laughed, dryly now, and said to Victoria, "Thanks, Tori, but I was asking Liz."

Nervous laughter, up and down the table.

Liz stood up, too, or maybe she just floated into a vertical alignment. "Yes," she said simply.

Someone pulled her chair back, and she walked around to the side of the table where Jack, abandoning his post as party leader, met her. He cradled her face between his hands. "I don't know what took us so long," he said in a voice of sheer wonder.

He lowered his mouth to hers in a kiss that sealed the past and told the future, and then they walked, hand in hand, out of the ballroom, leaving the exclusive little group to fend for itself.

The tent was overflowing with oddly dressed humanity. Liz had told everyone, "Anything goes," and sure enough, anything went. From the modestly costumed upstairs maid to the fella who'd wrapped himself up in exactly one thousand twinkle lights and said he was the millennium, it was an eclectic group. Gilded Age costumes were as popular as New Age: ostrich feathers, rhinestones, and miles of fake pearls held their own against guardian angels, benign witches, and other cosmic creations.

Meredith Kinney and virtually all of the dinner guests wandered through the tent on their way to other Bellevue Avenue parties, adding their glitz and glamor to the funky scene. Every well-dressed one of them wanted to know who this Liz was who'd stolen their Jack out from under their noses.

Liz was introduced by Jack to all of his socialite friends— some of them catty, some of them nice. Even the lady who'd stamped her foot had somehow managed to be there; Liz hadn't noticed her in the ballroom, and she hardly noticed her now.

There was too much to do, too much to oversee, too much to just plain enjoy. It was a wonderful event, filled with good humor and charm and fun. People were dancing. People were making wishes and throwing two-dollar sun-disks into the polymer fountain. People were *begging* the millennium man to plug himself into the battery pack he was storing behind the cappuccino table. He'd light up the lights, and then his audience would light up with glee. If there was an apt symbol for the night, it was the millennium man.

Both the palmist and the phrenologist were doing gang-buster business. Why not? One was professional and the

other was free. Victoria, who was walking around in a
dreamy delirium and hugging everyone she could, had her
palm read, while Dr. Ben gave the phrenologist a try.

Afterward, Ben said to Liz and Jack, "Professor Thacker
said I oughta have my head examined if I really believe he
can tell me anything based on the shape of my head. I told
him I *was* having my head examined. He said I was the
fourth one to crack that joke. I guess I'm not so brilliant after
all."

"I told Ben to see the palmist, but he won't go," said
Tori, her arm locked tightly around Ben's. Her voice was
high with excitement as she said, "She told *me* that I'm
going to have a big surprise tonight." She gave Liz a wildly
meaningful look.

Victoria was sure, from things Ben had hinted, that he was
going to pop the question tonight. "It's in the air," she'd
told Liz during a congratulatory hug.

Ben and Victoria moved on, and Liz dipped a fat red
strawberry into the fondue of melted chocolate, then held it
over a napkin and aimed it at Jack's waiting mouth. He took
it in one bite, savoring it.

Liz murmured with a wicked smile, "Do you think anyone
noticed that for a while we weren't at the dinner *or* under
the tent?"

"Hmmm, that was *great*. You I mean, not the fruit," said
Jack, kissing her with chocolate breath. "Of course they no-
ticed. Do you think they're fools? And who cares anyway?
Have I told you I love you?"

"In the last five minutes? I don't think so." She pursed
her lips in a thoughtful frown. "No, I'm sure I would've
remembered."

"I love you, darling. I love you."

No time for any more banter than that; Liz was grabbed
and dragged over to the small wooden platform that served
as a dance floor; one of the boards had collapsed. And so it

went, with Jack cornering her for words of love and quick, stolen kisses, and others hauling her off to some other new crisis that—thankfully—wasn't a crisis at all.

When the gathering had reached its peak—in noise, in attendance, in gaiety—pretty Irish black-haired Deirdre, who'd dressed as a Victorian nanny, came rushing up to Liz and Jack. "You won't *believe* who's here, mum," she said. All night she'd been doing that—calling everyone mum.

Liz took a wild guess. "Princess Diana."

"How did y'*know*, then?" asked Deirdre, thunderstruck. " 'Twas all planned, was it? You might have tole me," she added, hurt.

"Deirdre, I was kidding just now," said Liz, laughing.

"But I'm not!" Deirdre said. "Come with me, and see for yourself, mum."

"She sounds convinced, m'dear," said Jack with a wink.

Something about that wink made Liz decide to follow Deirdre as she wound her way through the crowd. She wouldn't put it past Jack. . . .

"Over there," said Deirdre, fluttering her hands excitedly. "Behind Glinda the Good Witch—see her? Not talking, just listening? Could it be, do y'think?"

In profile, Liz had to admit, there was a resemblance. Something about the incredibly elegant line of the woman's neck and back as she inclined her head attentively made Liz pause and consider. The woman was dressed in a generic outfit, neither Gilded Age nor New. The point of the dress, a plain black gown with long, open sleeves, seemed to be to *not* attract attention. The three-quarter silver mask she wore was striking, but only because all else was so severe.

"If only we could see more than her chin," Deirdre murmured. "But the chin is right."

"Or her hair," Liz said, caught up in the fantasy. "Too bad about that turban thing."

They stood there for a moment, trying to be as discreet as

they could. Liz said, "She wouldn't still be around. Would she?"

"Where can she go?" asked Deirdre. "It's always the same. Better here than in England. Their press is even worse than yours."

Jack came up behind Liz just then and wrapped his arms around her waist. Resting his chin playfully on her shoulder, he looked off where she was looking. "Well? Have you made a positive ID?"

It was still so new, this wonderful, spontaneous public display of his love for her. Liz let the sensation sink in, right down to her toes, before she said, "*You* know if she's here or not. Admit it."

"Me?" he said, kissing her cheek. "How would *I* know?"

"Lizzie, Lizzie!" came Victoria's hiss behind them. She was with Ben, as manic as ever, to the point where Liz was beginning to worry. By now Tori—having accomplished her pin-mission in spades—should be settling down. But her green eyes were bright with leftover intrigue as she whispered, "Someone said she's definitely here. It's definite. Silver dress, black mask. Have you seen—?"

"Well for God's sake!" boomed a voice directly in front of their group. A big man with a loud mouth was approaching them in the first stages of a bear hug. "Bony Maroney, bless my soul! I haven't seen you in years! You haven't put on a pound or shrunk an inch!"

Victoria stared at him, frozen in place.

The man, dressed as either Dracula or the Count of Monte Cristo, wrapped his arms around her in a death-grip and rocked her back and forth. "Judy Maroney, how *are* you? Good lord, and Paul? Still working on the Space Shuttle? Those two kids of yours—they must be scaring the bejesus out of you by now!"

Liz watched with a mounting sense of horror as Victoria's eyes seemed to lose focus, then shut tight in pain. Before anybody could do anything, Victoria let out a shattering scream, then collapsed in the arms of her well-wisher.

The man held her, limp in his arms, and said in a shocked voice, "My god—what did I do?"

Ben and Jack rushed to take her from him, and then Ben, smaller than Jack but with a will of steel, lifted the prostrate woman into his arms and began elbowing his way through the merriment. Liz was aware of a buzz of concern as Ben took the most direct route to the house, with Jack and her following close behind. Inside the house, Netta, already out of costume, ran to pull back the bedding in a bedroom upstairs.

Liz, shaking from the experience, was thinking, *Is it possible? Is her insane theory possible?* Had Judy Maroney tried to reclaim her self? Who screamed, in that case? And who is being carried up these stairs?

Ben laid the unconscious woman on a mahogany fourposter bed in a well-appointed, feminine room that was in fact Mrs. Eastman's. "It's the only one that's made up," Netta explained hurriedly.

They gathered around the bed as Ben checked Victoria's— Judy's?—vital signs. "She should be okay. She's had an unbelievable shock."

But he didn't sound nearly as certain of himself as Liz thought he should, and so she waited, with Ben, with Jack, with Netta, for whoever it was to regain consciousness.

They waited an unbearably long time. It seemed to Liz— and apparently to Ben—that the woman who lay there should have come around by now. Liz began to have the morbid sensation that they were gathered around a deathbed. She shuddered, and Jack put his arm around her.

They waited.

At last, the slender woman in the silver gown and starthreaded hair began to recover. Her eyes fluttered open; she sighed heavily. Fully awake now, she saw Ben before she saw the others. "Ben . . . ," she said softly. He sat down on the bed beside her.

Ah—still Tori, thought Liz with mixed emotions.

She watched, holding her breath, as Tori sat up in bed and said, "Oh . . . *Ben,*" and broke down into an agonizing series of sobs, slipping headlong into the morass of pain she'd tried so hard to avoid for the last five years.

And then Liz knew, and everyone knew, that neither Judy nor Tori would ever be the same again.

There was nothing Jack or Liz could do now, so they left her in the arms of Ben, the best possible therapy for her pain, and slipped out of the room. Netta, blowing her nose in a huge white handkerchief, went off to make tea for them. Jack and Liz, reluctant to go far, sat down on the top stair of the vast and elegant second-floor landing.

"The healing will start now, I think," said Jack, taking Liz's hand in his. "It's not going to be fast or easy."

"But Ben will be there for her. So will we." They sat silently for a moment, and then Liz added, "Thank God Caroline's over at my place. She certainly didn't need to see or hear this."

Jack smiled reflectively. "Caroline told me it was her first sleepover, ever. She was so excited. I have to say, the kid's a lot less of a monster nowadays."

"A *lot* less," Liz agreed.

"I wonder what's happened to change all that," Jack said, bemused.

"*You've* happened. She adores you. I can tell by the way she talks about you to Susy. 'Jack this. Jack that.' Susy's become a little jealous, I think."

Jack lifted Liz's hand to his lips and kissed it. "That won't be a problem soon." He laughed softly and said, "We're going to have one hell of a mish-mash family."

Which brought the subject, inevitably, to Caroline's little

brother. "Any luck tracking down Bradley's father?" Liz asked Jack.

Jack shook his head. "I have someone checking down leads, but Stacey dated a lot of men," he said a little grimly.

"You sound as if you're not all that anxious to find the guy."

Jack tapped her hand, still in his, against his thigh absently as he thought about her remark. "You're right," he said at last. "I guess I'm not. I seem to be developing a taste for finishing someone else's half-chewed vegetables."

Or maybe you just want a son. The thought welled up, as she knew it must, and then receded, like a wave from a beach.

They had talked about her condition, briefly, when they lay in each other's arms a couple of hours earlier. Jack had been abject in his apologies, ardent in his reassurances.

"Babies or no babies—how could I live without you?" he'd said to her then. "Just the thought of it has been making me sick these last few weeks. When I saw you with the pin, I swear: I felt my heart stop. You were so . . . *beautiful*— glowing, almost. That's when I knew I couldn't make the same mistake that Christopher Eastman had made with Ophelia."

Liz then told Jack what she hadn't told him so far: that it was Christopher Eastman who'd gotten Ophelia pregnant.

And Jack surprised her by saying, "I know. I went to see Ophelia's grave. I saw the end-dates on the grave of her son and put two and two together."

So the air had been cleared, once and for all. But Liz knew to expect an occasional wave to roll in, and then out, if ever the talk came back to babies again.

She sighed and said, "I have to go check on things. They'll be setting up the costume contest now. I wish I felt more like celebrating," she added, standing up.

Jack got up, too, and slipped his arms around her and

kissed her. "Tori will be fine," he said again. "I'll check with them and then go out and join you. Isn't this about the time they form a line to do the bunny hop?"

On that silly note she left him, then walked down the elaborately carved walnut staircase, open to all the grandeur that was East Gate. She had absolutely no idea where they'd live after they were married, only that they'd have plenty of family to fill the bedrooms, wherever it was.

She took a shortcut through the kitchen on her way to the tent, and there she found Netta sharing tea with a sixtyish, well-dressed woman. A carry-on bag sat on the floor near them. The woman looked up at Liz with an air of surprise and expectation. Without a doubt, she was Jack Eastman's mother.

Netta, who'd been so deep in conversation that she'd scarcely registered that Liz had walked in on it, said, "Ah, and here she is now. Elizabeth Coppersmith, this is Jack's mother, Barbara Eastman."

Barbara Eastman stood up to shake Liz's hand. She was an attractive woman with a firm handshake who looked her age, neither more nor less, and didn't seem overly bothered by the fact that she was holed up in the kitchen with an old servant rather than gliding up the grand staircase to her rooms, like the mistress of the manor she so clearly was.

"Netta has told me some—probably not a fraction of—the news," she explained with a wry look that reminded Liz of Jack.

It was obvious that she knew of Liz's status. Just as clearly, she seemed to be sizing up the idea of having a daughter-in-law after all these years. Liz felt her cheeks betray a certain amount of insecurity, and she was suddenly glad that she was dressed to kill.

"It's been a busy summer," said Liz with her usual understatement.

"Even for Newport," her future mother-in-law agreed.

She added, "I'm sure we have lots to talk about," and then turned to Netta. "Jack will be surprised that I'm here. I really should see him before—"

Here some of the superb self-confidence seemed to drain away, because it was clear to all of them that after Barbara Eastman talked to her son, she didn't know what she'd do. Liz felt a surge of sympathy for the woman: during her absence, an army of invaders had overrun all that she thought was hers—even her bed.

"Well, if you'll excuse me," said Liz quickly. "I'm pleased to have met you," she added.

Barbara Eastman smiled in noncommittal agreement and said softly, "I must find Jack."

Liz went out to the tent and found that the costume parade and contest were already in progress; Katherine, the executive director of Anne's Place, had stepped into the breach and kept things—literally—marching along. Liz, not daring to return to the house, was able to preside over the whole thing and watch with a certain amount of pleasure as Katherine awarded the grand prize to the obvious choice and everyone's favorite, the millennium man. He plugged himself in for the occasion and stayed plugged in, despite the heat, for almost ten minutes.

After that, the guests began drifting off in small clusters until there was no one left besides Liz and the help; and then they, too, finally packed up and left. Liz hadn't seen Jack since they'd sat together on the landing stair, which was hardly surprising. Alone under the empty tent, she sat down on a chair near the fake-marble fountain and closed her eyes, listening to the sound of the trickling water, letting herself be comforted by it.

She should go home. Her parents must be wondering. She should at least turn off the little white lights. But she felt suddenly alone without Jack, and afraid of the dark.

Is this what it will be like, now that we've committed to

each other? She decided that it would, and that it wasn't all bad.

"Can anyone make a wish?"

Liz opened her eyes and saw Jack's mother standing next to the fountain. Her carry-on bag was at her side.

"Sure," Liz said with a steady look. "Wish away."

Barbara Eastman took a change purse from her coach bag, then took out a silver coin from it. She tossed it in with what had to be the saddest smile that Liz ever saw. Then she turned to Liz.

"Good night," she said. "It looks like you did a wonderful job."

"Thank you. Good night."

Liz watched as Jack's mother picked up the bag and, with her head held high, walked in the direction of the carriage house.

Jack came out almost immediately afterward. He'd gotten rid of his tuxedo jacket, his waistcoat, and his tie. His shirt-sleeves were rolled up to the elbow. His hair looked more uncombed than ever. But the smile on his face when he saw Liz was worth all the white lights in the world.

He took her in his arms, as if he'd been away at sea, and they kissed long and deep.

"Ben sent out for something for Tori," he said. "She's sleeping soundly now. He'll stay with her, of course."

"And your mother?"

Jack glanced in the direction of the carriage house and sighed. "She feels a debt. I don't know if she feels love."

Liz fingered the small pin that lay over her heart. "I wish she did," she said quietly, pressing her cheek to Jack's chest. She wanted to reassure herself that his own heart was still beating. "I wish she felt what I do."

"Some things are meant to be," Jack murmured in a faraway voice. "And some things . . . aren't."

"And we—?"

"—are fated. It's so clear to me now."

Epilogue

"*S*usy Eastman! Will you explain to me why you're inside watching television on a beautiful day like this?"

Susy looked up at her mother and said, "It's *Sesame Street,* Mommy," as if that explained everything.

"Makes no difference," Liz said, heading for the remote control. "I don't want you turning into a couch potato."

Without taking her eyes from the tube, Susy said, "I'm not a couch potato. I'm a *sofa* potato. Caroline says rich people say 'sofa.' "

"Well, Caroline is wrong, and we're not rich." Liz picked up the remote and shot Big Bird out of the TV sky. "Now git."

Susy groaned at the injustice of it all, then scampered out of the Great Room to join Bradley and Caroline. Liz, carrying her cup of decaf, went over to poke the dying fire back to life, then sat on one arm of the leather easy chair where Jack sat hovering over the sports section of the Saturday paper.

"Did you hear that?" she asked her husband.

"Hmmm," he said without looking up. "Something about vegetables."

"Hey. Coach." She folded his paper over itself. "Remember me?"

Jack looked up with a quiet smile. "Of course. You're my

life's blood, the cream in my coffee, the object of my adoration—*but*. You haven't pitched three straight shutouts for the Red Sox.''

She rolled her eyes and said, "How can I possibly compete?''

Jack reached over and rubbed her swollen belly with his hand. "Keep this up, I'll have my own franchise soon.''

"I *don't* think so," she said, smiling.

"Seriously, Liz: how do you feel?''

Liz shrugged and said, "Great. Better than with Susy. I think I've convinced myself that this is a miraculous pregnancy.''

Jack's look turned sly. "Want me to run through how it happened one more time?''

As near as they could figure, Liz had gotten pregnant on the night of the fund-raiser, between dinner and the bunny hop. The night had been filled with miracles; this was just the biggest one. Liz kissed the top of Jack's head and said, "Enjoy your paper while you can.''

The doorbell rang and Liz sang out, "Never mind, Netta; I'll get it.''

She walked down the long marble floor of the entry hall, covered with skid marks from the bicycle race that Netta and Liz's parents had engineered on the night before, and swung open one of the massive double doors that faced onto the circular graveled path outside.

The caller was Detective Gilbert, whom she hadn't seen since the day she sat at the station, reading through the dozen stolen letters, looking in vain for clues to Eddy Wragg's motives.

Her first reaction was panic—surely Wragg had escaped—but the bemused smile under the big mustache on the detective's handsome, fine-boned face reassured her.

He suspended a folded, crumpled, dirty letter from two fingers in front of her. "Guess what the janitor at the shelter found when he changed a light bulb in one of the ceiling fixtures?''

"No way!" she said, mimicking Caroline's favorite phrase. "Come in, come *in*," she cried, grabbing the detective by the arm and dragging him over the threshold.

Liz pelted him with questions that had no answers as she hurried him into the Great Room where Jack still clung, without hope now, to his paper.

Detective Gilbert said, "The handwriting's clear enough, and so's the motive. This Victoria St. Onge character seems to've had another one of her fits of kleptomania, and—well, read it yourself."

He handed Liz the soiled sheet of paper. Nestling on the rolled arm of Jack's leather chair, she unfolded the last known letter of Victoria St. Onge, dated the month before the sand-pail dinner party.

" 'My dear Mercy,' she read aloud,

I believe I have finally succeeded in storming the gate—East Gate, that is. I truly believe it would be a simpler matter to climb over the wall to Mrs. Astor's Beechwood than it is to gain entry into the inner circle of John and Lavinia Eastman. However, by insinuating myself aboard their yacht as the guest of a guest, I did manage to make some headway.

John Eastman has no use at all for me—I am forced to that conclusion, since he scarcely said a word to me, but kept in the company of two or three close friends who shared his love of sporting pursuits.

Liz glanced up at Jack with a wry look and then resumed.

Lavinia Eastman, however, appeared to find me amusing, and it is on her that I pin my hopes. I should add that it may all come to nothing, since, alas, I have been naughty again.

Jack snapped to attention as Liz read on:

One of the ladies came aboard wearing an extraordinarily long rope of black Tahitian pearls, bound by a diamond clasp the size of a pie-cherry. Fearing she might lose it overboard, the guest removed her necklace and left it atop a bureau in one of the staterooms.

It did not remain there long.

I suppose it was owing to her extreme vanity—in any case, I took it upon myself to relieve her of the jewelry and tucked it out of sight until such time as I could retrieve it. As you know, I have a head for such things.

At the end of the cruise the necklace was discovered missing. The crew and servants, naturally, were questioned closely. One of them, a steward, was taken into custody, as he had a previous experience of petty theft. (Mrs. Eastman is too soft-hearted by half.) Perhaps an examination of the yacht will turn up the jewels. But—perhaps not. We shall see.

Detective Gilbert interrupted at that point and said, "The rest of the letter is a description of fabric."

Liz glanced over the remainder of the letter. "So it is." She looked up and said to Jack, "Have you ever heard anything of this incident?"

He shook his head. "I can call my dad—although it's a little early for him, California time."

"It's not too early for Palm Beach. You could call your mother."

"Yeah, okay." He turned to Gilbert. "Do you mind waiting?"

"Not at all. I was thinking—if no one has any information, would you object to a search of your yacht? I understand it's been in the family since the time of this letter?"

"Can do. Just give me a minute to make the call first."

He went out to call Barbara Eastman. Detective Gilbert, who'd never been at East Gate before, looked around and said, "Lotsa room for a growing family."

Liz smiled. "That end—with the toys and bulletproof slipcovers—has been handed over to the kids. It's tough when you don't have a rumpus room in the basement."

The two shared a working-class laugh together and chatted about kids, and then Jack came back.

"No luck there," he said. "She's never heard anything about it. When did you want to search the boat?"

"Now!" said Liz. "Can we?"

In five minutes they were on the road, Detective Gilbert in his car, Jack and Liz in theirs.

"If Susy finds out about this, we're dead," said Liz. "But I think she bought the bit about seeing the lawyer."

"Y'know, I used to be a pretty honest guy before I had kids," Jack said thoughtfully. "Now I lie all the time."

Liz sighed and said, "It's easier than arguing with them. Life's too short. How's your mother?" Liz added, her train of thought ending up with Barbara Eastman.

"Doing well. She misses him, of course. But at least she got him up and running again. It leaves her free to go ahead with the divorce without guilt."

Automatically she and Jack reached for each other's hands. It was amazing, Liz realized, how in tune they were about everything to do with love. About everything, really. Her one great lapse was baseball; his, parties for grown-ups.

After a thoughtful silence, she said, "Do you think I should have an all-women-personal shower for Tori, or should we have an appliance shower, with couples, for Ben and her?"

"God. All-women-personal. Please. I'm begging you."

With that simple maneuver, Liz made her announcement to Jack that she'd be taking over the Great Room for an extravaganza unmatched since—well, since his birthday a month earlier.

She squeezed his hand. "I love you, you know."

He smiled. "Me too, you conniving witch." After a minute or so, he said, "What do you think about a baseball theme for Bradley's birthday? June—it's baseball season. . . . Just a thought," he said absently. "Oh, wait. By then the baby—"

"—will still be too young to blow up Bradley's party," Liz said, remembering her infamous debut at East Gate.

"Plenty of time to do that," Jack said reassuringly. Then: "Why are we going to the boat, anyway? There's not going to be any necklace there. It's had a hundred years to be found."

"But it hasn't been, as far as we know. You have to humor me and Detective Gilbert on this. We won't take long."

They searched, all three of them, for four straight hours. The boat was ice-cold below, but Liz pretended that she didn't notice. Starting with the staterooms, they turned the boat inside out, pulling out the drawers, taking up the floorboards, taking up the berthboards—anything that wasn't screwed down was removed, searched, and replaced. From there they moved into the main salon, repeating the process; and from there to the galley, the wheelhouse, even the engine room and the foc'sle.

No pearls.

Liz had taken frequent quick breaks and made the men coffee while they continued the search—Detective Gilbert, with the discipline born of his years on the force; and Jack, with mounting impatience and concern for Liz.

The recovered letter got picked up and reread until they all knew it by heart. Something about it bothered Liz; she couldn't figure out what. It was while she was taking her third pregnancy-induced pee of the search that it hit her. No one would write, "I have a head for such things." In that context they'd say, "I have a penchant," or, "I have a weakness," or whatever.

Head. It was almost a Freudian slip.

On a hunch, she decided to search the bathroom she was in—the *head,* as Susy would undoubtedly insist she call it. Small, exquisite cupboards were too recently painted to give her much hope. But they were still empty of supplies, since the boating season hadn't begun yet, and Liz was able to feel behind them and all around without much trouble.

At the back of the linen closet was a small horizontal hole—meant for air circulation between the closet and the hull—which was just big enough for Liz to slip her hand into. With mounting hopes she probed the dark gap, feeling for jewels and finding nothing but very, very cold air.

Disappointed, she tried another ventilation hole, and then another. In the third one she felt something.

Fat round beads, a string of them.

"Jack!" she screamed at the top of her lungs. "Come quick!"

He showed up in five seconds with a look of panic on his face, matched by Detective Gilbert, who stood peering over his shoulder into the small compartment.

She was half-kneeling in a bizarre contortion with her hand still in the hole. "I've got 'em! I've got 'em!"

"What're you *doing*?" cried Jack, scandalized. "You'll hurt yourself, twisting like that!"

"I'm fine, I'm fine. I just . . . don't . . . want . . . to drop them," she said, carefully unhooking the strand from something sharp that protruded out of the back of the closet—a too-long screw tip, she assumed.

With infinite care and in utter silence she began pulling the rope of pearls through the hole, fearful that at any moment the century-old string that held them might be too rotten to hold, and she'd lose it all. But the string held, and she was able to pass the rope of pearls intact to Jack.

At first glance, the pearls seemed ruined. They were covered with green fuzz, unpleasant to hold. But even in that condition, there was no denying their majesty. "They are *huge*," Liz said, staring in awe at the moldy beads.

The diamond that was mounted on the clasp wasn't as big as a pie-cherry—more the size of a plump raisin. Maybe Elizabeth Taylor wouldn't be impressed, but Liz sure was.

She rubbed the mossy coating from one of the beads, revealing an exquisitely dark pearl: dusky, gray, as exotic as the Pacific islands it came from.

"Wow," whispered Detective Gilbert.

Jack handed the necklace carefully to the detective. "Who was the owner, I wonder? Who are the heirs?"

Those questions never occurred to Liz. Her knee-jerk response had been: finders keepers. She blushed to realize that she hadn't thought beyond that. It made her love Jack all over again, just for his integrity.

"We can find out," said Detective Gilbert, fingering the stone. "Between the *Daily News* and the police archives, we should be able to tell. I predict a bunch of lawsuits, though."

Jack was thinking of something else besides lawsuits. "Hold it. . . . I wonder if it's possible—yeah. Has to be."

He laughed at some recollection and said, "Last year Cynthia said that someone called the yard, asking the name of the Eastman yacht. She told him the *Déjà Vu* without thinking, then asked me if that was all right. I said sure and never thought about it again, even after the fan-belt episode. After all, David Penny obviously knew the boat; he wouldn't have been the one to call."

"You're thinking it was—who—Wragg?" asked Liz.

"Yep. And I think the moron saw the *DeeJay* and got the two names confused—hell, they're both old wooden boats—

and ransacked the *DeeJay* instead of the Déjà Vu. Wait'll I tell Jay. He'll think it was worth it just to be able to tell the story over sundowners.''

"Well, that's that," said Detective Gilbert. "The case may finally be closed."

It was hard to tell who was the most relieved. "Just make sure somebody tells Wragg that we found this, okay?" asked Liz.

They stepped out of the boat into a brisk, cold, southwest breeze. Spring came hard to cities by the sea.

Detective Gilbert flipped up the collar of his jacket and said, "Nice yard you have here."

"It's been touch and go," Jack said, "but I think we've turned the corner. The International Yacht Race is sending a fair amount of business our way."

Liz slipped her arm through Jack's and said exuberantly, "And Jack's not selling, so those jerks can just put *that* in their pipe and smoke it."

Both men looked at her strangely, but she didn't care. She was wonderfully content with finding the pearls, wonderfully pleased with herself for figuring it out. Susy would have to be told: Liz wanted credit from her nautical daughter even more than she wanted it from Jack. *Head.* Ha.

They went back up the ramp that led from the float to the pier above. Detective Gilbert shook their hands and wished them well with the new baby, and then he hurried to get out of the wind.

"All set to go home, Columbo?" asked Jack.

"You bet."

Liz turned and looked back at the *Déjà Vu,* pulling restlessly on its docklines. She could—almost—see Christopher Eastman on the afterdeck, looking up at her with a glint in his eye and a laugh on his lips.

She blew a kiss down from the pier: it got carried away on the wind.

Joan Johnston